MY BEST MAN

MY BEST MAN

ANDY SCHELL

KENSINGTON BOOKS
http://www.kensingtonbooks.com

KENSINGTON BOOKS are published by

Kensington Publishing Corp.
850 Third Avenue
New York, NY 10022

Library of Congress Card Catalogue Number: 99-067617
ISBN 1-57566-549-2

First Printing: May, 2000
10 9 8 7 6 5 4 3 2 1

Printed in the United States of America

For Jonathan and Maria . . .
and Madalyn too.

ACKNOWLEDGMENTS

My premier thanks go to Ed Karvoski, Jr., without whom this manuscript may not have made its way to an agent and publisher.

I'm forever indebted to Pam Satran, who was with me from the first word to the last, and beyond. Thanks, Pam.

I most sincerely thank my editor, John Scognamiglio, for his wise and gentle counsel, and for making this experience a pleasure.

Much gratitude goes to my agent, Alison Picard, for enthusiastically taking me on, and finding the perfect home for the manuscript.

Special thanks to Pam, John Barrows, and Christine Meinecke for plodding through the first draft.

Undying gratitude to my writers group, The Fictional Sluts: Dave Betz, Joel Gardner, Ginny Horton, Pam Satran, Bill Taeusch, and the original bad girl, Cameron Tuttle. You're a deft bunch of drunks.

Love and thanks to both sets of parents, Robin and Kay Jones, and Peter and Lillian Louie. And to all my extended siblings: Fritz, Sam, Ai, Mei, Sue, Rick, John, Alan, Bev, Lee, Stephanie, Ron, Jana, and Bill.

Thanks to my writing partner on script projects, Todd Stites.

Thanks to the following people for their ongoing support: Larry Scibilia, Ty and Leslee Harman, Chris White, John and Nancy

Barrows, Marsha Carrington, Marika Van Adelsberg, Nate Grant, Craig Udit, Roger Hanson, Jim Fleming, Scott Peterson, Judy Pimentel, Beth Silver, Kelly Daniels, Cheryl Neese, Susan Bourn, Barbara Bennett, Jane Bemmerl, Chris Meinecke, Keith McKechnie, Rick Smith, Michelle Gurnick, Peter Kater, Doug Ferguson, Jane Neiderbrach, Julie Underwood, Betty Ferguson, Amy Shelton-Cole, Bruce Shelton, Sallie Strole, Fritz and Kathleen Shelton, Jane Metcalfe, Steven Petrow, Barbara Kuhr, John Plunkett, Julia Sweeney, Darrel Wingo, Joe Keery, Stacia Goad, Susie Stark, Alan Novidor, Tommy Mullins, Debra Pollock, Maureen Anderson, Dennis Reh, Jane Smith, Joe Zohar, George McGrath, Tracy Newman, Robin Schiff, Jeff Greenberg, Milinda McNeely, Jan Stack, Tom Temple, Barbara Klingbiel, Koji Takei, and Marquita Stanfield.

Highest regards to those who make me laugh until I bleed: Jonathan Louie, Larry Scibilia (that guy drinks too much coffee), Jimmy Tucker, Rodney Morrison, Carrie Earll, Misti Langenhoffer, Roz Rissler, David Cushing, Karen Robinson, Krischa Mayben, Deb Pollock, Stacia Goad, Janet Gunn, Soomi Goldmark, Mike Higgins, Madalyn Hill, Melody Fee, Kelly Whitt, Judy Pimentel, Bill Reeves, Tad Cockrell, Mini Silver, Marty Olson, Kimberly Curry, Sam Johnson, Steve McGriff, Shirley Prestia, Randy Bennett, Craig Strong, Bridget Sienna, Julia Sweeney, Ty Harman, Leslee Ross, Scott Hartman, Andi Matheny, Peggy Etra, Cathy Barnett, and Todd Stites.

Thanks to Anne Lamott for writing ''Bird by Bird.''

CHAPTER ONE

"How many heterosexuals work as airline stewards?" my mother asks me. I'm in the Kansas City International Airport, and a man's voice is blasting over the loudspeaker, announcing my departure to Dallas. I can hardly hear my mother in the waxy receiver of the pay phone. "It's Donald who's wondering. He's concerned you're in the wrong environment to fulfill your father's wishes."

I cut her off. "Mom, they're announcing my flight. I'll call you from Dallas."

"This is the year!" she says, instead of good-bye.

Hanging up the phone, I ask aloud, "For what?"

I skulk down the aisle, throw my suitcase into the overhead bin, and collapse into a passenger seat. I've only been flying for three months, but it already seems rote—probably because I don't really want to be a flight attendant. When I was a boy my father always told me that I would attend law school and that I would graduate first in my class, and I believed him. How did I end up becoming a flight attendant? Well, after things turned to shit with my father, I figured out the job he would least likely approve of and then applied. It was my way of getting back at him for reneging on all his promises. I've always reacted to my father in one way or another.

First, I opted out of prep school and demanded I be allowed to attend public high school with the real kids. And when Dad took away my Fiat convertible, after I told the family I was gay, I hustled up enough bucks to buy a used VW bug. No one in my family had ever driven a used car, let alone one with an Amnesty International sticker on the bumper, and my mother was so appalled she wouldn't let me park it in the driveway. Nor had anyone in my family attended a state university. But what was I supposed to do? It would have been awfully difficult to pony up tuition to a private university on student loans. So while my brother, Winston, was sent to Northwestern for his MBA, all expenses paid—and no one can rack up expenses like Winston—I left college to pass out plastic trays of warmed-over Salisbury steak at 30,000 feet.

Today I'm a passenger. Looking out the window to the frozen tundra that surrounds the Kansas City Airport, I think of the slightly warmer environs of my destination. The balmy temperatures of Texas may make it bearable for me to live on the street—in the event I don't find an apartment, make a life, gather food, get laid. It's only the first month of 1984, but something tells me this is going to be a long year.

I open the January in-flight magazine and do what all flight attendants at the airline do: go to the *Flight Attendant of the Month* page—though we call it *Slut of the Month*, since the rumor is that you have to fuck the big, sweaty, redneck Manager of Flight Crews in order to be chosen. No guy has made it. There, on the page, in her sexy little stewardess uniform, is a Texas babe with thick blond hair and a hey-big-spender look on her face. Her name is Amity Stone, and the copy says that she likes "eating barbecue, riding horses, and searching the Texas sky for an occasional falling star." *Please.* I picture her eating a hunk of barbecued Appaloosa while getting hit on the head with a meteor.

"Are you laughing at me?" a female voice with a Texas accent as thick as a jungle asks.

I wipe the grin off my face, look up, and there she is: Amity Stone, *Slut of the Month.* Her hand is resting on my seat back, and her head is cocked. Her perfume is heavy and her makeup is artfully applied. She's more beautiful than the likeness in the magazine—she actually looks like a young Grace Kelly. I'm intimidated. Not because she's beautiful—women don't affect me that way—but because I can tell she's incredibly confident, and with my ego freshly smashed, I'm not. "Not at *you,*" I say.

Her blue eyes highlight me like spotlights. "Then what, Bubba?"

I realize that *Bubba* is a salutation, like *sir,* or *mister,* or *creep.* "It's your bio," I say, trying to get out of this. "I like it."

She bends down, knees together, and quietly decrees, "I heave at the smell of barbecue, and the only time I rode a horse it made my little Lady so sore I had to cancel all my dates for a week, and the only star I want to catch is Richard Gere. *Capiche,* Bubba?"

"Hey, I'm just jealous," I stammer, laughing it off, "because they'll never pick me."

"You're one of us—a flight attendant?"

"Yep."

"That's great!" *Grite!* She says it as if she has just won a hundred dollars. Not a thousand or a million, but a hundred. It is the perfect amount of enthusiasm to bestow upon a stranger. "Jacqueline," she calls to her coworker. "Jackie!"

Jacqueline looks up the aisle like a giraffe scouting the horizon. She's so tall she nearly has to slump from hitting her head on the low ceiling of the DC-9 jet.

"He's a flight attendant for us," Amity happily explains.

Jacqueline approaches us, a model sauntering down a catwalk, neither smiling nor frowning. Just vacant. Like a wall somebody forgot to paint. Her face is long, angular, odd. Her copper hair is beautiful, and she has freckles on her face and hands. "Oh, that's good, I guess. Do you like it?" Her Texas accent is almost Californian.

"Sure," I crow, trying to look confident. "I'll like it a lot more now that I won't be commuting from Kansas, where men are men, and sheep are women."

Amity runs her unclad ring finger over her bottom lip. "Kansas boys are cute. Those sheep ought to consider themselves lucky."

"My boyfriend just dumped me," I say, envisioning a voodoo doll of Matthew with pins stuck in its eyes. "Kansas guys aren't *that* cute."

She smiles, as if we're old friends. "It's his loss. Don't worry. There are plenty of men in this world, and you've picked the perfect career to meet them all."

I return the smile. Offer a handshake. "I'm Harry."

She shakes. "I'm hairy too, but I drop into the spa for a bikini wax."

"Harry Ford." I laugh.

"My mom drove a Ford," Jacqueline says, coming to life. "For a long time. She drove a Ford that was green. It was this big old green station wagon thing. I'm pretty sure it was a Ford. Green. Yeah, I think it was a green Ford." She flips her hair with her hand, turns, and heads back up the aisle, shutting the overhead bins as she goes.

"*Green Ford*," I chant mystically.

Amity smiles with Southern sarcasm. "She just got out of an institution." We hear the thud of the front door being shut, and the engines begin to spool. "I'm Amity Stone, but I guess you know that, because I'm the *Slut of the Month!* It's such a pleasure meeting you, Harry." *Hay-ree.* "I hope we get to fly together sometime." *Some Tom.* She follows Jacqueline to the front of the plane, leaving behind her perfume, heavy and full of spice, to soak my face.

Does she really hope we fly together sometime? God, I'd like to latch on to her right now. This is just what I need to get my life started, a girl*friend* who can make me laugh. My training classmates and I were schooled in the fine art of stewardessing in Dallas, but after graduating we were supposed to scatter across the country to fulfill our initial one-year assignments. My domicile choices in order of preference were New York, Los Angeles, Honolulu, Boston, Chicago, and Dallas. I was one of only three class members assigned to Dallas. But I have no one there to call a friend, since I immediately moved back to Kansas to live with Matthew. But now I'm bound for Big D, where people eat fried vegetables, wear snakeskin boots, and diphthongize the word *couch*. And treat Northerners like enemies in the Civil War.

Could Amity be one of those rare Southerners who would *want* to hang out with a Yankee? I can't believe I told her, "I'm just jealous ..." How losery. Matthew crushed my confidence when he told me I'd become stagnant, shallow, not interested in personal growth. Considering I lacked the funds for a higher education, I thought my choice to become a flight attendant was an acceptable diversion, even if passing out oily little pillows to people who sleep upright isn't what I intend to do for the rest of my life. I thought being a flight attendant gave a certain working-class cachet to a gay guy in his early twenties, but Matthew likened it to becoming a hairdresser or an interior decorator. And of course, my brother, Winston, gave me all kinds of shit. When I pointed out that, unlike him, Mom and Dad had cut me off, and that by working for an airline I could still afford to fly to Paris, he said, "Yes, but it's *standby*."

As the plane taxis out for takeoff, I watch Amity and Jacqueline in the aisle demonstrating the emergency equipment while the other flight attendant dishes out all that industry speak: "At this time ..." and "In the unlikely event of ..." and "For your own comfort and safety ..." It didn't take me long to realize that it's all a crock that won't help you in any way when the plane slams into a mountain at five hundred miles an hour. But Jacqueline looks as if she's hearing it for the first time and it actually means something. She concentrates on every word, straining to follow along. When she drops her demonstration oxygen mask from the ceiling a little too early, she lets it dangle there awhile, while the speaking flight attendant catches up.

Amity, on the other hand, looks like one of those models on *The Price Is Right*, all smiles and perfect timing as she demonstrates the seat belt, safety card, and oxygen mask as if they're exciting prizes won by all.

During the flight, I study Amity further, watch her movements. She seems to serve every drink, offer each bag of peanuts, and answer any question as if she were starring in a film based on her life. I would love to be that confident. That *steady*. In my college days, I was. It's only been a few months since I left campus life, but something's happened to me. It's as if I can't adjust to the world outside school. I'm no longer the jester in the theater department (with law school out of my means, I opted to use my oratory skills on the stage) but the loser in the life department. I miss the security of university life. I miss my old friends. And most confusing of all, I miss my father.

"What's the matter, Harry?" Amity and Jacqueline are standing over me in the aisle, the drink cart between them. I'm not full-on crying, with sobs or anything, but the tears are flowing steadily down my face. I look up, don't answer, because the lump in my throat feels like a new tennis ball. Amity abandons the cart and sits beside me. "What is it?"

I swallow the fuzzy ball. "I was just thinking about my dad," I tell her. "He passed away recently."

"Jackie," Amity says, looking up at Jacqueline, "you're going to have to drive that thing by yourself. I need to talk to Harry."

"Nu-uh," Jacqueline protests, "you're not doing this to me again. Nu-uh."

"*Jackie.*"

"No, Amity, forget it." Jacqueline then looks at me. "She's

always doing this. She stops and talks to guys all the time and leaves me serving the drinks. Forget it.''

"Come on,'' I say, wiping my eyes, prodding Amity to stand and step into the aisle. I follow her and squeeze between the beverage cart and the seats to replace Jacqueline. "We'll take over,'' I offer.

"Cool.'' Jacqueline takes off her wings and hands them to me, then disappears to the back galley.

I pin the wings on my street clothes. Amity and I look at each other, then turn to our respective passengers. "Would you like something to drink?'' Then back to each other. "He was a surgeon,'' I tell her, using tongs to put ice into the plastic cup. I accidentally spill a couple of cubes.

"Just dip a cup into the ice bucket, darlin','' Amity instructs, "and use it to fill the other cup. We only use those fancy-ass tongs when airline management is on board.''

I disregard what I learned in training and do as she says; it's infinitely easier. I can't believe I've been struggling with those stupid tongs for three months. "My dad was an orthopedic surgeon who smoked two packs a day. He was actually shocked when he was diagnosed.'' I pour ginger ale into the cup and hand it to the passenger. "He thought his tax bracket excluded him from cancer.''

Her face is kind, sympathetic. "Are you doing any kind of therapy?''

"I write poetry,'' I tell her. "That's my therapy.''

"I'd love to have you read it to me sometime. Were you and your dad close?''

"When I was young, yes, very close. He was a great dad. A control freak, but I didn't mind because he gave me more attention than other kids got from their dads.''

"Coca-Cola, please,'' a man in a fedora hat requests.

"Is Pepsi OK?'' I ask him.

"Yes, sir,'' he answers.

Amity tells me in an unsubtle stage whisper, "Midwesterners

and Texans are polite, Harry. They don't care what you give them. It's the New Yorkers and Californians who expect you to wipe their butts over the difference between a Coke and a Pepsi.''

I hand the man his Pepsi and then look around, expecting people to be shocked by her words, but the locals seem to smile and nod in agreement while reading their newspapers and magazines. ''My father's work schedule had a way of sucking up his life, but whenever he had time, he was right there. Tennis, golf, horseback riding—whatever I was involved in, he'd help me, make me better. When he got cancer, I wanted to do the same for him—make him better. But he wouldn't let me.''

''Sometimes doctors make the worst patients, huh?'' Amity says sympathetically, handing peanuts and drinks to her passengers.

I picture my father sitting in the garage, his Cadillac running while he floats away in the carbon monoxide. ''He went quickly,'' I say.

Amity is focused on me rather than the teenage boy with the baby face who is focused on her—while I focus on him. Another unrealized triangle. ''Would you like something to drink?'' she asks him, still looking at me.

''I'd like a rum and soda with a lime,'' I answer, then look at the boy. ''How about you?''

''Sounds good,'' the teenage kid says.

Amity puts ice in the cup, empties the little rum bottle, adds soda, and places a speared lime into the drink.

''How old are you?'' I ask him.

''Sixteen.''

Amity hands him the cocktail. ''Don't tell your momma or your daddy,'' she whispers. He nods OK. She winks at him, and he blushes, making himself even cuter.

I was warned in training that attendants can be fired for serving alcohol to minors, but Amity doesn't seem concerned. I look across to the two passengers on my side of the aisle who obviously disapprove of our actions. I wait for them to order. They don't. "Would you like something to drink?" They request a black coffee and a diet drink. I pour the coffee, continue. "My dad was smoking even more the past year because he was stressed-out about a malpractice suit. Some guy lost his foot in a car accident and my dad had to reattach it, and he put it on sideways or something like that."

Amity hands a glass of Pepsi to a businessman who seems to be engrossed in our conversation. "G'yaw," she replies.

"It's more complicated than that, but basically he screwed up." I hand out the diet cola and the coffee. These people, so quiet before, are quick to remind me about the peanuts. I give them extras and roll my eyes while looking at Amity. "What is it with these peanuts?" I ask as we push the cart on to the next row.

"They help people poop," Amity explains. The woman sitting in the aisle seat looks horrified. Amity smiles, turns on the charm, and asks, "Would you care for a beverage, ma'am?"

"I'd like a Diet Seven-Up," the woman snips, "and *no* peanuts."

"I'll take hers," the guy sitting next to her says.

Amity hands the man two bags of peanuts, winks, and says, "Hope everything comes out OK." Then she pours the woman her beverage, lays the napkin gently onto her tray, and sets the drink down precisely, as if this were a Japanese tea service.

I continue. "My boyfriend, Matthew . . ."

When the rock-solid guy in the Texas Rangers baseball cap hears me, he looks as if he's going to puke. When I pause to take his drink order, he looks at me in disgust and shakes his head. I keep forgetting that I'm not insulated by academia anymore, that some people in the real world won't take a drink from a gay person.

"Matthew was one of those phony-baloney people who majored in psychology so he wouldn't have to deal with his own feelings. My dad's body is barely cold, and my boyfriend doesn't think a thing about breaking up with me. Drink, ma'am?"

The woman declines, not because I'm gay, I think, but because she's creeped out by talk of my dad's dead body.

"What about your momma?" Amity asks.

"She's already remarried," I answer.

"G'yaw, Bubba. People move fast around you! Beverage, sir?"

The gentleman orders a hot Bloody Mary.

"One spicy B.M. coming down the pike," Amity announces as if the peanuts are working on *her*.

"My mom is one of those resilient Midwest women," I say. "Onward and upward. She wastes no time." I hand out two Pepsis and notice that my drawer of peanuts is empty. "I need poop inducers."

She happily throws me two bags, I catch one, miss the other. "Gay guys can't catch!" she yells. People turn in their seats. I'm embarrassed, but there's something so honest about her I know she's not trying to harass me. Somehow, I ignore the stares. We move on.

By the time we get to the last row, I've poured out more of my innards than I have soda, juice, and coffee. I've explained that with my father gone, my boyfriend gone, and my mother's new surname and life, I feel left behind. Lost. No family. No school peers. Nobody to *hang* with. The only thing I've edited is the existence of my brother. I just can't stand to talk about him right now—not since the reading of the will. Through it all, Amity is an extraordinary listener, as if everything I'm saying is absolutely fascinating. She has an instinct for when to be quiet and when to make a joke, and even though I'm a little needy now, she's cool enough not to make me feel like some pathetic washout. I'm grateful.

Near the end of the flight, I stand with Amity and Jacqueline in the rear galley. Amity breaks open a bottle of champagne she's taken from first class and pours rations into three Styrofoam cups— so no passenger will know what we're drinking—and we toast to "New friends!" as Amity warmly puts it. The flight attendant at the front of the plane, in first class, ignores us. "How come she hasn't come back here?" I ask.

"She's one of those girls who makes the mistake of thinking that, because she's *working* first class, she *is* first class. Misguided."

I laugh. We down the champagne. I learn that Jacqueline and Amity are roommates, both twenty-six years old. They share a house near the DCU campus in Dallas. They each give me their phone numbers to their separate phone lines, and I tell them that I'm in the process of moving and will call with my new number. The truth is, Matthew ended it so quickly that I have nothing set up.

When the flight lands, I politely say my good-byes at the front door and tell Amity it was nice to meet her. She agrees, then yells, " 'Bye, Harry! Love your guts!" Once I'm off the jet I decide to wait until Amity deplanes and ask her if she'd like to go for a late lunch. I'm standing there, in the gate area, when she exits the jetway, and just as I'm ready to approach her, this really hot guy in a khaki-colored business suit takes her into his arms and kisses her lips and then her neck. He picks up her luggage, and they stroll away while the loudspeaker announces the departure of a flight bound for Memphis.

Good for her.

"Hey," a guy says. He's also in a suit, also sexy. I recognize him from the flight. He's very tall and lanky with sandy hair and an almost blond beard that is trimmed close to his face. "Sorry to hear about your boyfriend." He must have been listening to our in-flight conversation. "Want to go for a beer?"

Good for me.

CHAPTER
TWO

It's 12:01 A.M., and the pain is excruciating. I'm doubled over, riding in the passenger seat of the lanky guy's car. After ten minutes that seem like twelve hours, we turn into the circular drive of the hospital, and he helps me out of his car and through the electronic doors. The emergency room is incredibly bright, and my agony is highlighted by the nuclear glow of a thousand fluorescent bulbs. As I limp toward the admitting desk, while leaning on the arm of this guy whose name I can't remember, I notice a woman with a bloody broken nose who's waiting in a chair beside a man. His cologne smells like *Wife Beater*—he's even wearing the white tank top underwear shirt. There's also a guy who's having some kind of allergic reaction; his head is redder than a ripe tomato while the rest of him is as white as a marshmallow. He uses a single fingernail to scratch his nose. And in the corner, a couple hold a sleeping child in both their arms and rock it back and forth as if it were in a hammock. Add the Duran Duran song playing in Muzak, the out-of-date *National Geographics* strewn about the room, and the noisy motor of the drinking fountain, and this place is a real party.

Our hostess, the woman at the admitting desk, looks like Divine's stunt double, with her big perfect hair and cat-eyed makeup. Her motionless forearms lay on the table like hunks of yeasty, rising bread dough. But her fingertips fly around the keyboard like manic hummingbirds. She looks like a huge thrift store mannequin that's retaining water. I never want to come to one of her parties again. "Age?" she asks, not looking at me.

"Twenty-three."

"Height?"

"Five-eight."

"Weight?"

"One forty-two."

Eyes brown, hair brown, shit brown. Come on, lady, can't you see I'm dying here? All you people care about is whether a guy has insurance anyway.

"What is your complaint?" she asks.

The pain strikes my lower abdomen like lightning. "Oh, my God!" I shriek, falling over. I can feel something explode inside of me.

"I've got to go," my new former friend nervously tells the admitting gal. He beelines for the door.

"Wait!" she calls. "Are you family? Friend?"

"He's got an insurance card in his wallet. I checked!" the guy yells over his shoulder before slipping out and into the night.

What's wrong? Why is he fleeing the scene? Did he do something to me? We just had good old normal sex, as any two guys would. But now the fireworks are in my stomach, and they're burning me up. As I start to pass out, I see a nurse and an intern running toward me.

When I wake, I hear a TV blaring the *All My Children* theme and see a curtain between me and my roommate. I discern I have a roommate because the scrimlike curtain makes silhouettes of the bloated, large-headed creatures gathered round his bed, and when they raise their fat hands to gesture, or eat fried chicken (I can smell it), their hands appear to be webbed. When they move slightly and allow me a view of the silhouetted patient, all I see is a large stomach on a slab. The visitors standing at the foot of his bed, beyond the curtain, all have big, wide, matching bottoms, so I figure they're all cursed with the same genetics and must be the poor sap's family fresh from the lake bed.

One of the creature shadows speaks. "That little gal is evil." *Ayvil.*

"She sure is." *She shore iyuz.*

The biggest shadow creature, the one who looks as if she's got a spark arrester on her head, says, "Erica ain't dumb. She'll catch on." *Ercka aint doom. Shill kich own.*

A voice escapes one of the butts at the end of the bed. "That guy ever wake up over there?"

The tremendous buttocks turns, I assume so that whatever is connected to them can look at me. Oh, God, get me out of here. I close my eyes, pretend I'm asleep. I've seen the bumper stickers stuck to tailgates of those dusty pickup trucks the moment I crossed over the state line: SECEDE! and US OUT OF TEXAS! I just don't take the citizens of the Lone Star State to be the kind of folksy neighbors who will shower goodwill upon a Yankee homosexual who is probably hospitalized because he got knocked up by someone who wasn't his own cousin. At best, they make jokes, the way they do about blacks and Mexicans. *Nigras and Mescuns.* And at worst, they'll throw stones, read me scripture, and make me watch *PTL with Jim and Tammy Faye.*

I keep my eyes closed for at least another hour. *All My Children* ends; *One Life to Live* begins. A nurse comes in to check me, and even though I'm starving, I pretend to be asleep. Finally, the puffy lake people become bored with the schizophrenic Nicki/Vicki story line on *One Life*, so they decide to wallow back to the estuary.

I ring for the nurse. She appears. Nurse Carbonada. She's a hundred years old and smells like broiled meat. "How are you feeling?" she wheezes.

"Fine."

"Your girlfriend was in here this morning. Wants you to know she'll be back this afternoon."

My girlfriend? That guy who brought me here? Gee, Nurse Carbonada is awfully hip.

"Hungry?" she asks.

"I guess. A little."

"You're restricted. I'll bring in what I can."

Before I can ask her what happened last night, she's gone. There's nothing lonelier than being in this hospital by myself and not knowing what circumstances brought me here. Strangely enough, I have the immediate longing for family. But who can I call? My father? Moot point. Although maybe he's already here, watching all this from above. I can't help but wonder if he loves me now, if he understands me in a way he couldn't before. Is he some divine spirit who's stopped passing judgment? He was good to me when I was a kid. Never physically affectionate, but always interactive. Showed me how to toss the tennis ball while serving. Bought me the best golf clubs and demonstrated the right wrist action when chipping onto the green. Taught me everything he'd learned of horses as a boy and bought me a wonderful gelding and schooled me into a knowledgeable equestrian, counseling me on form and helping me train my horse and enter horse shows.

I'll never forget the night everything changed. We were seated around the dining room table, eating dinner, my mother rambling on about "those jakey Carters" and how the White House had become a "hillbilly retreat for poorly dressed beer drinkers" when I said I had something to say. And my mother joked, "If you're going to announce that you're dating Amy Carter, I forbid you to speak." Which was absurd because Amy Carter was ten years old at the time, but I saw my opportunity for the perfect segue.

"No," I said, "I'd rather date her brother Chip." It wasn't true. Chip was kind of goofy looking and his jeans fit too low on his ass for him to be gay, but it got the point across.

My mother knew the moment I said it that I was serious, and she quickly retracted. "With a little makeup, that Amy could be a lovely girl."

But it was too late. And with only a little further discussion, in which Winston was quite silent, my father as well, I explained that I was gay and I didn't see any sense in lying about it and politely declined to see the therapist my mother recommended who'd done wonders convincing the Westholt's daughter that she didn't want to be a longshoreman and hopefully life would go on.

And just when I thought I would get out of my confession alive, my father rose from his chair and slammed his fist down so hard he broke two wineglasses, and decreed, "We are the Fords, goddamn it. The *Kansas Fords!* We're the most powerful oil-and-gas family, not to mention majority landholders, in the state of Kansas, and we will not be taken down by teenage faggotry," which I thought was a magnificent use of the word, and he assured me that, if I was going to live a gay life, then I would live a miserable *anonymous* gay life. And so I did. I stayed in my room most of the time and wrote anonymous poetry and daydreamed about my anonymous invented relationship with the tennis player Guillermo Vilas.

I could call my brother. But do I really want to speak to him? Forget it. He's so fucking smug since the reading of the will. It was just like when I was ten years old and he was twelve and my father called a family meeting to inform me that I would not be allowed to attend summer camp in Colorado, as Winston would, since I'd thoughtlessly ruined my mother's brand-new white Berber carpet in the living room with my greasy cowboy boots. I'll never know how he crammed his feet into them or where he got the grease that was smeared into the soles. I only know that he trudged around the whole room until it was completely defiled, then cheerfully turned me in for the crime. He sat there, the chosen son, the good son, barely containing himself, as Father decreed I would stay home for the summer, not even allowed to ride my beloved horse. And he sat there, almost fourteen years later, barely containing himself, as our family attorney, Sam Johnson, spelled it out, the one condition upon which my financial future depends. I think Winston knew all along—I think Dad told him about the stipulation before he died— that he stood to inherit my part of the trust if I'm not married by my twenty-fourth birthday. "*Legally* married," Sam Johnson stressed, looking at me, "for a continuing period of *ten* years." Winston knows I've been up on my soapbox since the age of seventeen, and that I'm too openly gay to sell out for the money, even if my little share is multiple millions. He's practically salivating at the thought of autumn ushering in my next birthday. I don't want to speak to him. Now or then.

My mother. I'll call my mom and let her know I'm hospitalized, and when she asks me what for, I'll just make something up. As long as I keep it light and breezy she won't care. A wart removal. Liposuction. In-patient pedicure. Something she can relate to. She's great at cheering people up under those circumstances. I turn to grab the phone and notice the flowers at my side. Somebody knows I'm here. As I twist and lift the card from the bouquet, my lower abdomen stings. I reach down and feel the stitches. I lift the sheets and look at the scar; it's big enough to call five inches. God, what happened to me? The note reads:

Darling,
    Out with the old, and in with the new! So happy you're in good hands! Your "special nurse" assures me there's no need to fly down, but if you say the word I'll be there!

Love,
Mom

Nurse Carbonada told my mother not to come? What the hell is going on?

"Hey, Bubba!" Amity sings, gliding into my room, flowers in one hand, a bottle of champagne in the other.

"Amity," I say, surprised. "How did you know I was here?"

She smiles, setting the stargazers down and fluffing them out. She puts the bottle of champagne next to them and turns the label toward me. It's decent bubbly, too decent for a hospital occasion. She sits on the edge of the bed, pulls my paycheck out of her cleavage, and drops it into my hands. "Well, they say whoever brought you here kind of dumped you off. And after your appendix burst, they had to rush you into surgery."

"My appendix. So it wasn't—"

"What?"

I look toward my roommate's shadow behind the curtain. "Never mind."

"Harry, who dropped you off here last night?"

God, she has good instincts. She knows just where to fish. "I just met him yesterday. Some big, tall, lanky guy."

"Lanky? Darlin', that's code for *dick the size of a luxury sedan.*" She starts laughing while smoothing out the bed covers. "For heaven's sake, Harry, that lanky guy had nothing to do with it. It was just your little ole vermiform appendix. It doesn't serve any purpose but to take up space in your life, live off your body, and then at the worst possible time go bad on you. There're *people* like that, you know."

I laugh, and my stitches hurt like hell. "Shit! Don't make me laugh." I breathe in, exhale. "Amity, how did you find me?"

"Well, besides your wallet and insurance card, there was the piece of paper in your pocket that had my phone number on it— and Jacqueline's too, but she wasn't home, so they spoke to me, and I put them in touch with your family."

"My family? But—"

"Through the airline, Harry. Of course I don't know your family, but I convinced the supervisor that you and I were good enough

friends that I needed to call your mother and assure her that everything was simpatico. She's a lovely woman, Harry. Just precious.
I promised her I'd take care of you.''

''See,'' Nurse Carbonada says, shuffling into the room. ''I told
you she'd come back.''

Man, life is fast. Yesterday I had an appendix; today I don't. I
have a new roommate whose family dwells in a lake. I have a
prehistoric nurse who thinks Amity is my girlfriend, and no doubt
my mother *hopes* Amity is my girlfriend, and Amity is *acting* like
my girlfriend. I wonder where the lanky guy went.

The nurse sets my meal tray down in front of me and leaves
before she hears the guy on the other side of the curtain call,
''Nurse? Nurse?''

Amity draws back the curtain slightly, peers in, and says,
''Vampira is gone, darlin'. What can I do for you?''

''Oh,'' I hear the guy say nervously. ''Never mind.''

''Come on now,'' Amity pursues. ''What is it?''

''No, really.''

''This is a hospital,'' she says in a motherly tone. ''Don't be
shy.''

''I need my bedpan emptied.'' He chuckles uncomfortably.

''No problem,'' Amity chirps. She disappears behind the curtain
and then reappears carefully carrying a metal bedpan out in front
of her. She looks sideways at me and winks, announcing, ''Pee-
pee!'' while walking into the bathroom with it. She empties it,
flushes the toilet, walks past me smiling, and steps beyond the
curtain to my compadre. ''Fresh as a daisy,'' she says. He thanks
her and she returns to the bathroom to wash her hands. ''Now,
Harry,'' she calls from the bathroom, ''I have to run errands today
and I may not make it back until after dinner. Are you going to be
OK?''

I hardly even know this girl and she's treating me like a best
friend. If it were any other time in my life I'd ask myself what's

wrong with this picture. But considering the state I'm in, this picture is frameable. "I'll be fine," I answer, opening up the envelope that holds my paycheck. It's still not enough money to get me started on this life in Dallas. And I can only imagine what the hospital bill will be.

"You're sure?" she asks, coming back into the room. I nod affirmatively, and she grabs her purse. "OK then, Bubba, I'm going to take off. They say we can get you out of here in just a couple days. I promise to push things along." She kisses me on the cheek and glides out of the room, singing over her shoulder, "See you tonight!"

"Man," the guy behind the curtain says, "you sure do have one fine lady there. And she don't even care about your sissy-boy cravings."

Sissy-boy cravings? Interesting way to put it. I guess he heard the part about the lanky guy. Yet he's still talking to me? Does this mean the banjo duet from *Deliverance* will start playing, and he'll rip back the curtain and tell me I have a *purdy little mouth*? "What are you in for?" I ask as if we're serving hard time.

"Swollen feet," he answers. "Circulation problems. Can't walk no more." *Cain't woke no mower.*

I relax somewhat, knowing that he can't get to me and that he hasn't had some kind of belly surgery that inspires him to rip back the curtain and lift up his gut and show me the scar. "That's tough. A guy's gotta be able to walk, huh?" I tell him, dipping a spoon into my fish broth.

"It ain't so bad. I can eat lyin' down and watch TV lyin' down. Only thing tough is takin' a shit."

"I can imagine." But I won't. In fact, I think it's time to think about little puppies and rainbows and unicorns and all things fresh and clean.

And about getting out of here.

CHAPTER
THREE

The first week out of the hospital my mother insisted on putting me up in a suite at the Mansion on Turtle Creek. On her days off, Amity visited me, and I was embarrassed to have her see me there, cloaked in the opulence and abundance of Dallas's finest hotel, but Amity loved it and delighted herself each visit by ordering various twenty-four-dollar room service items for me.

But the gravy train is over, I'm healed, as well as financially cut off again, and now I'm back at work for the first time since the surgery. Amity insists on flying with me. "With the stitches removed, I have to make sure your stomach doesn't fly open when the plane depressurizes!" she hoots. She has this off-the-wall way of making me feel wanted. How can I not like her? It's as if she's some character an actress would play—only she's more interesting. And Amity has met me at my weakest, most vulnerable, and insecure, yet easily looks beyond the maudlin sap who cried on the airplane and convalesced in the hospital. She sees the waggish devil from my college days who even I only hope still exists somewhere inside me.

We're assigned to fly with one of my other two training classmates in Dallas. Bart is a god. He has the most incredible legs and ass I've ever seen. Out of uniform, he wears Wrangler jeans and cowboy boots and shirts that show off his muscles. A former high school football jock from one of those interchangeable suburbs north of Dallas, he's Texan to the bone. He loves to tell jokes that put down Yanks like me. All he has to do is shake a woman's hand and look her in the eye, and she'll want to fuck him. He rolls great joints.

This is the first time I've seen Bart since training, and we're huddled with Amity in the front galley of the DC-9 on our way to St. Louis, our first destination of the day. Amity breaks in, "I want to tell a gay joke, but I'm sure Harry's already heard it."

"Why?" Bart asks.

"Because he's gay." *Guy*, it sounds like.

Bart nearly shits a chicken-fried steak. "You are?"

"Of course he is," Amity says. She looks at me. "You don't mind me saying so, do you, Harry?"

"Not at all," I answer nonchalantly. I want her to like me, to think I'm as comfortable as she is. But the truth is, while I'm a pretty candid guy myself, I'm stunned a little by her perpetually openhanded game. She's just so unabashed. So casual with her candor. I half expect her to get on the P.A. system and announce, "Ladies and Gentlemen, at this time, for your own comfort and safety, Harry Ford is gay."

Bart is shocked because I hadn't divulged my orientation to anyone in my training class. It's funny what you learn about yourself when you change your surroundings. I always prided myself that I came out to my family at the age of seventeen and that I lived an open life in a family whose heraldic crest probably looked like one of those red-and-white CLOSED signs in the window of a dry cleaner. But my flight attendant classmates just seemed so much narrower than my college chums, and I knew my friendships with them were finite, so I kept my sexuality to myself.

I also hadn't told anyone I was gay during flight attendant training class because I figured the airline could fire me if they wanted.

There aren't any employment laws to protect me, and after all, it was obvious they were trying to hire "straight." Out of the twelve guys in my class, I was the only gay one. Straight male flight attendant? I thought that was an oxymoron. Maybe at other airlines, but not at this one. For the first time since the age of seventeen, I strategically crawled into the closet. Fortunately, I only lasted two months inside before I came jumping out, figuring, "Fuck it. Let them fire me if they want."

"How does a guy know when his roommate is gay?" Amity asks, launching into the joke. Pause, punch line. "When his dick tastes like shit!" I laugh, and Bart does too, but neither of us louder than Amity. "OK, y'all, time to feed and water the cattle," she commands.

Amity works the first-class section, and the first few rows of coach, and Bart and I drive the cart in the back of the bus. Bart's not really cut out for this work. He's more accustomed to holding a football than a coffeepot, and he's only truly comfortable when he has a can of beer in his hand, which is just long enough to hand it over to a passenger. But he's so gorgeous that few people care that his thumb is in their drink or that he's forgotten the cream for their coffee. Between my socially adept upbringing, and my subsequent poverty during the college years, I'm pretty well suited to the tasks at hand, and Bart often defers to me for help in the delicate operation of spearing a wedge of lime with a swizzle stick without touching it with your fingers or separating two napkins stuck together. When someone asks me for decaf, and I realize we're out of the little instant packets, I traipse to the front galley to procure some from Amity. "You spear your limes ahead of time?" I ask, noticing her cupful of sticks stuck through lime wedges.

"It's the only way. Whether you just picked your nose or not, you gotta take those things in your fingers and *shove* them on the stick. I don't have time to do all that ceremonial bullshit in the aisle with everyone watching.''

She's the master. I'm the student. "We're out of decaf," I tell her.

"Why bother?" she says, grabbing a cup and pouring it full of regular coffee. "Give them this."

"But they'll be wired up for Jesus," I laugh.

"No, they won't. They'll think it's decaf and it won't do a damn thing to them. Power of the mind, baby, power of the mind."

When all the cattle have been fed and watered, and we're all back in the galley, Bart gives me the old line. "I don't think you're really gay. You just haven't had the kind of woman that would show you you're not."

Amity winks at me before taking a glass of water out to a passenger.

"That is such a crock of shit," I tell him, smiling. "You straight people always think you've got it figured out. What if *you're* gay and you don't know it because you just haven't found the right *guy*?"

"What if?" he says, his accent making magic of the question, his thumbs in the belt loops of his uniform pants, his fingers hanging down to the natural bulge of his crotch. He looks at me with a shit-eating grin on his face.

I'd drink this guy's bathwater and he knows it.

Of course we're one big happy threesome by the third flight of the day. It truly is a bonding experience to serve little bags of peanuts to people sitting upright in rows of chairs. Amity breaks out the in-flight champagne in Styrofoam, and we illegally indulge while she teaches us that if, ten napkins are stuck together, we should give the passenger ten napkins, because it isn't worth your valuable time separating them. And even if you're working a flight to Europe, when someone asks how long the flight is, we should always say, "About an hour." And if the captain asks for lemonade, we should tell him we're out, because it isn't worth the trouble to fix lemonade for a guy who (in her case) only wants to "stick his hand up my skirt and play grab ass." And when I ask her what a woman captain wants, she says, "To stick her hand up my skirt and play grab ass." So we learn that lemonade is out of the question. And finally: "Always have a stick of gum sitting out of the wrapper, close by, to take the champagne off your breath in a hurry."

By the end of the day, as we approach Stapleton Airport in Denver, the captain tells us that we'll be landing in a heavy snowstorm, and that operations are limited to a single runway, where we'll make an instrument approach for landing. We circle the city, and all we see out the window are what look like huge shreds of coconut cascading from heaven. "I *love* snow," Amity says dreamily. "If I ever have to be in a crash, I want to go down in snow."

Bart and I look at each other uncomfortably. "Could you be in that crash some other time, Amity?" I ask her.

"Yeah, let's just land and get to the hotel," Bart adds.

By that evening, on the ground, the three of us are practically best friends, smoking pot in the hotel room, watching HBO. Bart takes the joint, places it between his lips, and asks if I want a *shotgun.* I nod, bring my mouth to his until our lips barely touch, and he blows the smoke into me while Amity watches; it's all I can do not to kiss him full on. As I pull my lips away from his, I look over at Amity, who gives me the slightest smile, and I know she's reading my mind. I'd *kill* for this guy.

After trudging down the snowy street for a dinner of steak and mashed potatoes, which Amity washes down with champagne, we return to Amity's hotel room, crank the heater, and settle on the bed, all three of us. We smoke more pot and listen to the Eurythmics on the little radio at the side of the bed.

Sweet dreams are made of this . . . .

Somehow this is all less innocent, more dangerous, than my college cavorting—which was solely limited to men. This is the real world, and we all have jobs, and Bart is a straight guy from Texas who played high school football, and I'm a Yankee who doesn't really understand him or Amity or their intentions at the moment. Bart takes his hand, slides it behind Amity's neck and pulls her mouth to his. While he kisses her, he slowly places his other hand on my thigh. He doesn't move it. He just keeps it there while he gently eats Amity's face. I follow the veins in his hands down to his long, sexy fingers. Should I reach out, take his hand, and move it to where I want it to be? Before I make a move, Bart pulls back from Amity. Turns to me. "Now you," he says.

I can't believe I'm going to kiss a real live straight cowboy. And by the way he kissed Amity, I know he's talented. "OK," I answer, my voice nervous. I reach my hand toward his shoulder to hang on, but he intercepts it and steers it toward Amity. He leans forward, twists, and pulls Amity to me. "You kiss her," he says.

Fuck. He's toying with me, setting me up, trying to see if I can get it going with a girl. I've never done it with a girl, and the only time I even came close, my dick made it clear it wasn't going to cooperate, so I made some lame excuse about not having a condom and bailed out.

"Come on, buddy," he says, coaxing me.

Shit. If he's trying to hand me the "right girl" so I can straighten out, I'm not into this. I should get up and go. But what if this is the beginning of all three of us together? If he sees me with Amity, will he join in? Maybe it can work. It would be worth it, seeing him naked, watching him make love. I lean over and place my lips against hers. I haven't kissed a girl since high school; it feels strange and even abnormal to have contact with such soft pink lips. The lack of beard or whisker stubble on her face makes her alien to me. She's soft and perfumed, and I try to stay tender with her. She starts moaning and kissing me harder, her tongue moving freely inside my mouth. I feel the bed move and realize that Bart is rising off the mattress. I continue to kiss Amity, but turn my head, to watch him undress. Instead, he tucks his shirt in. He's leaving.

"Where are you going?" I ask, breaking from Amity.

"You don't need me now, cowboy," he says slyly.

If he only knew. My dick is softer than a warm stick of butter, and unless he stays and rolls his piece of corn on it, it's going to stay that way. Why hasn't Amity said anything? And why did she go along with this whole setup? Did they plan this together on the airplane today? My uneasy eyes slide their gaze to Amity, and she understands. "I think you'd better stay, Bart," she says breathlessly.

Bart stands there, doesn't move. He closes his eyes, rubs his eyebrow, looks uncomfortable. For all his swagger and tease earlier, I can tell it's something he can't do. "Yes, I think you'd better stay, Bart," I echo, rolling off the mattress. "And I'll be taking my leave."

I walk past Bart, who gives me a single sexy nod of his gorgeous jock-boy head. "You sure?" he asks.

"I'm sure."

Amity jumps up and walks me to the door, then opens it. "Are you OK, Harry?" she whispers. "I had nothing to do with this."

I'm embarrassed. I feel clumsy. "I'm fine," I tell her. "He's a stud. Go for it."

"Don't worry. I'll do you proud. He'll be limping home to his stall, darlin'."

I smile, step out into the hall.

"You're a good kisser, Harry. Are we still friends?"

I nod yes.

She kisses me again, this time on the cheek, and I head into the hall.

I enter my room next door and fall onto the bed, full of conflict and question. The question isn't whether I'm gay. I am. The question is whether I could have done it without Bart somehow involved, and I think the answer is no. Minute's pass, but I can't get the thought of him out of my head. His thick wrists, the veins in his neck, his tongue lapping at Amity's face. What would his perfect ass look like out of those Wrangler jeans? Do his feet really fill those big, wide cowboy boots? I'm aroused again, and soon my erection is spurred on by the sounds coming from the other side of the wall.

I've got to hear them. I rip off my clothes and throw them on the floor. Then I run to the bathroom, grab an empty water glass, and return to the bed with it. I stand on the bed and place the glass on the wall, just to the edge of the huge framed knockoff of van Gogh's water lilies, and press my ear to the cold glass, absorbing the echo of Bart and Amity making love.

"Ah, ah, ah," he moans as if his horse is cantering on the wrong lead over pavement. It's a rough ride, but he's thoroughly enjoying it.

Amity breaks in, "Oh, baby, you drive me *wild!*"

The bed creaks and crunches, and I hear one of their heads moving against the wall.

"Yee haw, baby. Yee haw!" Amity whoops.

Yee haw? Is he riding on top of her like a horse? Is he holding on to her hair like reins, his big, sexy forearms flexing as he steers her right, then left, then pulls back on her? Is she some porno Trigger, rearing up into his big, sexy chest while he takes her from behind? No, wait: She said he'd go to his stall limping, so is *she* on top? Is he stretched out below her, his muscled legs reaching for miles, his big arms holding her shoulders while she rides him to the edge of the cliff in a full gallop?

In my excitement, the glass slips from my hand, and as it falls toward the end table, I try to catch it, but in my haste I knock the monstrous van Gogh off the wall, and it comes crashing down onto the headboard like thunder and flies sideways onto the end table, breaking the water glass and smashing into the phone, which flies off the table with a booming ring. I turn to jump off the bed and catch myself in the mirror, naked, horrified, my stick of butter frozen hard.

I carefully step around the broken glass and grab the painting, lifting it away. As I set it on the other bed, I realize the rodeo on the other side of the wall has shut down. Ceased all events. There's not a sound from the riders. Shit. I can only imagine what it must have sounded like to them. I gingerly place the receiver back on the hook and lift the phone to the table. As I'm setting it down, it rings.

I let it ring. Four times. Then slowly lift the handset. "Yes?"

"You all right over there, big guy?" Bart asks.

"Yes."

"Anything broken, Bubba?"

I look at my penis. "No."

"Well . . ." he says. I hear Amity giggle in the background.

"I'm going to take a shower now," I tell him.

"Keep the water cold, buddy. Keep the water cold."

The next three days of the trip, Bart holds Amity's hand when she steps out of the crew van, carries her luggage through the airport, opens any doors for her, orders her champagne at dinner, and fucks her as if she's a sheep from Kansas.

And the two of them adopt me as their favorite son. We're one little happy airline family. Our failed attempt at sex hasn't hurt Amity's and my relationship in the least. Nor mine and Bart's. On the contrary, we have something to bind us and also make us laugh. And that's how it is in the airline business, I'm told. People get incredibly close for a few days, and then they don't see each other for maybe another year or two or five.

But I have a feeling that, if I stick with Amity, I'll have some kind of a family here in Texas. And that's what I intend to do.

*   *   *

The night of our arrival back in Dallas, Amity suggests Bart come to her house for a drink. She also enthusiastically invites me to come along, but I decline, since I get the feeling that Bart wants another rodeo ride, and I don't want to be the clown who distracts the bull this time. Amity and I agree to get together as soon as our days off coincide, and I bid her and Bart good night.

My days at the Mansion are over, my paycheck isn't enough for me to make a deposit on an apartment, and I can't spend money for even a sleazy hotel room (because my student loan payments are starting, and my hospital bills will be coming in). So I decide to sleep in the one of the four commuter bunks in the flight attendant lounge. It won't be long, just over a week, before my next paycheck, and until then, I can crash on a bunk.

But tonight, the bunks are all taken, and I'm forced to curl up on a sofa in the main lounge while attendants come and go. I'm almost asleep when I hear Amity's voice. "Christ on a crutch, Harry. What are you doing?"

I open my eyes. "Sleeping," I say foolishly. "What are you doing here?"

"I was all the way in the parking lot when I realized I left my vest," she says, grabbing it off the back of a chair. "And of course I'd hate to lose a single piece of this god-awful uniform. Why are you sleeping in the lounge?"

I sit up. "I'm a little tight on funds. I need a couple weeks to get on my feet."

"Harry, you're a Ford, but not an Edsel. Sleeping in the lounge is worse than living below the underpass. Wait here," she orders.

"Where are you going?" I ask.

She calls over her shoulder while gliding out of the lounge, "Bart's waiting out front—I'll get rid of him."

"But—" Before I can argue, she's out the door.

In a few minutes she returns. "Come on. You're going home with me."

"I feel guilty," I tell her, picking up my luggage.

"Why? Bart's got a home—you don't."

"But he wanted to be with you tonight."

She smiles, holding the door open for me. "Not anymore. I told him I just started my period."

It's a white wood-framed, one-story house that sits on a corner near the Dallas Congregational University campus. As she puts the key in the lock, I cup my hands to the glass door and look past the enclosed porch into the living room. The lights are on, and I see a shiny hardwood floor that looks as if it was polished by hand, a wood-framed lithograph of one of those English horse-and-hound hunting scenes, and a single elegant wingback chair sitting confidently alone. It is so well ordered, so the opposite of my chaotic life at the moment.

"Where's Jacqueline?" I ask.

"Didn't I tell you? Jacqueline moved out."

"So fast?" I can tell by the quick way she says it there's something more to the story. "What happened?"

"Girl stuff. I won't bore you with the details."

"But you and Jacqueline seemed like good friends," I protest.

Like a *Star Search* spokesmodel, she sweeps her arms upward and across while moving into the house, her heels barely making a sound on the hardwood floor as she walks. "This is the living room," she announces, throwing her arms apart. I expect the walls to slide open and reveal a speedboat and a gas grill. She rests her hand on the fireplace mantel—the fireplace that has been sealed off and no longer burns wood—and looks into the mirror above it. Instead of looking at herself, she looks at the reflection of me and smiles into the glass.

"I get the feeling you don't want to talk about Jacqueline," I tell her.

She takes her glance from me, her smile fades, and she stares at her own reflection. "Sometimes people aren't at all what they appear to be," she tells herself. For a moment she stares at her visage, unblinking. And she looks as if she might even cry. Then, like a wind-up toy that is suddenly rewound to its tightest turn, she smiles and chirps, "Let's have a drink!" and flings me into the kitchen, which is too small to house such a big mood swing. As she opens the refrigerator, I can sense she's aware of my scrutiny, which is why she bypasses the Diet Dr Pepper and nail polish to go straight for the only other item in her refrigerator: champagne.

She pops the cork, fills two flutes, hands one to me, then glides back through the living room and the hallway so smoothly that the champagne in her glass doesn't even move. I look to see if she has wheels on the bottom of her shoes. We arrive at the doorway of the vacant bedroom. "This is your bedroom if you want it, Harry Ford," she offers. "I'm a great roommate."

I'm stunned. I thought she was offering me a room for the night, not something permanent. "You're serious?"

"Serious as Dan Rather sitting on a corncob."

I peer into the bedroom; it's carpeted and has windows in two different walls. "You'd offer a stranger a place to live?" I ask.

"Harry!" she says, hitting me on the shoulder, spilling a little of my champagne. "You're not a stranger. Do you consider me a stranger?"

"No," I answer sheepishly, still wondering what happened to Jacqueline.

"You need a place to stay. I need someone to share with. So let's be roommates."

"But I don't even have a bed," I tell her.

"No problemo, amigo," she tells me, going into the hallway and opening the closet door. She hauls out a deflated full-size mattress. "I don't have a pump so I guess we're just going to have to blow up this bad boy ourselves," she says. I follow her to the living room where she puts *Thriller* on the turntable and starts it up. She takes me by the hand and leads me back to the carpeted square hallway that sits in the center of the house, dividing the bedrooms from the bathroom and living room. I feel like a little boy being led to school. We sit on the floor and smoke from the bong.

"I'm so glad you're here, Harry. I think we're going to be wonderful roommates." *Room mites.*

I'm flattered. "Me too, Amity. Thanks for helping me out, coming to the hospital, and now offering me a place."

"I know you'd do the same for me," she says matter-of-factly. She grabs the bong, stuffs it full of marijuana, and offers it to me. I use the plastic lighter and light up. I smile at her as I inhale. She smiles back. Her hair is a mop of gold, falling down upon her shoulders like sunlight onto a beautiful ridge. Her face is lightly brushed with color, and she is wearing the same perfume as the day we met. But when she sticks her painted lips around the bong and sucks like a Hoover, she's all action. It's a fetching quality I notice right away—her ability to meld the feminine with gusto. She's take charge, confident, one of the guys. I can't help but like her, because, for whatever reason, whether we're straight or gay, guys like guys—especially when they're women.

We blow and blow that air mattress, stoned out of our minds. The more oxygen we surrender, the higher we get, as if we're sitting on our own private mountain. We start laughing about Michael Jackson, who's wailing in the background.

"Sings like Tarzan, looks like Jane," I choke.

"Looks like his mother," Amity corrects.

"What?"

"Everybody always thinks he's trying to look like Diana Ross, but just look at a picture of his mother—*that's* who he's trying to look like. It's all subconscious, I'm sure. Anyway, I don't care

what he looks like. He's rich!'' Amity screams. ''If he wants to
fuck me, I'll shut my eyes and turn him into Billy Dee Williams.''

''I couldn't do it with him, even with my eyes closed.''

''He can wear his little dust-and-particle mask while we make
love!''

I take a sip of water to offset my cotton mouth. ''Are you
dusty?''

''Of course not. Lemon Pledge, baby. But you know Michael.
He's got to be sure before he impregnates me. I can't wait to have
Michael Jackson's alien baby!'' *Bye-bee!*

We laugh until we choke and pee our pants and think we'll die
if we don't catch a breath. And we know if someone comes into
the house and asks us what we're laughing at we'll laugh even
harder.

And this is the moment I know I'm saved—that I will survive
post-school, post-suicide, post-breakup, real-world, no-inheritance
adult life. Because there's somebody in Dallas, Texas, who doesn't
want me for the value of my family name or money or my willing-
ness to make her laugh—because Michael Jackson can supply it
all.

And that night, as I stretch out on my air mattress, borrowed
covers pulled up to my neck, I lie back and stop worrying about
where I'm going to be five minutes from now. And for the first
time in weeks, I drift quickly off to sleep, thanks to Amity—plus
my waning marijuana-induced stupor.

''No! Help me! No!''

Amity is screaming! I kick the covers off. Roll out of bed. Run
into a wall. Out. Into her room. ''Amity?''

She turns the light on beside her bed and sits up. ''Harry,'' she
says, clutching her heart. ''Go back to bed.''

''What's the matter, Amity? Are you OK?''

''Nightmare,'' she whispers, staring at the wall ahead of her.

"That silly old nightmare." She turns the light off and rolls onto her side. "Go," she whispers.

I'm left standing in the dark. Awkwardly, I feel my way out of her room, and grope the wall to make the turn into my own room. Settling down onto my air mattress, I have to wonder what she meant by *that silly old nightmare*. Though clearly in terror, she spoke coolly and tried to brush it off, as if describing an annoying but harmless cousin who showed up uninvited at a party. But there was more to it, I could tell. Something in her eyes told me it was far more familiar than that and far more frightening.

For a moment I get a sick feeling. Have I done the wrong thing by moving in here? Do I really know this girl? There's always more to people than you think. I like to think of the *more* as good, but what if it's not?

Forget it. It's probably just my mind going paranoid on all this smoke. In fact, that's probably it: the pot. She was having a stoner nightmare, and here I am making a big deal of it. Creating some big dark secret that doesn't really exist. Right? Maybe. I don't know. What happened to my blissful sleep? I'm hungry. Shit, all she has is Diet Dr Pepper and champagne. Never mind. I'm too wired to sleep. This air mattress feels as if it's floating on a body of water. When I move, it tilts, and I fear it will capsize if I'm not careful. This blanket is irritating every nerve cell in my body. I kick it off, but then grow cold. I drag it back on. I wait for sleep. Am I too stoned? Or not stoned enough?

Should I really be sleeping here at all?

CHAPTER
FOUR

I stay. I sleep on the sheets she provides, wash my hair with her shampoo, and listen to her records on her old beater of a stereo. And when she's sleeping at home and not with her boyfriend, I attempt to grow accustomed to her occasional nightmares. On the flight attendant seniority list, she is senior and I am junior, so we cross paths only occasionally at first. On a day off, I fly back to Kansas and reclaim my car from Matthew, a 1968 Volkswagen Beetle, and drive it back to Dallas. The poor old car has seen sixteen years of service, and it barely limps down to Texas. I coax it along, knowing that, if it breaks down, I'm fucked, because I just don't have the money to fix it.

My second weekend in Dallas, Amity is down in Houston on a date. She says it's a flight attendant thing—going out of town for a date. You don't have to clean your house, you impress your date with your mobility, and you're guaranteed to have sex, because when it's over, you fly away.

I'm jealous that she's in Houston with a guy. I wish it were me. But now that I'm feeling somewhat more secure, and my stitches are dissolved, I'm brave enough to strike out on my own for a night.

I head over to the gay bars. I luck out and find a parking place

right in the thick of it on Cedar Springs, and as I step out of my
'68 VW, I hear a gaggle of guys catcall my Kansas license plate.
"Girl, you need to ask the Wizard for a new car!" I look at them
and laugh, as if they're just having fun with me, and they look back
as if I've broken a rule by smiling at a stranger. A different guy
says, "He ought to ask the Wizard for a friend." That hurts. They
walk on, singing "If I Only Had a Friend." My confidence is
weakened.

I unknowingly choose a bar that's infamous for its heavy S&M:
Stand and Model. The place is named LBJ's and I'm amazed that
the Johnsons haven't sued. It's all glass and chrome and pretense.
The floor is actually carpeted with now filthy dark green short pile
carpet that does nothing to soak up the deafening sound of the
thump-thump gay-boy music. Behind the main bar is a wall-to-wall
mirror that the bartenders use for preening rituals during their few
off moments: flick of the hair, teeth check, suck in the cheeks,
change the angle. The patrons use the mirror for the same thing;
these guys in Dallas act like peacocks. I order a beer, stand two
feet from where I paid the bartender, and check my hair in the
mirror until I'm pushed aside, little by little, by people with biceps
who know each other. The place is packed, and no one speaks to
me. I look for, but don't find, a sign that says: GUYS WITH SMALL
ARMS MEET HERE. I squeeze myself over to a new area near steps
that lead to an elevated platform. I park awhile and try to look
relaxed, friendly. Friendly doesn't work here. Every time I glance
at someone he looks away, as if he doesn't want to be the one to
tell me I've been turned down by the Barbizon School. As the place
fills to its limits, I'm pushed farther up the stairs until I'm on the
shiny platform surrounded by a chrome railing.

Before I know it, the lights go off, and a spotlight slaps itself
onto the platform and I can feel its heat, and standing inside that
spotlight is a god with a microphone. "OK!" he says. "It's contest
night!" A few guys whoop and holler, but most everybody looks

toward the platform stage with scrutinizing smirks, their mental scorecards ready. The MC, in jeans and a white tank top, has biceps the size of hams and thighs as big as toddlers. His face is stunning, even under all that bronzer. "We're tired of girls being the only ones who enter wet T-shirt contests, right?"

The crowd livens a bit more and applauds and yells its agreement.

"So let's see 'em, boys! Show us those pecs!" Nobody comes forward, and I can see he's getting anxious. "Come on. There's a fifty-dollar prize!" The gorgeous carny barker with the biceps and thighs is too close, and I'm trying hard to escape his range. As he scouts, he makes eye contact with me. I push back into the people behind me, but they respond by giving me a *hard* shove, and I land in the arms of the MC god. "OK, here he is!" he shouts.

The crowd goes wild.

I want to die. I look behind me and see the guy who said I should ask the Wizard for a friend. He and his friends are laughing hysterically at me. They pushed me. They fucking pushed me into the contest.

"What's your name?" the god asks, putting his arm around my shoulders the way a gym coach would.

"I'm not in the contest," I say, the microphone magnifying my twidly voice a hundred times.

"You are now!" the guy says, and as he backs off, some guy out of nowhere sprays me down with a hose. I want to scream. I'm not even wearing a T-shirt. My favorite long-sleeved flannel shirt is instantly soaked and stuck to my skin. The primping crowd of boys goes wild as splashes of water ricochet off my little no-pecs chest and splatter their faces. I'm practically in shock, the water is so cold. I try to leave, push against the mean gaggle. They huddle like a trio of sissy defensive linemen and hold me back. The MC asks the crowd, "What do you think?"

The crowd, seeing my humiliation, goes *wild*. I'm so desperate and losery, they *love* it. I don't know how they can applaud so forcefully when they're laughing so hard.

Again, I push hard past the gaggle, and this time I escape. As I press through the crowd, I hear catcalls and get slapped on the ass. Somehow I find the door and get out. The winter air is cold against my wet shirt. Thank God my car is close. I lock the doors, fall back against the seat.

What a fucking nightmare. Most gay guys will tell you they hate those obnoxious straight guys—big, mean, steroid-pumped jerks who work construction or man the oil rigs, who whistle and holler at women with big tits. But everyone in the place tonight was acting just like them—they were screaming for big tits in a wet shirt and acting like pigs. "What a bunch of fucking assholes," I say aloud, starting the car.

The car chugs to life, and I slide the heater knob over. Aw, hell, who am I kidding? If I hadn't been on stage, I'd have been ogling any guy with a decent chest and catcalling too. I'm just pissed off my chest is so small. Everybody tells me I have a cute butt—so why couldn't it have been a wet butt contest? I release the clutch, pull away, and drive to the nearest pay phone, where I dial information for the number of the neighborhood's 24-Hour Nautilus. The guy at the gym sounds garbled, as if he's in the middle of swallowing a mouthful of supplements, but I understand his directions well enough to jump back into the VW and take a left, then the first right, onto Oak Lawn, and about a quarter of a mile later there it is: a 24-Hour Nautilus. I wheel in and turn the VW off. Before I can talk myself out of it, I haul out and march inside, all wet and dripping. The guy behind the counter thinks I'm nuts until I pull out my credit card and he sees that I really do want to buy a membership right here, right now. I haven't allowed myself to charge on my new credit cards I've obtained since landing my job because I'm already so far in debt. But this is an emergency. As I'm filling out the forms, I feel someone staring at me. I look up to see a well-built guy with jet black hair and eyes the color of green glacier ice. He's leaving, his gym bag over his shoulder, and he casts his glance on me long enough to make me think he's interested. I can't believe it. He's way out of my league, but I know how to read the signs. I hurriedly put my signature all over the pages and try to make it out to the parking lot in time to catch him. Too late. He's driving off in his shiny black BMW. But then he stops—and so does my heart. Do I walk over to his car? The driver's window rolls down, his sexy pumped arm comes out, his hand holding a white piece of paper, a card it seems. I walk over, step up to his window, and look in to see a masculine face that's even more gorgeous than I remember from minutes ago. In the dark, his glacier green eyes glow more stunning yet, and before I say a word he tells me in a sexy drawl, "I've got to get home." Then he hands me his card, his wedding ring catching the glow of the parking lot lights, and drives away.

I look at his card:

> *JT Reardon*
> *Sales*
> *Fairway BMW*

And only his business number is on the card. Great. He wants to sell me a car.

Since moving in, I've not seen a lot of Amity because she's been spending nights with her boyfriend, Troy, the guy who whisked her away from the airport the day I met her.

"Come sit on the bathtub, Harry, and talk to me while I poo up for my date with Troy." *Poo up* is her phrase for the production of putting on her makeup and doing her hair, she explains. I soon find out it's a minimum two-hour production, and it's always done with the help of a glass of champagne and a toke off the bong.

"What happened to Bart?" I ask, sitting on the edge of the bathtub, watching her from the backside. She wears a pair of men's boxer shorts and a flimsy camisole. I love that she's so relaxed in front of me.

"I'm still seeing Bart," she answers, locking her eyelashes into her eyelash curler. "But he's hard to get to know, Harry. He still lives with his parents in Plano. I went out to their house, and all Bart wanted to do was watch TV. That's just not this girl's style." *Stawl.* She switches the curler to the other eye, causing the strap on her flimsy camisole to fall over one shoulder. "And every time I sleep with him he's wearing the same boxer shorts," she giggles, wrinkling her nose. "You change *your* underwear, don't you, Harry." It is a statement, not a question, to extol my virtue and erode Bart's. She starts extracting the rollers from her hair, and each shock of hair falls and bounces like an uncoiling snake. "You know why his ass looks so good in those jeans, don't you?"

"Why?"

"He buys women's jeans. They fit his ass better and make his box look big." She unleashes the last roller, turns, and screams, "Medusa!" while her coils of snakes fly in all directions.

"Don't touch me," I beg, laughing.

"It's too late!" she says, playfully putting a finger on my chin. "Now you know why my last name is Stone!" She starts fluffing out the snakes, one by one, using a hair pick and her hands, and each shock of hair triples in size. Soon she has the whole thing jacked out to *there*, and I'm sitting under its mass. It's like when I was a boy, growing up in Kansas, and I would play golf with my father while the afternoon clouds grew larger and larger and closer and closer as they silently exploded over the Western plains, and everything on earth was in their shadow.

I'm amazed watching her transformation. I had no idea how much a product of her cosmetics she is. Not that she's not beautiful without them, but I realize the Amity I've known in these couple of weeks is more of a visual creation than I thought. What's more amazing is that she's just as unabashed about herself in situ as she is about everything else. She's not reticent in the least to make the transition from Plain Amity to Glamorous Amity right before my eyes and stop in the middle of it all to sit on the toilet and pee while I sit across from her on the tub and talk. Man, I didn't know girls were this casual. My mom never peed in front of me—I'm not sure she peed at all. And she certainly never let me see her without any makeup on. The fact that Amity is taking the mystery out of it kind of makes it all the more mysterious.

"He still has a killer ass," I say, getting back to Bart. I love the idea of this country-boy jock buying women's jeans, and I refuse to let her ruin my image of him.

"I like what's in front of the ass," she says, candidly. "Dicks!" She goes into her bedroom, and like a puppy with a new master, I follow. "A girl should never kiss and tell," she says, taking a preppy-looking plaid dress—navy, maroon, and beige with a white collar—off the hanger. "But we're roommates, right, Harry?"

"Right."

"Bart doesn't like getting his dick sucked. I don't know why. When I get down there he pushes my head away. All he wants to do is fuck me. And I just don't know about that."

What can I say? I don't like it when all somebody wants to do is fuck *me*.

"He just doesn't have the class of say . . . a member of the Ford family from Kansas," she declares.

Shit. She knows about my family. "And what do you know about the Fords?" I ask tentatively.

"Everybody knows about the Kansas Fords, Bubba. Your momma throws that charity ball every year, and your daddy's one of the few who inherited wealth but still had a distinguished career." Then she adds reverently, "God rest his soul."

My warning flags go up. In college, there was a kid in my dorm who knew everything there was to know about my father and the Fords. It was as if he'd read every mention in every little newspaper column. He'd refer to my mom, dad, and brother by their first names. It only made me steer clear of him. "How come you haven't told me you know who my family is?" I ask.

"How come you haven't told me yourself?" she counters.

"I did," I answer defensively "The day we met. I spilled my guts, if you remember."

"You didn't tell me you were a *Ford.*"

The hair on my neck rises. I hate when people use my family name *with emphasis*. "I've always found it easier to be a regular Joe than an irregular Ford," I explain, "and I decided when I started this airline life that I'd keep my lineage a secret. Does it matter?" If it does, I'm out of here.

"Not in the least, Harry. Your family isn't much different from mine."

I realize I've been selfish. I've been so wrapped up in my family dramas, I've never really taken the time to ask about Amity's family. "Tell me about them," I urge.

"I'd rather not," she answers.

"Come on," I goad. "What are they like?"

"I'm from money too," Amity says, stepping into her dress. She faces the mirror, not me, but I see her reflection and her visage is guarded. "But like you, I'm sort of disconnected from my family. They're from Fort Worth, you know."

"What's Fort Worth like?" I ask, the ignorant Yankee.

"Fort Worth is old money, Harry. The good families, families like yours, are from Fort Worth. Not Dallas," she says with contempt, "where everyone's nigger rich."

It sounds ugly to hear the word *nigger*—particularly when it's spoken with a Southern accent. I've noticed that the people I've met in Texas get away with saying it by not actually using the word to call a black person a *nigger*, but by using it in phrases. If someone is nouveau riche, as my mother says in Kansas, they're deemed *nigger rich* in Texas. Likewise, if something is broken and has been shoddily repaired, it is *nigger rigged,* rather than jury-rigged. "You've said you have a brother and a sister, right?"

"Right," she says. "Zip me up."

I reach behind her back and zip her up. "Are you the youngest, oldest? Fucked-up middle child?"

"Oldest," she blurts. "I'm very well adjusted. My whole family is."

"So why are you estranged from them?"

"My own choice. It's personal, Bubba."

"But you say your family has money *and* is well adjusted? What did you do, make them out of papier-mâché in kindergarten?"

She smiles, while slipping diamond droplets into her lobes, but her face tightens and looks strange—as if she *did* make them out of papier-mâché. "Whoa," Amity says. "Whoa, Bubba. We've talked about my family longer than we've talked about yours." She finishes with the earrings and positions her hands in the time-out signal.

"You're right," I acknowledge. "Fair is fair. No more family talk." Still, hers must be the first moneyed family on earth that is well adjusted. Hard to believe.

When Troy arrives, she has me answer the door. We shake hands and head for the sofa in the little sitting room off the kitchen. Right away I can tell he is friendly, outgoing, thick. Like if you asked him what the capital of Texas was, he'd say, "The T." He is preppy to the nth. A big, blond prep boy in khakis and a plaid button-down shirt. Webbed belt, polished loafers, the whole nine yards. Not nearly as mysterious as that day I saw him at the airport. Now I understand the dress Amity has chosen. And when Amity makes her entrance, she is the perfect preppy date. I notice she's more reserved, somewhat proper, in her manner with Troy, which really surprises me, because this is the first time I've seen her hold back.

We all get stoned together on some pot I bought before leaving Kansas, and Troy and I grow stupider while Amity becomes more alert. It is really the most intense pot I've ever had—I bought it from a town cop, who I assume took it after busting some student. It smells like a ground-up pine tree, and I keep it in a baggie that has pictures of Mickey Mouse on it. After Troy and Amity leave, my beeper goes off. I'm so fucked up I can hardly dial the phone, and I want to die when they tell me I have to make it out to the airport for the last departure to Houston. I can't even *function* when I'm stoned.

As usual, I'm assigned to our smallest, least glamorous aircraft, the DC-9. The two girls I fly with, Beverly and Angela, look at me with great suspicion. Maybe I'm paranoid, but I'm sure they know I'm stoned. I've doused my eyeballs with Visine, but they're still redder than diaper rash and drier than lint. I blink every two seconds, and though I keep using Visine, it's like pointlessly adding water to dead potted plants.

"Are you all right?" *All rot?* Beverly asks, as we prepare the cart in the galley. She's a hefty gal with large hips, fat ankles, and heavy earrings. She put her hand to her mouth and whispered about me to Angela after I introduced myself in the flight attendant lounge.

"Fine. Why?"

She tells me, accusingly, "Your eyes look funny."

The truth is, her eyes look funny too. I wonder if Mary Kay has anything left in her inventory. "I have allergies," I lie.

"Maybe you should see a doctor," she suggests snidely.

"Maybe you should too," I answer, fumbling a cup of condiment packets that lands on the floor.

She's perplexed. "Why should I see a doctor?"

I'm on the floor, picking up these stupid little packets of coffee *whitener*, and my marijuana-induced paranoia makes me want to hide inside the stinky lavatory until we get to Houston. "I don't know. When was your last . . . inspection?"

"For what?"

I don't know. I'm stoned out of my mind! "Um . . . your levels."

"What levels?"

"Oil."

"My oil levels? What the hell are you talking about?" she asks, her beefy ankles inches from my face.

"You could be low," I caution.

"I think your brain levels are low," she snips. "Come on. We need to get these people their drinks before we land."

I peel the last packet off the scummy floor and stand up before I realize she's extended the shelf on the end of the cart. My head hits it as I rise, and a can of Pepsi falls to the floor and punctures, spewing both of us with a spray of sticky soda. She screams and clings to the emergency door while the can spins around, blowing Pepsi onto everything in its radius.

Fuck this stupid job. I want my inheritance.

CHAPTER FIVE

"Hurry, Harry! I'm so nervous Troy's going to come home!"

It's the middle of the day. He's at work, but we're both nervous. Amity has used her key to get into Troy's apartment, and we are cleaning out everything that belongs to her. It isn't much—just a few pieces of jewelry, some pictures, clothing. But she is throwing it all into a bag as if he were coming up the steps with a gun.

"He just doesn't understand," she says, hurriedly grabbing a shirt off a hanger. "I'm not going to marry him. He was a *frat boy*, Harry. They never grow up. They talk so *loud*. They chew with their mouths open. They don't wash their balls. Forget it. Troy just wants a country club wife." *Wawf.* "Is that everything?" she asks. "Wait! I'm going to take a couple pairs of his boxer shorts. After all, I bought them for him." She opens his underwear drawer and helps herself. Then she runs to the kitchen, grabs a diet soda out of the *icebox*, as she refers to it, and yells, "Let's go!"

"Aren't you going to leave him a note or something?"

"I already did. I mailed it yesterday. He should get it today." *To die.*

She puts her sunglasses on, and I escort her to the parking lot as if she were a movie star coming out of an abortion clinic. We hustle into my VW and quickly roll away.

"I'm so hungry I could eat the ass end out of a rag doll!" she says as we speed down Skillman.

I laugh. "What are you hungry for?"

"Cowboy Bill's Chicken," she says, rubbing her hands together. Her hands are the only thing that don't match the rest of her. They're younger than she is, like the hands of a child, with perfectly manicured fingernails. "Rotisserie chicken, Harry—it's the best." She lets out a big sigh as if she were a stage actress who wants the people in the far-off reaches of the balcony to hear her.

"What?" I ask, eyes on the road.

"Every time I go to Cowboy Bill's Chicken, I think about my ex-boyfriend Jerod. He was a cowboy artist from Fort Worth. Oh, Harry, I loved him so much. I really did. He was *wonderful*. Real cowboys from Fort Worth are gentlemen, not like the city cowboys in Dallas—they're not cowboys at all."

"He was an artist?" I ask, stopping at a light.

"Yes. He painted Texas landscapes and did sculpture. Harry, Jerod made love to me better than anyone I've ever been with," she says breathlessly, putting her hand between her legs.

The light turns green. She moans, her hand between her legs. "God, Amity, don't have an orgasm," I laugh, stepping on the gas.

"Why not?" she asks seriously. As I drive on, she licks her fingers and moves her hand inside her blue jeans. "He always knew to wet his fingers before putting them inside me," she pants, sounding like a Texan Marilyn Monroe.

"Shit, Amity. Are you jacking off?" I ask, not believing this.

"Jerod had the greenest eyes," she moans, working herself. "And his stubble scratched my face till it hurt." She smiles at the memory while moving her hand faster. "He wore sleeveless flannel shirts that showed off his big, strong arms," she wails, "and he loved to spank me if I took too long getting ready to go out!"

What am I supposed to do? I'm laughing, I think, out of nervousness, but she's so steeped in Jerod's memory she doesn't care. Maybe I should give her a moment alone. "Do you want me to stop the car?" I ask.

"No! Go faster!"

I step on the pedal, the VW spurts ahead in a jerk, and Amity cries out. I can't believe she's jacking off (when a woman does it, is it called jacking off?) right in front of me in my car. Whatever it's called, I assume they usually do it in private. Obviously my mother is incorrect in telling me that "a woman doesn't have great needs" or that "as long as you don't *tell* her you're gay, she'll never notice." She hasn't met Amity.

"Faster!" Amity shouts.

"I'm going to get a ticket!" I yell as the little engine pushes harder. We're on a city street, and I'm nearly up to fifty miles an hour on the speedometer. I check for cops.

"Jerod was a gentleman—he never came before I did. Change lanes!" she says.

I swerve over to the next lane, and she squeals with the motion. I'm embarrassed. I wish we were at Cowboy Bill's so she could just duck into the bathroom or something.

"He did push-ups on the kitchen table! Go back!" she commands.

Sitting so close to her, feeling her state of excitement, I realize my face is flushed and my hands are so clammy I can hardly steer the old bug back to the other lane.

She squeals as I make the lane change. "Jerod's dick was thicker than a buffalo in China," she screams, throwing herself back in the seat and writhing like a snake on gravel. "Harry, roll the windows down!" she calls out while twisting and jerking herself into an orgasm. "I'm so wet we're going to drown in this car like Mary Jo Kopechne!"

* * *

"Darlin'," she chirps, to the teenage boy at the drive-through window at Cowboy Bill's Chicken, "do you have any of those little moist towelette packets? My fingers are sticky." She's leaning over me, smiling at the little guy.

We're stopped inside of a huge recreation of a Stetson hat that has a hole in it for cars to drive through. The kid at the window is dressed in a red-and-white gingham shirt, bolo tie, and cowboy hat. "Yes, ma'am. I'll throw some extras in the sack."

"You're a peach, sweetheart."

We take our roasted chicken and vegetables home, and I expect Amity to shower off or clean herself up or do whatever girls do after they jack off, but I guess the moist towelettes were sufficient. She simply plops into the wingback chair and picks pieces of chicken off the bone while sipping champagne and flipping through *D* Magazine. The cover story of the February issue is "Dallas's Most Eligible Men."

"I've got to get me a rich one, Harry. Someone who will help us *both* out. Me and you."

"We don't need anyone to help us," I say, gnawing on a thigh.

"Harry, we're flight attendants, not financiers. I'm accustomed to a certain lifestyle." *Lawfstawl.* "And I'm sure, considering your family background, you're accustomed to certain comforts as well."

I'm sitting on the floor beside her. "Yes, I am. What's the problem?"

Her voice turns soft, her manner gracious. "I just thought, since you're working this job, and driving your car, that maybe you're on your own, like me."

"Sort of," I shrug, putting my chicken down. "But I took this job because I wanted to. I was bored with school—the last thing I wanted to do was keep going. Sure, my family sees the world in a certain way, but I thought it would be fun to see the world differently. And my car—well . . ." I stare at the wall. "I've always loved my old VW, and I don't see why I have to drive a new car."

"I'm embarrassed," Amity says. "I don't want you to ever feel you have to justify yourself to me. Listen. I'm up front about it— I like money. And I've dated plenty of guys because of it."

Which makes me doubt her family is anything like mine. Unless she's done something to displease them, there is no reason for her to date guys for money if she can get it from her family.

"But this is different, you and me," she continues. "You're my *friend*, and I don't give a damn about your family's name because I would never think of you in that way."

"I appreciate you saying that. But you know, I do have money." I'm not exactly lying. I *do* have money. I'm just not married enough to get my hands on it. Do I tell her? I know what she'll do. She'll impetuously say, "Let's get married!" But as much as I'd like my inheritance, it's not worth living a lie to get it.

Amity and I peruse the pages of *D* together, finding the choices laughable. A Budweiser delivery man. A party designer. A wood craftsman. "G'yaw! Whoa, Bubba!" She makes the time-out sign. "Who came up with these jokers? Guys who drive beer trucks are too *groovy*—they use blow-dryers and wear musk cologne."

"Is there such a thing as a straight party designer?" I ask.

"Letitia Baldridge," Amity answers. "Even though she looks like a big ole drag queen, I'm pretty sure she's straight. She designed Jacqueline Kennedy's parties."

"*Men*," I clarify.

"Who cares?" Amity says, forfeiting the question. "Party designers, closet organizers, motivational speakers—they should all be shot so we can get on with our lives! Give me a filthy rich, boring-as-rice, trapped-in-suspenders *banker* any day of the week. Cash money, baby!" Amity falls to the floor on her back and moves her arms and legs over the hardwoods as if she's trying to make a snow angel.

"Hey," I laugh, poking her with my foot. "What if you had some guy who *wasn't* boring as rice and trapped in suspenders, but who still had lots of money? What if the guy with money was fun and made you laugh and had a cute butt?''

"I'd be in heaven, Harry," she answers, lying on her back. "And I'd love the hell out of him. Now tell me something."

"Yes, Amity?"

"Do you have a cute butt, Harry?"

"You tell me," I answer coyly.

"I'd say it's beyond being a cute butt, Harry," she growls. "Frankly, you've got a *great ass*."

That night, at the gym, the car salesman with the glacier ice eyes, JT, is there pumping up his pecs. He hoists the bar onto the bench clips and walks over to me as I'm down on a mat doing crunches. "How come I haven't heard from you?"

I continue with the sit-ups. "Maybe you have." I grin. "You don't even know my name."

"JT Reardon," he says, putting out his hand to shake.

"Harry Ford," I say, shaking it. "And I'm not in the market for a car or I'd definitely call you."

"I do more than sell cars," he assures me. Then he goes back to his bench presses.

I come home from the gym to find Amity sitting in her darkened room on her bed, painting her nails by the light of her little bed lamp while listening to Troy crying into the phone machine in great sobs. The bottle of champagne is empty, and there's only a little bit left in her glass. "See how loud he is?" she asks. "Can't you tell his balls smell like Brie cheese?"

"Jesus, Amity," I laugh. "He's torn up. He's not talking—he's crying."

"I know. Those frat boys are such big titty babies. I can't listen to this anymore." She turns the volume off, gulps down the last bit of champagne.

I toss my gym bag onto the floor. "Isn't that kind of callous?"

"Well," she says, "sometimes a girl's gotta do what a girl's gotta do."

"Would it kill you to talk to him?" I ask, feeling one of my biceps. It's growing a little, and I like the tight feeling of the engorged muscle.

"Listen, Bubba. Troy was starting to claim squatter's rights," she says with narrowed eyes, "and *nobody* owns me." She picks up the bottle and tries to pour herself more champagne before she realizes it's empty. She slowly sets it down. "Nobody can tell me what to do. Not Troy or my family or anyone."

"Hey, I'm your friend. Remember?"

She jerks as if she's switched gears without using the clutch and laughs. "Be a darlin' and go to the kitchen and get me a can of Raid so I can kill this bug that's up my ass." I smile and she goes back to painting her toes, and as I pick up my gym bag and leave her darkened room, I realize she houses another darkened room inside her.

At the end of the month, President Reagan announces his candidacy for reelection. There's no way I'll vote for him. He's just so *old*.

I am invited by a college friend, Iris, to a Pink Party in New York, and I'm concerned about attending because I don't have any clothing that is pink. She assures me that it isn't necessary. I decide to fly to the Cayman Islands first, then up to New York. Amity loves that I am jetting off by myself, and I'm aware that I've ascended a notch in her book.

As an airline employee, I fly from Dallas to Grand Cayman for a total of twenty dollars. First class. Who needs family money? Though it is *standby*. I land at night and check into a moldy American franchise hotel. The turquoise carpet and drapes are sprouting penicillin, the sheets smell like someone's dirty scalp, and the air conditioner is spewing a damp Legionnaire's breeze. I just want to get back on the plane and fly around the stratosphere in first class.

In the bathroom, I brush my teeth and prepare to wash my face by attempting to unleash the little bar of soap that is trapped in paper. I get so frustrated trying to uncase it that I practically pop a blood vessel. Finally I smash it against the counter, rip it open, and take out little chips to wash with. Since the chips are mixed with the oceanic tap water, I get no lather at all.

After brushing my teeth with saltwater and Colgate, I slip into the dirty-scalp sheets and pull the bedspread up to my chin. Traveling is so glamorous.

The next day I lie in the sun to disinfect. After hanging out on the sand awhile, I take a walk down the beach. I soon sense that I'm being followed, and when I turn around there's a guy who has big muscular legs walking twenty yards behind me in a Speedo. After the third time I glance back he says to me in a sexy voice, "The farther you walk, the longer it takes us to get back to your hotel room." How can I resist that?

Our sex together is lingering, tropical, salty—as if we're floating in the sea. Our bodies meld into a gradual, steady, warm build that arcs with the end of the afternoon. It's weird, but I think of Amity while I'm with him. I fantasize that she's here on this island with me and this hot boy with thick thighs. I know she likes *scenarios*, and this is one I'm sure she'd love, so I bring her here in my imagination. I'm aware that I'm starting to want to share everything I do with her—as if it's not valid unless she's a part of it.

As evening approaches the island, we sit by the pool and enjoy a sunset that is the same pink and orange as the grenadine and orange juice in our drinks. Turns out he's a dancer from the cruise ship anchored in the distance, and he has to return to the ship for the nine o'clock show. Before he leaves, I suggest grabbing a couple of cocktail napkins and using them to write down our phone numbers.

"I don't do that," he says casually.

"Oh, because you're on a ship?"

"No, I just don't give my number out. I'm not looking for a relationship."

"OK," I say, trying to be nonchalant. The truth is, my feelings are hurt, regardless of the fact that he's a stranger. I suppose I *am* looking for a relationship. Why do I always have to pretend I'm not? Am I the only gay guy my age who's looking for a steady thing? It's not as if I want some boring suburban life in one of those *tribe neighborhoods* where everyone has the same red-tile roof and two-car garage. Believe me, I have no desire to drive a station wagon and cook casserole recipes that call for truckloads of cream of mushroom soup. I just want a mate who would live in a cool apartment with me, maybe even a house (slate roof), and share his life, his soul, his body. Someone who would make me laugh. Someone who's smart. Someone who votes. Someone who would let me walk through the door after a long trip and say, "Honey, I'm homo!"

The next two days an island boy with body odor pesters me to let him experiment with his bisexuality. Not the relationship I'm looking for. I decline and depart the warm sands of Cayman for the icy insanity of New York.

New York is frozen. Solid. Iris and her roommates live in Hell's Kitchen on a street that is famous for its rats—the kind of rats that sit on top of the garbage cans and catcall women in high heels. If you carry groceries past them, they ask, "Got anything good?" Rats you could saddle up and ride to the Bronx. I always think I should bring a ham or a plate of enchiladas, which I could throw onto the sidewalk to divert their attention while I make a frenzied dash to the stairs of the building. Arriving from the islands, I have nothing but a half-empty container of Tic-Tacs. I pop the lid, scatter them onto the snowy pavement, and make a run for it before I realize there are no rats in waiting. They must have frozen to death.

Iris congratulates me for making it to her door, and though she assures me my sunburned skin will qualify me for the color-coded soiree, or at the very least I can chew a piece of pink bubble gum with my mouth open, I return to the streets to buy a pink sweater, thinking it will be sufficient for my debut. Of course, everyone arrives at the party in these incredibly pink, incredibly well-thought-out ensembles that border on Broadway set design. The party is thrown by an actor/magician named Aaron, who happens to live in Iris's building, which is actually a funeral parlor on the bottom floor. Aaron is part of the famous drag entertainer Chad Barclay's entourage, though I have no idea who Chad Barclay is. Chad is working on a play titled *Theatrica: She's Hitched with Librium.* I love the title and try to be as funny. Of course, that never works.

I'm a bit uncomfortable at the party, because everyone is an actor or writer, or painter or something worthy, and I realize my journey into the skies is kind of an embarrassment. I stop telling people I'm a steward and just say, ''I travel,'' in a way that makes them not ask further.

Halfway through the party I lose Iris, but decide to find her because friendships like hers are what I miss most about my life in Dallas, and I'm only in New York for two days. Someone says they saw her and Aaron headed for the roof earlier. I scout the outside hall and find the steep ladder steps that lead to the opening in the building's roof. I climb slowly, because I'm a little drunk, and pop my head into the frigid winter night. I hear what sounds like a scuffle. I look to the right and see Iris and Aaron standing ten feet away on the roof. Aaron is driving her back forcefully. Iris is crying. It's all very Hitchcock—the cool blonde in the gorgeous dress; the dynamic fellow, a magician by trade, shadowing her on a rooftop in New York. Is he trying to kill her?

No. He's fucking her.

Iris had told me over the phone that she was having a little affair with Aaron. Iris and I have been tight friends since school, and we've wondered aloud what it would be like to sleep together, but never really felt the need to find out. I *am* gay, after all. But then again, so is Aaron.

At the moment, he has her off-the-shoulder 1950's dress gathered up in his hands, and he's using it for balance as he rocks into her, steadily, driving her back, until they brace against an air duct. My first thought is, "How's he maintaining a hard-on? It's *freezing*." My second thought is, "How's he maintaining a hard-on? He's *gay*." As for my first question: He's left his pants on, and though his dick is pulled through the fly of his pants, it's certainly not waving in the midnight air. As for my second question: Iris has her hands around his neck, she's kissing all over his face, and she's so excited she's crying, and he seems to be equally enthralled, meeting her kisses with wild passion. So I guess he's not *that* gay. Still, I find this fascinating, and since they're completely unaware of me, I continue to watch.

I'm cold. My ears are hurting already, and my fingers are nearly frozen to the pipe I'm using to steady myself. But I keep watching. I can't believe that Aaron is giving it to her so cocksure and that Iris is abandoning herself so freely and getting so much pleasure from him. I remember what Amity sounded like when she was being ridden to the finish line by Bart, and I wonder if she'd be so vocal coming down the home stretch with someone like Aaron—or me?

CHAPTER SIX

"**A**mity and I are just roommates," I declare, standing in the kitchen with my mother.

"I know that," my mother says, mixing curry powder into mayonnaise—a very exotic dip for the Midwest. She's making it herself, because she's scaled back our family maid, Marzetta, to minimal hours on account of Donald, her new husband, who believes anything worth doing should be done by yourself. I watch her hands as she stirs. Like Amity's, they're too young for the rest of her, but only because my mother has had not only a face-lift, but a hand-lift also. My late father's golfing buddy, Bud Orenstein, the plastic surgeon, tried his experimental hand-lift surgery on my mother and it actually worked. Of course, she has little scars at her wrist points, but those are covered by gold bracelets cut to a snug fit so that they never move from their camouflage position.

My mother is secretly relieved that Matthew and I have broken up, she tells me. It's much easier to talk to her friends about me, she explains, now that I'm living with a *girl* down in Dallas. And whoever this Amity is, she is good enough for my mother. "All I said is you should bring her up here to visit sometime. It's important that I meet her." She smoothes her auburn hair with her left land.

"Why in the world is it important you meet her?"

She places the dish of curry dip on the platter and spreads the crudités around it. "She could be the beginning of something new and wonderful for you."

My mother, like Bart, like so many people, thinks I just haven't found the right girl. She doesn't believe that *anyone* is gay. She thinks that Liberace has "a rare form of masculinity" and that Richard Simmons is just "playing a role." She thinks if I'll just *get on with it*, I'll be happy.

If all learning was by example, perhaps I would. The day after my father killed himself, she sweetly instructed the maid to take his Cadillac, the very one that had put him to sleep, and return it to the dealership for credit. And a month later, she used that credit toward the purchase of a new car for her new husband, my new stepfather, Donald, a retired general in the air force who fought in the Korean War, as well as in Vietnam. He's sixty-something years old, but has the body of a forty year old. He's handsome, in a John Wayne kind of way, though *his* hands look as if they were transplanted from a gorilla. I suspect the reason he still has a full head of hair is because he's not given any of it permission to *fall out*.

They met at a golf tournament at the country club. It was one of those mixer things where you draw your partner's name from a golf hat. Donald, whose wife had succumbed to cancer just six months prior, drew my mother's name. When she identified herself, he went to her, kissed her hand, carried her clubs to the cart, and from the way she tells it practically hit every shot for her along the eighteen holes. My biological father, from a fine family that taught him every rule of etiquette known to the civil world, had to be prompted to accomplish even the simplest gesture, such as holding a door open for my mother. He was a man's man, and he had little patience for women. So naturally, when my mother met Donald, she attained the nirvana never offered by my father: the state of bliss that comes from surrendering every decision to someone else who then makes you feel as if the decision is yours. I think she's crazy. Golf is already a stupid game, and I can only imagine how ridiculous it gets when someone is hitting your shots for you. But she put it in no uncertain terms: "I don't care if Donald's collar is as blue as your father's blood," she told me, after announcing their elopement. "He's the best man for me at this point in life."

"What is her family like?" my mother asks.

How can I answer? Whenever I mention her family, Amity dodges me. "I haven't met them yet."

"All in good time," my mother says, picking up the tray of vegetables. We join her husband in the great room. General Donald left his living quarters in the retired officers' village of the air base to move into my parents' (mother's) house on the edge of the country club. How could my mother bring this carpetbagger into our lives? He looks so comfortable, sipping his glass of scotch by the fire, his feet on the needlepoint-covered ottoman, his boots still on. "This isn't a bunch of crap from Levitz," I want to scream. "My grandmother did that needlepoint, so take your boots off, soldier!"

I was eight years old when I sat with Grammie at her summer ranch in Colorado, and we drank lemonade while she stitched that ottoman cover. I'd come down with a mild case of chicken pox the week I was supposed to fly off to Italy with my family for a three-week holiday, and so, being quarantined, my family went on without me and left me in the care of Marzetta—instructing her to send me on to my grandmother's ranch when I was well enough to travel. Those two weeks at Grammie's are magic in my memory. In the morning we ate bacon and pancakes, and Grammie let me have a small cup of coffee with lots of cream and sugar in it. We rode horses in the grassy valley below the house. My grandmother was regal, yet trustworthy and unaffected, and for a woman of good breeding, she rode comfortably in the saddle, like a cowgirl of fifteen. In the afternoons, we listened to records on the porch—

everything from Patsy Cline to exotic bamboo music from a phonograph she'd obtained while on an adventure tour of the Solomon Islands in the South Pacific. And when we'd accidentally leave a record in the sun too long and it warped, she'd take it off the turntable and walk to the edge of the porch, high above the valley below, and fling the record far into the distance like a Frisbee. "Good-bye, Benny Goodman!" she'd yell while transforming his bowed recording into a spinning flying saucer. She taught me how to throw a Frisbee that way, with old warped vinyl records.

In the late afternoon, we'd hike down to the stream and cast our rods for rainbow trout. And in the evening we'd take our catch to Fish Fry Point, where my grandfather had built a stone fireplace with a grill for cooking our bounty. We'd eat our fish right out of the pan, then roast marshmallows over the fire for dessert. Fish and marshmallows. Ginger ale to drink. Then Grammie would read from her latest book—Steinbeck's *Cannery Row,* or Wallace Stegner's *A Shooting Star*—until the real stars would appear, and we'd hike back to the house by the light of the moon, our handheld flashlights puncturing the trail with quick stabs of light as we walked.

Her friend Louise came to visit us during the second week of my stay. Louise was married to a man much like Grammie's husband, my grandfather. They were stern men, not overly comfortable around their wives, and they liked to go hunting together in Wyoming and drink rye straight from the bottle. I loved Louise nearly as much as my grandmother. She was risqué, as my mother said, and wore loose fitting dresses that were always revealing a shoulder or half a bosom. Long earrings dangled from her pierced ears, and by the time she started in on her second martini, those earrings would begin to dance and slap her in the face as she moved her head to laugh and tell stories of her hapless year at the helm of the Women's League of Denver, where she was the only president ever to be impeached for refusing to honor the mayor with a luncheon. "He was a politically racist son of a bitch who just happened to be sleeping with his adorable black maid,'' she said, offering me a sip of her martini. Grammie would scold Louise for using profanity in my company, but I could tell she loved the wild delivery of Louise's stories as much as I.

Together, Louise and Grammie finished stitching that ottoman cover during the second week of my visit, taking turns as one or the other tired of the detail. Upon my departure, they handed it to me at the airport, wrapped in paper printed with cowboys and lariats, to give to my mother. And when I cried as they put me on the plane to fly home, Louise said, ''Buck up, Harry. I'll take care of your grandmother,'' as if I was worried to leave her alone, instead of the truth that I was sad to leave them both.

Outside the sliding glass doors, I watch a fierce north wind rush in and push the cold rain to the freezing point. Everything seems to be icing over in front of my eyes. In the yard, skeletons of pin oaks stand shaking, their bare arms raised, as if Donald has slid open the door and yelled, ''Don't move or I'll shoot!'' Beyond the yard, the brown dormant fairway grasses of the golf course look like huge straw mats large enough for Donald to wipe his big gorilla feet on. I can't help wonder how much money Donald will see from my dead father.

The moment is dying for conversation, so I tell them both about my horrific flight into Wichita today. ''The turbulence was so bad that the flight attendant was knocking into seats and slamming against the sides of the overhead bins, but she refused to sit down. She just kept serving watery drinks and those Hello Kitty–size bags of peanuts. I was waiting for her head to hit the ceiling and break off and go rolling down the aisle, smiling.''

Donald doesn't understand my sense of humor and looks at me as if I'm callous.

''They shot three approaches,'' I continue, ''before they were able to land the plane. Every time they tried a different runway, the wind would change again. I thought we were going to crash into bits and pieces in some wheat field bordering the airport. And the stewardess was so perky, I'll bet she would have trudged through rubble with a beverage tray embedded in her forehead while she offered decks of playing cards to the survivors.''

"It couldn't have been that bad, or they wouldn't have landed the plane,'' Donald says staunchly, a glass of Glenlivet dwarfed in his simian hands. The TV is broadcasting the Olympics in Sarajevo. At the moment, no one is watching.

Curling competition.

"It was the worst flight I've ever been on,'' I state emphatically, feeling my status as an airline attendant gives me authority.

"*I'll* tell you about a scary flight,'' he says, stretching out, more comfortable still.

Here we go. A war story. I've only met this guy twice, but both times he was full of war lore. The first day we met, my mother insisted he tell his land mine story. The one where a recruit gets his arm blown through the air, and when it lands in the tree, it salutes the guy's own dying body. The curling competition is starting to look good.

" 'Nam,'' he says, shaking his head. "It was mission number 742. Flying out of Vung Tau.''

"You go ahead with your story,'' my mother says to Donald. "Harry and I will be listening from the kitchen.'' She nods for me to follow her.

I'm shocked. The other two times I was around them, she doted on him relentlessly and hung on his every word—even when he was reading closing shares from the New York Stock Exchange aloud.

"Just another ordinary day for a Caribou pilot . . .'' I hear him say as my mother and I step into the kitchen. His voice is muted by the TV.

"I want to tell you, I've got a little lump,'' my mother says, adding more vodka to her gimlet with one hand, patting her breast with the other. "And I'm going in next week to have it looked at."

Oh, my God, I survived my flight, and now it's my mother, her feet on the ground, who's in danger. "What do you think, Mom?" I ask, knowing she must have some kind of intuition.

"It was June. The Tet Offensive, which had started in January, was over. The flight was routine to Saigon . . ." Donald continues from the living room.

"Yes," my mother calls to Donald, "The Tet Offensive!" as if it's a wonderful Broadway play. She whispers to me, "I haven't told Donald. He's been through so much, losing his wife recently. I'm sure he's had enough cancer for one year. Besides, it's a big job having to step into the shoes of your father and all. Barbie Botter has completely snubbed him. She won't even mention him in her column—nothing about us as a couple either."

Barbie Botter is the society columnist for the local paper. She's married to a banking executive who's been having a long-term affair with a blond TV news anchor from a local affiliate of one of the national broadcasting companies. Barbie and the news anchor were once pictured at a Wichita charity event giving each other air kisses, and if you looked close you could see Barbie's fingers, around the anchor's waist, were curled back and positioned so that Barbie was flipping her the bird. "Forget about Barbie Botter. Mom, *what do you think?*"

"I've had lumps before. Many times," she says, sipping her drink. But then her brow wrinkles and she looks slightly uneasy, a terrible sign coming from my mother because she's the kind of woman who's cheerful even during televised executions and killer tornadoes. "This time, I don't know."

"The commander said they wouldn't last another night. They'd all be killed if we didn't scoop 'em up," Donald proclaims.

"So what did you do?" my mother calls out, before turning to me and saying, "This really is one of his best stories."

"Mom," I tell her, reaching out for her tight-skinned hand, "I can't believe you're telling me this. What if you have cancer?"

"I'll beat it!" she sings as if it's as simple as beating an egg. "Your father wasn't right to do what he did," she adds with very little judgment.

"I agree," I say, smiling gently. "Are you going to tell the general about the lump?"

"When we landed on that little dirt airstrip, those young Vietnamese boys were waiting for us—proud little shits, they were."

"Well, Donald!" my mother yells, pulling her hand from mine and putting it to her throat. She keeps it there—to cover the wrinkles. "Of course I'll tell him," she quietly tells me. "But let's have a nice visit while you're here. I'll tell him after you go."

Donald's voice grows louder. ". . . catastrophic left engine failure!"

It makes me sad to see her nirvana shaken, to see her faced with a decision she cannot surrender to Donald. "Mom, I love you," I tell her.

"And I love you," she says, setting her vodka gimlet down. She pulls me to her damaged breast and hugs me close, whispering in my ear, "Right or wrong, I have to carry out your father's wishes, follow the codicil in the will. You understand, don't you?"

I hold tight, afraid to let go, but don't understand. Why won't my mother just negate the whole thing and set me free? She has a sense of duty to my father, but what about her sense of duty to me? He's dead, I'm alive. I can't help but think she's using my father's instructions as a last resort for her own attempt to straighten me out and send me off into the sunset with a wife. It makes me angry that my mother would do this. But now she may possibly have cancer. And I love every little nip and tuck of her. I want her to feel better, to heal, to live. I almost tell her about Amity—how my feelings for her are more genuine than they've been for anyone outside of the family. That, believe it or not, I very well may feel love for a girl. But caution tells me to say nothing, for it would be too big an opening for my mother, and she would thrust me upon a stage that had no exit. "Yes, Mother," I whisper back. "I understand."

"I feathered the engine, and we were slowly inching down, just barely above the treetops, and the Mekong River was out in front of us a little ways," Donald says with dramatic warning.

"Come on," my mother says, trying to pull me back out to the living room.

I resist. "Wait. Have you told Winston?"

"Oh, heavens, no. He doesn't understand these things the way you do. I'll only tell him if it's malignant. Promise you won't mention it to him."

I can hardly bear to speak to him. "Of course," I tell her.

"Good. Now *come on*," she says, dragging me toward the living room. "Donald's about to land the plane!"

"Anyways," Donald says, as if we've never left, "we brought her in and set her down, and just as we rolled out and turned off the runway, we lost the other engine. If it had happened two minutes earlier in the air, we'd have crashed and burned."

My mother looks at me like, "See?" She is fully smitten with this general from Georgia, who impresses her with his gallantry and heroism. And I see that she's happy and taken care of. Perhaps in a way she never was before.

Grammie answers the door herself. She's almost eighty years old now, and years of riding horses and other athletic activities have taken their toll. She walks with a lame gait, supported by a cane, and her hands are riddled with arthritis, but she's still the trustworthy and regal matriarch of the Ford family, and her stance and carriage, though painful, still reflect it.

"Hey, Grammie."

She smiles. Laughs. "Harry." We embrace, and she fills my senses with the scent of childhood, the same citrus-and-spice mixture from the cologne bottles she has ordered from California since I was a child. "Come in. Marzetta is making sandwiches." Grammie explains that she has inherited Marzetta almost full-time since Donald has reduced her hours, and she loves Marzetta so much she hired someone else to do most of the work, so Marzetta is free to enjoy life. "What's it like being a poor airline attendant?" Grammie asks.

"Oh, well," I laugh, while following her into the kitchen, "it's great. You only have to pay half the rent, because you're forced to have a roommate. You never have to worry about your car being stolen, because nobody wants it. And you never have to worry about shopping for clothes—just throw on a uniform. Hey!" I say, seeing Marzetta. "How's my *real* mother?"

"She's proud," Marzetta beams. "I hear you're an airline steward, son. That's the job I always wanted. I used to dream about flying the troops to Europe during the Second World War. 'Course, they didn't let colored girls like me be stewardesses back then. So it was just a nice dream."

"I'll tell you what," I say. "I like flying with black girls most of all. They don't take any guff from anyone. The passengers behave better when a sister is on board. Us white women get no respect."

"Oooh!" she laughs.

"Come on. Let's sit," Grammie commands. She sees the two sandwich plates Marzetta puts before us and asks, "Where's yours?"

Marzetta shakes her head. "I'm off to the drugstore. I'm needing some foot cream." She waves good-bye, grabs the keys to the car Grammie bought her, and heads out the door.

My grandmother nods. "Drive on." She takes a bite of her sandwich. "So who is this girl your mother wants to meet?"

"Amity?"

Grammie is silent for a moment, then smiles. "You know, the

word *amity* is often used when describing peaceful relations between two nations. Have you two made a pact? Like two nations?''

"Meaning?''

My grandmother quickly gives up on the chicken sandwich and makes for the chocolate-covered graham cookies. "Do you plan to marry her for your inheritance?''

I frown while biting into my sandwich. "No.''

"Does she know you're gay?'' she asks, picking up a piece of chocolate that has broken off her cookie and fallen on her plate.

It's amazing to me that my grandmother is perfectly comfortable saying the word *gay*, but my mother can't utter it. "Sure, Gram. We have no secrets, Amity and I.''

"Good. We have too many secrets in this family already.''

"Like what?'' I ask.

She lifts her finger to her mouth and presses the little piece of chocolate to her lips, then licks it away. "If I told, they wouldn't be secrets,'' she answers, winking. "Harry,'' she continues, cocking her head, thinking, "how come you've never asked me for money?''

"I don't know,'' I tell her. "Your money is your money.''

"But I have an abundance of it.''

"That's true. OK, Gram, since you brought it up, how come you've never offered me any?''

"Because I've had no greater pleasure than watching you break some of this family's rustiest old chains. I like what you've become, Harry. For now, I'm afraid money might rock your boat, maybe even tip it over.''

"I can swim,'' I tell her confidently. "Don't worry. I'll get mine.''

"Be careful, my boy. Just make sure you get it the old-fashioned way.''

"Inherit it?'' I ask, a devilish smile on my face. "I intend to.''

"Not at the expense of your self,'' she cautions. "I see your mother pushing you. Donald too. I imagine your father is still pushing you, even though he's gone. But I'm telling you not to make decisions to please other people. Please yourself. Be yourself.''

"Don't worry, Gram. I'm hopelessly born to the breed—it's just not the same breed as the rest of my family. Which means I'll probably have a life of blissful poverty while remaining my own man—whatever the heck that means.''

"You're anything but hopeless, kid. I wish I'd had a life like yours.''

I tease her. "You wish you were born a gay guy?''

"Not exactly,'' she laughs. "Listen. Forget about the money, Harry. Everything will fall into place. Just promise me you'll be honest with yourself. The word *amity* also means friendship.''

"And that's what we have. Don't worry about Amity and me. We won't do anything foolish.''

"Good. Because that would suck.''

"Suck?'' Now I pick up a cookie. "Grammie, who taught you the word *suck*?''

"TV.''

"*My* Grammie? My Steinbeck and Stegner Grammie? What's going on?''

"I'm old now, honey. Can't read. My eyes don't work on the page. I watch TV and eat candy. That's it. I'm done with marriage, horses, travel, and even philanthropy. I gave them my all for most of my life. Put up with a cold husband. Loved those horses as much as my children. Traveled the world in order to learn about people. And donated millions of dollars plus my own two hands to every charity that crossed my heart. But my life is near its end, and I'm stupid and sweet with TV and candy.''

"Hey, whatever works. To thine own self be true,'' I say, squeezing her hand.

"Precisely what I'm saying to you, my boy.''

*   *   *

It's not a week later that I come home from the gym to find a message on my answering machine from my mother. She has breast cancer. She's already had a modified radical mastectomy, she jauntily informs me, and the doctor believes that he's gotten all the cancer. The good news is that while she was in the hospital she got Bud Orenstein to come in and give her a tummy tuck and that soon she'll be able to have her breasts reconstructed to something nice and perky, but don't tell anyone. And not to worry, she doesn't have to do chemotherapy, but simply has to endure a little radiation, which she intends to look upon as a quick trip to the tanning bed. *Beep.* End of message.

I've never blamed my mother for cutting me off financially. I know that it was my father's doing and that she's of a particular generation and feminine ilk that acquiesces to all demands masculine. And though I think she's often shallow and ridiculous beyond words, I love her and I'm scared that she has cancer so soon after losing my father. I call her and tell her I'll be on a flight to Kansas that day. She says there's no reason to come—the general is taking care of her every need. I refuse to believe that I, her son of twenty-three years, can be replaced by her husband of three months.

The airline gives me a leave of absence and I go to Kansas. When I bring her flowers, she says, ''Put them over by the flowers the general gave me.'' When I bring her the morning paper, she says, ''Oh, honey, thanks, but the general brought the paper already.'' When I bring her favorite candy bar, a Heath bar, she says, ''The general made me homemade toffee.'' A general who makes toffee? Forget it. I'm glad she's happy and taken care of, but I decide to head back to Dallas, where at least someone appreciates me.

CHAPTER SEVEN

"**D**on't fuck with me!"

It's late at night. It can't be one of Amity's nightmares because it's a man's voice. It sounds as if he's outside the house, but I can't be sure. I sit up in bed, hear Amity say something in a hushed tone.

"Don't fuck with me, Amity!"

I get out of bed and step into the hall. Amity sounds strained, but controlled. I can't really tell what she is saying. The man interrupts her. Angry. Accusing. Shouting something. I know who it is: Troy. He's finally confronting her for leaving him. I step into her room.

"Is everything OK?"

"Yes, Harry!" She is at her window, a few feet from her bed, wearing nothing but a man's dress shirt.

Outside the window is a Latin guy with glasses, not Troy. He looks at me, doesn't give a shit who I am. "I mean it," he warns, looking back at Amity.

"I think you need to go," she says, nervous but in command.

The guy slams his fist against the frame of the window and takes off.

"Who was that, Amity?"

Amity shuts the window, locks it, and escorts me into the sitting room, where she grabs some rolling papers and my pot. "You don't mind, do you?" Of course I don't. I'm amazed that even with shaking fingers, she rolls the joint with precision and expediency— as if she formerly worked on a joint-rolling assembly line. "Ahhh," she moans, exhaling the smoke. "Harry," she says, handing me the doobie, "that was Miguel Arturo. He's a flight attendant with the airline. I don't know what's wrong with him. I really think he must be some kind of a stalker." She rises from the sofa and heads for the kitchen.

"Really?"

"You saw him," she calls from the kitchen. "I was in bed, and he just started banging on my window. He wouldn't go away until I opened it and we talked." I hear a champagne cork pop and bubbly being poured. She returns with two glasses, hands one to me. "I just wasn't going to let him into the house. I mean, g'yaw, Harry, I only flew a trip with him. I fucked him because he reminded me of Dex Dexter from *Dynasty* and his parents own a hotel in New Orleans, but it's not like we dated or anything!" She takes a long hit off the joint, speaks the next sentence with puffs of smoke popping out of her mouth. "I think something's not quite right in his head. I can tell he's desperate to be taken seriously. He must have never had any attention, his mom running the Bates Motel and all. I think he has some kind of mental problem."

"Obviously he's fucked up," I say, bolstering her analysis. Amity is so funny, so cool. I can't imagine people being angry at her—unless they were sitting behind her in a movie theater and couldn't see the screen because of her hair.

We finish the joint and she drinks both glasses of champagne after I decline mine. I ask her if she's calmed down enough to go to sleep. She says she's not sure if she feels safe, and so I offer to sleep with her in her bed. "Would you?" she asks.

"Sure," I tell her bravely. She refills both glasses and carries them to her bedside. After we get into bed and pull the covers over us, I'm not so sure. I don't know why, but it feels strange for the two of us to do this. The last time we were in bed together was in Denver, and I was kissing her. I'm thinking about it, and I can tell she is too. I'm really stoned, and my mind is wandering all over the place while my body lies rigidly still. I'm an island in the sheets, and my heart is pounding out indigenous rhythms of warning. I'm afraid if I move my legs they might brush against her. Every time I swallow I feel it's being broadcast through a bullhorn. Of course that's probably crazy, but I'm stoned and paranoid—and gay.

"Harry," she whispers, "thank you for protecting me."

"You're welcome," I say.

She leans over and kisses me sweetly on the lips. My eyes are open, and so are hers. She looks at me and smiles. We kiss again, our mouths closed, but our lips soft and relaxed. It's pleasant. Not full of heated passion, and not the kind of kisses that make me want to rip off my clothes, but nice. Soft. Loving.

She pulls back and sinks into her pillow. "And thank you for kissing me," she says, evidently wanting nothing more. Then she rolls over and puts her arm across my chest, and within a minute she's out. Fast asleep. With a satisfied smile on her face.

"She's out on a trip. Chicago, I think."

"What's her name again?"

"Amity Stone."

"Amity Stone. God, that sounds familiar. I know I've heard that name before," my friend, Randy, says, looking up to the ceiling to grab an invisible memory. Randy's a knock-dead handsome Jewish-Italian guy who speaks with a Texas accent. He lives with his boyfriend in Austin. I met him in college. He was in the theater department for five minutes before transferring to a school in Texas to major in fashion merchandising. I've flown over to Austin on my day off, and this is the first time I've seen him in two years. We're sitting at the kitchen table, eating a spread of salami, crackers, pickles, rye bread, and cold potatoes—washing it all down with a couple of cold beers.

"She's wild. We're always having fun. I swear, Randy, there's nobody like her."

"What's different about her?"

"She just doesn't have that internal cautionary mechanism, that off switch that most of us have. You know, the one that keeps you from being *too* honest or *too* carefree or *too* sexual."

"Let's go straight to the sexual part. What do you mean? *Too* sexual?"

"She goes for it. If she wants some guy, she fucks him. Period."

"Definitely a shiksa."

"And I just know, no matter who she's in bed with, she's a *top*."

"A shiksa with a dicksa."

"And she's straight on with me about the fact that she likes money and guys with big dicks. I don't know why she's hanging out with me—I'm not getting any inheritance from my father, and I don't have a big dick."

"And you're gay," Randy laughs, putting salami onto a cracker. "It's a good thing you're just friends, because unless you get a dick job and rob a bank, she'd probably drop you like a hot-potato salad."

"No shit," I chuckle.

"Still . . . I know I've heard that name before," he says, scanning his memory again. "Amity Stone."

"I'm not in the running anyway," I go on, "because she has a new boyfriend. Some guy named Matt Hunter—goes by Hunt. He's this strapping redheaded boy with great teeth who comes roaring up in his BMW 2002 and hops out like he's hopping off a horse. The weird thing is that he's a fraternity brother of the last guy she dated—some dude whose balls smell like Brie cheese."

Randy spews out a chunk of pickle.

I continue. "He's really friendly to me in a very sexual kind of way, which I thought was hot until Amity told me he admitted he used to go to gay bars with a couple friends who would wait out in the parking lot while he would flirt with a guy inside, lure him out to the car with a promise of sex, and then beat the stuffing out of him with his friends."

"How sick is that?" Randy says, disgusted.

I bite a chunk of pickle. "I know. Amity told me so nonchalantly, as if to say, 'Isn't that funny, Harry?' I got pretty angry about it, and it really disturbed me that she looks at him as if he's the finest man in the world. But then I realized, that's how she looked at Troy, the other guy, and he didn't last long. So I just kept my mouth shut."

"I know who she is!" Randy says, almost choking on his beer as well as his epiphany. "She's the girl from CCT who sued the professor."

"What do you mean?" I ask, taking a swig of beer.

"Amity Stone. She slept with her professor at a Christian college in Fort Worth, and he ended up giving her a B in the class, so she sued him," Randy says excitedly. "Of course she expected an A. And from what I heard, she gives the kind of blow jobs that earn an A+."

I'm uncomfortable that Randy is treating Amity as a juicy gossip tidbit. "Who told you about this?"

"My friend Kevin. He went to CCT. He said they kept it low profile, but it still made the papers. She sued the guy for sleeping with her and not giving her an A. He lost his job, and the university settled out of court, *and* she got her grade changed to an A."

"Well, she *should* have sued," I say defensively. "I would have."

"You blew your professors for better grades?" he asks.

"I should have," I answer as if it's perfectly normal. "How much money did she get?"

"No one would say. But Kevin heard it was like a hundred thousand or something. I can't believe she's your roommate! Kevin said she's hysterical. He met her at a party once. He said every guy at the party wanted to go home with her."

"I told you she's great." I can't help but wonder what she did with all the money.

"He said she was coked out of her mind though," Randy cautions. "Is she still doing that stuff?"

Maybe that's where the money went—up her nose. "No, she just smokes pot like the rest of us," I assure him.

"Be glad," Randy says, taking another sip of beer. "Cocaine is fun, but it sure grabs hold of you."

On the flight home I think about our conversation. I guess it's no surprise that Amity has a *reputation*. The truth is, she's the kind of woman who has a reputation the moment she walks into a room. I just thought it was a more fun-loving and innocent reputation than the one Randy described. Who knows, maybe the story has become legend over the last few years and been blown way out of its original proportions. I mean, how many students have slept with their professors? Thousands? Millions, probably. Amity was smart enough to make a deal out of it, that's all.

Still, it gives me a bit of pause. My father took me aside when I was very young and explained in plain English that all my life there would be people who would associate with me because of my money. And he constantly drilled caution into me in that regard. But hell, I don't have any money now. And frankly, it's Amity who is the provider at the moment, putting a roof over my head for a reduced rent. She sees my life, my car, my clothes. She's way too smart not to notice I have nothing to offer. Not at the moment, at least.

CHAPTER EIGHT

March rolls around, and Jacqueline, Amity's friend from the airline, starts coming around again. One fallow day, when the tulips are trying to peek out of the ground, and the magnolias are thinking about blooming, and the dormant ragweed is envisioning the coming summer kill, she comes over and we all sit in the living room—two of us on the floor and whoever in the wingback—and drink icy Stolichnaya from the bottle we keep in the freezer. Jacqueline can drink. Like a pro. And she likes to smoke cigarettes while explaining the latest thing she's learned. She waves a cigarette around and says, "Do you know what a peninsula is? It's land surrounded by water on three sides. So here's the land," she holds the cigarette out, "and on three sides is water. Here, here, and here. Water, water, water." She puts the cigarette back to her lips, takes a sloppy drag, leaving lipstick smeared on the filter, and continues. "Water, water, water, land. Land, water, water, water. A peninsula is—"

"OK, Jackie!" Amity shouts. "You're beatin' that horse to death!"

Jacqueline is beautiful in her own unusual way. It's not just that she's six feet tall. It's that every part of her is long. Her fingers, nose, legs, eyelashes—they're all long. And her hair is thick and luxurious, like the hair of those girls in shampoo commercials. And she has a wide, lush, pouty mouth. Amity still has never told me why Jacqueline moved out on her so fast, other than to say they were having problems in their friendship. I guess they've patched things up.

"Can you believe how boring that debate was last night?" Amity asks. "That Walter Mondale is about as exciting as a day-old biscuit in lukewarm gravy."

We watched Gary Hart, Walter Mondale, and Jesse Jackson debate each other on television last night for the Democratic nomination for president. "You don't care about taxes and Medicare?" I say sarcastically.

"What *is* Medicare?" Jacqueline asks. "You always read and hear about Medicare. Medicare. What is Medicare?"

"It's when you're old, and you poop your pants, and the government pays for your diapers," I tell her.

"Cool."

"I could definitely spend a night with that Gary Hart guy," Amity says. "Which one did you want to sleep with?"

"I can't believe it. You play that game too?" I ask, laughing. "Well, being a white boy from the Midwest, I kind of have a thing for dark, exotic men."

"Don't tell us Jesse Jackson!" Amity yelps.

"All right then. Gary Hart, but only when he has a really dark tan."

"What's wrong with Jesse Jackson?" Jackie asks. "I think he's sexy."

"Mrs. Jesse Jackson," Amity mocks dreamily. "Jacqueline Jackson. Jackie Jackson. JJ."

"And if he wins," Jackie decrees with a jutted chin, "I'll be the First Lady, and it'll be a White House full of ice-cold Stoly and fat doobies, and Kevin Bacon and Daryl Hannah will come to dinner and Corey Hart will sing for us. Corey Hart."

"Wouldn't President Jackson rather have Eddie Murphy and Rae Dawn Chong come to dinner while Aretha sings?" Amity asks.

"I'll determine the guests," Jackie proclaims.

"So you'll be a queen, like Nancy Reagan?" I ask.

"Speaking of queens," Amity jumps in, "Queen Noor is coming to Dallas later this month."

"Who's that?" Jacqueline asks, throwing down an icy shot of vodka.

"The Queen of Jordan," Amity answers, taking the bottle from Jacqueline and filling her little shot glass.

"Where's that?"

"It's in the Middle East, right, Harry?" Amity says.

"Right," I say. "It's not a peninsula though."

Jacqueline complains, "I just was trying to explain what a peninsula is. When you have like this piece of land that juts—"

"OK, Jackie—that horse is never going to get across the finish line! Forget about peninsulas, girl. You and me need to be taking our lessons from the queen," Amity tells her, getting back to business. She downs her vodka and shudders as if she's having an orgasm. "She was an American girl, a Princeton grad, architecture, and she knew *exactly* what she was doing. God, I wish I could have concentrated in school. I just wanted to fuck the professors."

Of course I immediately think of the professor story Randy told me. And realize, in her own way, Amity is confessing the truth. We laugh and snort our Stoly. Jacqueline snubs her cigarette out and lies down on the hardwoods. "So how is she the Queen of Jordan Almonds?"

Amity's eyes flash with intrigue. "The king divorced his first two wives, and his third was killed in a helicopter crash, *so they say.*"

"What do you say, Amity?" I ask, fascinated that she always seems to have a take on things.

She's been reading *Wired,* the biography of John Belushi, and she's taken to raising an eyebrow, one of his famous moves. It makes whatever she says seem more significant. "Those divorces were getting too expensive. He did something to that helicopter!" Left brow high.

"Sugar in the gas tank?"

"Probably, man," Jackie says, doing leg lifts. "Who's gonna know? Who's gonna check it out? He's the king."

Amity continues with her lesson. "Lisa Halaby, the American girl, was his architect on a project, and she worked some kind of magic on him and got him to marry her. She worked it big time."

"You've been doing your homework," I say.

Amity looks at me with mysterious conviction. "Harry, it's a fairy tale life. I love fairy tale lives." She stands up to head for the kitchen and accidentally releases a little fart. "Oops," she says regally, like Queen Noor. "The queen has spoken."

Jacqueline and I lose it.

In Amity's white Ford Granada that is nearly as old as my Volkswagen, Amity and I head down Northwest Highway toward Northpark Mall. Even though it is gray and rainy, Amity drives with her sunglasses on. She points out the many Mercedes, Jaguars, and BMWs zooming around us on the four-lane road.

"A person's car is a reflection of his lifestyle," she says seriously. Then she yells, "And look at this piece of shit we're driving in! People are going to think we're homeless!" She laughs and screams and swerves into the fast lane.

I hold on to the door handle. "Homeless people don't drive cars, Amity."

"They do in Dallas!"

Somehow I believe her.

"Who sees your house?" she asks. "Nobody if you don't ask them over. But *everybody* sees your car. A man can live in a ditch as long as he's driving a Mercedes." *Mer-sigh-dees.*

While on the subject of cars, I tell her about JT, the BMW salesman who struts his stuff at the gym.

"You know he'll let you do it!" Amity says. "Buy a car from him; then break it in by fucking him in the backseat."

"I don't need a new car."

"Well at least go on a test drive," she urges, eyebrows raised. It's not a bad idea.

She pulls the Granada into a parking space at the mall, cracks her window, and decrees, "Power nap!" Then she reclines her seat, shuts her eyes, and within thirty seconds she's asleep. Out. Completely dead to the world. And I sit there, while the rain drizzles down, and she Z's out. I'm not tired, so I watch the studly valets in red jackets park the Mercedes and BMWs of large-haired, starving ladies wrapped in fur coats to shield themselves from the blustery, arctic, Texas spring days that sometimes dip below fifty degrees. Brrrr. They *need* those fur coats, in case their German sedans malfunction, and they're stranded on the side of the road during a *blue norther*. Sure, they have car phones, but it's hard to dial when you're freezing—and the chances of breaking a nail are greater under stress. Though my mother is the Kansas version of these women, there's something a little more lifelike about her. Maybe because she lacks the hokey accent.

"Out!" Amity blurts, springing up like a corpse from a coffin.

"Ahhh!" I say, grabbing my heart. "You scared the shit out of me!"

"Power nap's over! Out of the car!"

I feel at home as we head down the escalator, past the mannequin-like saleswomen who use their ring fingers (because all a ring finger does is hold a ring, so it's cleaner and less stressed-out, Amity claims) to smooth eye refirmer onto prospective clients' hopeful faces, and into the Mid-Life Cafe, as Amity calls it, where she orders a tuna salad on loose leaf lettuce, so I do too. My mother used to take me on trips to Kansas City to shop at department stores like this, until my father told her to stop or I'd turn out queer.

I notice Amity sits taller in her chair at Maxwell's than she does at home. Taking a cue from her surroundings, she reapplies her lipstick. First, she uses her white starched napkin to wipe off the red stain from her lips. By the time she's removed the old color, her napkin looks like a blood-soaked tourniquet. Then she opens a compact to access a mirror. Using a ruby-colored pencil two shades darker than her lipstick, she lines the outsides of her lips, expanding their borders by following the cosmetic manifest destiny. Then she takes the actual lipstick and sensually fills in her lips with a red that resembles M&M red dye #2. Then she takes the tourniquet and blots her lips several times, making it bloodier still. She finishes by doing a final check in her little, feminine purse mirror.

Then the food comes, and she wipes it all off and eats.

And when she finishes eating, she performs the whole procedure again.

I notice as we walk out of the cafe that almost every woman in the place is holding a blood-soaked tourniquet in her lap and staring into a little purse mirror.

Before we leave the mall, Amity tells me she wants to get her watchband replaced. I follow her into the upscale watch store, and she approaches the salesman. Staring at her with a pissy look on his face, he painfully asks, "May I help you?" He might as well be saying, "Is there any help for you?" He's fluffy and immaculate. His dyed-blond hair has been blow-dried and sprayed into a stiff meringue. The manicured nails of his pudgy little hands poke confidently out of his expensive suit sleeves, and the ring finger of his left hand is adorned with a showy diamond wedding ring in the shape of the state of Texas. His fine cologne hangs over the room like an impermeable velvet awning, and I imagine it's called *Evil Saleswoman Man*.

"Yes," Amity says sweetly. "I just need a replacement for this band.'' She takes the downscale watch off her wrist and lays it out on the counter. The bright lights of the glass case are unkind to the cheap black leather band, which is cracked and frayed on the sides.

He picks up the watch by one end and dangles it between his bulbous fingers as if he were holding a dead rat by the tail. ''It appears you put some wear and tear on your timepiece,'' he observes with a sniff.

''This is my work watch,'' Amity tells him, undaunted, ''it's seen a lot of action.''

''Do you work construction?'' he asks brazenly, adding a smile to get away with it.

Why doesn't he just slap her in the face? Christ, I can't believe he'd insult her so boldly. I look at Amity, wait for her to give it right back.

''Yes, I *do* work construction. I built this mall, darlin','' she answers, smiling.

She's all class—with a sense of humor too. God, my mom really would love her. The salesman definitely doesn't. ''Maybe you should purchase a *nylon* band this time,'' he suggests haughtily.

I hate this mean, Southern class stuff that goes on in Texas. No one in Kansas would treat Amity this way. Well, maybe Winston would. Yes, he'd love to wave his Cartier watch in front of Amity's face while scornfully looking at her substandard wristwatch. He's been that way since we were kids—measuring his good fortune by what others lack. When my mother bought us new shoes, he always insisted on having a different design that cost more than mine, and he would throw such a fit that my mother always acquiesced to his emotive theatrics. When eating at the club, even as young children, he'd insist that I order first and then make sure to order something more elaborate and expensive. And he loved the ceremonial handing down of his blue blazer to me each year, as he received his new one.

''Nylon is fine with me,'' Amity says casually. ''It's just for work.'' She thinks, then adds, ''And play. And casual affairs. And dressy affairs. Come to think of it, maybe we better go a step above nylon, darlin'.''

''A step above nylon?'' the clerk chuckles.

I can't stand to see him treat her this way for one more second. ''Have you never replaced your Rolex?'' I ask her, a disbelieving look on my face.

Amity looks at me. It clicks. ''No,'' she sighs, playing along.

I look at the salesman. ''Silly girl, she left it in the hotel room in Monte Carlo.''

''I did not,'' she argues. ''It was in Paris. I still had it in Monte Carlo. I lost it in Paris after we spent the day with that duke and duchess from Austria—or Atlanta—I get the two mixed up.''

''Yucky couple,'' I tell him. ''All they did was change clothes and eat. Change clothes and eat.''

''Until the duchess practically rammed her tongue down my throat in the powder room at the Ritz,'' Amity tells the salesman dishily. ''That was when I realized she wanted to *remove* clothes and eat.''

''And then eat some more,'' I add, winking at the salesman. I turn to Amity. ''But I really think you lost it in Monte Carlo. I think you traded it for chits or chips or whatever they call those little gambling denominations the night we got tanked with Princess Stephanie and made those recordings and ended up sleeping on the Grimaldi yacht.''

''And which Rolex model did you own?'' the man asks sarcastically.

Amity and I take a few steps over to the glass case that houses everything Rolex. ''Was it that one?'' I ask, pointing to the timepiece encircled with diamonds.

''For heaven's sake, Harry, don't you remember Barcelona? I explained the meaning of *gaudy* in relation to the work of *Gaudí?*

That Rolex is *Gaudí*. No, darlin', mine was the simple, tasteful standard model," she says, pointing to it.

"Of course. Let's replace it," I say, grabbing the wallet from my pocket and taking out one of the two new credit cards I've acquired since landing my steward job. All I've bought is a gym membership for myself. It's time to buy something for Amity. I turn to the clerk. "That one. We'll take it." Amity looks at me with awe, an eyebrow raised. The sales clerk has his doubts. But I keep my eyes drilled into him, as if to say, "Get the watch, girlie." He does. Amity's right eyebrow raises to meet her left one, and her eyeballs expand like little helium balloons. "Put it on," I suggest. She's in shock as she realizes our game has transcended into reality. She places it on her wrist, locks it into place. It fits perfectly. And looks gorgeous. She takes her youthful hand and runs it through her blond hair. "It is so nice to finally have my watch back," she tells me with a shit-eating grin on her face. She almost has to stifle a laugh.

I know it's crazy. I have no money. And she already has a watch, but it's such a pathetic little thing, barely ticking along. And if there were ever a woman who was meant to have a nice flashy watch, it's Amity. Besides, I just can't stand to see the saleswomanman treat her with such contempt. I use the credit card with the five-thousand-dollar limit. I figure I'll have a couple thousand dollars to spare. I sign the credit slip, and Amity digs her nails into my arm and says, "Thank you, Harry. Thank you!" She presses her nose against mine and kisses me slowly on the lips. I feel not only her lips, but the sales clerk's tension. She unlocks our lips, smiles at the clerk, and says, "It is so wonderful you've devoted your life to helping others. I just know there's a special place in heaven for you."

The clerk rolls his eyes. "What about this?" he asks, once again holding up the tail of the barely ticking dead rat.

"Good Lord, Aunt Stephanie, just throw that piece of shit in the trash," Amity chimes, grabbing me by the arm and leading me out. "I've got my Rolex back!" And as we leave the store, Amity mutters, "I'll bet his mother lives with him and his wife. And when his wife goes out, his mother puts him in a diaper and spanks him and feeds him apple sauce."

"Hell's bells!" Amity says, pounding on the steering wheel of her old Granada. It won't start. The engine turns over, but it makes a horrible noise, as if there are shards of glass in the starter. "The Lord baby Jesus loves to fuck with me! He knows I got a new watch today, so he trashed my car."

"Do you have AAA?" I ask her.

"No. Couldn't afford the membership. You?"

"Nope."

"Well," she says, slumping down into the seat, "I'm sure going to pay for it now, Bubba. Five times more than that AAA membership would ever cost."

We have the sexy Maxwell-Grey valet boys call us a tow, and we wait an hour for the guy to show up. We ride in the truck, pulling the old Granada behind us, and when we get to the repair shop, the mechanic tells Amity it needs a new starter. I pull out a different credit card—to pay the tow guy and the repair man. And Amity keeps fussing about how we're going to pay off the bills and insists on taking the Rolex back, but I tell her not to worry. Somehow we'll get by.

"This is the third time in a year that this piece of shit has broken down on me," she sighs. "Oh, well. Now this gorgeous watch on my wrist will tell what time it is when my car breaks down. Why didn't you get yourself a watch, Harry? Huh?"

"Because I'm happy with my Timex," I tell her matter-of-factly.

I've been plugging along since I was seventeen, making my way in the world and knowing that it's possible to survive on my wits. I really *am* happy with my Timex, my casual clothes, my familiar old car. But I have to say it's a kick to meet someone who likes the opulent things my family likes and who actually gets *excited* about ownership rather than feeling it's an inalienable right.

Amity, Jackie, and I have just finished eating dinner at the Highland Park Cafeteria—a large cafeteria that caters to the kind of families I've been running from my entire life: white, conservative, suburban clans tribed out in Ralph Lauren and Laura Ashley ensembles. The place was loaded with parents whose children were miniature versions of themselves. Absolute clones in penny loafers and espadrilles, their wee hands folded while saying grace, their tongues orange from smuggled sips of fruit punch. The food was great, but there was something disturbing about seeing three-year-old girls with hairdos and makeup, and four-year-old boys who look like investment bankers, asking Jesus Christ, their Lord and Savior, to bless their squares of Jell-O.

We climb into Jacqueline's old silver-colored Volvo. "Let's drive through Highland Park!" Amity suggests.

Ever amiable, Jacqueline steers toward the money.

"Can you believe that woman thought her husband was choking?" Amity asks, referring to a woman who began yelling out for a doctor in the cafeteria.

"He just didn't want to talk to her," Jackie offers. "He wasn't choking. That's why she threatened to do the Heimlich maneuver on him—to get him talking."

I laugh, rolling down my window to invite the cool spring air into the car. "I thought she was saying Heinrich."

"I'd love to do the Heinrich maneuver," Amity answers. "Ja ja, to those German boys!"

"They wear dark socks and sandals over their dirty feet," Jackie complains. "They have dirty feet that smell."

"So suck their dicks, Jackie, not their feet," Amity answers frankly.

Jacqueline looks disgusted and lights a cigarette.

As we roll into Highland Park, Amity shakes and shivers over the wealthy neighborhood full of old-money homes. My parents have friends who live here, and my family visited one summer when I was twelve, but I let Amity think I'm seeing it for the first time.

Amity's stomach is full but her eyes are hungry. She claims an affinity with the tasteful, venerable properties of Highland Park and the families who go with them. It makes me nervous to see her so attracted to the world from which I came. I know that her family is not from the same station, not with the way she views it. "Jackie, are we *ever* going to live here? Girl, we've got to get ourselves the right guy."

"I don't want a boyfriend," Jacqueline declares.

"Who would? After Arthur!" *Author.*

"Who's Arthur?" I ask.

"My old boyfriend," Jacqueline yells above The Motels, who are blasting on the radio. "Arthur was an asshole. He was an asshole." She pronounces his name as *Author* also.

"He wrecked Jacqueline's Jaguar," Amity says, lighting a joint. "He has no conscience."

"You ought to know," Jacqueline tells Amity.

I wait for Amity to explain herself, but she raises the joint to her lips and sucks in without a word. It's a pretty cavalier response to someone who's accused you of having no conscience.

"What was that about?" I ask.

Amity ignores me, looks out the window.

"You guys have a secret?" I pry.

"Arthur was an asshole," Jacqueline repeats for the third time.

Amity and Jacqueline seem to agree that the secret is theirs, so I push no farther. I take the joint, inhale a large hit, and watch the world go by. In the front seat, the girls look great together—like Grace Kelly and an offbeat runway model motoring in a junk heap. As the dope soaks into me, I have a creeping feeling of contentment. My belly is full and I'm driving around with two bad-ass stewardesses, one of them capturing my heart. Life isn't at all bad. I realize I've succeeded in being happy in my life with nothing—and that means I'm entitled to something. And someone. And if the right guy isn't going to be that someone, maybe I should open my eyes to the gift in front of me.

Only the lonely can play.

CHAPTER NINE

April comes, and on its first day, Marvin Gaye's father shoots him dead, and Amity takes to playing "Sexual Healing" on the stereo for the rest of the month. My ex, Matthew, calls me to tell me he's taken up with the boy next door, who, he shamelessly tells me, is a *haircutter!* Some twenty-one year old who skipped college for hair-burning school is kissing Matthew's beautifully educated lips, but I wasn't good enough as a flight attendant? Oh, yeah, he tells me: "Derrick is from money. Tasteful St. Louis banking family. And they don't care that he's gay."

That fucking Matthew. I knew it. It's what he wanted all along: a free ride. A bank to pay off his student loans. One of the reasons I was attracted to him was that he was from a middle-class family and had to put himself through school and had chosen to strive toward a selfless career. Selfless my ass. He'd been waiting all along for the day when I'd graduate from student takeout food to haute cuisine and dump my VW for a BMW. And that's why he dumped me after the reading of the will—as soon as he learned I wouldn't have a dowry until I was a practicing heterosexual.

How could I be so stupid?

* * *

In his suit, at the BMW dealership, JT is tall, dynamic, and even sexier than when he's wearing shorts and a tank top at the gym. I look into his green glacier eyes and tell him I'd like to take a test drive. "Listen," he tells me, handing me the keys to a new black 325 with leather interior. "I've got an appointment with another customer in five minutes. Why don't you take this baby out for a spin—take your time. Maybe take it home and show it off to your . . . ? Anybody at home, Harry?"

"A girl," I say. "She's just a friend. Your situation's a little different, huh?" I ask, motioning to his wedding ring.

"Nah," he says, a roguish grin on his face, "just a girl."

Black. Five speed. Leather interior. Killer stereo. Sunroof. I drive out of the lot and steer straight for home.

"Oh, my Gawd!" Amity screams, running out the back door. "Harry! I love it! Is it yours?"

"Hell, no. I'm just trying to get laid," I laugh, yelling out the window.

"Life's a game show, baby. Go for the fuck *and* the car."

"Get in," I yell. "It'll turn into a pumpkin if I don't get it back soon." I scroll back the sunroof, and through the opening I can see the campus water tower.

"A Beamer!" she whoops, running toward the car. She touches the hood, then falls onto it and hugs the car as if it's her gigantic newborn child. She then pushes off and rushes to the driver's window to peer in. "Wait," she says. "I'm going to run in and twist one up." She flies into the house to roll a joint. I check out the stereo, put the seats back, honk the horn. "I'm coming!" she screams through a window, answering my honks.

"I was just trying to hear what it sounds like," I yell.

"No, I mean I'm *coming!*" she pants, faking an orgasm. Then she climaxes like a porn star on Gatorade and slams the window shut. Two seconds later she flies out the back door, locks it, and runs toward the car while sticking a freshly twisted joint behind her ear, the way a secretary stows a pencil. I hold the driver's door open for her. "Me?"

"You don't want to drive it?" I ask incredulously.

"Why not," she squeals, jumping in. "Ahhh," she sighs, "the smell of a new car makes little Virginia get all wiggly." She engages the cigarette lighter and fires up the joint. "So," she says, grabbing the stick shift and putting it into reverse, "is the sales guy's shifter this big?"

"I haven't found out yet. He's married, you know."

"Married men are perfect, Harry. They'll always buy you things, and the sex is great because those married guys *never* get any at home." She guns the car, pops the clutch, and jets off down the street. "And it's so easy to get out of those relationships if things go wrong."

"Is that so?" I laugh. "I was thinking about marrying you, Amity," I tell her jokingly. "Does that mean I'll have great sex with other guys?"

"*Nobody* gives it up better than Mrs. Harry Ford!" she screams, wind flying in through the sunroof.

By the time we're rolling down University Avenue, our usual route to the airport, past upper-middle-class homes designed to look like Tara, with yards full of huge oak trees and feminine flower beds, we're stoned out of our minds. The sun pours in through the roof, Boy George sings "Karma Chameleon" on the radio, and we smoke the joint down to the nub. God, Winston wouldn't recognize me. Neither would Matthew. Nor my mother. I'm probably closer than ever to the person they wish I would be. "We better get this thing back," I yell over the radio as we approach a four-way stop. "I've had it for almost half an hour. Let's roll down all the windows to get rid of the pot smell and be sure to toss the roach out."

While I fumble with the window controls on the console, Amity fishes the roach out of the ashtray.

Slam! Boom! We're smashed against our shoulder belts.

"Shit!" I croak.

"Fuck me on Sunday!" Amity yells.

We're over a curb and smashed into a stop sign.

"Fuck!" I yell, the metal sign bent in front of us, the gash it leaves in the hood horrifying to our eyes.

"Oh, my Gawd!" Amity inhales. She's still holding the roach. Even smashing into a stop sign can't cause her to part with it.

"Back up! Back up!"

She puts the car in reverse and plunks back down over the curb. We jump out and survey the damage. It's not good. The bumper is indented in a decidedly V shape, and the front grill and top of the hood is gashed in.

"Babe, I'm so sorry," Amity moans.

A cop car, from around the corner of nowhere, flashes his lights, gives a single *whoop* from his siren.

"Shit! Where did *he* come from?" She drops the roach and quickly covers it with her foot. Smooth as a card shark she reaches into her pocket and slips me a piece of gum while hardly moving her arm. "*You* were driving, Harry."

"What?" I ask, my heart racing. I awkwardly shove the gum into my mouth while she starts to chew her own. "Why me?"

"I've been drinking champagne, Harry. I won't pass a test if he gives me one."

The officer approaches the car. The absolute stereotype. A big, fat, doughy white guy with puffy fingers that are probably full of mayonnaise. He's got no neck and too much forehead, and his cheeks look as if they're storing walnuts. He checks out Amity as he asks, "Who's the driver?"

"Me," I answer.

He looks at me and with his backwoods accent says, "License?"

I hand him my Kansas license. He grabs it with his swollen hands, holds it into the sun to see better. I get the feeling he can't read. I swear he's just staring at it, turning it over, looking for my picture. Surprisingly, he seems oblivious to the pot smoke that's still seeping out of the car. Maybe, with all the windows down and the sunroof open and Amity's perfume, he doesn't smell it. Maybe it's because he's breathing through his mouth.

"You don't got no license plates, Kansas," he drawls as if my name is Kansas.

"We're just test-driving it, Officer."

When he laughs, I see that even his tongue is fat. "Hell of a way to test-drive it, son. We're going to have to file a report."

Amity slams into save-your-ass mode. She jumps into the conversation, her accent thicker than I've ever heard it. "Officer, my husband and I are just so excited!" *Exsawted!* "He's planning on buying this new car, and this is his first time to drive it, and one of us was trying to adjust the side mirrors so we could see properly while the other found the control for the headlights." *Hay-ud-lawts.* "Did we do something wrong?"

He looks past me to the smiling Southern belle. A young Grace Kelly. "Why'd you need the headlights?"

"It's always safer to drive with the headlights on. Even during the day," she says smoothly.

All of a sudden he becomes polite. "Yur right. That's good defensive drivin'. You married to Kansas here, ma'am?"

"Just recently," Amity glows, taking my hand. "Don't you worry. I'll make a Texan out of him yet."

I know she's just playing this out in order for us to escape, but no one has held my hand and claimed me since the day my mother dropped me off at my first day of kindergarten. I hold tight to Amity's hand.

He noisily inhales through his fat throat. "No doubt. Well, you've bent the stop sign. Damaged city property."

"Oh, but just hardly." She grabs the officer, grinding the roach into oblivion with her instep as she leads the cop to the sign. "Look, a big ole strong man like you can bend this thing back. No problem."

"You think so," he asks, putting his hands on his doughy hips and puffing his sagging chest up.

"Go on," she purrs. "Help us out. I know you can do it."

The cop pushes against the sign. It doesn't move.

"Harry, get over there and help the officer," Amity conducts.

Together, we're able to push the sign until it's almost vertical.

"There!" Amity decrees. "Good as new." She walks over to the cop and grabs his fatty biceps. "You're so *strong*. Forget those firemen. If my pussy's ever stuck in a tree, I'm going to call *you*."

The cop blushes. "What about the car?" he asks.

"You know it's less than five-hundred dollars damage, Officer. There's no need for a report. It's going to be embarrassing enough having to return it this way to the BMW dealership." *Bay-Em-Dubbya Daylership.*

He looks at her. Thinks. Thinks about her pussy. Then he says, "I shouldn't be doin' this, but all right. You get that car turned in, y'here? And make sure you set them mirrors 'fore you drive off."

She relaxes, smiles, cocks her head. "We certainly will, Officer. Thank you."

He returns the license to me and walks back to his car. We sit and for a moment do nothing. Then I start the car, turn the headlights on, and drive away cautiously. We slowly inch down the western stretch of University, lined with brick duplexes inhabited by grand-mothers who sit on their porches and knit pot holders while watching cops pull over stoned Yankees. "Shit," I say, practically slumped over the wheel.

"Bubba, I'm *so* sorry. I'll pay for the damage," Amity says, anxiously rubbing one eyebrow.

"Don't worry, sweetheart. It wasn't your fault. Neither of us were watching the road."

"I just don't ever want to cause you pain, Harry Ford," she says seriously. "I can't believe I've done this to you."

"Hey, if it weren't for you, that cop would have filed a report. You saved my ass."

"This is University Park, Bubba. They don't like outsiders. He knew right away you were a Yankee, Harry. You need to develop your Texas accent. And use a few phrases like 'Y'all' this and 'Y'all' that. When you're working, say to the passengers, 'Drink up. We're *fixin'* to land.' And instead of 'How are you?' say 'You all right?' And when you agree with how somebody is feeling, say 'Myself.' Can you remember all that?"

My theater training pays off. "You bet your sweet ass." *Yew bet yur sweet ayuss.*

"Good boy, Harry."

"Here's what we're prepared to offer you," JT says, tapping his pen on a legal pad. I've dropped Amity off at home, and I'm sitting in JT's office, the glass windows obscured by miniblinds he's rotated shut. "You buy the car, and we overlook the damage. *Or* you buy the car, and we can fix the damage at below cost—only six hundred dollars—and we'll simply tie it into your payments. Or you don't buy, and we go through your insurance company, and I'm afraid the damage is set at thirty-two hundred."

He doesn't know that I don't carry collision coverage on the VW, so I'm not covered for the BMW. I'd have to come up with over three thousand dollars and get nothing in return. "I'm not sure I qualify financially to buy the car," I tell him sheepishly.

"Harry," he says sexily, as if he wants to rip my clothes off, "*everybody* qualifies. I'm tight with Gary, our wonder boy in the finance department. I'll push it through for you."

"Man, I don't know," I say, pressing my palm into my forehead. "I mean, I don't really need a new car. I don't know if a BMW's even my style. I really didn't come here expecting to buy a car."

"Then why did you come here?" JT asks, biting his pen through smiling teeth, both his eyebrows raised.

I move my hand down my face and rest my chin in it. Look at him. Grin.

"Look, Harry. Your car's almost twenty years old. It's time. There's nothing wrong with driving a BMW. You're not going to turn into a capitalist pig or yuppie scum or whatever it is you're afraid of. We can transfer your Amnesty International sticker from the Volkswagen to the BMW," he teases. "You'll still have enough money to write those checks to Greenpeace. But you'll love driving this car, I'm telling you. And if for any reason you find you can't afford it, you can return it at any time, and we'll buy it back from you."

My grin changes from good-natured to wry. "For a lot less than I paid."

"That's a fallacy. We can give you almost what you paid. Really. There's no risk, buddy. Your little accident today was just life telling you to wake up. Come on, Harry. Don't you want to grab life by the balls?"

I think about his balls. And the third credit card that arrived yesterday, with the preapproved seven-thousand-dollar spending limit. "What the fuck? I'll do it."

"Great," he says, standing and coming around to meet me on the other side of the desk. I stand and we shake hands. He holds on to my hand and tells me, his face inches from mine, "I've never had a customer I didn't satisfy." He's so hot my clothes are going to ignite.

He finagles the paperwork, and I sign on the fifty-two dotted lines, and with the credit card down payment, and a small amount on another credit card, and the trade-in with the VW, and the rest financed through the credit union at the airline, my payments are only $512.47 a month for four years. And since I make $17,000.00 a year as a flight attendant, it will only cost me, after taxes, about

two-thirds of my salary a year for four years—which means I have
to eat nothing but those little squares of cafeteria Jell-O for breakfast,
lunch, and dinner for four years.

As we're wrapping up the transaction, shaking hands outside by
the car, JT penetrates me with his arctic eyes, hands me a card,
and says, "This card is different from the one I gave you at the
gym. It has my private number on it. My wife doesn't answer my
private phone. And I want you to call me if there's anything else
I can do to make you feel satisfied."

Is this what I would be like if I married Amity? Would I end
up being a hungry animal on the prowl for the *real* nourishment I
need? I'm sometimes wondering if I'm falling in love with her,
and I know I love being with her, but I also know I'd never be
able to deny my natural feelings for men. Would it be fair to offer
myself to her if I could never tender my body in full? Maybe not,
but it's my heart that wants her, and isn't my heart more important?

"Call me soon. Don't make me wait," he whispers.

Shit. At the moment, my dick has so much more feeling than
my heart.

We have eye sex for a second; then I drive away. In a new
Beamer with a dented hood and bumper.

When the bills start coming in, I make the minimum payment
on the Rolex, and somehow eke out the first car payment. It leaves
me with nothing in the bank. I can't even afford a square of Jell-O.
Amity graciously pays the rent in full, as an apology for denting
the BMW. But I still don't have any money for food or bills. I
decide to call my mother. I know she's sympathetic, and now that
my father is gone she'll be more apt to help me. I also know he
kept a tight rein on her, and she's been brainwashed into thinking
it's for my own good (translate: future heterosexuality) for her to
withhold, which spikes my anger. After all, Winston has received
a Brink's truck worth of cash over the years, while I've toed my

own humble line, never inching over. The least she can do is give me a loan. I'll pay it back. With interest, if she wants.

"How's Amity?" she asks almost before we've even said hello.

"Fine, Mother. She's out on a trip," I answer into the phone.

"And your children?"

I'm always stunned when my mother dishes out a little sarcasm; it seems so incongruous with her jaunty personality. "They're fine, Mother. Harry Jr. has the best batting stats in Little League, and Amber and Amity recently won the Mother-Daughter Pageant. And how are things with the general?"

"Just fine. He bought me a new water fountain for the backyard and installed it himself," she answers proudly, shifting right back into the surrealism of her real world.

"I got a BMW," I blurt, shifting into my own current realism.

"Oh, thank God," she says. "I was always afraid someone was going to recognize you in that VW!"

I was sure she was going to say, "I was always afraid that someone was going to *hit you head-on, and you'd be killed.*" That's what most mothers of rear-engine drivers say. "Well," I answer positively, "BMWs are very recognizable, very acceptable cars."

"You'll have to tell Winston."

"Well, I sort of got it for me—and for Amity." I'm shameless. I didn't plan this lie—it just came out. But I'm completely prepared for its effect.

"Harry Ford," my mother gushes, "I'm so proud of you! Thinking of Amity before yourself. I've had a hunch things would come to this."

"Well, don't get too excited, Mom. It looks like I'm going to need your help. You know I've never asked for much, and it's long been made clear by Dad that any requests would have been denied anyway. And even with him gone, I know the conditions of the will have been clearly spelled out, but I was wondering if I could ask you for a small *loan*. I'm in kind of a bind."

"I'm perfectly willing to consider it. When are you two coming up? We can talk about it then."

Fuck, I set myself up. If I bring the girl, I get the loan. If not, I suffer. Why is everything with my mother a negotiation? "Mom, are you trying to blackmail me?"

"Oh, for heaven's sake, I'm not blackmailing you. It's just so much easier to talk about these money things face to face. The general and I are free two weekends from now. How about you two?"

"I'm new at my job, you know. Sometimes it's hard for me to get the weekend off but I'll try. And I'll talk to Amity."

"Good. Those BMWs are really very affordable when your finances are in order." Subtext: Those BMWs are really very affordable when your *fiancée* is in order.

"Mother, how are you doing?" I ask tenderly. "I mean the cancer."

"The C-word is nowhere in sight. What I'm worried about is the A-word, honey. This AIDS thing is looking more like a homosexual-related disease every day. They just isolated the virus, you know. It's a virus, Harry. You can get it from other men. I'm glad you're with Amity now."

I know she's trying to manipulate me, and I could certainly argue that viruses aren't gender specific, but I do feel safer being with Amity. "It's scary, isn't it?"

"Not a good phone topic. Sorry. Let's end on an up note. I go in for my new breasts next month. I'm ordering a perky little set like Sally Field has."

"Is there anything on Sally Field that *isn't* perky?"

"No," she answers, "and we should all strive to be just like her."

"Well, I'm glad you're working on it," I tell her. "Everyone likes breasts that have a positive attitude."

* * *

Amity's out flying, and I'm feeling pent-up. Every time I dial JT's private phone, I only dial half the numbers before I hang up. I'd just feel weird, sneaking around with some guy who has a wife. It's not right. I decide to try the gay bars again. Maybe, with my new, improved gym body, it'll be different. Of course a cold wind blows in from the north, and I have to cover up.

I try a different bar, one with a Country-Western kind of theme. The floor is wooden and worn and covered with sawdust or wood chips or maybe carcasses of dead insects—I can't tell because the lights are so dim. The bartender's station sits in the middle of the place, and there's a huge wooden bar with stools that sit in a rectangle all around it. From the jukebox, George Strait sings to the gays, an irony that goes unnoticed by the cowboys at this here homo hoedown, who are acting just as standoffish as the dudes in the S&M bar. Their boots are scuffless and their starched blue jeans and Western shirts have been creased by irons. I suspect their boxer shorts are starched and ironed as well. And they probably put a little dab of cologne on their dick heads.

I just can't get into it. I'm not tall (even in cowboy boots) and handsome like these guys. Even though I've been building up my body at the gym, I'm still average in height and referred to as *cute*. And cute doesn't compete with square jaw lines or massive biceps and hulking chests. Worst of all, there's no starch in my jeans. Everyone continues not to talk to me, and I continue to feel stupid. Stupid because I doubt I'd genuinely be interested in anyone here anyway.

I find a pay phone and call JT. He answers, asks me what I want to do. "Anything," I yell over the pain and heartache of George's twang.

"I can't pass that up, can I?" he answers. I can't tell if he's whispering into the phone or if it's the music in the background that makes him difficult to hear. I hang up. Saddle up. Head out.

We rendezvous at a park off Lover's Lane (how perfect), close to Snider Plaza. I arrive first, shut off the engine. Wait. Headlights appear. It's an old green Ford. I think of the day I met Jacqueline. Wonder if it's her mother's car. It pulls up beside me. Stops. A head nods. It's him. I wait for him to join me, but he nods for me to come over there.

"Hi," he says, more nervous, less confident than when he shook my hand at the dealership.

"Hi. You drive a Ford?"

"My wife's. She's using my car tonight." He wastes no time. "So what do you want to do?"

"I don't know. You want to trade blow jobs?"

He nods. Looks around to see if anyone is coming. Coast is clear. He unzips his zipper, takes out his dick, which I can barely see in the dark, and reaches for my head. He shoves me down on his already hard dick and fills my mouth with it completely, instantly. It's kind of salty, and I have a flashback to when I was twelve years old and my father took me to watch the local baseball farm team, the Wichita Aeros, and I picked the sexiest player with the biggest basket and used the binoculars to watch him the whole game, and when my dad got me a hot dog, I removed it from the bun, and while watching my baseball fantasy, stuck the whole thing in my mouth at once. I got away with it for several innings, until Winston, so astute to my desires, tattled on me. Though my father took a hard swipe at Winston for his claim, causing him to cry, he never did take me to a baseball game again.

I try to take a moment to catch my breath, but JT is shoving me down, and pulling me up, working my head like a hand pump from the get-go. I press my hands against his thighs to brace myself. I feel the starch in his jeans. "Someone's coming!" he warns, grabbing a handful of my hair and yanking my head up so hard I get whiplash.

I sit up. We wait. A small compact car drives around the circle, passes us, and drives out of the park. JT watches it in the rearview mirror. When it's gone, he grabs my head again and says, "OK!"

Man, what's the rush? He's pumping my head like Helen Keller pumps the water well. My nose is running. My eyes are watering. Then all of a sudden he says, "Now!" and holds my head down until I swallow. Then he lets me loose.

"That was great," he says, zipping up. Then he starts the engine of the green Ford and says, "I'll take care of you next time." Then he puts out his hand to shake, as if we've clenched another car deal.

After he's gone, I sit in my car and laugh. After wiping the water from my eyes and blowing my nose, I realize why straight women are obsessed with waterproof mascara and those little pocket packs of tissues. And no wonder a lot of them would rather eat a good bar of chocolate and read a good book than fuck their three-minute husbands.

At least I'm safe from AIDS. They say straight men don't get it, so I guess JT is protected. But if he's straight, what's he doing with me? What a crock of shit. I'm an idiot. That guy didn't connect with me any more than he connects with his wife—or any of the hundreds of other people he's probably done it with. Shit, I've yet to meet a guy who *is* willing to connect—truly connect—the way Amity and I do. Maybe I *should* marry Amity. Not only do I love her, but it may help me to stay alive.

CHAPTER
TEN

The bills keep rolling in—for the dinners I offer to charge, the fancy cowboy boots Amity yearns for, concert tickets—you name it, I charge it. But along with the overdue notices, the phone calls start. I'm amazed at the tenacity of these people—the collection agencies—who call eight times a day. And though I feel like I'm sinking under it all, it's worth it. Amity is so happy with me that Hunt fades out of the picture. I'm satisfied to have him gone because I've never liked having him around after hearing his bar story of beating up fags. It's weird, this competitiveness I have with her boyfriends. I know I can't satisfy her in the same way they can, but for some reason I want to try. Before she goes out on a date, I become wildly entertaining and make her laugh as much as possible so her date seems substandard and boring in comparison. I bring home little sugar cakes from her favorite Mexican bakery and pick up her laundry from the cleaners, and now that it's warm enough, I wash her car once a week.

If actions speak louder than words, then Amity must know how I feel. But since I've made no verbal declaration, she takes on another beau, Wade. Wade is a flight attendant who believes in the power of green algae. He's tall and has a good body, but he's thick in the head, Amity says. ''Dumber than a jar of hair.'' He doesn't make her laugh, because he's always promoting the benefits of green algae. She laments, "I've tried to tell him I don't need more oxygen. I need more *clothes*." I can tell she's bored with the whole thing, and it's almost as if she's daring me to tell her to get rid of him. I ask her what she sees in him, and she tells me his mother has an oceanfront house in Pebble Beach, and that's what she *sees* in him. She's planning a trip to Pebble Beach with Wade near the end of the month. "You must think I'm awful," she tells me.

"Not at all," I assure her. "You're just with the wrong guy."

"I *hate* this," Amity says of her period. She's lying on the sofa, a hot-water bottle on her abdomen. "Muffie is miserable, Harry." Muffie is another name for her Virginia. Virginia, Muffie, Libby, Lady. I really think she has a schizophrenic pussy.

"What can I do for you?" I ask.

"Will you drive me to Ben Franklin? I'm craving penny candy." *Pinny Caindee.*

The five-and-dime is only blocks away in Snider Plaza. We both go into the store. If Amity's getting penny candy, then I want some too. She loads up on all kinds of bite-size confections: saltwater taffy, caramels, Tootsie Rolls, Bit O'Honeys, candy corn, jelly beans, Dots, licorice—you name it. I get some jawbreakers and Hot Tamales.

Back at home, we sit on the sofa, get stoned, and eat. And she eats it all. Everything. Then she wants to go to a movie. I drive us in her car to see *Romancing the Stone*, and we have to travel on Central Expressway to get to the theater.

Central Expressway, nicknamed Suicide Express by the locals, is an infamous freeway in Dallas on which people die horrible deaths. Every day. It has only two lanes in each direction, no shoulder (only walls), and insidious curves. There are no on ramps where you can build up speed to merge. The traffic hurls along at 70 mph, so anyone entering the expressway must go from a complete stop to 70 mph, while concentrating on the curve ahead, and trying not to hit the side wall. Did I mention Texas allows open containers of alcohol while driving?

"Here, Harry. Take another hit off the joint."

"No!" I scream. "You're trying to make me kill us both!" My heart is thumping. I'm at the edge of Mockingbird Lane, ready to turn on to Suicide Express.

"It'll make you drive better, I swear," Amity pleads, laughing. She cranks up the stereo louder so that the Thompson Twins are shouting "Doctor! Doctor!"

"You're going to *need* a fucking doctor if you give me any more of that pot!" I yell.

"OK, OK. Get ready!" she shouts, bracing herself, pushing against the dash.

I put it in first gear and hold the clutch in. Then I step on the gas.

Amity whoops, "Go!"

I pop the clutch, the tires squeal, our heads snap back, and we jettison into the traffic, screaming like passengers in a crashing airplane. "We're going to die! We're going to die big time!" *Big Tom!*

As we pass the brightly colored candy counter at the movie theater Amity makes an *ugh* sound and looks as if she's going to vomit. We sit in the back of the theater and watch the movie, and halfway through Amity whispers that she wants a diet drink. I get her favorite, Diet Dr Pepper, and return with popcorn too. She pushes the popcorn into her mouth as if all these meetings Reagan is having with Gorbachov are just for show and the Soviets are going to drop the bomb at any moment. She washes it down with a huge gulp of Diet Dr Pepper. After the salty popcorn is gone, Amity gets up and leaves. She returns with malted milk balls. Christ, two hours ago she ate enough candy to satisfy a busload of kindergartners. An hour later she was ready to puke at the sight of the candy case in the lobby. And now she's wolfing malted milk balls as if they're a cure for cancer. I can't figure her out.

At the end of the film, when Michael Douglas and Kathleen Turner are reunited, Amity reaches over and takes my hand. I look sideways at her in the dark while the movie screen lights up her face. She's not looking at me, but focusing on the movie. Yet she's quietly holding my hand with no explanation.

It really is the strangest, most tender moment. Sometimes Matthew and I held hands during movies, but it always seemed like a statement. A we're-just-as-good-as-anyone-else gesture. We would sit there, clenched in unity, and when the lights went up after the picture ended, and all the straight couples had unclasped and were gathering their coats, we'd wait a few moments longer to ensure the effect of our statement. Of course, that took the romance out of it and made it a political gesture. And though political gestures are necessary, they're seldom sexy. So this public act of handholding with Amity is a provocative, new, *free* feeling. Straight people have it so easy.

Two days later, Amity is over her period but now has a raging yeast infection, something I'm not at all familiar with, but she assures me it's true. I offer my services, and since she doesn't want to poo up to go to the drug store (because women in Texas feel obligated to wear a ball gown to a 7-11, and even Amity suffers this burden), she sends me to the pharmacist for Monistat cream.

"Hep Yew?" the lady pharmacist who looks like Dolly Parton asks.

"I'm picking up a prescription for Amity Stone."

"What's the prescription?"

"Monistat."

"And you are?"

Not suffering from a yeast infection, Dolly. "Harry Ford, her roommate."

She gets the stuff, has me sign the log, inspects my name as if

I'm a scam artist, and carefully hands me the pussy cream as if it's kryptonite. I rip it from her hands and hustle to the register.

When I bring it home, Amity yips, "Relief!" She takes the medicine and rushes into the bathroom, and for the first time since I met her, she closes the door. I start to head for the kitchen to get a Diet Dr Pepper, but she yells out, "You're so good to me, Harry. No guy would ever help a girl with this. Thank you, babe."

"You're welcome," I call.

"Do you know how hard it is to lie down on a cold bathroom floor and do this?" she asks.

"I know it sucks. Every time I get a yeast infection I vow it's my last," I answer.

"It's not a picnic in the park, is it?" she responds, as if I'm serious. "I mean, here I am, fixin' to shoot Libby in the bull's-eye with chilly cream! It's about as pleasant as a drive-by shooting."

I imagine her with a loaded gun pointed at her crotch. "Do you shoot it like a gun?"

"Sort of. Well, not really," she yells. "I mean, you won't hear a bang or anything."

"Are you doing it now?"

"Are you ready?" she asks, as if I have anything to do with it.

"Maybe I should take a hit off the bong first," I joke.

"Good idea, babe, but hurry. I'm freezing lying on this tile!"

"Just get it over with," I tell her. "I don't need drugs for this."

"*I* do," she says. "Fire up that bong and pass it through the door."

I laugh and grab the bong off the hallway floor. There's still pot left in the bowl, so I open the door a crack and slide it in on the floor, followed by the lighter.

"Grazie!" she yells. I hear the bubbling of the water in the chamber, followed by silence, followed by exhalation. "OK, Harry, here we go. Medicine time for Muffie!"

"I'm ready." I keep thinking about the vaginal monikers

invented by the straight guys in my college dorm: hairy carport, love taco, Cindy's trap door. But girls always seem to give it feminine names or liken it to a flower. Georgia O'Keefe made it downright glorious. What in the hell is going on behind that bathroom door?

"Ahhhh!" Amity screams. Then she starts singing in a high-pitched voice:

> *When you see Libby Libby Libby*
> *on your table table table,*
> *you better pet her, pet her, pet her,*
> *while you're able able able!*

"Is it over?" I ask.

"It will be in a couple days, darlin'. But at the moment it's like a Jane Fonda workout. I *feel the burn!*"

The next week, the day before she's to leave on her trip with Wade, I say, "Don't go. Let's buzz down to Padre Island and cross the border to Mexico." Padre Island is off the gulf coast of southern Texas, where college students spend their spring break burning through their parents' money by drinking cases of Jack Daniel's Whiskey and puking it over the sides of chartered "booze cruise" barges. It's also a favorite junket of Dallas-based flight attendants, just a nonstop flight from Dallas to Brownsville, the gateway city, and we can be down there in just over an hour.

"Harry," Amity says, "I thought you were supposed to be working a three-day trip tomorrow?"

I was. But yesterday I signed it over to a flight attendant who wanted the hours. I don't mind her going out with someone besides me, but *Wade?* I mean, he's a nice guy and all, but he doesn't even make her laugh. "I'm not working this week. Let's go to Padre. We'll bake and drink Margaritas."

"What about Wade and his blue green algae?" Amity wonders, doing her doe-eyed look.

"Tell him you're in search of a blue green cocktail instead."

We wear sufficient clothing for the flight down, but pack nothing but swimsuits and the boxer shorts Amity lifted from Troy, since it's now full-on summer and we're into minimalist attire. Our flight down to Brownsville is staffed by a woman with clownish makeup. Amity whispers, "Barnum and Bailey, y'all." The attendant also has the longest, biggest hair I've seen in Texas yet. I check to see if her name tag says, "Rapunzel." In contrast, our flight's captain, also a woman, has hair shorn so severely that we're able to see her scalp. "Well I guess those two even themselves out," Amity says, brushing the crumbs off her seat cushion before sitting down.

"What do you mean?"

"The captain and Rapunzel are lovers. They think nobody knows, but it's a common fact."

I buckle my seat belt. "That hair has *got* to be heavy. At some point it's going to snap her neck."

"Good, she's senior to us. We'll both move up a number on the seniority list." Amity checks her own hair's reflection in the little purse mirror she carries. "Harry, promise if my hair ever gets that big, you'll write me a note."

We order two glasses of champagne from the woman with the colossal coif, and when she brings them, we inspect them for hair. All clear, we sip them and snack on the little bags of dry-roasted nuts with MSG glaze, while flipping through the in-flight magazine to check out the *Slut of the Month*, a girl Amity claims has had more abortions than there are Osmond children.

As the jet turns to make its final approach to the runway in Brownsville, Amity states, "My parents have a second home on the island."

I'm surprised she didn't mention it before. "Are they there now?"

"I don't know," she says, looking out the window to the lush farmland of the Rio Grande Valley as it grows closer and closer.

My parents have a home in Colorado, and I can't imagine going to Aspen and not staying in the family house—even though I'd have to sneak us in with my extra key. "You don't want to stay with them?"

"No," she says. "If they're there, they'll only make us crazy. We didn't bring any nice clothes, and they'll want to drag us to the Yacht Club and make us play bridge all day while sipping Manhattans."

"Sounds awful," I admit.

"We're not even going to call them," she states.

"I understand," I answer. But I don't believe her parents have a home on Padre Island. What is this thing with her family? Does she even have a family?

Amity takes off her sunglasses and holds my hand. Her eyes sparkle as she changes her entire chemistry to address me. "Let's not talk about my family. This is going to be a wonderful two days together, Harry. Just you and me. We don't need anyone else, do we?"

"No, we don't."

"Power nap!" she barks without a segue, breaking regulations by reclining her seat fully before landing. In seconds she's out cold. The jet's gear drops with a thud, and the engines whine while we line up with the runway. We come roaring in and touch down with a hard bounce—as if we've been shot out of the sky—and the pilots deploy the thrust reversers with full force, as if the runway were the length of a Band-Aid. The shrill noise is deafening as the reverse thrust slows the aircraft. We're still moving at a good clip when the captain steers the jet onto a taxiway as if she's making a left turn through a yellow stoplight. Everyone on board is thrown against the right side of his seat. And Amity sleeps through all of it.

As the pilots shut down the engines at the gate, I lean over to gently wake her. Just as I'm about to touch her shoulder, she pops up like a piece of toast from a toaster. "Let's go!"

"Ahhh!" I jolt, slamming back against my own armrest. "God, Amity! Why do you do that?"

"Do what?" she asks, grabbing her tote.

I approach the rental desk to rent a cheap car. After handing over my credit card, the agent informs me my authorization has been denied. I make a lame joke and hand her another card. Denied again. Fuck. These card people are closing in on me. I've *got* to get these payments out. It's just that even my minimum payments are too high now for me to have any money to live. I'm afraid to try my third and last card, and luckily I don't have to when Amity dives in and saves the day, happily producing her credit card to the agent. "Sorry," I tell her, embarrassed. "I'll pay you back as soon as we get home."

"Don't worry about it, Harry," she smiles, fully sincere. "We're a team."

We find a reasonable hotel next to the ocean. Amity checks us in, and we head immediately for the beach.

The almost tepid ocean is like a Kansas horizon right before a tornado, but the charcoal darkness of the water is sliced with lines of rolling white waves. The patches of sky are the same brilliant blues of any Caribbean horizon and strung together with huge cumulus clouds looking like giant popcorn floating by. We dig our toes into the warm sand. Let the sun soak into our skin. Walk with our feet in the water. Snack on chips. Flip through fashion magazines.

In the late afternoon, after we're tanned and warmed and talked out, we grab the rental car and head across the border to Matamoros, Mexico.

We stroll through the dusty dirt streets of Mexico, dressed in our boxer shorts and short sleeved button downs. We're energized by the brass of the mariachi music floating out of a nearby bar as we inspect ashtrays, rugs, velvet paintings, and maracas laid out on the brilliant blankets of the street vendors. When I offer to buy Amity a pair of maracas, she tells me she already has a pair, then shakes her titties. I laugh, and so do the local men on the street, while their wives scold them and usher them back into the shops or on their way.

We decide we're hungry for local flavor of a more edible character, so we dine in a restaurant that looks like something from the Hollywood of the 1940's. Large round tables with white starched tablecloths and napkins, big red velvet chairs, a huge dance floor in the middle of the restaurant, and a large live orchestra that plays while we eat.

There is something special about this day, this evening, this dinner. Amity's hair is curly, full, and gorgeous, and her ears are adorned with gold hoop earrings, and this combination makes her look almost like a *Latin* Grace Kelly. And though she's wearing only a starched white men's short-sleeved dress shirt, boxer shorts, and little leather slip-on shoes, she's glamorous beyond words. She leaves the top two buttons of her shirt open, and the string of pearls around her neck spills into her freckled cleavage.

And tonight she looks at me as if I'm the finest man in the world. And I completely forget that I've seen her look at Bart this way. And Troy. And Hunt. And probably Wade. And Miguel Arturo. And while she gazes at me with magic in her eyes, I can't help but notice the waiters appraise my status. *Nice score, amigo,* their faces tell me. And the bass player in the band nods his approval. And the couple at the next table, who are only mildly enjoying themselves, seem to look at Amity and me with melancholy envy. Man, this is it. The thing that everyone is looking for. I feel like the one guy in the room who every other guy wants to be.

Amity, in between bites of lobster and sips of beer, stops and holds my hand and bathes me with her eyes, but doesn't even try to add language to the moment before she gently releases my fingers and returns to the food. Maybe there hasn't been language invented yet for two people like us in a situation like this.

While the orchestra plays, a Mexican gentleman with a large, old-fashioned camera goes table to table. He stops and raises his camera to capture us. Amity leans over, I hold a bottle of beer in my right hand and put my left arm around her, and she puts both her hands under the table on my leg, where she slides one hand inside my boxer shorts and moves it upward until it almost touches my dick. We look into the camera. *Flash!* Her hand is gone.

We look at each other and burst with laughter. ''You almost touched my lobster,'' I tell her.

After dinner we move onto the dance floor and shake it out with the band to some killer merengue. We're a little drunk—on margaritas, beer, and most definitely, each other. We don't even notice that everyone else is dressed formally until the maître d' comes onto the dance floor to inform us there is no dancing in underwear. We laugh, dance back to our seats, feed each other dessert, and pay the check—both of us contributing, me using my little stash of cash.

We hold hands on the return drive to Padre, and once back, Amity says, ''Let's take a romantic walk on the beach.'' The moon is full enough that we can see the sand below our toes and the waves rolling in beyond the shore. We stroll, holding our shoes in one hand, each other in the other, while the warm wind washes over the sea and onto our faces. I look down and in the moonlight see little creatures running at our feet. Crabs? Wait. What's that one with the curled tail? A scorpion? A scorpion! ''Amity, there're scorpions on the beach!''

''Where?'' she screams.

''There!'' I say, pointing to the creature with the erectile little tail.

''Run!''

We break hands and run toward the hotel, dodging crabs and scorpions and anything else our imaginations might give form. We get to the door, and Amity says, "Hurry!" as I try to get the key into the lock. We fly into the room and fall onto the bed, laughing. She pulls herself up to me and says, "I love you, Harry Ford." And before I can answer she slides down my body, pulling off my boxers as she descends.

This is a strange moment for a gay guy, believe me. It's as if all my life I've eaten Almond Joys, and for the first time I'm about to sink into a Mounds. It's just so much softer and smoother, and though it's supposed to be sweet, I'm not sure I'll taste the sugar in it—and I'll definitely be missing the nuts.

But as if she senses my apprehension, she doesn't make me take a bite at all, but bites it herself, so to speak. It doesn't matter that my dick isn't hard in the beginning, she *makes* it hard. And forget that I called her a Mounds—she's a fucking Payday, with more nuts than any guy. And I'm losing my mind, because the one thing I've always heard that women have in common is that they can't give head. I've heard wrong; Amity is far beyond even any *gay man*. She sucks me as if she's dying of thirst, and I'm the only source for a thousand miles, as if she's *desperate* for my release. I'm rolling all over the bed, sometimes pushing her off because it's so intense, and she's following me, hungrily reconnecting, begging me to give it up, moaning, whining, totally *in need*.

When I come, I scream like a sixteen year old getting his first hummer, and she screams too, her mouth full. Then she swallows. And then we both collapse as if we've been shot.

We lie there for several minutes, both of us catching our breath. I feel guilty all of a sudden. I should do something for her, right? If not, I'm just like JT, the car salesman. But what will I do? I've never flicked the switch on Cindy's trap door. I wouldn't know what the hell I'm doing. I'd be the amateur of all time. "So?" I say halfheartedly, my dick starting to soften. "What about you?"

"Don't worry," she answers, exhaling. "I already did. We came together."

I'm so relieved I take her wet hand and hold it. I hear her head rustle against the pillow as she turns to me. I turn mine and look into her eyes.

"Just hold my hand," she says delicately, "and I'll be happy." And she soon is sleeping—without nightmares.

CHAPTER
ELEVEN

As Amity pulls the BMW up to the house, we both see the official-looking piece of paper taped to the front door. Never mind that I'm not poor white trash. I *have* put ninety cents' worth of gas in my VW because that was the sum of change in my ashtray, and I *have* lived on convenience store hot dogs after I blew my measly paycheck while at college. I know what that piece of paper is.

"Creditors," Amity mutters with contempt.

"How do you know?" I ask sheepishly as we step out of the car.

Amity goes to the mailbox, grabs the mail, and sorts through it. "It's happened to me, Harry. Only once, but it sucks. That's why I date rich guys."

"Until now." Fuck. I can't believe I said that. "I mean . . . I guess we're not really dating. Which is good . . . because—"

"Relax, Harry. We don't need a title."

"I know," I chuckle defensively. But it's true: Life is different after that blow job. Somehow, I'm more of a man. And somehow, Amity is too. And I'm just not sure what that makes the two of us together. Am I a straight guy just because I got a blow job from a girl? Is she a gay guy just because she sucks dick like a man?

I read the notice. The credit company says they'll be sending someone to the house again "in the near future." Fools. Don't they know I have no future. "What the fuck am I going to do?"

"Don't worry, Harry. I'm all lined up to go out with this big-bucks guy named Kim."

"A guy named Kim?"

"Why not? There was a boy named Sue. Listen, Harry. Kim is filthy rich and his midlife crisis is burning a hole in his pocket. He needs a girl like me who can cash those checks as fast as he can write them. I'll make sure some of those checks have your name on them."

It's amazing. She must know my family is worth more than two hundred million dollars, and she's not only never asked me for a penny, but she's willing to help me out. But I don't care how much money he has—Amity shouldn't have to date him if she doesn't want to. Besides, I can't help but feel jealous. "You're not dating some middle-aged got rocks in order to pay off my bills, especially a guy named Kim," I say, disgusted. I realize what has to be done. "We just need to go to Kansas and meet my mother," I sigh. I lift our bags from the trunk, carry them in.

"What are you talking about, Harry?" Amity asks.

"I'll explain later. Let's get stoned."

"Uh-oh," she warns, looking at the pile of mail in her hand. "Just like clockwork. They always know."

I set our bags down in the house. "What?"

"You got two new credit cards while we were gone."

"Fuck!" I laugh.

"It's like they can smell you when you're desperate, so they just keep sending you more temptation. Come on," she orders, pulling on my arm. "We gotta freeze these bad boys."

"What the hell are you talking about?"

She reaches into the cupboard in the kitchen and pulls out two midsize Tupperware bowls, then instructs me to remove the credit cards from the envelopes. She takes a piece of ice from the tray in the freezer, wets it, and sticks it to another piece of ice. "Get a couple pieces of ice and do what I'm doing," she tells me.

"What *are* we doing, Amity?"

"We're freezing your assets, babe. You gotta make these bad boys unavailable for impulse purchases." She shows me how to wet the little tower of cubes and stick the card onto it, then set each of them into a bowl carefully, credit card balanced on top, and fill the bowl until water is five inches over and under the card. "You gotta have the credit card frozen right in the middle of the block of ice so you have to wait *hours* before you use that card—and by the time it thaws you've come to your senses, and you just put it back in the freezer."

"You're crazy," I laugh, grabbing her around the waist and kissing her. "You definitely need to meet my mother."

The next day, as I walk by myself through the airport terminal, pulling my luggage on my little luggage cart, I have a confidence I didn't have before Padre Island. I feel more authentic, as if I'm finally a citizen of the world. It's hard to explain, but I mostly go through life thinking that everyone else is stamped with APPROVED while I'm left blank. But after my tryst with Amity, I'm stamped. One of them.

After we're airborne, a girl I'm working with says, "So you're Amity's latest?"

"Latest? I guess." I'm flattered to be chosen by one of the most beautiful, mysterious women at the airline. I smile. "Yes."

"What's it like living with Amity Stone?" she says with half a smirk on her face.

"Everyone always asks me that at work," I tell her. "It's great. We're always laughing. I love it."

"Do you guys sleep together?"

Man, this girl isn't shy. But then again, most flight attendants aren't. They'll tell you anything and expect the same. My second month on the job I flew with a girl who shared all the gory details of her impending divorce and said, "I haven't had sex with my husband in three years, but I'm finally having orgasms again because I'm sleeping with my therapist, and would you mind taking a bag of peanuts and a Miller Lite out to the guy with the cowboy hat in row eight?"

"Amity says never kiss and tell," I say, finally answering her question.

"It's a good philosophy," the girl agrees, "especially for Amity."

"Hey, I know all about the professor at CCT," I say assuredly. "Big deal."

"I don't know anything about a professor," the girl answers. "I was talking about her first husband, *the millionaire.*"

"I know about him too," I scoff. A lie. She told me she's never been married, and naturally I believed her. Does this girl have her facts right? Surely this can't be true. Why wouldn't Amity just tell me if she had been married?

Not an hour after I return home from my trip, as I'm getting totally stoned on pot, the yard boys appear. Amity, who is out flying, has told me about them, and though I've yet to see them, they are legend in our household. Now I know why: they're *gods.* They bail out of a very expensive, candy apple red Chevy truck, three of them, and they're so beefy and muscled and practically naked that I expect them to turn the volume up on the radio— "Union of the Snake" by Duran Duran is playing in the truck— and use the hand clippers to snip off their little short shorts and bump and grind in G-strings on the front lawn.

Amity says that the house we're living in is one of the hundreds of properties owned by one of those Dallas *families* with a name I definitely recognize, because my parents are friends of friends. And the particular son that manages and looks over this property is gay. So the yard boys he hires are like the A-list at Chippendales.

I go from room to room, looking through windows to check them out. I can't stand it. I have to pull my dick out. I drop my pants around my ankles and use one hand to separate the miniblinds, the other to warm my dick.

The beefiest yard boy, the one with a buzz cut and a tattoo on his exploding biceps, is just beyond the glass. His triceps flex as he trims the grass next to the house with the weed eater. I'm a pud whacker—he's a weed whacker. It's a beautiful relationship.

I look down, past the bulge in his shorts; his legs are shaved. Hotski wow-wow. This big moose, with biceps and a tattoo, shaves his legs. It's a mixture of feminine and masculine that sends me through the roof. Shit, he's moving on, just as I swear I'm going to come!

My pants at my ankles, I hobble like a doped-up, perverted Easter bunny into Amity's room to follow. I make it to the window, push the lace coverings away, separate the miniblinds. I'm stroking away when her phone rings, and the machine picks up. "Hi, honey," the woman's voice says, "it's your mom and dad. We really miss you, and we're worried because we haven't heard from you in a while. You all right? Please call us, Amy, and let us know you're all right. You know we'll be there in a heartbeat if you need us."

I feel so weird, jerking off while Amity's mother is talking. I concentrate on the yard stud when her father comes on. "That's right, darlin'. Your momma and I miss you somethin' awful. You call, OK? 'Bye now."

" 'Bye!" her mother's voice adds before they hang up.

God, they sound nice.

The yard stud, the yard stud. Back to business.

Ding-dong.

Shit! Someone's at the door! Someone's at the fucking door! Oh, God. What if it's one of the yard boys? I pull my pants up as the doorbell continues to ring insistently. If it *is* a yard boy, I can tell by the way he rings that he's a top.

I stuff my stiff dick into my pants and think of puppies and squirrels and innocent little things to make it go down. It's not working, and as I move toward the front door I go for the old standby, Heidi Schaeffer. Heidi was a fat little German girl in grammar school whose bottom never smelled right, particularly after recess. I've used the visual and olfactory memory of Heidi to squelch hard-ons for years.

I'm only *semi* by the time I open the door. The scent of freshly cut grass pours in, washing Heidi's bottom from my nostrils.

"Mr. Ford?" the ancient couple asks in unison. It's hot and they're sweating, bundled in their Sunday clothes.

"Yes?" I feel gravity pulling my softening dick down.

"We're from the Healthy Retriever Credit Agency," the old woman says, watching my dick move in my pants. "May we have a couple minutes of your time?"

They're old. They look as if they're going to die. What am I going to do, slam the door in their faces? "Sure, come on in."

They each lift their feet over the threshold as if they're stepping over a great chasm. I direct the woman to the wingback chair. I get a folding chair from the closet for the gentleman, whom I ease into the seat. I stand. "How can I help you?"

Father Time clears his throat, tries to speak. Nothing comes out. He clears his throat again. "We're here on behalf of Foremost Inter-Bank, as well as Ala-Corp," he says, reading his papers. "It seems you owe a total of . . . ." He can't find the figure on the page. He struggles for it, adjusts his glasses. Gives up. "I'm as blind as Jose Feliciano, but without the musical background," he explains.

"Can I help you?" I offer.

Whistler's mother thinks I'm talking to her. "Do you have ice water?" She looks ashen, dizzy, not long for this world.

"Yes, of course," I say, hustling to the kitchen. I grab ice to put into glasses and see the frozen credit cards in Tupperware containers. God, these people are bill collectors? They make Nurse

Carbonada look like a candy striper. They're Mesozoic at best. This is terrible. They shouldn't be out in the Texas heat, hunting down delinquent bill payers who buy BMWs. I feel so guilty. "Here," I say gently, offering them cold water. "I think I owe close to fifteen thousand dollars. Unless you count the balance on the car I recently bought, which is financed through my credit union. Then it's about forty thousand total."

"OK," the man answers.

"Yes, probably," the woman adds.

"Are you two married?"

"Sixty-one years," the woman responds, lacking the enthusiasm I'd expect from such a statement.

These poor people. They've got to be over eighty years old, and they're working this horrendous job where desperate, bankrupt people must scream at them, spit on them, and treat them like shit. I'll bet it's this lousy savings-and-loan crisis. I'll bet they lost all their retirement savings, and this is how they survive. Don't they know McDonald's hires senior citizens? They could work in an air-conditioned building, and no one would scream or spit on them for offering up Big Macs and soft-serve cones. I can't stand it. I run into the kitchen, open the freezer, grab the Tupperware, turn it over and pop out the large bowls of ice. I carry them to the creditors. "Look! I'm serious about not going into any more debt. I've frozen my cards. And I'll get you the money, I promise!"

"You will?" the man asks, surprised.

"I will," I decree, sincerely, balancing the ice hunks in my freezing hands. "Do they give you a bonus for making a quick collection?" I picture them being able to retire on the bonus from my speedy payoff, living a life of relaxation, wintering in Scottsdale, summering in Vancouver.

"They?" the man asks, ice water dribbling a little down his craggy chin.

"Whoever owns the company," I say.

"*We* own the company," the old woman says. "We got tired of cruise ships and grandchildren and vacations and watching our stocks split and our dividends be reinvested. So we started a business." She downs her ice water.

I want to stick a vacuum hose down her throat and suck it back up. Then I want to throw it in her baggy face. "How nice for you," I chirp, pert and perky as I possibly can be, my hands too cold to ever stroke my dick again, these two dinosaurs who deserved to die in the ice age with all the rest of them smiling in my miserable face.

To think, these old fossils cost me a yard-boy orgasm!

Three days later, Amity comes back from her work trip.

"I thought you were supposed to get home yesterday?" I ask, pouring us glasses of sun tea I brewed on the back porch.

"We got rerouted. Extra night in Memphis. I got fucked by the ghost of Elvis!"

"How was it?"

"He drugged me. I can't remember," she says, taking her glass of tea.

She walks to the bathroom. I follow her and sit on the tub while she sits on the toilet. As her stream of pee shoots into the bowl, I tell her about the blood-sucking dinosaurs that came calling for money.

"I practically fed them and clothed them," I say. "I wanted to buy them a cottage and pay for their medications."

Amity whips off a few squares of toilet paper, wipes once, flushes. "My bill collector was this nervous little Japanese guy," she laughs while rinsing her cervical cap, a European form of birth control she finds superior to any available in the States. "I let him do his spiel; then I threw him down on the hardwoods and fucked the shit out of him. Raped him, baby!" *Riped him, bye-bee!* "I never got another notice." She places the cervical cap in a small bowl and fills the bowl with mint mouthwash.

I motion to the mouthwash. "Does that make your Lady smell like pussymint?"

"Pussymint!" Amity screams. She heads back to the couch in the sitting room.

"Wait," I say, following her. "I haven't told you the worst part about these bill people. They came while the yard boys were here."

"Harry saw the yard boys," Amity announces, plopping onto the couch.

She lies down on one end, I on the other, our legs touching as we face each other. "When the two thousand year old couple knocked on the door, I was jacking off to the yard boys. I swear to God, my pants were around my ankles, and I was fantasizing about getting laid by the gorgeous tattooed moose with the weed whacker."

"Harry, we're going to have to put a cervical cap up your butt."

"No shit," I tell her.

"Yes shit," she answers. "In the cervical cap."

"Your mom and dad called," I tell her.

She looks nervous, fidgety. "When?"

"While I was jacking off."

She tries to laugh, but it's not much of an effort.

"Do they call you Amy?"

"It's my nickname. Short for Amity. What did they say?"

"Just that they love you. Want you to call them. By the way, I flew with a girl who says you were married," I blurt out. It's not nice of me—hitting her with this when she's already weakened by mention of her parents. It's what Winston would have done.

She's stiffens, looks me square in the eye. "Would it matter if I was?"

"Not at all. That's why I don't understand why you didn't tell me about it."

She sighs. Takes a moment to gather her thoughts. "It was ugly." She looks past the back of the sofa to the light beyond the lace curtains. "I had a lot of pressure from my family to marry him. It wasn't good chemistry with Arlen. After leaving that god-awful Christian wench he was married to, he just wanted a little trophy to carry around and give him sex on demand. He never really liked me. I fell in love with Jerod right after marrying him. He suspected and had me followed—and his goons discovered me and Jerod making love in the bathroom of a Black-Eyed Pea."

"Those little peas have bathrooms inside of them?"

"The restaurant chain, silly! They have the *best* fried corn."

"How the hell do you fry corn?" I ask.

"The whole ear. Dip that bad boy in batter and throw it in oil." *Ole.* "Come on. This is serious," she says, her face adopting a sad look. "Arlen had me ripped to shreds. He even disregarded the prenup. Of course I couldn't fight him—he was too powerful. So I was left penniless. My daddy threatened to kill him."

"Sounds like a Country-Western song. How come he was so vicious?"

"Because I was kind of a bad girl. Arlen was wealthy, Harry. He was from a family like yours. He was married when we met, and his wife was this megareligious woman from a similar family. Their marriage was an arrangement. But poor Arlen—well, you know those Christian women: They just can't give head. Or dance. Or laugh. I'm not even sure they like to eat."

I flash back to my high school friend Doug Samuelson, whose parents were divorced. Doug had a mother who was this fundamentalist Christian nutball who plastered JESUS=SAVINGS and I AM BENEATH HIM bumper stickers on everything. You couldn't see out the windows of their house because they were all covered with bumper stickers. My mother forbid me to go to *that awful neighborhood,* but I liked hanging out with Doug because he would smoke pot and jerk off with me, and I loved watching his dick go up and down because he was uncircumcised. He wasn't gay. He just liked to smoke pot and jerk off because he knew it wasn't condoned by

the Bible, and he loved doing *anything* that wasn't condoned by
the Bible. His psycho mother served poor Doug and his sister
charred fish sticks every night of their lives for six years, until
Doug's junior year of school when he threatened to kill her. The
judge let him off with counseling after determining he suffered
from *frozen fish rage*, and he got to go live with his dad.

"I broke up their marriage, and it was an ugly divorce that cost
Arlen *a lot*, emotionally and financially. Right after I married him
I started having a little cocaine problem. And I fell in love with
Jerod. And Arlen hung me out to dry. I didn't get a penny."

"Did you marry him for the money?" I ask.

"Yes," she answers. "Yes, Harry, I did."

I take a drink of tea. OK, it's time to tell her everything just as
she's done with me. She spilled her guts, offered me unfettered
veracity, and obviously she's sensitive to my position in life.
"Amity, remember when I said we need to visit my mother?"

"Yes, Harry."

"There's a reason. See, the deal is, I'm broke. Busted. It doesn't
matter how much money my family has, they won't give me any."

Amity looks sweetly into my eyes. "G'yaw, Bubba. I'm sorry."

"My father fucked me over in favor of Winston, *the straight
son.* Dad was so mean the last few years, always holding it over
my head that I could have everything Winston did if I were willing
to play the game, become straight."

"That's so unfair, Harry. You can't just wipe the logo off a
Louis Vuitton bag and call it Chanel. A Louis is a Louis."

"Dallas women and their analogies," I say, shaking my head,
"but you've got it right."

She hits me on the leg. "I'm from Fort Worth!"

"Anyway," I proceed, taking a sip of my drink, "my father is
messing with me, even from the grave." Amity looks at me, remains
silent. "He stipulated in his will that I would forfeit my share of
the estate if I wasn't legally married by my twenty-fourth birthday.

In just a few months, my percentage of my family's holdings will pass to Winston, my older brother.''

"Well, we'll just have to get married, Harry.'' She says it matter-of-factly, just as I thought she would.

"Amity, I'm gay.''

"I know—your dick tastes like shit!''

I playfully kick her, and we both almost fall off the sofa. After hauling ourselves back into place, I continue. "But everybody knows I'm gay. I've been resolute about it since I was seventeen.''

"All the better, Bubba. Listen, any other guy in your shoes would go out, find some naive little country gal, and marry her. And he'd spend his nights leaving her at home while he prowls around some city park, looking for a boo-foo in the bushes. But that's not you—or me. We're on the level with each other, Harry. We know exactly what's going on. So marry me and get your money.''

"It's not that simple. I have to stay married and living with my *wife* for a minimum of ten years. If I get divorced before that, all my inherited assets, and any profits from their investment, are deemed immediately receivable by the family estate.''

"There's *always* a way around these things,'' she says confidently, as if she practices law.

"There's never a way around my father,'' I caution.

She thinks. For longer than usual. And just when it appears she has something serious to say, she changes tack and sounds as perky as my mother. "So we'll stay married for ten years.''

"Amity, that's a huge commitment.''

She sits up, takes my hand. "Why? Why should anything be any different than it is right now? You have your lovers, I have mine. And, well, considering Padre Island, sometimes we might even have each other.'' She finishes the last statement with her left eyebrow arcing nearly into her hairline.

She's right. It would be a prosperous honest arrangement. But I have to ask, "What's in it for you?"

She cocks her head, gives me the demure Amity. "Why, Harry, have I ever bullshitted you about my tastes? Bubba, I don't want your fortune. That's yours. But I meant it when I said I love you on Padre Island. And if I get to spend the next ten years hanging out with a wonderful guy who makes me laugh and buys me a few pretty dresses and a first-class ticket to Paris along the way, then I consider myself lucky. I don't want your money."

"What about having a life, Amity? What about a *real* husband? Don't you want to fall in love, marry some great guy, have children?"

Her face sobers, her eyes lock into mine. "No. I don't. Those aren't my dreams, Harry."

"I don't know. I guess I never planned on having *all* those things. And I know I could never get married to a man, because that doesn't happen in America. But I do have my dreams, and I kind of hope that one day I'll find a nice guy, settle down, get a house."

"I'm a nice guy. We have a house. So bring your boyfriends over!"

"You *are* a nice guy, and this is a great house. It would just be a pretty big step to get married even if we do love each other. Shit, my father sure has given me a lot to think about."

Amity pats my leg and rises from the sofa. "Well, I think we should at least get engaged. You've got to get these bill collectors off our porch!"

CHAPTER TWELVE

Our flight is about to land in Wichita. Amity is still in the lavatory of the jet. I've never seen her like this, so nervous. When she returns to her seat, her hair is larger than ever. Her perfume pungent. Her lips shiny. It's like opening night, and she's sweating it out before the curtain goes up.

At the gate, my mom and the general are waiting. When she sees us, Mother raises her arms and beams like the Statue of Liberty. Her doctors believe that they got all the cancer and that she'll have a complete recovery. She looks wonderfully alive in her peach-colored linen suit. Donald yells, "Hey!" but with his Alabama accent I imagine he's saying, *"Hay!"* Then, before we come any closer, my mother has a camera and is snapping photos.

Dressed in her little red-and-black Talbot's ensemble, her arm linked in mine, Amity shines it on. As I escort her out into the terminal, the camera's electronic flash popping over and over, she smiles like a movie star, and everyone in the gate area of the Wichita Mid-Continent Airport stares at her as if she's the most beautiful and glamorous thing they've ever seen. And at that moment, I wish Brian Manes, that dumb-ass wrestler in high school who hassled me to no end and called me a faggot every day of school for three years, could see me now. But since he's not here, it's satisfaction enough to know that he'll never get a blow job like the one I got.

"Harry!" my mother says, grabbing my face in her hands and kissing my cheek. She turns to Amity and reaches out her hand. "Amity dear." Amity shakes and smiles and *nauce to meet yew*'s my mom, and my mother turns to me and nods with an impressed look on her face. Of course I could have wheeled Karen Ann Quinlan out on a gurney and my mother would have thought, "What a delightful girl. Nonsense about this coma thing—she's just *thinking*."

Amity offers a handshake to Donald, who holds her hand a little longer than my mother does, and then a little longer still. Donald then shakes my hand and slaps me so hard on the back that I cough up a piece of lung.

We exit through the sliding glass doors of the terminal into the muggy summer air brimming with the smell of earth and wheat. It's sunny and hot. The puffy clouds serve only as decoration to the unrelenting Kansas sky. Donald has parked illegally in the holding area for hotel vans. I used to park there, five years before, when I was home from college for the summer, and working a piddly-ass job for pocket change by driving a van for the Sheraton Airport Hotel while Winston apprenticed at a downtown investment firm. I'd wait for the Braniff hostesses in their Halston uniforms to appear from the terminal so that I could whisk them away to their hotel jail cells. Haughty sky goddesses. They never tipped, which is why, now that I'm a flight attendant, no matter how poor I am, I tip double.

Donald wheels the Cadillac out of the airport and points it east, onto the flat infinity of Highway 54. The farmland outskirts of the city are soon replaced with rows of small brick houses and too many architecturally uninspired, single-storied, round churches with big brown crosses on their roofs. I'm never sure what the denomination of each church is, just that they all employ the same architect.

As we approach downtown, my mother narrates the city by explaining the "Keeper of the Plains" sculpture at the foot of the river, the sculpture we're unable to see from the highway. She points out the huge, low, circular roof of the Century 21 Civic Center. "That's where they have beauty pageants and ice shows and traveling art exhibits," my mother says. "And in the Fourth National Bank Building, there's a Calder sculpture," she adds, trying to impress. Amity nods and replies at all the right moments.

My family home borders the country club golf course and is a tasteful eight-thousand-square-foot ranch-style house with a wood shingle roof. It sits upon several acres of wooded lawns, and the entire property is encircled with a white wooden fence that is repainted every year. The entry to the property is gated, and my mother reaches up to her visor and clicks the remote control that triggers the gate. "Amity's here!" she sings to the gate as it swings open.

We drive past a grove of pin oaks and roll up to the house and unload. Entering the house, my mother leads us through the oak-floored foyer, over the white carpet, and out to the west wing, while Amity immediately compliments her on her lovely homestead. My mother's decorating tastes have never changed with trends and fashion—she has always been a lover of fine American antiques, and she's traveled the country most of her life in search of the finest Early American pieces. You can practically hear the buffalo stampede and frontier women giving birth as you walk past kerosene lamps, wooden rocking chairs, old school desks, the collection of horse bridles hanging on the wall, and flour and sugar storage bins now filled with spicy potpourri. A varied collection of grandfather wall clocks ticks away the silence in each room, including the room given to Amity and me. It's different from where I slept with my ex-boyfriend. Matthew and I only visited when my father was away, and we were assigned a room with two twin beds. My mother made no secret that she was only mildly comfortable having my boyfriend and me in the house, and that no sex was to occur. The rules are changed. Amity and I get our own bed. Queen size. My mother makes it clear that Amity is the queen, not I. No, now I am the *king*. I can practically hear my mother proclaim, "Long live the royal couple!"

In the late afternoon, after I've walked Amity around the house and grounds, and we're sitting in the living room, playing get-to-know-you, the front door swings open unexpectedly.

Winston.

He's standing in the foyer wearing a double-breasted suit and a condescending smile, the only kind he owns. I had no idea he was coming, and I want to kill my mother the moment I see him. I know she's arranged this and conveniently not told me. There's no question he's here in order to attend the unveiling of his baby brother's girlfriend.

"I finally made it," he says, as if we've all been waiting for him. "Sorry I'm late. I told the airline I understand that coach passengers get what they pay for, but when someone flies first class, they should be guaranteed to arrive on time." He dumps his Bill Blass blazer on the old wooden school bench in the foyer. He's stunning, as always. Just over six feet tall. Brown wavy hair, hazel eyes, and tan as a lifeguard. "Hello, Mother," he sings, kissing her on the cheek. He nods to Donald. "Ronald." Then he turns, ignores me, and sighs, "And you must be Enmity."

Amity cocks her head, smiles, and offers her hand. "And *you* must be Winston."

He shakes her hand while looking her up and down. "Nice shoes." Then he finally looks at me. "Hello, baby brother. How's *tricks*?"

Winston always hits the first serve. "I met a really hot BMW salesman," I say, smashing the ball back over the net.

"Don't start!" our mother snaps. "Donald, pour Winston a drink."

"What do you want," Donald growls.

"What are you drinking, Enmity?" Winston asks.

"Champagne."

"What a charming little accent. I'll have the same. *Sham-pine.*"
He enters the living room and sits in the chair Donald had occupied.
"So, that's right, Jerry," he says, looking at me. "I hear you bought
a BMW."

"I mean it, Winston," Mother cautions.

"I just asked him about the car, not how he clinched the big
deal."

"It's nice," I say. "I'm beginning to realize that I like nice
things."

He looks accusingly at Amity. "No doubt you've inspired this
change in Gary's tastes."

"Oh, I think it's Harry who inspires me," she glows, feet crossed
at the ankles, champagne glass held by the stem.

My mother is enraptured with Amity, Winston appears to want
to slap her, and Donald looks as if he wants to fuck her.

"We make each other laugh," I state. "Do you and whomever
you're dating this month do that?"

"It's Patty," Winston hisses. "You've met her."

"Have I? They all seem the same," I tell him.

"You and Gravity will have to fly *standby* to Chicago and dine
with us."

Mother scolds him. "Her name is Amity, Winston."

"That's what I said."

"We'd love to," Amity states. "I'd really like to meet this
Patty."

Something's going on between the two of them, Winston and
Amity, and it's not the routine competition between Winston and
anyone—over who has the best clothing, hairstyle, and good taste.
And it's not just the fact that this is the girl who could potentially
decrease his inheritance by millions. No, even though Winston is

being his usual awful self, I detect a slight crack in the armor. Is Amity on to him? Does she suspect what I've always suspected?

Since it's nearly evening, Donald dons an apron and prepares Cornish game hens for cooking on the grill. We all sit on the patio by the pool and continue to drink. Mom and Donald scotch, Amity and Winston champagne, and I beer. Mom is chipper, animated, and downright obsequious at times. In between taking pictures of us in every situation, she makes sure that everyone's drinks are full and that the table is set just right and that the conversation never lags for a moment. "I can tell by that accent that you're a Texan, Amity. We have friends in Dallas. Where are you from in Texas?"

Amity tilts her head, and I know the F-word is coming. "Fort Worth, Mrs. Ford."

"For heaven's sake," my mother says, "call me Susan."

She never asked my ex-boyfriend, Matthew, to call her Susan. And when he did, I watched the hair on her neck rise just slightly. This is serious—her immediate allowance of first name rights to Amity—and I see Winston's venom rising in his throat.

Amity sees it as well. "Fort Worth, *Susan*."

"Fort Worth," my mom repeats. "I've been to Dallas, but not Fort Worth. We have friends in Highland Park."

"Of course," Amity smiles.

"Fort Worth?" I ask teasingly. "Isn't that an old abandoned frontier town with cowshit on the streets?"

Amity renounces her perfect manners to throw a cracker at me. "Harry! Don't talk about my home town like that."

I know why she threw the cracker. Winston has been watching her, inspecting her for authenticity, finding her perhaps a bit too studied, too polished. She's a smart girl to have thrown that cracker.

"I knew a guy in the Air Force from Fort Worth," Donald says. "One of the nicest guys I ever met."

"See?" Amity answers, vindicated.

I pick the cracker up, dust it off, and eat it.

''Harry!'' my brother Winston says distastefully. He hates anything to be dirty or improper. Including food. He washes bananas with soap and water before he peels and eats them.

''What?'' I ask, crumbs flying out of my mouth as I aspirate the *wh*.

Amity giggles.

He dismisses me and turns to Amity. ''Is your family still there?'' Winston asks, also holding his champagne glass by the stem, so as not to increase the temperature of the sparkling wine. ''In Fort Worth?''

''My folks are.'' Amity smiles. ''My momma and my daddy, and my grandmother too.''

Winston digs a little deeper. ''Does you grandmother live with your *momma* and your *daddy*?'' he asks, doing Elvis versions of the words.

''Oh, no,'' Amity answers. ''Grandmother has her own house. Of course it's too large for her at this point, but she just can't bear to leave it.''

I can hear Winston thinking, *How large? And in what part of town?*

''That guy from Fort Worth,'' Donald continues, ''had a wife and two young daughters. They'd be about your age by now. You know the Hedelsons? Ever heard of a family of that name?''

''No, sir.'' Amity answers, placing cheese on a cracker. ''I sure haven't.''

''He left the service. Became a dog breeder. Never knew anyone who knew so much about Rottweilers.''

Amity smiles, reminisces. ''We had a German dog too. Weimaraner. Duchess.''

''We had a Duchess!'' my mother exclaims. ''But ours was a dachshund.''

''A weenie dog!'' Amity spouts, looking at Winston. She's off the track again, confusing Winston with her irreverent bravado. ''That's German too.''

"So where did you go to college, Amity?" Winston asks.

Uh-oh. He's used her real name. This means he's going for the kill. I think she senses it. She sits ever so higher in her chair. Answers, "CCT in Fort Worth."

He smiles that smile. "And what does CCT stand for? Cold Calculating Tech?"

Amity laughs. "No. Christian College of Texas."

"Education *is* a religious experience," my mother declares for Amity's benefit.

Amity exhales. "I agree, Susan." She takes a sip of champagne.

"A good cabernet is a religious experience, *Susan*," Winston says.

"Don't be facetious," Mother answers.

"So," Winston continues, ready for the big hit, "when did you graduate?"

She hesitates. Will she tell the truth? "I didn't," she answers, her hands crossed in her lap.

"*You didn't graduate?* Don't you feel it's a burden—being uneducated?"

"Winston!" my mother shrieks.

"For Christ's sake, you little shit!" Donald barks.

I want to kill him, but as Winston raises his chin slightly in victory, Amity rallies. "It's OK. He's right. It is a bit of a burden at times. You see, the reason I left was to get married. Sadly, the marriage never happened. But I'm proud of myself for following my heart." With a hint of tears in her eyes, she uncrosses her hands and reaches them both out to take mine in hers. "I've been waiting all my life for the *right* person to come along. And I believe he has. And don't think that I don't know everything there is to know about Harry and his past. I do. But when love calls, a person has no choice but to answer."

God, this is so cornball. I feel as if I'm in some syndicated soap opera that couldn't even make it to the major networks. The only thing that makes it work is Amity. She's so committed, so convincing, that even Winston can't decide if it's an act or not.

Amity raises our hands in the air and gives me that look that says I'm the finest man in the world and finishes, "And that's why I've proudly agreed to become Mrs. Harry Ford."

My mother puts her hand to her cheek so hard she accidentally slaps herself. Donald knocks over his chair when he stands and congratulates me, nearly shaking my hand off. He tells me I'm doing the right thing and how proud my father would be. My mother grabs the camera and flashes on our Kodak moment. Then she drops the camera on a chair cushion and hugs us both with manic energy. "When did this happen? I can't believe it! You never gave me any reason to think this visit was so important!" she squawks.

"It was a recent decision," I choke. I'm too shocked to say anything else, but try to play it out, because I know Winston is watching. It's not that we haven't discussed it, but to hear it go from a possibility to a reality leaves me so stunned that all I can do is put my arm around Amity while she coos in my grasp and bats her eyelashes at Winston.

"Well done," Winston says, reaching out his hand. I extend mine to shake, but I realize he's talking to Amity.

"Thank you," Amity says, shaking it in triumph. "I look forward to knowing you."

"I'm calling your aunt Shirley!" my mother says, running into the house like a bird on fire.

Energized by her triumph, Amity turns to me and suggests, "Let's take a stroll through the yard." She takes me by the arm and leads me away. Winston lowers himself onto the chaise longue, disgusted, while Donald rights his chair, shakes his head, and tends to the other birds on fire, the game hens on the grill.

"I can't believe you did that," I whisper, not angry but stupefied.

"Just keep walking, Bubba," Amity whispers back.

The yard is impeccably manicured, no longer by gardeners, my mother has told me, but by Donald. Amity makes it appear we're walking arm in arm, young lovers on a saunter through the garden, but it's more like she's an attendant in a psychiatric hospital, holding up the dazed patient on her arm, lest he fall face first into a pyracantha bush from the news he's getting married before he's even been discharged. We stroll past native grasses and sunflowers, marigolds and impatiens, petunias and geraniums, past the new water fountain, past the ancient oak and sycamore trees at the edge of the property, and when we're out of earshot, almost to the edge of the fairway, Amity says sincerely, "I'm sorry, Harry. I had to do it. Your brother is gayer than you'll *ever* be."

I knew it! I've always known it! I hadn't told her that he was—mostly because he's never come out, even to me. And it's only been a *sense* I've had—never confirmed by anyone. And I knew she'd tell me if she sensed it, because Amity's not-so-remote detection is as sharp as any gay guy's. I can see she is blown out of the water by this unexpected grasp of Winston. "Do you think so?" I ask innocently.

"I *know* so, Bubba. That boy's about as straight as a circle jerk in a bathhouse!"

My eyes grow wide. "How do you know what goes on in a bathhouse?"

"Never mind!" she answers, the whites of her eyes flashing. "Listen, Harry. I'm sorry, but I just couldn't let that bona fide queer take all your heterosexual money. It would be as ironic as a Baptist beauty pageant."

I can smell the stagnant water from the pond by the sixteenth hole of the golf course. "I've carried these doubts around for years, but deep down I think I've always known. None of my friends has ever met him because Winston and I keep such distance between us, so I've never had anyone who could make an analysis."

"He's gay," Amity says. "How can you stand it? Why don't you expose him?"

"What am I supposed to do, ask his girlfriend if his dick tastes like shit?"

"His *girlfriend* isn't Patty, but some guy named Pat, I guarantee you."

"What difference does it make? He can live his life any way he wants. If he's willing to deny what he is and live a lie just for money, then that's his own miserable business. I've never wanted that kind of a life, and he knows it. It's why he hates me."

"Misery wants company?"

"You got it. God," I laugh, watching a foursome tee off in the distance, "are we really doing this? Are we getting married?"

"We can't turn back now," Amity says forcefully. Then she changes expression. "Unless you want. I can write your momma a note after we return to Dallas. Tell her we decided to call it off. Is that what you want, Harry?" she asks, searching my eyes for a clue.

"My mother's probably in the house calling all her friends, booking the church, the caterers, the photographer. It'll be in the *Eagle-Beacon* tomorrow."

"What's that?"

"The local paper." I pause. "My mother will make this *huge*."

"And we'll laugh through the whole thing," Amity promises. She rubs my back in circles with her palm. "Don't worry, Harry. We'll pull it off."

The foursome drives away in their little golf carts. "I've always known in my heart that Winston was gay. But he's so powerful. And mean. He was mean as a kid, and he's mean as an adult. I think I knew the day he ratted on me to my father that I was sucking my baseball hot dog like it was a dick."

Amity bursts out laughing.

"I'm serious," I contend. "He recognized too well what was going on. He totally understood my desires. They were his—only he was successful at masking them. He somehow fooled Father.

And Mother. And most everyone else. But he hasn't fooled you. And he knows it. You better watch out, Amity. Those handsome queers are the most vicious.''

She says nothing more, but wears her smile like a weapon.

That night, in the bedroom next to Winston's, Amity takes great pleasure in seducing me, not even asking me if I want to do this. There's something weird for me about being naked in front of a girl. I'm slightly uncomfortable for her to be looking at me with lust, which is probably the way a straight guy feels in a locker room when he knows another guy is looking at him. But unlike the straight guy in the locker room who can quickly put his clothes on and leave, I have nowhere to go. We lie down on the bed, and she brings her face to mine. As on our layover in Denver, it feels strange to kiss Amity's soft, feminine lips. It doesn't do the trick for me, but she's forceful tonight, so animal in the way she has sex that, after a few minutes, I'm spurred—forced—into action. Meaning, she's a great top, staying in control, filling my emotional void with friction, keeping me going when necessary with her hands and tongue and torso. As she slides down my stomach, leaving her waves of hair splashing all over my chest, I grip the pillow in my hands. And when she goes for it, with even more hardihood than the first time, I can't help but think about those farm team baseball players of my youth. I close my eyes and travel back to those guys in their tight striped pants with their jockstraps showing through and their caps on their sunburned heads. How their hands were rugged sexy instruments of power. And how they constantly pulled on their dicks, while standing around spitting mouthfuls of tobacco or chewing globs of bubble gum. Once, after I caught a pop fly (the greatest moment of my spectator life), the pitcher of the opposing team, from Omaha, came over and signed it after the game. When he finished signing it, he tossed it back at me and gave me the sexiest wink of an eye I've ever seen.

He's winking at me now, as Amity pushes me to the edge,

then pulls me back. Again to the edge. Again back. She's totally controlling me with her mouth. And as I thrash and strain and moan, I half expect my mother to open the door, snap a picture of us, and say, "Thanks, kids!"

Finally, right before I pop, Amity pulls away from my dick and slides herself up to me, pushing me inside her soaking wet Virginia. I've never been inside a woman, and it feels different from any past sexual experience. Softer. Not as tight. But warmer, more slippery, and certainly pleasurable. I was sure this would never happen to me, and to be losing my heterosexual virginity with someone I love makes it more exciting still. Is this it, the moment that I'm a bona fide heterosexual? As the moment comes, and I fill the state of Virginia to its borders, I let go with a low "Ahhhhhh."

Amity, on the other end of the pendulum, is screaming, "Oh, babe! Oh, yes! *Oh . . . maw . . . Gawd!*" She collapses on top of me and smiles wickedly, satisfied.

I think that last amplified "Oh, my God!" was for Winston's sake.

The next day, Amity and I are bonded in a way we weren't before. There's a connection in our eyes, and my mother sees it, which makes me nervous enough that I decide to squire Amity out of the house and show her the sights of my childhood before my mother sets the wedding date for *today.*

We drive east, less than an hour, out into the country, where there's a famous drive-in that's been serving up burgers and shakes since the beginning of the automobile; it was one of the few places my parents would take us that didn't require jacket and tie.

Amity and I order two banana milkshakes. They're the best banana milkshakes in the world—made with homemade ice cream, milk straight from the cow, and chunks of banana—and we sit in the car, like two teenagers on a date, and drink them while watching the cattlefolk of this small Kansas town trod out of the place with greasy bags of burgers and onion rings.

A large gal struggles out of her car, practically tearing the door off with her weight.

Amity giggles. "G'yaw, Harry. She can hardly walk. Were the girls in your high school like that?"

"No, most of them were pretty normal size. It happens two years later. By twenty years of age they're having babies, and it's all over. They're bigger than buses."

"The babies?"

"The moms. Well, actually, the babies too."

"I'm *never* having children," she says, her voice low, her accent dissipated. It's a voice I've never heard. It's as if all the cameras and lights have been turned off on the movie set where she's starring in a film based on her life, and she's sitting, secluded, in her trailer, after everyone has gone home.

I look over at her. See significant pain of insignificance.

She cranks it back up. "I can't believe you went to high school here!"

"Well, not here. In Wichita. But me neither," I stutter, steeped in painful memories of my own. For all of my bravado about attending a public school, once I did it wasn't so great. Most of the kids in my grade looked down on me and called me Richie Rich. They were either intimidated by my name, ignored me, or thought I was a faggot by virtue of the sports I chose: tennis and golf. It was hard making new friends at a new school in my senior year. And of course I couldn't let on to my folks that it was a mistake, that I would have probably been better off staying in the academy and graduating there.

My grandmother was the only one I confided in. She'd let me come to her house and drink a beer and pour out my lonely teenage troubles. She never judged me and always made an effort to ask, "Have you met a boy you like?" *No one* ever asked me questions like that. And it was through her that I slowly realized that it was OK to be who I am.

But now I realize that, if I'd had Amity then, I would have saved myself a great deal of that teenage pain and perhaps Amity's pain as well. We'd have bonded immediately—I know it. And though I was born the way I am, maybe I could have gained some confidence about my sexuality by hanging around her. As much as I wanted one, I certainly never had a boyfriend in those days. Maybe I would have been better off with someone like Amity, and maybe she would have been better off with someone like me.

That night we have the big "coming-out" party. Only, this coming out is what my mother has hoped for all along. My mother has gathered certain relatives—Grammie (my father's mother), my aunt and uncle (my mother's sister and her husband), and their kids, my cousins, one boy and two girls, all in their early twenties. And like my brother and me, none of them are married. So here I am, the gay kid, home with a girlfriend, and my mother is absolutely exploding with the unexpected news that I'm the first to be married.

Amity, in full poo up, drives with me over to my grandmother's home. I'm nervous about Grammie meeting Amity. Obviously, I haven't spoken to her about Amity's and my hasty engagement. And this won't be the time or place for me to explain fully.

As we pull into the driveway, Grammie, in a handsome deep maroon silk blouse and matching pants, is sitting on a bench beneath a grand old oak tree in the front yard of her Tudor home in Eastborough. She waves at the sight of us, and we wave back before getting out of the car and walking over to her. "Hello," she calls as we approach.

"Hey, Grammie," I say, bending over and hugging her gently. I step back and hold her hand. "Grammie, this is Amity."

Amity cocks her head, reaches out for Grammie's free hand, and lays the accent on each syllable. "Grammie Ford, I've heard so much about you." The truth is, I've told her very little about Grammie. Amity is turning on the charm autopilot.

"And I've heard something about you," my grandmother

answers sweetly, while looking at me. "Your mother called me
last night and told me the aim of our gathering this evening has
changed."

"That's right," Amity answers, letting go of Grammie's hand
and replacing it with mine. "Harry and I are engaged." Amity is
a little too confident. And she realizes immediately that her confidence has no effect on my grandmother.

There is a moment of uncomfortable silence. I'm holding both
their hands, and though no one is moving a muscle, it feels as if
these two women are pulling me in opposite directions. I look at
Grammie, who is smiling, but neutral. "It was kind of sudden,
Grandmother." I rarely call her Grandmother. She knows I'm
slightly off edge.

"Life is always full of surprises," she answers. "Sit down."
We all release hands, and Amity sits on one side of her, I on the
other. Grammie turns to Amity. "Harry tells me you two have no
secrets—is this true?"

"Absolutely," Amity answers firmly.

"Why are you marrying my grandson?" she asks directly. She's
not aggressive or distrusting in manner, merely honest.

"I *do* love Harry," Amity answers, her feathers just the slightest
bit ruffled. She can tell my grandmother is real, not easily flattered
or manipulated as my mother can be.

My grandmother asks, "Is that why you're marrying him?"

Amity looks at me. Before I can offer help, she quickly reclaims
her perfect instincts and follows them accordingly. "No. I'm marrying him to help him get his inheritance." Dead on.

"Thank you, dear," Grammie answers. "The last thing this
family needs is another pile of horse manure." She pats both of
our legs. "So. What about true love?"

"She really does love me, Gram, and I love her too," I answer.

"But not like you would another boy," she reminds me. Turning
to Amity she says, "And no matter how much you may feel for

my grandson, you know he simply isn't able to feel the same in return?''

I'm amazed that my grandmother is so steadfast in her knowledge of me. "We know, Grammie," I say, starting to sound defensive. "We've talked all this out. We know what we're doing."

"I'm sorry, but I don't think you do," my grandmother tells us. "I know the provisions of your father's will. He talked about it with me. I strongly disagreed with him about it. Ten years you have to stay married. Ten years. Believe me, the next decade will be the most significant of all. It's the only time in your life that your body will remain young while your mind will ripen. It's a precious combination that lasts only for a short time. I fear you'll be making a mistake by this marriage. If you are planning on coupling in your lives, it's during this period that you should offer yourselves fully—to the *right* person, each of you."

Amity dispassionately explains, "I've told Harry he's free to sow his wild oats. Be with whoever he needs to be with. He's offered me equal treatment."

"It's not the same," my grandmother answers, shaking her head sadly. "The years will pass. You'll never be able to go back."

"Grammie," I say quietly, "trust us. We're not going to screw our lives up over this. It's the only way. Dad forced my hand, and now I have to play it."

My grandmother sighs, takes a moment to think. "I could fix all this by giving you money," she says, exasperated.

I look ahead, then over at Amity. She looks back at me, and we both remain silent. It's true. She could put a stop to it. But as soon as I realize the possibility of it, she speaks up again.

"No," she says, resolutely. "I've trusted you since you were a little boy to do the right thing, and you always have. You're better than the rest of us in that way. I respect your decision, Harry. I just felt the need to give you my two cents."

I smile and tell her, "Well, that's two cents more than anyone else has given me in this family.'' She chuckles, and Amity looks uncomfortable. ''Come on, Gram. Don't worry. Just give it time. Everything will work out OK. Let's go to dinner.''

We arrive at the club to find my mother again beaming like the Statue of Liberty, her family gathered around her. Amity and I approach with my grandmother on my arm, as if the royal couple is now escorting the queen mother, and my mother starts in with the picture taking. Amity knows my mother is making this evening an event, and there's nothing Amity likes more than an event, especially when she's the theme. My relatives are slightly nervous, my female cousins stifling excitable giggles. Amity rises to the occasion with flair and grace, shaking everyone's hands and repeating names as she goes. My uncle Jack, like Donald when he met her, holds Amity's hand a little too long and greets her with his face so close to hers that I'm sure she is intoxicated by the gin on his breath. She continues on before he can jam his tongue down her throat, and by the time she's done, she's soaked every hand with her perfume, and we all smell like the Esteé Lauder section of the cosmetics department at Maxwell-Grey.

As much as I despise him, I'm feeling sorry for my brother, Winston. He's brought several girls to various gatherings over the years, and my family's never made a fuss over his dates the way they're making a fuss over Amity tonight. It's the engagement, I'm sure, but maybe I was wrong about my mother and father, maybe deep in their hearts they knew these women of Winston's weren't the real McCoy. They were props. He's always used ex-sorority, husband-seeking girls to put himself at ease. Even with our father gone, I don't see him changing. He never talks romantically about women. Never kisses them in front of the family. Never asks them to stay over. Yet they *love* being with him. He actually can be exceedingly charming when he wants to be. He looks incredible in a suit. Has a great sense of humor. Impeccable style. And when not being a cad, he's the quintessential gentleman in the classic sense of the word. He stands when a lady enters the room, opens doors for her, seats her at a table, selects the wine for her. The problem is, he would also enjoy dressing her, styling her hair, teaching her how to walk, and entering her in a pageant if he could. But I suspect the last thing he'd want to do is to sleep with her.

And Amity knows this. And that's why he's threatened by her.

The competitive part of me is amused. It's quite ironic that the ''straight'' brother has no respect for his women and the gay one now does. But the other part of me is saddened that Winston has never understood that truth is the great emancipator. I take no pleasure in his self-imposed prison, and in a way I find it cruel that my mother is so desperate for some *genuine* heterosexuality within her sons that she'll forsake the past pretenses offered by my brother, in order to flaunt the authenticity of this real, live, dick-smoking girlfriend of her formerly gay child. I admit, I love the attention almost as much as Amity does, and it's fun being so worshiped by my extended family, but I embrace no joy in Winston's predicament, regardless of what a shit he is.

We drink cocktails and more cocktails. And Amity answers all the stock questions about Texas, Fort Worth, and her accent. Somehow the subject turns to cooking, and Amity, whose *icebox* still holds nothing but champagne, Diet Dr Pepper, and nail polish, claims she's an expert pie maker. ''I'm famous for making pie.''

My aunt Shirley, blessed with a sick sense of humor, starts laughing, and I know right away why. With her accent, it sounds like Amity has said, ''I'm famous for making Pa.'' Aunt Shirley explains to the group what she thought Amity said, and my family, all of them possessing a wicked wit, joins in laughter at the thought of this beautiful and cultured girl saying, in a polite and acceptable way, that she's famous for fucking her father.

Amity, ever the good-time gal, takes it in stride and laughs along. She even good-naturedly shakes her finger at Aunt Shirley. But now there is a crack in her mask so small that even Winston doesn't see it, probably because he's concentrating on concealing his own. And inside that microscopic fissure of Amity's, that only I can see, the pain of something awful is revisited. And I have a feeling that if all the lights and cameras were turned off on this dinner and we were alone and she spoke, she would sound as she did earlier in the day when she swore with an authentic voice that she would *never* have children.

Before we're seated for dinner, I excuse myself for the restroom, and my cousin Brad, home from Yale, comes with me. He's a big handsome guy. A soccer player. Quite intelligent, but macho, definitely a jock. We're standing at the urinals, an empty one between us, and he's got a shit-eating grin on his face. He says to me, "She's pretty wild. All that hair. That accent. This is really something."

I know what he's trying to say. This is really something that not only have I brought home a girl, but one who looks like *that*. "I'm totally in love with her, Brad. Can you believe it?"

He pauses. Decides to tell the truth. "Not really."

We look at each other, start laughing, splashing our pee onto the sides of the urinals. "I know, I know," I tell him. "Everyone thought I'd end up with my high school drama teacher, Mr. Sweeney."

"Something like that," Brad says. "This is a better choice, man. Why'd you do it?"

"She makes me laugh," I say. I can tell he still doubts me. "And she gives good head." Now he doesn't.

"She can even bake a pie," he adds.

Man, this is so sexist. I can't believe I'm standing at a urinal, taking a piss, talking about how my fiancée can give head and bake a pie. My lesbian friend from college, Debbie, would punch me in the mouth if she heard me talk like this. It's such a guy thing—to talk about *chicks* while you shake the pee off the head of your dick, then skip the hand washing and head out. I don't even check my hair in the mirror.

I can't believe I just peed like a straight guy.

Everyone is feasting on their prime rib or pork loin or duck or whatever they ordered. The black waiters, in their white waiter's jackets, keep the water glasses and the wineglasses filled. A trio plays in the background. And Winston compliments my grandmother for the third time this evening—only this time he adds a little fire. "Grammie, that's such a lovely silk blouse. Alacrity has been eyeing it all night. You'll have to leave it to her in your will."

My mother slams her knife on her plate.

Grammie smiles and tells Winston, "Maybe I will."

Amity jumps right in. "I do love silk, Mrs. Ford," she says to my grandmother, "but I'm not interested in taking the clothes off anybody's back—unless it's coming directly from the silkworm itself!"

Everybody laughs, including Winston with a forced *sotto profundo*.

"Actually, silkworms aren't worms at all," Amity explains, buoyantly still afloat after Winston's shot across the bow. "They're caterpillars. We just refer to them as silkworms."

"I never knew that," my grandmother says. "And I've been all the way to Japan to buy a kimono robe."

"I remember that robe," Aunt Shirley chimes in. "Midnight blue with yellow swans on a river. Pagodas in the background."

"How lovely," Amity says. "Did you know it takes about three thousand silkworms to make a kimono?"

Everyone is charmed. They're all looking to Amity now, enjoying her trivia. Winston is rolling his eyes and cutting his meat. "Go on, Calamity. Tell us more," he snivels.

"They're little eating machines, y'all. They have to increase their body weight ten thousand times during their lives—and they only live about twenty-eight days!"

"So do some girlfriends," Winston digs.

"Like *Patty*?" I ask, poking him back.

My mother steers the conversation back to Amity. "What do silkworms eat?"

"Ham hocks and grits?" Winston spouts with a bad Southern accent.

"They just *love* mulberry leaves," Amity chirps, ignoring Winston.

"Don't we all," Winston chirps back.

"A little known fact is that they're very fragile," Amity states, no longer ignoring Winston but looking pointedly at him. "Anything can upset a freshly hatched worm: the bark of a *dog*, the crow of a *cock*, a foul *smell*." She's labeling Winston as she goes.

"What about a female dog?" Winston asks, striking right back.

"Oh, I'm sure she could upset a worm," Amity replies, "if she put her mind to it."

Aunt Shirley takes an off ramp from the Competition Highway. "What about a horrible singer?"

Everyone laughs as the small trio with a female vocalist labors on the far side of the room. Aunt Shirley, with her wickedly caustic wit, nearly collapses with laughter as the off-key vocalist hits a dreadfully wrong note while butchering "Fly Me to the Moon." Her slack tempo and dull ear betray an obvious overdose of Valium.

"She's got to be deaf," my aunt wheezes with laughter. "She ought to just *sign* the words."

"Mother," Ellie, her oldest daughter, scolds. Ellie is home for summer break from law school at Tulane.

"For God's sake, it sounds like she's singing 'Drive Me to the Moon,' " Aunt Shirley counters.

Mary, her other daughter, who was studying English literature at Sarah Lawrence, but scandalously dropped out to open her own bookstore in Boston, comes to her mother's defense. "She *is* pretty awful."

''Wait till she scats,'' my aunt chokes, practically falling into her plate. ''Let's write a request on a napkin and make her sing really fast.''

We're all laughing now. Thinking of fast songs.

'' 'Fascinating Rhythm,' '' I suggest.

'' 'Anything Goes,' '' Amity says, scoring a winning laugh from the gallery.

''The Theme from *HR Puffinstuff!*'' Mary adds.

''I'll bet no one's ever requested that before,'' my uncle Jack contends.

''Why not request something really hard to sing like an aria from an opera?'' Winston suggests, ever the wicked one.

''Good idea,'' Aunt Shirley says, laughing harder still, tears pooling in her eyes.

Donald doesn't really understand our family's humor, and he tries to defend the poor gal. ''I don't think she's that bad. Why not let her do what she's prepared?''

Boos and hisses ensue, and everyone strikes him down. My mother comes to his defense. She never questions him, but we know she secretly enjoys the game because she's secretly still one of us.

Winston, to impress Amity, snaps his fingers and condescendingly summons a black waiter. We all cringe at his manner, but we know he always addresses *the help* in this way, and we're used to it. He requests a cocktail napkin and a pen.

''What's a good aria?'' he asks.

''The one from *Madame Butterfly,*'' Aunt Shirley suggests. ''And make her sing it in G sharp.''

''What does it sound like?'' Brad asks.

Silence. Then a couple feeble attempts to hum it.

''We all know what it sounds like,'' Winston dismisses.

''I'll sing a little,'' Amity offers, smiling wickedly at Winston.

My mother is overly impressed. ''You will?''

''Sing us a little!'' Donald cries.

"Yes," Uncle Jack agrees.

"But sing it quietly, so she can't hear you," Aunt Shirley cautions, referring to the *legit* singer.

Winston looks pissed off. Amity has stolen his thunder.

She sings twenty seconds of the aria. She's soft and has no vibrato, but she sings it evenly and on-key.

Everyone applauds. Everyone but Winston.

After dinner, Winston quickly volunteers to take my grandmother home—I assume to accomplish two things: remove himself from "Amity Night" and ingratiate himself further with Grandmother in order to receive more in her will. The rest of us stay behind and make our way to the piano bar. My family has always been too stuffy to indulge themselves with drunken, off-key singing while sipping cordials, as a few select families do after dinner. But having Amity among us has made the evening a very special occasion, and everyone seems years younger and somehow more childlike around her.

After a few songs like "I Left My Heart In San Francisco," which Brad changed to "I Left My Harp In Sam's Clam Disco," and "Guantanamera," which everyone modified to "One Ton Tomato," Amity leads everyone in her favorite little song—the "Bee I Bo, Bee I Bo, Bee I Bicky Bo, Bee I Bo, Bicky By Bo Boo." Or something like that. It's from a scene in a Three Stooges movie. We're all drunk, and we butcher it into further nonsense, which only makes it more fun. And by this time Amity has charmed everyone: my family, the waiters, the busboys, the pianist at the bar. My mother is sailing with happiness, waving her wineglass in the air and singing so unbelievably off-key, as she does in Episcopal church, that I fear our glasses may shatter at any moment.

And in the middle of all this boozy—dare I say *gay* frivolity— I suddenly become a little sad. Because I realize how much my mother wants me to be straight. And even though she loves me dearly, and there's never been such levity in her heart as there is this evening, here, with Amity, I find it all to be a little false. And I realize that it wouldn't even matter if my mother *did* know that in the short time I've known Amity, she's fucked Bart, Troy, Hunt, Miguel, Wade, and me. As long as Amity is willing to provide legitimacy to her son's life, she's in the fold.

And poor Winston. He's been driving me to this moment since the day at the baseball park. He can't stand my attempt to be legitimate, to be gay, to be myself. He's resented that I've refused to walk the same straight line that he does, making it impossible for all of us to have a comfortable prosperous life. But now that I'm finally doing it he's trying to derail me. Forget it. I'm marrying Amity. And getting my inheritance. For all the right reasons.

CHAPTER
THIRTEEN

Amity's five-year-anniversary "Award Ceremony" with the airline is tonight. It's only June, but it's the hottest day of the year so far. The stagnant air is dripping with humidity, causing leaves on the trees that line our street to hang heavy and cast shadows of resignation on the baking pavement. Like Wichita, Dallas has no oceans or mountains to temper its weather, or even give its air a salt or pine scent. The heated Texas earth forces the air to rise up high into the atmosphere, where it cools and forms huge cumulonimbus structures that serve as a patchwork blanket riddled with holes. The sun blazes through the voids in vertical streams that bear down on us as if we're ants under a magnifying glass.

We have both of the wall-unit air conditioners blasting in the house (we bought a second one, after cashing the enormous check my mother wrote me the day we left Wichita), so we're somewhat relieved from the heat as we get ready for the big hoedown. The party is being held in a ballroom of some downtown hotel and requires formal attire. These events are renowned at the airline. It's a chance for all the employees to put on their TV star clothes and go up on stage and accept awards for things like "Five Years of Perfect Attendance" (you have no life) and "Most Inspirational

Employee'' (misguided zealot), but most importantly, stand around and get drunk while gossiping about whoever is out of earshot. It's that magic night when the stewardesses get their chance to meet the unknowing wives of the pilots they've fucked on their layovers. Then all the employees sit at tables of eight and eat gristly prime rib while the president of the airline, Mr. Gherkin, a highly religious man who doesn't drink or smoke (and has a legendarily tiny penis), tells them he wouldn't be able to live without his devoted workers. Amity showed me a recap of last year's ceremony in an old issue of the employee paper. It was a gushy article with lots of splashy pictures that culminated in the coverage and photo of the ''Employee of the Year,'' a dead ticket agent who had died in a single-car accident and was lauded for her ''irrepressible good humor, kindness, and honesty.'' Amity told me the inside story was that there were *two* sets of tire tracks on that fated highway; the ticket agent was a prissy bitch with breast implants who, after she'd threatened to go to his wife, was run off the road by the executive VP she'd been having an affair with.

I sit on the edge of the tub and watch while Amity patiently separates her hair into clumps and puts those clumps into rollers, winding them up, one by one. She's dropped the formality of boxer shorts and camisole and stands naked, her freshly showered ass to my face.

''Hey, baby, did you know that Eva Catrell is going to be there tonight with her shit-kicker boyfriend?''

My first trip at the airline I flew with Eva Catrell, who tried to get me to fuck her while we were on a layover in Amarillo. I had dinner with her, and she suggested we go back to her room, where she gave me a Valium and poured me a drink, and we lay down on her bed. She told me she always brought her vibrator on her layovers, but loved when she didn't have to use it. Get it? This gal was rough around the edges, tougher than most of the *guys* I'd slept with. ''Rode hard and put up wet,'' as Amity would say. When I realized she wasn't offering me her vibrator as a loan, I got off the bed and headed for the door, but before I got out of the room, she stuck her tongue down my throat. The next day, she drank Bloody Marys on the last flight and insisted on taking me home with her, since it was too late to commute to Kansas. I begged off and let her drop me at what I claimed was a friend's apartment house— where I called a cab to take me to a hotel.

"Oh great," I say.

"Don't worry," Amity answers, finishing up on her hair. "I'm sure she didn't tell her boyfriend that she French-kissed you, Harry!"

"I bet her pussy tastes like sourdough biscuits and campfire logs."

Amity screams with laughter. "Ooh, baby, you gotta get some of that!"

"No, I don't," I say. "I'm just getting to know little Virginia here."

Amity turns around, naked, her hair in rollers, barely any makeup on, and somehow looks like the most elegant woman on Earth. "And little Virginia is quite pleased to know you," she answers with gracious esteem.

We're heading down Mockingbird, in my dented but paid-off BMW (another benefit from Mom's generously written check), on our way to Central Expressway, and I ask Amity, "Did you read that the House of Representatives passed legislation that cuts federal money to states who have drinking ages below twenty-one?" Texas's legal drinking age is nineteen. "So they say Texas is going to probably raise the drinking age."

"That's not fair!" Amity whines, toking on a joint. She's wearing a dark maroon floor-length velvet dress that has a slit up the side. "How are young drivers going to cope with Suicide Express?"

"They could drink lots of 3.2 beer."

"That's not good enough, Harry. You need a shot of whiskey to get on this bad boy."

"Amity, that's a great idea! We should set up a series of H&A Roadside Whiskey Stands at every on ramp. Sell little shots of Jack Daniel's to people about to enter the expressway."

"Yes!" *Yay-yus!* "And give them little pep talks like, 'Y'all are great!' and 'Go git 'em!' "

"And sell double shots to those fat, fraidy-cat housewives in those tanky station wagons, and give advice like, 'Punch the shit out of the accelerator and close your eyes!' "

We quit joking, have a moment of silence, as we approach the expressway.

"Get ready," Amity whispers, pretending to straighten up.

Our mission is to catapult onto Suicide Express, head south, and somehow arrive downtown alive. I'm behind the wheel, but Amity's hair is so jacked up it's practically blocking my sight. "Move your hair," I order.

"I'd need a crane," she answers.

There's a car sitting on my tail, which makes me even more nervous than usual. The air conditioner is blasting. I call to Amity to turn it off for extra power.

"Air off!" she calls, my copilot. "Take a hit, baby. Take a hit," she encourages, holding the joint to my lips.

I suck in. All the way. Gun the engine. Pop the clutch. Jettison the Beamer into traffic and exhale the smoke.

"Yay!" Amity yells. "We're alive!" She accidentally drops the joint, and by the time we find it there's a hole burned in the vanilla-colored leather seat.

We're stoned out of reality, riding up the escalator to the ballroom, both of us grinning at the high cheese factor of the big event. On the escalator, she slips one leg through the slit on her dress and hikes it onto the step above her. Her legs are so tanned and smooth she doesn't have to wear panty hose. "Squirrel shot!" she yells, showing me her bare crotch. We roll off the escalator laughing so hard that everyone in proximity stares. We stop first at a table where they give Amity her five-year service pin—a 747 that's rising for takeoff. Amity pins it on so that it's pointing downward toward her breast—a 747 crashing into a mountain. Then she's handed two drink tickets that entitle us to one cocktail each. Any more and we'll have to pay. Tacky. We know we're "Couple of the Month" for the moment—the Texas Babe and the Gay Yankee—so we play it to the hilt, going table to table, as if we're the President and the First Lady at a fund-raiser, while various Southern belles scream with delight at seeing Amity and carefully hug her while stabbing her with a dull kitchen knife in the truth of their imaginations. Amity's hair gets caught in another stewardess's hair clip, and everyone gets a good laugh when the women are unable to separate. The guys shake my hand, hard, and slap me on the back, I presume, because I'm the gent lucky enough to land Amity Stone, former *Slut of the Month.*

I wander off to get us our two free drinks, and when I return she's not there. And I can't locate her in the crowd. So here I am, among these straight guys—some with ill-fitting polyester suits over their big bellies and horseshit on the heels of their cowboy boots; others looking downright elegant, like male models in tuxes and tails; and all of them highly heterosexual.

Some guy about a foot taller than I am nods, strikes up a conversation. "Did you watch the game yesterday?"

Was there a figure skating competition on TV?

"Nolan Ryan is the man," he continues, not waiting for me to answer. "They can't pay that guy enough as far as I'm concerned."

I stand there with a glass of champagne in one hand, my dark rum and soda with a twist in the other. "Definitely."

"Who's your favorite team in the American League?"

"The 49ers."

He looks at me as if I've cut a fart. "That's football."

"Right."

"I'm talking about baseball."

"Oh!" I have to think quick. "I thought you were talking about Nolan *Cromwell*." I know Nolan Cromwell is a football player because he's a local Kansas boy who made good by going on to be a star in the NFL. But that was with Los Angeles, I think. The Rams. "I just heard the name Nolan, and that's why I thought you were talking about football," I explain.

"It's June," the guy says. "Football season is over."

"Right," I say. "It's too hot for them to wear those outfits."

He sort of frowns, swills the spit back at the bottom of his beer bottle, and says, "Excuse me."

Strike one. That's baseball, right? I slam my rum and soda, set it down. Fuck the coupon. I'll pay for another one.

I start to head for a couple of flight attendants I recognize, but before I reach them, an operations agent who recognizes me calls out, "Hey, Harry, I didn't know you were dating Amity Stone." He's never said two words to me at the airline, but tonight he calls me by name and acts as if we're buddies.

He's standing with two other guys. I stop to answer. They all hold beer bottles while I clutch Amity's champagne glass. "Yeah, we've been dating for a few months," I say with a confessional grin. "We live together."

"You *live* together?" He wriggles uncomfortably, as if he's just shit in his tuxedo.

"Well . . . yeah," I say, a questioning smile on my face.

One of his buddies speaks up. "Old Perry here went out with your girl."

I'm not defensive. Broaden my smile. "Hey, we're casual. I mean, I don't blame you—she's a beautiful girl."

"How long have you two been living together?" he asks.

"Since January," I tell him.

I watch him do the math in his head, and I know he's slept with her since then, because he looks a little red in the face. He takes a sip of his drink. His buddies laugh, shift their feet in their uncomfortable shoes.

"It's no big deal. We've only started *really* dating in the last couple months," I assure him.

He relaxes. Frees up. "Man, she's pretty fine, huh?"

"She sure is."

"I've never known any girl like that," he says. His friends laugh again.

I know that he's referring to her blow jobs and that he's enlightened his buddies. I let my face tell him I know what he's talking about. "Me either. She's incredible."

"Hey," the guy who has yet to speak blurts out, "you know who I think is hot? That Jennifer Beals. Man, I'd do her in a minute."

Please. That horrible perm?

"No shit," Perry says. "And the way she can move—you could bend her over from the front and do her in the back."

It was a stunt double! She can't bend like that—or even *act*.

"Did you see the porno version?" one guy asks. "No shit. There's a porno movie out called *Flashpuss*."

Oh those poor women in porno. White legs and bruises. Plastic high heels. Blue eye shadow. They should unionize.

Perry's buddies howl and give each other high fives. He turns to me and raises his hand. I raise my free hand to high-five him. And miss. And fall into him and spill Amity's champagne on his tux.

He backs off. "Shit!"

One of his buddies: "Whoa!"

"Oh, God, I'm so sorry." I set the champagne glass down on the nearest table and grab a napkin. Without thinking, I start wiping him off.

He backs off as if I'm some kind of faggy flight attendant. "I'll do it," he says, trying to be polite in his disgust.

His friends look at me differently. Chuckle.

Strike two. It's a lousy baseball season.

Reunited in another part of the ballroom, I hand Amity the glass of champagne. Since the spill, there's half a swallow left in the bottom of the glass.

She looks at the paltry amount. "This pathetic airline." *Airlawn.* "This is just typical of their idea for a free employee drink."

"I'll get you another one," I say, feeling like an idiot for not replacing it already. I just want to get out of this place.

"Don't worry, babe. We're about to eat. There's supposed to be red wine with dinner."

"I wonder what church they stole it from."

"The Catholics, I hope. They always have the best booze."

We turn and practically bump into Eva Catrell and her boyfriend. He *is* a shit kicker. His hair is combed straight forward, and the knot of his tie is thick. His hands are as rough as Eva's voice, and he's drinking beer from a bottle. He didn't even try to put on clean cowboy boots. No doubt he drives a pickup with a rifle hanging in the back.

Amity turns on her smile, full bright, and looks at Eva in that Southern way that says, "Sorry, darlin'. I win."

I'm uncomfortable, but I smile, and Eva smiles and we all kind of say hi for one second before Eva raises an arm of her beaded dress and pushes her boyfriend on. He has no idea.

For a moment we stand and watch the women—some in ball gowns, others in thousand-dollar cocktail dresses—lead their uncomfortable dates, imprisoned in their tuxes and dark suits from table to table. Taped orchestra music is playing, and slide shots of airline workers are being flashed up on a big screen. We watch the screen to see a shot of a fat guy throwing luggage into the cargo bin of a DC-10, then scan the party crowd to see him now wearing a ridiculous light blue tux with ruffled lapels, his buddies slapping him on the back.

The ten-foot-tall picture of the mousy ticket agent, with greasy straight hair, hoisting a piece of luggage onto a scale, belies the glamorous girl in the indigo, off-the-shoulder, beaded gown, her hair now swept up into a French twist. Every once in a while there's a random shot of our passengers, who, for this presentation, are solely aristocratic families and high-powered business travelers rather than our usual cargo.

After gristly prime rib, the awards begin. The CEO and President, Mr. Gherkin, the religious zealot who measures about five feet tall in his lifts, takes the stage. He stands behind a podium, pulls the microphone down to his mouth, and unconsciously adjusts his toupee. The parade of aviation heroes begins.

Best Voice, Reservations Agent Category. Most Permanent Smile, Flight Attendant. Best Landings, Pilot. Most Christian Baggage Handler. Most Pleasing Secretary. Best Groomed, Janitorial Staff. Most Optimistic Mechanic. And on it goes until we're drowning in a sea of hugs and kisses, and the acceptance speeches are waxing gushier and more illiterate with each new award. Amity and I are kicking each other under the table, laughing into our wineglasses as if they're spit cups at the dentist, using our napkins to cover our hyena mouths. And then . . .

"For her ability to keep everyone happy, passengers and fellow employees alike, for always maintaining her poise and charm, and for always offering an encouraging word and kind compliment to anyone and everyone she meets, the award for Most Congenial Flight Attendant, 1984, goes to . . . Amity Stone!"

For one second, she looks at me with this hysterical bullshit face, and reaches under the table to grab my crotch, and when that second is over, she transforms herself into an Academy Award winner, rises to the applause, gives the crowd a brief wave of acknowledgment, and walks glamorously toward the stage to accept her award.

As she steps up to the dais, the creepy little president comes out from behind the podium, his lips still wet from the last babe he bussed, and plants a kiss on Amity's lips that's just a little more than Christian. She stomachs it beautifully, accepts her little silver 747-shaped award, and takes to the microphone.

"Y'all are so sweet!" There's almost a tear in each eye, and she looks deeply touched. "I can't believe I've been honored with this wonderful award. G'yaw, how am I going to live up to this? Does this mean I'm always going to have to be nice, even if JR Ewing is on my flight?"

The crowd chuckles.

"This is a wonderful airline. I just want to say thank you to everyone that I've flown with in the last year and how much I'm looking forward to meeting all the new people who come on board as we grow. And to Mr. Gherkin, our president: Thanks for giving me a job—I promise to never tell your wife our little secret."

The audience howls and applauds, and Amity winks at the president, who is laughing uncomfortably. And then, with magic sincerity, her blue eyes become the same two spotlights as on the day we met, and she looks right at me and finishes, "And I want to thank Harry Ford, my fiancée, for making 1984 a year for new beginnings."

Home run. Out of the park. With the bases loaded.

Everyone applauds, I look over at Perry's table, and see that he's watching me, not Amity. I look back to Amity, she lifts her award and motions to me, and I nod, and suddenly this is the finest, most legitimate award program on earth.

We're tanked, flying down Suicide Express with the moonroof open, headed for a restaurant in the Knox-Henderson area for dessert and coffee. Amity's screaming, "I'm an award winner! I'm an award winner, baby!" She holds the award up and announces, "Best Stewardess in a Foreign Bra and Panties!" And then she throws the statuette out the hole in the roof.

"Amity! What are you doing!" I try to watch it in the rearview mirror careening into the dark. I look to see if it hits another car. I can't find it.

"I don't want that cheesy award, Harry," she laughs. "They give those things to the butt suckers and brownnosers. Besides, that thing was cheap. We can do better than *that*."

Dressed in black-tie elegance, Amity and I are the best dressed couple in the restaurant. The place is packed, and we confidently squeeze our way into the bar. There's a devilishly handsome waiter, about six feet four inches tall, with blond hair and blue eyes. He's immediately attracted to Amity, I can tell. We're sitting at the bar, and every time he approaches to get drinks for his dining tables, he gives her a glance. But he's smart, and he smiles at me as well. It works—I'm not jealous. In fact, he's so gorgeous, I would want anyone I know to have him, including me. Amity and I acknowledge what's happening, and she loves the attention and approval she's getting from both me and the waiter.

We're finally seated, and we find out that we have a different waiter, a Latin guy who's really hot looking and energetic, who introduces himself as Nicolo. He's around 5'8", with a beautiful strong nose and dark eyes, and a perfect body with one of those tight asses that's got scoops on the sides, quite evident to me in his stretched-to-breaking black pants. He says hello and reaches out with the menus, but accidentally drops them and they crash onto a wineglass and break it.

"Boom!" Amity laughs.

He grimaces and apologizes, but I'm hardly listening to him because he's just so fucking handsome, and I had just the right amount of red wine with dinner to make me feel sexy, so I'm boldly staring him down. He picks up the broken pieces of glass and tries to tell us what the specials are, but he's too flustered to remember.

"Don't worry," I tell him, laughing. "We only want dessert and coffee." I give him my I've-been-drinking-red-wine smile, and before he leaves I notice he rests his glance on me a little longer than any straight guy would. Man, he's definitely my type.

After he serves us coffee and two pieces of Chocolate Death Cake, that he almost drops in our laps, and we remind him that we need forks in order to eat them, Amity and I replay the evening in our heads and laugh while loading up on sugar and caffeine.

I excuse myself to go to the bathroom, and as I approach a table of eight, four couples of men and women, I hear cussing. "Fuck that!" and "Bullshit!" and other garbage is being spewed onto our waiter, Nicolo, who stands at the table with his arms at his side. I slow down to listen to what the problem is.

The waiter, his voice tense, tells a guy, "You asked for a Caesar *and* the buffalo wings."

"No, I didn't, *Pancho*," the guy says derisively.

"Tim, don't start," a woman warns. I hear "faggot" slip out of one of the other guy's mouths.

"He's screwed everything up from the beginning," a woman says to her date. And then I hear the word "faggot" again.

"Hey!" I say, stepping up to the table. "What gives you the right to talk to this guy like that?" I'm angry and shaking.

The table is silenced for a moment before one of the guys says, "Who the hell are you?"

I had a businessman treat me unkindly on the airplane my first month on the job. He called me a faggot because I couldn't find a place for his carry-on luggage. And I had to stand there and take it because it's my job to smile and keep my mouth shut. But another passenger came to my defense and really let the businessman have it for being so rude. Now is my chance to do the same for the waiter. I start to answer, and realize that Hunt, the guy Amity used to date, is part of this group. "I'm a friend of Hunt's here," I say as soon as I see Hunt. I walk over to his chair, put my hand on the back of it. "How's it going, Hunt?" I'm pissed off and dripping with sarcasm.

He answers slowly. "Pretty good, Harry. How are things with you?"

"Who is this guy?" one of the other guys says.

There are at least twelve empty beer glasses sitting on the table. The women look embarrassed. A redheaded gal with spiky hair says, "Tim, just let it go. You ate the damn appetizer. Just pay for it."

"I'm not so good," I tell Hunt, answering his question. "Why don't you tell your friends here that *faggot* isn't a very nice word."

"Well I guess you already have," he drawls.

"Who *is* this guy?" his friend asks again.

"Tim, just shut up and pay the check!" the redhead spurts.

"I'm a faggot," I tell the guy, "which means I'm allowed to use the word. But you're not allowed, unless you're one too."

"No fucking way," the guy laughs disgustedly.

"Hunt here has experience with guys like me. He'll tell you what we don't appreciate."

A couple of the girls look sickened and turn to Hunt. The drunken belligerent guy, Tim, rises from his chair. "Look, you Yankee smart-ass punk—"

"Tim!" the redhead yells.

"Tim," Hunt echoes. "Let it go. I'll explain later. Let's just get the fuck out of here." He slaps down several big bills, and one of the women says, "Don't leave him a tip," while looking pointedly at the waiter.

I step backward as Hunt pushes back from his chair, and they all leave. Tim gets in another, "Fucking faggots." But Hunt presses him forward past Nicolo and me.

"Man," Nicolo says after they're gone, "you are my hero." He's potently masculine in a way most guys aren't. There's not a trace of sissy in him, and I'm surprised they were calling him a faggot. Maybe they were just trying to put him down in what they thought was the worst possible way.

"Aw shucks," I say jokingly, flushed in the face. "I don't know if I've ever been anyone's hero."

"You are now," he says, drilling a hole into me with his black licorice eyes. "Nicolo," he says, introducing himself again, this time offering his hand.

"Harry," I tell him, shaking his hand.

"So how did you know that guy?" Nicolo asks.

"He dated my roommate—the girl I'm with tonight. He told her he used to proposition gay guys in bars and then take them out to the car and beat them up with his buddies. Never gave me any shit though. He was always real nice to me."

"And your roommate dated him? What's the matter with her?" he asks seriously.

"Nothing," I say, slightly offended. "Her business is her business. She's just my roommate." It's a weird moment. I'm slightly insulted that he insinuates Amity is inferior in some way for dating Hunt. And at the same time, I purposefully mislead him, telling him Amity and I are just roommates.

"I'm glad that's not your date you are with," he says with his Spanish accent.

"Why is that?" I ask.

"Because I would like you to have coffee and dessert with me, not her."

Wow. He's bold when he's not being a waiter. The way he says it, it almost sounds as if he doesn't like Amity. It bothers me, but I can't refuse—he looks too much like Guillermo Vilas. "I'd like that," I tell him, smiling. After all, Amity said I could bring my boyfriends over to our house after we're married. And I sure would love having this one as a boyfriend. "Well, excuse me," I tell him, starting for the bathroom.

"Harry," he tells me, offering straight white teeth from behind aubergine lips, "it was a pleasure to meet you."

My motor is officially running. "You too."

By the time I return to the table, Amity has whipped the other waiter, Thomas, into a sexually frustrated frenzy, and he's smiling at her every chance he gets as he passes by. I tell her about Nicolo and what happened with Hunt, and she said she watched it all from her seat. So now we're hyped up on sugar, caffeine, and waiters. It is confusing though. I mean, Amity is my date, and I'm hers. She just endorsed my virtue to the longtime employees of the airline, and I've never felt so connected to her. But our natural inclination is to cruise these sexy waiters. I'm beginning to realize that, besides being similar to a gay guy in the way she gives blow jobs, Amity is also similar to gay guys, *all guys,* in that she constantly has a roving eye. Engaged or not, the fact is we both like guys. "Let's take these boys home," I suggest, giving in to my ego or my penis-brain.

Amity smiles and says, "No, Harry," with her experienced counsel. "We'll just give them our phone numbers tonight," she says, writing our names and numbers down on a napkin and leaving it on the table. "You and I will go home *together.*"

I feel like an idiot. Of course she's right. We're a couple. And this is our night to be together. Considering her loving acknowledgment of me at the awards dinner, I hope I haven't hurt her feelings.

Or is she just playing a hand of cards?

That night, at home, in her bed, we lie side by side and talk.

"Thomas and Nicolo," she says to the ceiling.

"Nicolo and Thomas," I answer, helping to create legends of our waiters' names.

"I can tell Thomas is a gentleman. I wonder where he's from?" Amity says, referring to her waiter. "He had some kind of European accent."

"That guy's pretty tall. Amsterdam?"

"Yes," Amity says breathlessly, "and Emily Post says the manners of Europeans and South Americans are more elegant than those of Americans."

"Does that mean he'll bow and say, 'May I eat your pussy *please*?' "

"*Ja, ja,*" Amity sings. "And I will say *bedankt!*"

"Well, it's all perfect. Because Nicolo is Latin American. And I know enough Spanish to say *gracias.*" Ah, the Spanish language. I think about my ex-boyfriend in Kansas. We met one day in Spanish class, went to my apartment to practice rolling our Rs, and finally rolled each other. Matthew was on the college swim team when we were undergrads; his body is killer still. He has sky blue eyes, big pecs with perfect nipples, and curly dark hair that falls almost to his wide, wide shoulders. An absolute wolf (our college term for a babe), and my ego is still shot that he dumped me. Amity picks up on my silence, my mood change.

"What is it, Harry?" she asks, reaching over and holding my hand in the dark.

"I was just thinking about Matthew."

"Do you still miss him?"

"Sometimes. I don't know why. He was such a jerk."

"Harry, this world has bigger things in store for you than Kansas. Matthew couldn't handle that. He knew when you took this flight attendant job that your life was going to change in wonderful ways, and he just wasn't ready to let that change happen to him. So he loved you enough to set you free. You're lucky. Do you understand?"

Where the heck did she come up with that simple analysis? Poor thing, for all her acumen in dealing with people, sometimes she really is naive. Matthew was a rotten snake who dumped me only because I would never see my inheritance. It amazes me that, for all the subterfuge and intrigue she casts upon the innocent King of Jordan, she's blind to the machinations of the guilty commoner known as Matthew.

"It's the same thing that happened with my boyfriend Richard," she continues. "I told Richard I'd marry him—but I just wanted to get out of the house. See, my parents were so cruel to me. They had money, but they never cared for me the way they cared for my brother and sister. I was restless. I was at school in Fort Worth, and I didn't really have any desire to finish. The only thing I ever got an A in was art. My final project was a self-portrait entitled 'Rug Burns On My Thighs.' "

"Was it hard earned, that A?" I ask, smiling.

She sits up, looks at me. "Why do you ask me that way?"

I chuckle. "Well, I heard you had a little trouble with a professor."

"How dare you?" Amity says, her brow wrinkled, her eyes burning a hole in me. "If you know something, don't act like you don't."

"OK," I say defensively. "I heard from a friend of mine that you slept with a professor and ended up suing him."

Tears fill her eyes. "Are you enjoying making me feel like trash, Harry Ford? You think you can just say anything you want because of who you are and I'm supposed to take it?"

"God, no. I've never acted like that with you. With anybody. What's the big deal? I thought it was funny."

"Real funny," she says, more caustic than I've ever seen her. "I work hard to make you feel worthy, Mr. Ford. I don't need to be shot out of the sky by your knowledge of my past," she finishes, grabbing a pillow and hugging it to her chest.

"You *work* to make me *feel*? What kind of a sentence is that?"

"I do work at it," she huffs.

"That makes me *feel* like you're not being real—that I'm some kind of project."

"Now wait," she says, backpedaling. "You're not a project. What I meant was . . . Oh never mind. You'll never understand me. How can you?"

"Why not? Besides, that's crazy. I do understand you," I argue.

"No," she answers, exasperated, "you don't. I thought I was so lucky to find you, Harry. I've never been able to find a man like you. This girl has so much love to give, but most men want to own me, and I just don't want a man like that. And here I thought I finally found the right man in you, Harry Ford.''

"You have,'' I say, wanting to be wanted, wanting this thing to ultimately work out. "I love you, Amity. I really do. I'm going to share my inheritance with you, surely you know that. Anything you need.''

"You give me all I need,'' she says, lying back on the bed. The tears are falling sideways down her cheeks. "I didn't mean to get so squirrely.'' She wipes at the tears with her ring finger. "Listen, Bubba. If we do get married, if we decide to go through with it, I just want a thin gold band on my finger. Nothing fancy. No diamonds, babe. Just a thin gold band. I don't want your money, and I don't care if you don't make love to me with your dick, as long as you save just a little piece of your heart for me.''

Her words assure me. "I always will,'' I tell her, reaching out for her hand.

After a small repose in silence, we begin speaking again and spend the rest of the night talking about lost loves, postcards never written, life's curves, dreams of the future, travel to exotic countries, and anything else our imaginations dredge. And though we seem to be closer than ever before, there's still something that isn't right, something we've yet to get unearthed between us.

Eventually, something amazing starts to happen outside the window of her bedroom. "Amity, look,'' I say. "The sun is rising. It's morning.'' And she casts her eyes toward the fiery red of a brand-new dawn, then looks back at me and kisses me lightly, once, on the lips, before closing her eyes and falling asleep. I close my eyes to the red sky while remembering the old sailor's adage, "Red sky at morning, sailors take warning.''

CHAPTER
FOURTEEN

One week later, on another humid Texas morning, Amity and I are on the sofa in the sitting room, avoiding the morning sun of the living room—it's already nearly eighty-five degrees outside according to Willard Scott, who's broadly broadcasting the weather of major cities from the little black-and-white TV sitting on the kitchen counter. I sip a glass of water while waiting for the coffeemaker to spit out a pot of java gasoline. Amity is drinking a glass of iced tea with lemon and somehow painting her toenails at the same time. The phone rings.

"That's for me," Amity states, setting down the bottle of polish.

"How do you know?"

She looks at her watch. "Because Susan and I agreed to talk at nine o'clock on Thursday morning, and it's nine o'clock on Thursday morning."

The phone continues to ring. "Susan? As in *my mother?*"

Amity nods affirmatively while picking up the receiver. "Hello, Susan. This is Amity," she sings. After a pause she chimes, "Oh, we're fine as frog hair. Just happier every day we spend together— every night too."

The night before, I'd stayed home while Amity was out on a date with Kim, the rich guy who's going through his midlife crisis.

It was laughingly absurd to come home from flying and find a note from my fiancée that read:

My Harry,

I'm out on a date! Love your guts!

Your Amity

We've agreed it is the way things should be for both of us—that we remain free to be with the correct sex, which for both of us is men. We talked about the experimental encounters we've had together, and she knows that, while I was able to do it, there was an aspect of detachment and curiosity that made it a novelty. I want something authentic, not a novelty. Amity agrees—for me and for herself. Men, it is.

"Absolutely, Susan. We planned it for today, I promise," Amity gushes as if my mother were sitting next to her.

Last night, while Amity and Kim were out, Troy called, crying as usual—only this time I listened carefully to his message because Amity wasn't home to turn the machine down or talk over it. He begged for her to tell him *why*. He just kept saying that all he needed was an explanation. "Why did you leave without a word? Not even a note or letter?" he kept crying.

Was there a note? I wondered.

"I look forward to seeing you too. Give the general my love. 'Bye!" *Bah!*

"What was that about?" I ask apprehensively.

"Susan wants us to get ourselves registered at Maxwell's immediately," Amity tells me, returning to her little bottle of polish and her toes.

"Fuck, we're not Muffie and Biff. I don't want to do any of that stupid shit."

"Harry Ford!" she scolds, sounding like Scarlett O'Hara. "Of course we will. This is the only time your mother will ever be able to do this, and we simply can't deny her. Stop being selfish.''

Imagine, chastised by Scarlett O'Hara. I look disgusted. Feel a little angry. I keep telling myself that Amity and I are in this together, that we have our heads on straight. But her head seems to be tilting more and more these days. And her smile of satisfaction is beginning to look a little too sincere. ''The fact is, my father's will said nothing about *registering* ourselves, throwing *engagement parties*, or even that we had to have a ceremony,'' I snort. ''It's not like we have to convince anyone or land ourselves a mention in Barbie Botter's column. We just have to get married, plain and simple. My mother can do all this foofy stuff when Winston gets married.''

''The only person Winton is interested in marrying is himself,'' she pops.

''Well, stop trying to make me into a straight boy,'' I snap. ''It's not worth the money.''

She changes tack. Her voice softens. ''Look, babe, this is the *one* time in our lives that either one of us is going to walk down a wedding aisle.'' She says it as if her other wedding didn't happen. ''Just because your momma is trying to make it a traditional scene, don't let that spoil it for us. It's a game. Let's make it fun. You'll step into your Armani tux, and I'll pour myself into a Calvin Klein wedding gown, and if your momma wants to knock us on the head with Nambe serving utensils and Baccarat goblets as we walk down the aisle, we'll just have to suffer through.''

''Something tells me you won't suffer, Miss Name Brand.''

''You be nice.'' *Yew bee nauce.*

''Tell me about your date,'' I say, heading into the kitchen for coffee. ''I need to talk about something *real* for a change.''

''Well, Kim is *real* wealthy. He just separated from his wife, and he's moving into a very expensive condominium. I think he's going to help us.''

I take a coffee cup down from the cupboard. "Great," I answer sarcastically. "And what do you mean by that, Amity?"

"With the rent, babe. I told him that I just don't make hardly any money as a flight attendant and that my roommate can't pay any rent until his bills are paid off. So when you meet him, you need to act like you just started flying and you don't pay rent."

"Amity, my mother paid off my bills—and yours." I pour the java, add half-and-half. "We don't need any help."

"I know, babe," she answers. I hear the clinking ice as she drains her iced tea. "But why get ourselves back in debt? You don't have your inheritance yet. We should take all the help we can get."

"It was me that was in debt, not you. And besides, it's *our* inheritance we're waiting for. It will be yours as well. So you don't *have* to date him," I offer, coming back to the sofa.

"Harry, I don't date someone unless I want to. Besides, he's great," she says, enthusiastically. "He's an electronics importer. Old family business. I told him I so desperately need one of those new multiple CD players." She does the pouting gesture, bottom lip out, eyes drooping. She quickly reanimates. "He also has several other businesses and part interest in a racehorse. He's going to take me to the Derby next year!"

"Winston goes to the Derby every year," I warn her. "He'll grill you like a steak if you show up with a guy named Kim."

"Wigs and glasses, baby. Wigs and glasses."

"What about your accent?"

She speaks in a perfectly British accent, "Not to worry, my dear Harry. I shall not expose myself in any way."

"Impressive. So how come you didn't spend the night with this guy?" I ask, fully ambivalent.

She looks shy. Reverts to her Texas twang. "First date. It just wouldn't be right." She's in her Emily Post mode.

"Where did you guys eat?" I ask, sipping my coffee.

"On the Border."

"Mexican food? He didn't take you to the French Room at the Adolphus?"

She snaps quickly from the demure Emily Post mode to the thinking girl. "Oh, no. *I* insisted on going to On The Border. There's plenty of time for truffles, foie gras, and lobster later on. First impressions are indelible—you've got to make these guys think you're low maintenance from the get-go. He'll always associate me with On The Border, even when we've moved on to the Adolphus. Believe me, babe, it's to my advantage to sit there and eat my inexpensive Mexican food. Besides, I had a taco salad! Have you heard of them? They're these new things—a big ole fried bowl of dough with everything but the *cocina* sink thrown in. By the time we left the restaurant, I was farting like Mama Cass's corpse. And oh!" she says, her eyes flashing. "I told him you're gay. So he doesn't know about us, of course." Then she changes her tone, to sex kitten, while sliding her hand over my back and down to my ass. "I don't want him to know how my man *really* makes me feel," she purrs. "I have to *pretend* I'm his girl, so he thinks you and I are just roommates." She pulls herself to me and whispers in my ear, "He'll never know I'm *your* girl."

It's as if we're fooling the whole world, but not ourselves. Or are we? She smiles devilishly at me and raises an eyebrow. This whole conversation has made me uncomfortable. In fact, this whole charade is starting to gross me out. "Amity, Troy called again last night."

She looks slightly agitated, rises, goes to the kitchen. "Just a minute, babe," she calls, "I need some more lemon and tea."

"He's just so pathetic," I yell. "Can't you at least talk to him?"

"I don't know what else there is to say!" she answers, exasperated. She wishes I'd drop it. I've been bringing it up now and then, and her Southern calm is being tested, I can tell.

"He didn't get your note," I say.

"Then I'll send another one!" she chirps. "Or I'll call him. Don't worry. I'll take care of Troy."

Amity is out on a date. I pick up the phone on the fourth ring, just before the machine clicks on, hoping that it's Nicolo, but knowing it's probably Amity offering to bring home food. "Hello?"

"Harry?"

"Yes?"

"Nicolo."

Two days. I've waited two whole days for this call, but it seems like forever. I was starting to wonder if he'd ever call. I had imaginary conversations in my head with him for practice, and I was so suave, cool, and funny that I almost wanted to date myself. "Hey, Nicolo," I answer, all those urbane conversation skills pounded out of me by my nervous heartbeat. "Hey, Nicolo." That's it. That's all I can say.

"How come a cute guy like you is home on a Monday night?" he asks quietly.

"Football."

"Who's playing?" he asks, almost in a whisper.

"I don't know," I laugh nervously, swallowing. "TV's not on. I never watch it."

He laughs. "I do not blame you. Besides, it's not really football. Football is what we play in Argentina. We use a lot more feet, and we have more balls," he says, flirting with me.

"I don't doubt it," I say, doing my best sexy-man voice—though I probably sound like a nervous telemarketer. "So where are you?"

"I'm at the library," he answers. "On a pay phone. That's why I sound so romantic, because I have to whisper."

"Damn," I answer, relaxing. "I thought you were trying to seduce me."

"Maybe I am."

I take the phone cord in my hand and twist it around my finger. "How will I know for sure?"

"The next time you see me, if I'm wearing a light yellow short-sleeve polo shirt, and a faded pair of button-fly jeans, then that means I'm trying to seduce you."

"Your two favorite pieces of clothing?"

"They work better than drugs and alcohol, and there's no hang-over."

"So you're a nice healthy Latin American boy, huh?"

"Mind and body."

"The body is evident. I'll have to get to know the mind."

"I'm hoping you will," he says strongly. "I knew when I saw you at the restaurant that I liked your looks, but after listening to you speak, I knew that I also liked the inside of you. It makes me want to offer the inside of me."

Whoa. He's not messing around. Man, it's hard to find this kind of forthright honesty from an American boy. I'm unbelievably flattered, but I'm also taken aback. "I'd like that," I answer sincerely.

"Good. I'm hoping to get a day off sometime next week. It's hard for me. I go to school full-time, and I work full-time."

"What are you studying?" I ask.

"Journalism. It's a family tradition."

"Your mom's side or your dad's?"

"Father. There is much to tell of my family history, my background. I'd like to share it with you if you're interested."

"I am," I assure him. "It's the best way to know someone."

"I'm glad you think so," he says. "Will you allow me to know your family as well?"

"As best as they can be known," I say wryly.

"Then we will talk of these things," he says, knowing that dissection of family doesn't lend its autopsy report to a pay phone discussion. "Call me later in the week? We'll plan a meeting?"

"Definitely. What's your number?"

I take down his number, and we sign off, both of us making it clear how eager we are to meet. Oh, boy, I can't believe it. Amity. My inheritance. And now, possibly, Nicolo. I could have it all. I could really have it all.

"I saw Gina Hyland at the bakery this morning," I tell Amity, referring to a flight attendant at the airline. The two of us are splayed in the hot Texas sun at the apartment pool down the street, and I'm spreading coconut oil on my stomach. "She said to tell you she had Victor on one of her flights. Who's Victor?"

Amity, who is spreading baby oil on her legs, quickly puts her sunglasses on. Something's weird. I can tell she's nervous. "An old boyfriend."

"Do you still see Victor?"

"Not often."

"Was that who you saw in Houston a few months ago for a date?"

I can tell she's trying to decide whether to tell me or not. "It's hard for me to talk about him," she says, bounding out of her chair and diving into the pool. I'm surprised by her sudden immersion— or is it sudden *diversion*? "Shit!" she yells, rising to the surface halfway across the pool. "I forgot I had my sunglasses on!" She takes the dripping glasses off and sets them on the side of the pool. "Listen, we've got to make us a plan for these waiter boys!" she says, hanging on the pool's edge.

"Nicolo called me last night while you were out," I say, giving in to her change of direction.

Amity screams with delight. "And Thomas called me! There was a message on my machine."

"I know," I say before I realize I've exposed my auditory peeping.

"Harry," Amity says softly, shifting gears again. "Emily Post says a husband must never listen in on his wife's phone calls or private conversations. Privacy must be respected.''

''Sorry. But what does it matter? We don't keep any secrets from each other anyway.''

She doesn't answer. And she never did tell me who Victor is. And how come I still haven't met her family? How come I still know so little about her upbringing? God, I hope I'm not fucking up here. My discussion with Nicolo about the importance of family and its bearing on personality has made me think twice about Amity. Yes, on the surface, I was comfortable with her immediately. Even more so than with Nicolo at the same stage. But why do I get the feeling I'll grow more comfortable with Nicolo over time while I seem to be growing less so with Amity as we proceed with this pact? What happened to that magic I felt for her in Mexico?

Hey, Harry. Wake up, buddy. You're gay and you're marrying a woman. And even if your marriage is a mutually agreed-upon pact with Amity, your pact involves money. Even if you do truly love and respect her, your decision was based on *money*.

Well, I guess that's OK. Not every relationship in life has the same priorities. I mean, at least I have all three aspects to my relationship with Amity, regardless of their order: money, love, respect. And whatever her secrets may be, they don't necessarily have anything to do with me. After all, my past has nothing to do with her.

''We'll make it fun, Bubba, I promise.''

We've cleaned up and dressed up, and we are now heading into Maxwell-Grey to register ourselves for wedding gifts. Amity is trying to convince me that this kind of bullshit can be fun, but I always think it smacks of grabby self-congratulation when couples do this kind of gift solicitation.

We enter the wedding department, and a woman descends upon us like a peregrine falcon on fresh mice. ''May I help you?'' she asks, inches from our faces. She's such a package she could fly on

Federal Express. Her red nails nearly blind us with their shine, her tiny face is painted into a geishalike mask, and her hair is the requisite Texas helmet that moves en masse. She's wearing a stylish suit-dress of red and black—the *in* colors for this year—and her red heels are so high that each step is a treacherous risk that could take her down. I *love* her.

"Harry Ford and I are engaged to be married," Amity states, proudly, "and we're here to register ourselves."

"I'm pleased you've chosen Maxwell-Grey." *Makeswill-Gry.* "My name is Kiki Cartwright. I'll be delighted to help you."

Kiki Cartwright. Great name. We follow her, staying back in case she falls, into a special area within the wedding department, where a tasteful, bone-colored sofa awaits. We sit. She offers us white wine or Perrier water.

"Champagne," Amity tells her. "We can't shop without it."

Kiki gives her a squinty saccharine smile and disappears.

"Look at this place," I tell Amity. "Everyone here is dead." It's true. There's not a single stained piece of clothing, a scuff mark on a shoe, a hair out of place, or a pockmark on the skin of anyone in view. No one except the mannequins and Kiki seems to have any kind of expression on his face. "Whatever happened to the love children of the sixties? Married people used to receive poetry as gifts."

"This is all a part of it," Amity explains, as if she's done this many times before. "Don't worry. We'll be out of here in no time."

"I'm giving you poetry as my gift," I tell her resolutely.

Amity smiles. "I can't think of anything I'd rather have from you, babe."

Kiki brings an open magnum, pours, and hands us the crystal glasses. "Do you like these glasses? They're available in the store. Many of our couples list them so that they can remember this special day." *Special die.*

"Very nice," Amity says. "Who makes them?"

"Baccarat," Kiki answers, seating herself on the edge of a chair across from us.

"I'm a Lalique girl," Amity says, no apology.

"Of course," Kiki says. "You look Lalique to me."

I notice another couple, who appear to be concluding their meeting, standing not ten feet away with their own sales-package woman, who is shaking their hands carefully so she won't break a nail, lest antifreeze ooze from the breaking point. The guy, who looks miserable, gives me a sympathetic nod. I nod back, even give a little wave of camaraderie. What's a straight guy to do? This is only a game. This is only a game. This is . . .

"Let's start with bedding," the sales package says. She's sitting so far out on the edge of her chair, I'm sure she's going to fall off and break, and I'd hate to see that happen because she's quite possibly the mother of a little girl who looks just like her. "Often our focus in the first stages of marriage is in the bedroom," she adds, trying to give a folksy wink. She doesn't pull it off, but I offer her a laugh to help her along. "Do you have any desire for linens, comforters, bedspreads?"

"Ralph Lauren all the way," Amity dictates swiftly.

I have a feeling that Kiki is the kind of woman who has intercourse standing up. So she doesn't mess up her hair. I don't blame her—it's a masterpiece. More curves than Central Expressway, but much better planned. "I like your hair," I say.

"Why, thank you," she says, nodding pleasantly. "I style it myself."

"Good job."

"You're so sweet." She looks at Amity. "You've landed yourself quite a gentleman."

"I certainly have," Amity answers. "If more of us gals married gay guys, we'd all be a lot happier."

"Aw, shucks," I say, smiling at Amity.

Kiki's face freezes with a deer-in-the-headlights look. Then she glances back at her printed forms and hastily asks, "Do you have specific needs in the bedroom?" She's instantly horrified by her timing.

Amity growls sexily, "Are you reading off the form? Or is that an open-ended question, darlin'?"

Kiki holds up the form and points to the question. "Right here on the list."

"Just put us down for everything," Amity giggles.

"Of course," the woman answers, nervously making a note.

"Does this go into a computer or something?" I ask, trying to smooth her out.

"Yes, Mr. Ford. You and your bride will get a computerized printout of everything you've listed, as well as a final printout of everything purchased," she answers.

I nibble a sassy little cucumber and red pepper sandwich from the tray on the table in front of us, look at Amity, try not to laugh.

"Let's move into the kitchen," Kiki suggests.

"Together?" I ask.

She doesn't get it.

"Yes," Amity says. "Harry and I aren't like those couples who focus on the bedroom. We like to focus on the kitchen."

"How marvelous," Kiki says, breathing a sigh of relief. "Do you both like to cook?"

"Heavens, no. We're horrible cooks. We use the kitchen for sex!"

Here she goes—shaken not stirred.

Kiki looks pained. She smiles a forced smile. "There's a place for everything," she says, trying to be a good sport.

"That's the trouble. There isn't. We need a big ole chopping block for Harry to lay me out on."

"Maxwell-Grey has them. We'll put it on the list," she says, refusing to be offended.

Amity leans forward so that both she and the sales package are on the edge of their seats. "And a sterling silver garlic press," she whispers. "It's nothing but a fancy nipple clamp, darlin'. You've *got* to try it."

"Great. Thank you," Kiki answers as if Amity has shared a stock tip.

I'm slamming my champagne. Looking around. Anything to keep from laughing.

"Oh! And a food processor! We definitely need one of those."

The saleswoman, assuming there's a catch, doesn't write.

Amity looks blankly at her. "For *processing.*"

Kiki looks relieved.

" 'Course, you've got to be careful what you put in those things," Amity adds. "After all, one little pureed weenie and there goes the marriage."

The woman finally stiffens, loses her grace. "I suppose."

Amity sings a Tammy Wynette hybrid:

D-I-V-O-R-C-E
That's what pureed weenie
means to me.

I'm spitting champagne through my nose. Amity's smiling. And Kiki is sliding back in her chair. Giving up.

"Look. Just put us down for everything," I say, using my little cocktail napkin to wipe my nose. "My mother will probably buy it all anyway."

Kiki Cartwright slides right back out to the edge of her chair, fully rejuvenated. "Yes, Mr. Ford!"

CHAPTER
FIFTEEN

mity has this thing about first dates. She prefers they be brunch or lunch. You can much easier steal yourself away from lunch than dinner in case the date turns out to be a nightmare. *Nawt-mayor.* She suggests we invite the waiter boys over for brunch and make nasty fruit plates.

"Nasty fruit plates, Harry! We slice the bacon into pieces and fry them up until they're nice and curly. Then we cut a banana in half, lengthwise, and lay it on the plate. Two big round slices of kiwi underneath, and you've got a nasty fruit plate!"

We sip champagne and take hits off the bong while we fry the bacon in the kitchen. It's only 10:00 in the morning and we're getting looped. After the bacon is fried, I slice the bananas down the middle and Amity peels the kiwi.

It isn't until we fix them up, on four different plates, that I see the curly bacon is pubic hair, the banana is a big penis, and the kiwi slices are testicles.

"Just look at those bad boys!" Amity squeals, referring to our creations. "Now, the finishing touch." She takes the bottle of creamy salad dressing, and pours a dribble down the shaft of each banana. The phone rings.

"Hello?" I say, into the receiver.

"Hi, honey. Is Amity there?"

"Nice to talk to you too, Mother," I answer, loading the semen-dribbled bananas into the refrigerator.

"Oh, I'm sorry, Harry, but I've a limited amount of time today. I have to go to the clinic for a follow-up."

Of course. She's still recovering from cancer. I feel guilty. "Sorry, Mom. How is everything?"

"Wonderful, honey. Bud Orenstein says that it's the best tummy tuck he's done and that I look like Suzanne Sommers. He just wants to check my muscle tone, but I'm running late. Is Amity there?"

Duped again. "What's going on with your cancer tuck?" I ask.

"What a perfect way of saying it! Everything's fine. Now really, darling, give me Amity."

I hand Amity the phone.

"Hi, Susan! How can I help you? Uh-huh. Right. Oh, yes. Great! I can't wait. I'll mark it on my calendar. See you then. Love your guts!" Amity hangs up the phone.

"She loves her own guts. They've been tucked away so nicely."

"And I'll do the same when the time comes," Amity says resolutely.

"So what's the skinny?" I ask.

"She's coming down to Dallas. We're going to go gown shopping."

"Just warn me so I can be out of town. Now look," I state, changing the subject. "You, me, and Nicolo are going to get off on eating these nasty fruit plates, but what about Thomas? He's straight. He doesn't want to eat a big dick dripping with jism."

"Oh my God, Harry! Should we have made him a pussy?"

We laugh so hard we fall on the kitchen floor.

"Come on, come on!" Amity says, pulling me up. "We've got to whip up an edible Libby."

We find out that kiwi is actually very vaginalike when squished into shape. And with the green color and the black seeds, we wind up with something wet, juicy, and so visually stunning that Georgia O'Keefe would be proud. We crumble the bacon on top of it and use a little round slice of banana as a belly button above it.

Amity cheers, "Voilà, y'all!"

"Voilà, y'all!" I imitate.

She jumps into the bathroom for a mini poo, the abbreviated version of the poo up. The full version takes two hours, and she doesn't have time. She takes off her clothes and squats in the tub. She's dark from yesterday's sun, and her tan lines make her look as if she's wearing a white bra and panties where her breasts, ass, and crotch have been shielded by her swimsuit. As water flows out of the spigot, she unabashedly uses a washcloth to wash her Muffie or Lady or whatever it's called today while I sit on the tub's edge. "We gotta make sure this isn't an all-day thing because I've got a date with Kim tonight," she says, now washing under her arms.

"Don't worry. The waiters probably have to work tonight."

She finishes up, and we both get dressed. I wear linen shorts with a belt and a starched, short-sleeved button-down. No shoes. It's too hot, and besides, my feet are tanned, so they *do* match my belt, as Amity insists they should. I'd really just like to wear a pair of gym shorts and a T-shirt, but Amity makes me dress Winstonesque.

The boys arrive together in Thomas's convertible Mustang.

Amity is turning up my short sleeves, making cuffs, while we watch them from the house. "Look at his car, Harry!" She smoothes my collar. "I'll have to wear a scarf when I go riding with him, or my hair could fly loose and kill someone in the next lane." We bolt from the door so they don't see us watching them. When they knock, Amity has me answer and then casually strolls into view behind me, wearing linen shorts of her own, a melon-colored blouse, and expensive European sandals over her tan feet and painted toes.

"Hi, y'all." She's resting her head on my shoulder, allowing it to be her frame.

Nicolo stands there, wearing a light yellow polo shirt, his dark-skinned biceps bursting out of the short sleeves while his muscled legs press against the faded button-fly jeans. The guys come in. Thomas kisses Amity, and Nicolo shakes my hand. When Amity reaches out to shake hands with Nicolo, he quietly says hello and shakes hands dispassionately. Like the night at the restaurant, I can tell he doesn't really like her. I think she can too. We show them the house and then bring them right back near the front door to the sun porch, and serve them mimosas. Then Amity pulls out a pre-twisted joint, and we all get stoned. Then Amity and I announce the nasty fruit plates. Nicolo and Thomas are relaxing, digging it, and we laugh while we all eat our fruity genitalia.

"We almost served you a dick," Amity cheerfully confesses to Thomas, who's slurping up his New Zealand-grown vagina.

"Yes, your pussy is very last minute," I add.

Amity tilts her head and takes a sip of champagne and orange juice. "Harry's so thoughtful. He helped me shape it just this morning."

"That's why it's so fresh," I claim.

"So what happened to my dick?" Thomas asks, jumping into the game with his very slight, very sexy European accent.

Amity smiles and tilts her head even more. "I ate it, darlin'."

And so our conversation goes, remaining on the light side to the extent that it almost escapes gravity. And I notice that the lighter it gets, the less patient Nicolo grows. Every time he tries to make a stab at something real, whether it's the Russian boycott of the Olympics or the ongoing presidential debates, Amity steers the conversation back to sex. And I can see that Nicolo doesn't really respect her, and in fact, I sense that he thinks she's rather shallow. It's not anything he says, but I can see it in his eyes when he looks at her. He even tries to discuss the Air Florida bankruptcy, perhaps thinking that Amity would at least be interested in something that has to do with the airline industry, but she steers the conversation back to sex again—and gets no protest from Thomas, who eventually picks her up and carries her into the bedroom while she pretends to kick and scream like a cavewoman.

Nicolo and I walk to my bedroom. Nicolo lies down on my bed, which is no longer the blow-up mattress, but a queen-size mattress and box springs that sit directly on the floor. Before I close the door, we hear from Amity's bedroom, "Oh, Thomas, you drive me *wild!*" Nicolo chuckles while I close the door and pull the shades. I light two candles and turn on the radio. Cyndi Lauper starts into "Time after Time" as I turn to Nicolo. He smiles, pats the empty bed next to him, and says, "Let's talk."

"It wasn't exactly what we were doing on the porch, was it?" I answer quietly.

"No," he claims, "we didn't saying anything. I want to learn of you, Harry." Never mind that he's gorgeous. His Spanish accent alone makes him sexy. I lie down beside him, and he takes my hand. "You said before that Kansas is your home. Tell me about Kansas."

His hand is warm, and his dark skin is reflective with the slight sheen of natural oils. I've never been with anything but white boys, but I've always craved his type. I like the feel of him and how he looks next to the white sheets. "Kansas is flat," I answer. My erection isn't.

"And?"

My heart is pounding, pushing against the skin of my chest. I want to kiss his aubergine lips. "Hot."

"And?"

"Humid."

"And?"

"What do you want?" I ask, desperately wanting to undress him.

"More."

More than a laugh? More than a refill on the champagne? More than a quick reply? I look at him, into his eyes. They're unbelievably beautiful, the first pair of dark eyes that I've found prettier than blue or green or hazel. His eyes are on the border where brown becomes black. And his luxuriant eyelashes remind me of the pocket combs I carried as a kid, with their thick black prongs emanating from the base of the comb. I used to run my fingers across them. I'd like to gently run my fingers across his lashes.

He bids, "Tell me the poetry of your home. I know it's inside your heart."

There is something about him that makes me not want to disappoint. I take a breath. Think. "Kansas . . . is like a dirt road that runs for infinity, never dipping or rising, never turning." He nods and closes his eyes, causing his lashes to fall like fans, and waits for me to continue. "And above the road is a sky so large it could hold the wings of every angel. And people say there's no ocean, but there is. In the early season, when the wheat is green, almost the color of seaweed, it rolls in waves, pushed by the wind, just like the top of the ocean. As summer wears on, the waves turn gold and stiffen slightly as if the tide has turned. Sometimes I'd ride my horse down a country road and stand on the side of a wheat field and pretend I was on a beach watching the waves roll by. I'd watch them carry life along, just like the sea. Then I'd close my eyes, breathe in, and change the scent of the damp earth and ripening grain into salty air. And sometimes when I opened my eyes, a meadowlark or a whippoorwill would land and roll up and down over the waves while deciding where it was headed next. And even though the waves rolled on for infinity, like the road and the sky, most often the meadowlark flew only as far as a neighbor's front porch because she couldn't see leaving such perfection behind."

He opens his eyes, satisfied. "This is your reward for telling me about Kansas," he says, lifting my hand to his mouth and gently kissing it.

"I can tell you about Missouri and Colorado too," I offer eagerly.

He laughs. "Just Kansas, hombre." He lowers my hand from his lips. "And why did you fly farther than your neighbor's porch?"

"Well . . . I had no choice, I guess. My family couldn't offer me the comfort of their precious little nest, so I took off."

"Then we are alike," Nicolo says, his beautiful lips forming a melancholy smile. "I'm here because of my family also. Though we were forced to flee our nest together—what was left of us."

"What do you mean?" I inquire, my erection subsiding.

"I am from Argentina, Harry. Do you know of our recent history?"

"Not really. Just that it's been kind of unstable down there, right?"

"When Peron returned to power eleven years ago, I was thirteen years old. The people of my country thought that we would be delivered to prosperity, that the end of bad times had come, that Peron would restore Argentina to the glory of its past. But my father believed that Argentina had never known glory, that its successes throughout its history were triumphs only of the rich and were short-lived and had always come at the expense of the common people—*la gente verdadera*, my father called them. He was a journalist for *Liberacion del Alma.*"

"Liberation of the soul," I translate.

"You speak Spanish? You want that we speak in Spanish?"

"No," I answer. "I only know a little."

He continues. "*Liberacion del Alma* was a paper that was not aligned with guerrilla factions. And not with the government. It was a neutral publication dedicated to telling truth through all eyes and letting the reader decide who was righteous. An interview with members of a Marxist guerrilla organization like the ERP would be published beside an essay from the Navy School of Mechanics, the evil military organization that my father knew operated clandestine concentration camps, and below that, you might read a passionate interview with Las Madres de la Plaza de Mayo, the mothers of the kidnapped civilians who were accused of being subversives. Though the paper was committed to allowing all thought and debate, my father was employed to offer his opinion on the last page. He wrote political editorials that were most often open-minded. It was when he aligned himself with Las Madres that he got in trouble. He believed they were right to speak out about the disappeared. So the government disappeared him.''

He's not crying, but he's inside of himself now, below the equator, I suppose, in the land of his past. ''What do you mean?'' I ask.

''*Los desaparecidos*. The disappeared. Thousands of people were kidnapped, tortured, murdered. They simply disappeared. Those who were found were floating in barrels in the River Plata or dropped on top of refuse dumps. It is said there were groups taken to the sky in airplanes and thrown to their deaths. I'll never know what happened to my father.''

''God,'' I whisper, ''there are some passengers on my flights I'd like to throw out of the plane, but I'd never do it.'' He looks incredulous, confused by my remark. Shit, me and my mouth. ''Sorry. I didn't mean it. Sometimes my timing is off. Why were they kidnapped? What did they do?''

''Nothing,'' he answers, shaking his head. ''The government called them subversives. But they were ordinary people, like you and me. Their biggest crime was that they had an opinion or belonged to a social group that helped others less fortunate or were lawyers with so-called subversive clients or whatever the excuse. It is hard to explain.''

I put my arm around him and stare at the wall, as he does, and try to imagine what he sees. ''Is that why you came to America?''

''No. We came because of my sister. She was an artist who vowed to expose my father's murderers. She was sure it was the work of the government. She blamed the federal police. But when she confronted them, in print and in her person, they cast the blame on the Argentine Anticommunist Alliance, who had written a strong rebuttal to one of my father's editorials, which was gladly published in *Liberacion del Alma*. But everyone knew the Alliance *was* the federal police, and they were making her walk in a circle, she believed, laughing behind her back. And when she pushed too hard and they weren't laughing anymore, they disappeared her.''

''Your sister too?'' All of a sudden the champagne and reefer is making me dizzy, uncomfortable. ''Did you find her?''

He shakes his head no. ''But my mother received word from a member of the Navy School, someone who called himself a *friend* because he was willing to offer the truth that both my father and sister were dead so we should not worry or try to find them. 'Go on with your lives,' he told us, 'but remain quiet.' My mother was devastating.''

''Devastated,'' I correct. Then I think, maybe she *was* devastating, I've never seen her.

''Yes, devastated. So she did what only a woman in her shoes could do. She joined Las Madres de la Plaza de Mayo, the group of women who publicly protested their disappeared family members— only she knew something the other mothers did not know: Most of the disappeareds were never coming back.''

''She's brave.''

''Yes,'' he says, lost in a memory, ''until they attempted to take me away.''

''You? Who?''

He snaps out of his trance, looks me in the eye. ''I don't know. It was the week of the World Cup games, 1978. Police in plainclothes grabbed my arms and legs while I was walking down the street and tried to force me into an unmarked government car.''

''You got away?''

''Yes, because there were so many *turistas* in town, and a group of Italians was on the street, and I started to scream to them in Italian. The police agents let me go, because they didn't want to make a scene in front of the *turistas*, in case someone from the international press could be watching. When I got home, I told my mother, and she broke down. She cried, a very broken woman. She made arrangements that week to get my brother and me and herself out of the country. She could suffer no more loss.''

I think about my perky mother and wonder how she would endure such tragedy and loss in her own family. Would she become a Mother of the Plaza by going shopping on the Country Club Plaza in Kansas City? Treat herself to a Smoothie? Would she be devastating? No. I'm too hard on her. She would rise to the occasion, use her Midwestern pluck to live on, reinvent the family as best as she could. That's my mother.

"So you see, Harry, I enjoy hearing the poetry of people's homelands. Because mine is stuck inside of my heart and it will be a very long day before it will come out again."

We're silent for a few minutes while the candles flicker and the radio plays Eurythmics, "Here Comes the Rain Again." It feels odd, lying here, holding hands, learning about the sorrowful past of this beautiful man beside me. But when Annie Lennox sings, "Talk to me, like lovers do," I know that Nicolo is doing just that—speaking to me with the honesty of a lover. And the oddity of it falls away, and it feels just right.

Nicolo smiles, sighs. "This happens when I drink too much. I become lonely for my family. I'm sorry, Harry. You probably just wanted to get me in bed and taste the meat that Argentina is famous for. No?"

I smile, grateful that his sense of humor is intact. This time I kiss *his* hand. "Who's left in your family?"

"My mother and my brother," he answers.

He's right. We are alike. Alike and so different.

He rolls off the bed, walks to the table, and carefully lifts the plate holding the burning candle. He carries it slowly back to bed and lowers himself next to me until the flame is flickering near my face. "Look into the flame," he says. "And tell me what you see."

I look through the dancing fire connected to the wick, and what I see is his handsome, dark-skinned hand, beyond its glow, holding the plate. "I see your hand," I answer, feeling stupid and literal. Shit, he likes poetry. I should have said something poetic.

"When you look into a flame you are looking into your future," he explains. Then he smiles sexily and says, "And what you see is me." He holds the candle in front of our faces, highlighting them with the swaggering flame, then suddenly blows it out, returning us to the middle gray light of the shade-darkened room. He puts the candle on the floor, rolls back to me, and wraps me in his muscular arms. Then he closes his eyes.

It's nightfall. Nicolo and Thomas are gone. Amity is pooing up for real—the whole two-hour show. I'm feeling almost dreamy, as if I'm still wrapped in Nicolo's arms. I sit on the side of the tub and watch. I don't know how she's doing it, but she seems to have this incredible energy, she is fluffing her hair and painting her face and staying very focused and task oriented. "Thomas was unbelievable, Harry. He can go and go and go. You should hear his accent while he makes love. 'I'm *coming*, Amity,' he said, but it sounded like he said, 'I'm *calming* Amity.' European love makes me melt. From the moment he stamped my passport, I was wetter than a canal in Amsterdam!"

I smile. Quietly laugh.

"How was your Latin lover? Tell me about Nicolo, Harry. Did he scramble your *huevos?*"

I sigh, contented. "We didn't have sex. We didn't even take our clothes off. We just talked."

"What? G'yaw, sounds like true love," she says flippantly. "You just talked the whole time?"

"No, we talked a little while; then we fell asleep in each other's arms. We were both kind of knocked over by the champagne."

"And each other?" Amity asks. She does the Belushi eyebrow, but her smile is slightly tense.

"Kind of," I say. I'm a little nervous about telling her my true feelings—that I think this guy is the sexiest, sweetest, most real person I've ever met—which is largely the way I felt about her when first we met. The fundamental difference is that Nicolo is a man. A man that I could instantly fall in love with and probably am. Even though my relationship with Amity is wide open, and honest as well, the whole situation seems loaded. How can I love two people at once?

"He doesn't like me," she says, putting her mascara on while she opens her mouth wide like a fish.

"How do you know?"

She pauses with the mascara wand. "Harry, don't bullshit me. You see it too."

"I think he likes you," I lie. "He just didn't like Hunt's friends calling him a faggot, and since you dated Hunt, he finds you guilty."

"I wish he wouldn't judge me," she says, going back to her mascara application.

"He's a wonderful man. He'll get over it."

"Harry, are you in love?"

"Amity, I just met the guy. How could I be in love?" I don't sound the least bit convincing.

She doesn't answer, but smiles. It's a smile I've not seen her wear; her lips aren't raised or lowered, but spread to camouflage whatever her feelings may be. She quickly resumes her mission of readiness, and before I know it, she's whipped herself back into a fresh and gorgeous woman in a black cocktail dress and pearls. "Libby's sore," she whines, slipping into her shoes. "Kim can have a blow job, but he's not sticking it in."

"You want me to tell him?" I ask, gallantly.

"You let me take care of that," Amity says.

Kim comes to the door, and this time she answers it herself.

She brings him in, and I'm surprised to see that he's Chinese or Japanese or something like that. He's a short, wired-up guy of about fifty who shakes my hand as if we've made a thirty-million-dollar business deal that entitles him to the whole thirty million. His black hair is dirty and unkempt, his face has a five o'clock shadow, but with his sparse whiskers it looks as if he's operating on daylight saving time. His clothes are jail cell fresh, and his breath smells like rotten sushi. I can't believe she's dating this guy. But Amity eagerly throws her Chanel purse over her shoulder, and *whoosh,* they're out of the house.

With the house to myself, I revel in the quiet. Falling into the wingback chair, I raise my hand to my nose. I can still smell Nicolo's natural scent. It's a powerful aphrodisiac, and I try to imagine him naked in my arms, kissing me. I'm feeling as if this is a day I'll never forget, like the day Amity and I had in Mexico. A day when every smell, every piece of clothing, every word will be remembered.

Later in the evening, I run out to Butch's Diner for dinner food. Recently, I've started eating all the fattening food I can and drinking protein shakes, because working out at the gym has made me hungrier. My body has been changing, and now that I've met Nicolo, I have more incentive to garner results. After I eat my takeout calories, I fall asleep in my room.

Later that night, I'm stirred slightly awake by sounds coming out of Amity's bedroom. "Oh, Kim, you drive me *wild!*" she squeals. There's something a little sick about it. She was just saying the same thing to Thomas this morning, and it makes me wonder which guy *really* drives her wild. And while the answer may be *both,* I have a feeling it could just as well be *neither.* I roll over and pull my feather pillow over my head and fall back into a deep sleep.

CHAPTER SIXTEEN

It's morning. Kim is smoking a cigarette, and Amity (topless) and he are sitting on the floor of my room, lotus style, in their underwear. Kim's underpants have yellow stains in the crotch, and the stains are these weird shapes that provoke me to analyze them as if I'm taking a Rorschach test. I swear I see a raccoon and a garden rake.

Amity tells him to sit still because she's going to pluck a gray hair from his head. I'm sure this is going to send his midlife crisis into a further tailspin, but he doesn't flinch. Possibly because he's so coked out of his mind at ten o'clock in the morning that his life is nothing but a big fat cabaret.

"Harry, read Kim some of your poetry," Amity commands. There's powder on her nose, and it isn't the kind she gets at Maxwell's cosmetics department.

"He doesn't want to hear a poem," I say, annoyed. There's something unseemly about being around a wired-up middle-aged guy who has pee-pee stains shaped like animals on his underwear at ten o'clock in the morning. I'm losing respect for Amity too— it's difficult to watch her coke-induced gushiness for this mutt before I've even had my morning cup of coffee.

"Come on!" she pleads.

"He doesn't want to," I repeat.

"Sure," he barks, scratching his ear.

I want to give him a flea bath, put him in a crate, and take him to the pound. And *insist* they neuter him before adopting him out. Oh hell, if I can improvise anew for Nicolo, I can certainly recite something old for Kim. I choose a poem I wrote when I was sixteen about a young boy who rides on a cloud looking for his lost horse. I decide on this poem because it is the one I will always know by heart—meaning I don't have to join the underwear party by getting out of bed to rustle through my file box.

> *He rode above the plains below*
> *Upon a castle of ice and snow*
> *O'er wheat fields and farms and creekbeds stony*
> *In search of his friend, his cinnamon pony.*

Amity tries to look interested while bending down with a rolled-up hundred dollar bill in her hand to snort a line of coke. She holds her hair back, but it falls into the powder and obliterates the line. "Damn!" she says, pulling back, grabbing the razor to reconvene the little nasal convention into a straight line.

> *They'd joined as friends when he was nine*
> *This Kansas boy and his pony fine*
> *And grew together, from boy and colt*
> *To handsome steed and young adult.*

Kim holds her hair back so she can stick the bill down and suck up the cocaine with her perfectly shaped nose and send herself flying into the atmosphere. After Amity's done, he pulls on her hair to guide her down to his Rorschach crotch. "Kim!" she says, mock horrified. He laughs while she looks at me disgusted and rolls her eyes. "Naughty boy," she sniffs, pinching her nose. He starts chopping more powder with the razor while Amity stares down into the glass of the mirror. "Go on, Harry," she says. "It's beautiful."

She hasn't heard a word, and this poem is more precious to me than others. Why in the fuck am I reciting it to them?

Along the way they learned to fly
O'er fences and gullies, to touch the sky.
No love had he, not yours nor mine,
Could touch the love of his pony fine.

Kim snorts up a huge line of blow, then reels back, eyes wide, and says something that I guess translates to "Killer shit, man!"

Amity giggles. "Don't you love Korean? It sounds so ... Korean!"

He pulls his head back, breathes in, holds out his hands. He's going to sneeze. Amity screams and grabs the little mirror holding all the powder, lifts it away from him, and holds it over her shoulder just in time for him to explode with a sneeze that sounds as if he's getting his head chopped off—four times. When he's through, there's a big green, phlegmy loogie hanging on his lips and chin.

"Nose floss!" Amity screams, holding her hand in front of her face so she doesn't blow the coke off her mirror while laughing.

Kim wipes the loogie off with the back of his hand and reaches for another cigarette.

I'm baring my soul for this guy?

"Go on, babe," Amity urges.

"I just finished," I tell her, lying.

"You did?"

"Sure. Didn't you listen?"

She nods as if she's been hanging on every word. "Yes, it was great!" *Grite!*

Kim blows a cloud of smoke into my face. "Very good." *Velly Goo.*

*   *   *

Four days later, after working a trip to Atlanta, I'm back in Dallas cruising in a black Jaguar sedan. The interior is incredibly fine leather, and the dash is mahogany, and the sound system beats the shit out of anything. There's a pack of cigarettes on the dash. I don't smoke, not usually, but I light one up, and add to my mystique—a twenty-three year old cruising the campus streets around DCU in a black Jag. I've never driven a Jaguar before because my parents were the Cadillac types, and I admit the power and design are intoxicating. I roll the electric window down and rest my arm as I drive. People look at me. On the street, in the next lane, at the stoplight. I pretend I don't see them, but I do. Fuck, I'm acting like Winston. Isn't it enough that I have my own dented-in BMW with a burned hole in the upholstery? What the hell is the matter with me?

Eventually, I park the Jaguar at Caldwell and Family, makers of fine clothing for the prep dogs at DCU, and I reach into my pocket and feel the five one hundred dollar bills. I hear Amity saying, minutes before, "Kim, you can't expect Harry to stay around while we're together at our house. We need our privacy and Harry needs his. I think you better send him shopping." And so Kim peeled off five bills and handed me the keys to his car. Amity walked me to the door and suggested I go to Caldwell and Family and get myself something nice, and when Kim wasn't looking, she pinched me on the ass and stuck her tongue in my ear. I walked to the car with a wet ear and a belief that I deserved the spree as a reward for putting up with Kim.

So here I am, in Caldwell and Family. The salesman is friendly, helpful. He probably saw me drive up in the black Jaguar, because he's not shoveling out the usual Dallas attitude thrown upon young Yankee lads. I'm fitted for a nice pair of khaki slacks and two button-down dress shirts. I see a khaki cotton jacket with red plaid lining, and though it's not quite the season yet, I take it.

I leave the shop and survey the surroundings, noticing a jewelry store. I stop in and decide to buy something for Amity since I'm really shopping with her hard-earned money. But as I wade through the necklaces, rings, and pendants and arrive at the fine writing instruments, I think of Nicolo and how he wants to be a journalist. If I buy him a pen, he can use it to take notes while investigating a story or while interviewing someone. After all, I've already bought Amity a car—sort of. I mean, she drives it as much as I do. So surely I can use the money to buy Nicolo a simple ink pen. I find a shiny sterling silver pen that is beautifully designed in the slightest curvature of the letter S. It fits perfectly in my hand, and it looks very elegant while I'm writing with it, testing it out. I tell the shop owner I'll take it if I can get it engraved right away. He says, "Of course." What shall I say? "With Love, Harry?" Too much, too fast. "With Love, From Your Hero?" Gag. I'm choking on my ego. I think I better go with inscribing his name on it. "Nicolo."

I drive toward the restaurant where Nicolo works. When I get there, I find he isn't working, but Thomas is. Thomas freely gives me Nicolo's address and directions to get there.

I pull up to the duplex and try to breathe my heart into a normal rhythm, but it doesn't work. I give up, grab the little gift-wrapped box, and head up to the door. Ring the bell twice.

A woman appears. His mother? She's about the right age, but she doesn't look anything like Evita. Come to think of it, I've never really seen Evita, just Patty Lupone pretending she's Evita on a poster. "Yes?" she asks from behind the screen door, her accent noticeable in just one word. Her black hair is pulled back from her face.

"Is Nicolo here?"

"He is at school," she says carefully.

I think about his stories, realize she's probably distrusting of strangers. "Can I leave something for him?" Oh, God, she probably thinks it's a bomb. "It's a gift."

"What is your name?"

"Harry. Harry Ford."

Behind the screen I see her smile. "Of course," she says, opening the door. "Come in."

"You know who I am?" I ask, stepping into the apartment.

"Nicolo speaks of you. You please him. He says you are funny."

I want to jump up and down and yelp with delight, "Nicolo told his mother about me! Nicolo told his mother about me!" But I calmly tell her, "Nicolo's cool. He pleases me too."

"And now you have bought him a gift."

"Yes."

"Would you like to drink coffee?"

"Sure."

She motions for me to sit, and as she turns and walks into the kitchen, I realize that her hair isn't pulled into a bun, but is hanging in a ponytail, which makes her seem less severe, less frightened. She's wearing a sleeveless dress that looks very seventies. The apartment is conservatively decorated, and the color scheme is mostly gold and deep blue. The wooden chair I'm sitting in probably came with them, as it distinctly *feels* like a foreign chair. The coffee must have been already brewed, as she returns directly with two cups.

I take the cup and saucer from her. "Thanks." She nods a welcome. I take a sip and only guess that I'm now drinking Argentinean coffee because the brew is megastrong and heavily sugared—stronger than a baby's fart and sweeter than his momma's milk, Amity would say.

"You met Nicolo at the restaurant?" his mother asks.

"Yes. I was there with my . . . friend. Nicolo waited on us."

"Do you like the food?"

I nod. "Oh, yes. It was great. I liked the service too."

"He is a terrible waiter," she laughs. "He comes home with food on his pants. But he is a very attentive, very kind boy. He is a beautiful singer. Someday if you are lucky he will sing for you."

"That would be nice," I say. As she lifts her coffee to her lips,

I notice that her hands—free of jewelry except for her wedding ring—are beautifully aged, full of life. There is elegance in their lines, veins, and creases, and I see that she's comfortable in using her hands, unlike my own mother. I want to make small talk, but I'm not quite sure what to say. Knowing her past has made me cautious. "How long have you lived here?"

"Five years," she answers.

I meant the apartment, not the US. I'm not sure if she understands. "Do you like it?"

"Very much. But I miss Argentina, to be truthful. It is my home. I had to leave. Did Nicolo tell you?"

"Yes," I answer, ashamed. I'm not sure why I feel this way. Maybe it's because I don't have any concept of difficulty or hardship. I certainly don't experience torture at the hands of my government—other than the suffering and agony I go through whenever Nancy Reagan appears on TV in one of her little red Adolfo dresses and insists that her ballet-dancing son is *all man*. "I'm sorry that you lost your husband and your daughter. I really am."

"You are sweet, like Nicolo says. Many people are awkward and unable to speak of it, but it is comforting for us to speak of our loved ones. Would you like to see pictures?"

"Sure."

She sets her coffee down and rises from her chair. "Come," she says, and I follow her across the room to the photographs she's lovingly hung in various, beautiful, handmade frames. "Here is my precious Graciela," she sighs, taking a photo from the wall. "She was the strength of all women."

The girl in the photo is small, but her energy nearly bursts the frame. She is smiling broadly and carrying a bag on her shoulder. The beret on her head makes her look as if she's in some kind of army. The Army of Dynamism maybe. In her hands is a small painting, but I can't tell of what. I smile and tell her, "I can feel her strength."

"I too," she answers, nodding her head. "And this is Gianni, my husband," she says, unhooking another picture from the wall. The man in the photograph is wearing an argyle sweater and dark pants. He's holding a rolled-up newspaper in one hand and a cigar in the other. His face is square, handsome, full of knowledge. His eyes are Nicolo's—almost black. At his feet is a little dog, a mutt of some kind.

"He's very good-looking," I say. "Nicolo looks like him."

"Yes," she smiles.

"Gianni, Graciela, and Nicolo. Italian names?"

"There are many Italians in Argentina," she explains. "Gianni's great-great grandfather came from Italy in 1857 to farm the land in the Santa Fe province. He gained title to his land and integrated his family culture with Argentina's."

"But your husband was a journalist, right? Or was he a farmer?"

"Gianni farm?" she asks, laughing at the question. "Crops need water, not words. His brother declined to farm also. To the salvation of their father, they have a sister, Angelica, who stayed and worked the land. She is handsome, manly, and lives with another woman on the farmland. I love her."

God, how wonderful to hear someone of my parents' generation be gentle and accepting of a gay person. "And where is Gianni's brother?"

She turns, hangs the picture back on the wall. "He is in Argentina," she answers, her back to me. "We owe him our lives. He helped us escape."

When she turns around to face me again, I see that her face is unsettled; there is a disturbance in her eyes. I swallow the last gulp of coffee. "Well, thanks for the coffee," I tell her, not wanting to push it and wondering if Amity has pushed Kim out of the house yet. "I better go. It was a pleasure meeting you."

"Enchanted," she says. "I make sure Nicolo receives the box," she adds, motioning to my present.

We shake hands, and she holds the door open while I depart. I feel her watching me as I walk to the street. There's something about her energy that levels me out, brings me back to my old self, and I feel embarrassed that I'm driving this Jaguar. I even wish I had my VW. I open the door, step in, start the car. Before I drive away, I look up to the duplex to see her standing in the doorway. She waves. I wave back. Drive away.

When I get back with the car, I reach back to grab my shirts, pants, and jacket from the hook behind me. A shirt falls off the hanger, and I try to reach behind me under the seat to grab it without having to crawl into the back. My fingers feel something cold, hard, made of steel. I get a horrible feeling and quickly lift my hand away. I step out, reach behind the driver's seat, lift the shirt off the back floor, and lean down to look under the seat. A gun. A pistol. Sitting there. No case. Just sitting there.

Amity and Kim come bursting out of the house. "Come on, Harry!" Amity says excitedly. "Kim wants to show us the new condo he just bought."

"Let me put this stuff in the house," I tell her. I motion for her to follow me, but she is oblivious to my gesturing, so I dump the clothes on my bed and head back out. I don't really want to be driving with this maniac and his gun, nor do I want Amity to do so. I decide to go along and see the condo to make sure she's safe.

We whiz down the Tollway to north Dallas, and do a walk-through of Kim's new place. It's the quintessential bachelor's pad, with wall-to-wall carpeting, ceiling fans, fireplaces, a wet bar, and sliding closet doors with mirrors on them so you can watch yourself from the bed as your blubbery midlife ass goes up and down while you pork girls half your age. I see Kim as a bad Southern Hugh Hefner in need of Reverend Moon and the Betty Ford Center. I'm getting an icky feeling, and at the same time I'm bored with having to fake my interest in this dump. It's totally empty: no furniture, no paintings, no *Seoul*. He's telling us what pieces are going to go where, but he can't seem to concentrate, and he's getting more and more agitated. I can tell Amity is slightly nervous, but she goes along with him, oohing and ahhing over his proposed design.

We get to the kitchen, and Kim picks up a carton of cigarettes, the only sustenance in the house, and takes out a pack. He tries to open the pack, but can't; his hands are shaking, and he can't get a grip. Out of nowhere he freaks out, screams at the cigarettes, and literally rips the pack of smokes in half, sending cigarettes flying in all directions as if they're scampering for their lives. They rain on the kitchen floor while Amity and I look at each other, then at Kim. Not the least bit fazed, he takes a bent cigarette from the floor, lights up, and tells us about the hanging cobalt light fixture he plans for above our heads.

The drive back to our house is tense. Kim is driving about a hundred miles an hour, passing left, passing right, ripping up the Tollway while Huey Lewis and the News' "I Want a New Drug" blasts on the radio as if it were his mantra. I'm waiting for some little old lady to change lanes in front of him without using her blinker and for him to pull out the gun and blow her away. I'm praying he doesn't get stopped, because it now dawns on me there was probably cocaine in the car the whole time I've been driving it. Like a big fucking baggie of the shit in the glove box. What if *I'd* gotten stopped by a cop? How would a nice white boy from the upper classes of Wichita explain the gun and the drugs and the car and the guy it belongs to and the girl who's entertaining him? I couldn't count on Kim to back me up. I picture the jury throwing the book at me, the armed Yankee homosexual with the stolen car and the stash of drugs. Though I definitely have my prison fantasies, I think I'd choose living freely with Amity or Nicolo over being some lifer's bitch.

Besides, one little felony and I'll never make *Slut of the Month* at the airline.

* * *

"Amity," I tell her after Kim is gone and she's ironing her uniform for work, "we have to talk."

"Yes, babe?" she asks, running the iron back and forth over her slacks with such manic energy it looks as if she's trying to erase her pants rather than iron them.

"Kim has a gun," I tell her.

She makes a *tsk* sound. "I know. He just loves the whole idea of a Wild West. Isn't that cute, him being Korean and all?"

"Aren't you worried?" I ask seriously. "You guys are pretty stoked, doing all that cocaine, driving around with a gun."

She flips her slacks over and attacks the other side. "Does he have it in the car again?" she asks, annoyed.

"Yes," I tell her. "It's under the seat."

"That little monster," she says affectionately. "I've told him to keep that thing in the house."

"Do you think you're safer with it in the house? I don't think he should have a gun at all, Amity. He's too out there. I'm worried about you."

"Harry, you're sweet, but don't you fret. I'll keep him in control. He's a short man, darlin'. Short-man complex. The littler the dick, the bigger the gun. Thank God he's big for an Oriental, or he'd be carrying a shotgun in the trunk!"

"Amity, I really don't think this is funny."

She pulls her pants off the board and slips into them, shuddering at their warmth. "I mean it, Harry. Don't torment yourself over Kim. He's harmless. Gun and all."

CHAPTER
SEVENTEEN

O ver the next few days, Nicolo and I talk on the phone inces-
santly like a couple of teenagers. He likes the pen I bought
him and tells me that he uses it at school to record lecture
notes. School keeps him busy; he's majoring in journalism at DCU,
the university that sits a block from my house. And of course, there
is his job at the restaurant. It seems as if every time he has a break
between classes I'm out flying or running errands or chauffeuring
Amity somewhere. Each time I come home to a message on my
machine saying he's free to drop by, I've missed him. I consider
calling in sick so that I can stay home by the phone, but I need to
work because my mother is now withholding the money again—
hinting that, until Amity and I set a date and appear in Wichita for
the big shebang in our honor, she can't send any money on because
"Well, you know how strongly your father felt about this." Funny,
she's so willing to move on with her own life, but digs up my dead
dad whenever she deals with mine.

So I fly to make money, and on my next trip I'm assigned to
fly with a girl who is an ex-cheerleader with the Dallas Cowboys.
She has a kick-ass body and the face of a model, which is why I
think it's really great that she comes to work with hardly any
makeup on, her blond hair pulled back in an elastic band, and a

stain on her uniform shirt before we've even set foot on the plane. Julie and I immediately hit it off.

Julie is the kind of flight attendant who says, "Here," and drops the peanuts in your lap. She'd serve a scotch and water to a twelve year old. She doesn't pick up trash or cross seat belts. She doesn't even point at the emergency exits during the demonstration—she just kind of nods while pushing back her cuticles. And she makes it clear that if the plane crashes she's the first one down the escape slides. "Follow me, motherfuckers!" she yells, simulating her escape drills, then laughs maniacally. How could I not like her?

On our last flight of the day she asks, "Have you ever done Ecstasy?"

I've heard of the new designer drug, but haven't done it. "No, have you?"

"Sure. Do you want to do some after we get in?"

"You have some with you?" I can't believe it when she nods yes. A stewardess who travels with Ecstasy. "Yeah, I'll try it."

We layover in Las Vegas, land of body odor and perfume. Dry heat and wet armpits. Parched tongues and moist legs. Purple spandex and clammy crotches. Dehydrated grandmothers and junkie waitresses. Cigarette smoke and urinal cakes. Burdened elevators and needless churches. Dusty gutters and damp cocktail napkins.

And airline crews with too much time on their hands.

Julie and I agree to meet by the pool. I walk through the clanging casino and catch the burdened elevator to the fourteenth floor, which is really the thirteenth floor, but since nothing is unlucky in Las Vegas the number thirteen is wiped out and replaced. Even the children in this town skip it—the next birthday after twelve is fourteen.

I change into my swimsuit, grab my sunglasses, and my Walkman, then head for the elevator.

At the pool, Julie is waiting. In her neon pink bikini, she's already given the pool boys a hard-on and quickly procured us two longue chairs, towels, and ice water. As soon as I lie down she slips me the pill. "Here."

"The whole thing?" I ask.

"Sure."

We both have portable Walkmans; all the flight attendants rushed out to get them so that they don't have to listen to pilots sit around hotel pools and talk about how the airline should be run. Julie and I listen to music for a while, bake in the sun, drink water. In about twenty minutes I realize that I've left my body and I'm hovering over the whole hotel. I pull my headphones off, look at her.

"Oh my God, Julie."

She smiles, pulls her headphones off. "Nice, huh?"

"I think I'm going to fly away."

She moans peacefully. "Call me from the Grand Canyon."

I can't hear very well. The public address system is piped out to the pool, and a woman is constantly paging people. "Mr. Rigglepert, Mr. Jerry Rigglepert, Mr. Court, Mr. Lobbler Court, Miss Koob, Miss Mary Koob, please pick up a white paging phone."

I start adding names to the list and saying them aloud. "Miss Peters, Miss Fonda Peters, Miss Quivers, Miss Virginia Quivers, Miss Muff, Miss Candy Muff, please pick up a white paging telephone."

It's not like pot where you laugh uncontrollably. It's like being on acid. And Quaaludes. And just a little bit of coke. So Julie and I start floating this name thing with quiet amusement.

She adds, "Miss Horse, Miss Rhoda Horse, Miss Skank, Miss Lotta Skank, Miss Case, Miss Charity Case, please pick up a white paging telephone."

A pilot shows up. A pretty-boy captain. Young and studly. He's married but dates a stewardess at the airline. So cliche. He automatically has the pool boys line his chair up with ours. He tries to educate us about the economics of substituting DC-10's for the

747's on the Hawaii routes. We're into the name thing. He doesn't get it. We leave.

Burdened elevator. Sunglasses on. Ride with the masses. Are those earrings or chandeliers? Freckles or bits of bacon? Fresh flowers. I smell fresh flowers.

The hallway now, floating forward, not really walking. We separate to change into clothes, then meet again.

Burdened elevator. Clanging casino. Doormen. Sidewalk. One hundred degrees at least. Into the nearest hotel. Two vodka and grapefruits to go. We raise the plastic cups of booze and citrus to our mouths. Float down the sidewalk. The sun melts our heads. The sidewalk liquefies our shoes.

"Caesar's," Julie says. "I love those things on those chicks' heads."

I see them in my mind: casino waitresses who walk around carrying trays of smokes and battery-operated earrings and call out, "Cigars, cigarettes, electric jewelry." Ancient Roman hairpieces, beehives of shit on their heads.

Cocktails evaporate. We beg the plastic cups to replenish, but they deny us. The gates of Caesar slide open. We exit hellfire and glide into Antarctica. We're polar bears craving cocktails. The grapefruit at Caesar's, a different hybrid, taps on our tongues. Surrender the twenties for quarters and sit.

Drop the coin. Pull the handle. Drop the coin. Pull the handle. Bang. You win.

The floor has disappeared. Ceiling too. Everything in between colored slightly outside the lines with thick Magic Markers offering a toxic high. Amplified living. Soundtrack traveling *through* our heads, flossing the cochlea. Tokens falling into trays, the sound of a thousand cymbals in an orchestra. Nerve cells in our skin on alert. A bald guy smoking, smoke washes over my skin, mixes with the cold oxygenated air that shoves me on the shoulder.

Julie has to pee. Myself. At the urinal, no dick. It shrank. To nothing.

We leave the casino, no genitals, but wealthy with quarters. The Pink Flamingo. It's pink. We see flamingos. This must be the place. Grapefruit. Vodka. Cash money.

Stand on one leg. Laugh. Drop the coin. Pull the handle. Drop the coin. Pull the handle.

Again we win. Time to go.

The MGM Grand. The catastrophic fire a few years earlier. The grapefruit and vodka will be excellent because they have to try harder—people were burned.

Drop the coin. Pull the handle. Drop the coin. Pull the handle.

It must be nighttime. Who knows from the inside of a casino? We sit on our stools, our quarters all eaten by the system. "So you're going to be Amity's next husband," Julie says.

I'm drunk and heady, but far below my earlier cruising altitude in the ionosphere. "Sort of."

"I heard she finally had an honest arrangement—that you knew about her past and that you guys were straight with each other." She starts laughing. "Get it?"

I laugh and realize I'm starting to feel my head again. "Straight as I'll ever be," I answer. "Yep, I know about Arlen and how she fucked up the marriage."

"I know it's none of my business, but did she ever go into detail about the money? I mean, the rumor was it was like a half a million or something, and then the next thing we knew, it's like six months later and she's left the cowboy and been taken down by that lawyer, Victor, and she's broke and in the treatment center."

My face is burning. I'm on fire within all this air-conditioning. I chuckle, act as casual as possible. "Cocaine makes you do fucked-up things." Treatment center? Was it that bad? *I didn't get a penny*, she told me. I think that's what she said, but my head's not so clear. "I'm not sure where the money went. She doesn't like to talk about it," I state, groping for the truth.

"I don't blame her. If I lost a Mercedes, a condo, and a Western art collection, I wouldn't want to talk about it either. It's a miracle she still has her job. Actually," she says, "that's not true. Steal a milk carton off the plane and you're fired. Do a bag of blow before you fly, and as long as you turn yourself in, they pity your ass and pay for your rehab. Then they give you one of those brownnoser awards at the annual jack-off ceremony. The system's fucked."

What is she saying? How much is true? I need to stop flying and land somewhere, but it will be a couple more hours before I can lower my gear and slow down enough to think.

"It's a good thing she found you," Julie continues. "First of all, because you're sweet. And I'll bet you can keep her off the coke and on the straight and narrow. She's so much fun. Everybody loves her, but from a distance because she's always on the edge, and to be honest, she's running out of edges—and domiciles. She transferred to New York after the last rehab thing, but then I heard she was based in Chicago for a while too. So when she came back to Dallas, everybody figured she'd burned through most of the route system. I guess she hoped she might have a few friends left here, but Jacqueline Deen is the only one who really seems to be there for her—which is totally incredible since Jacqueline was burned by Amity almost worse than anybody. And now that it's turned out like this, you and her, everybody is just rolling their eyes. It's amazing how she makes things happen. She said, after Arlen, that when she married again, it would be for permanent financial security and that she wouldn't fuck it up next time. And there she was, last week, at some party at a pilot's house, telling everyone you're inheriting land worth eighteen million and stocks worth twenty or whatever it was and oil wells worth another ten million. I'll say this for her—she always seems to land on her feet—just before she lands on her ass. A word of warning."

"Right." I smile. I calmly hold the slot machine's handle for support, stare at the last draw: two jokers and a lemon. Are the gods laughing at me? Does Amity have a secret past? Has she only been interested in *permanent financial security* all along? Never, *never* have I given her numbers. And though I haven't looked at the will since I tucked it away with my important papers, Julie is close to being right on. Which means Amity is right on. How does she know? God, I'd gladly give her half of everything—as long as she loves me and doesn't *expect* it. I'm not an instrument. I don't want to be played. "She and I are in this together," I tell Julie as much as I tell myself. "We're on the level with each other." No matter what I say, I can't fool myself the way I'm fooling Julie.

"You're pretty cool, Harry," Julie tells me. "Amity may have finally found the one person who can help her put it all together." She finishes her drink, turns to set it down, and falls off her stool.

I jump down to help her. "Julie!"

She's laughing so hard I can't scrape her off the carpet. "I guess I've reached my limit," she says into the carpet fibers.

"Me too," I answer. "Me too."

As I work the next day, I try to put the pieces together in my head. Randy said the lawsuit with the college professor yielded her a hundred thousand dollars. And Julie said she took away half a million dollars from the marriage to Arlen. I try to comfort myself by remembering that Amity told me all about these relationships, sparing no details. But the truth is, she told me about the professor and Arlen *after* I confronted her about them. And she falsely claimed that Arlen left her penniless. The financial numbers of my inheritance keep floating through my head. Amity must have gone through my private things while I was out flying and found my father's will. Oh God, I can't stomach the thought that she may be taking me for a ride, that perhaps she's interested in my money more than she is me. I fall into the lavatory and throw up.

We lay over that afternoon in Los Angeles. At the pool, Julie, myself, the other flight attendant, and the captain, a halfway cool guy from Cuba, soak in the sun, sipping mimosas. My body is slack, slightly wrecked from last night's excess, and the champagne and orange juice take the edge off. We start chatting with a group of seven hard-core Eastern Airlines flight attendants. They order up more cheap champagne and orange juice. And soon we're all soaked in mimosas as well as the sun.

I'm beginning to find out why Eastern's crews are legendary radicals within the industry. These girls are rough. I sure as hell wouldn't want to run into one in a dark aircraft aisle. At the moment, they're trashing a bunch of Delta flight attendants across the pool, who shared the van ride from the airport to the hotel. After educating us about "those uppity bitches from Delta," who never acknowledged the Eastern attendants during the ride, the Eastern women are fully worked up. They take their revenge.

"Hey, honey!" a hard Eastern stew with blond hair and black roots yells to a lily white Delta gal. "You're going to blind us all!"

"Yeah," her friend joins in, "you better lie *under* your towel!"

The Delta belle squirms in her chaise, flips a page in her magazine, pretends not to hear.

"Better yet, Snow White," another Eastern gal yells, "why don't you go choke on a poison apple!"

The Delta gal remains silent, but makes a sarcastic face, as if to say, *very funny.*

The toughest Eastern stew of all, the one with the precancerous tan, a slight gut, and a cigarette in her hand yells, "What's the matter, honey? Captain got your tongue?"

"No way," the black-rooted blond adds. "Those bitches are virgins, even the married ones."

The third one joins back in. "The only warm pussy in her house is sitting on top of the refrigerator!"

I feel as if I'm watching some women's prison B-flick from the 1950's.

The Delta gal leans over to her two flying partners and quietly whispers. Then the three of them giggle and look superior.

The cancer-tan stewardess yells, "Cunts!"

It's like the bomb dropped on Hiroshima. The Southern belles are completely annihilated, destroyed. They grab the scatterings of their magazines and diet Cokes and leave the pool.

The Eastern stews whistle and catcall them as they leave. Then they start telling jokes. They tell every tasteless joke of the week, and then one mentions she knows a great fudge-packer joke.

I've never heard the term before, but of course I know *fudge packer* means gay. Now what do I do? I'm supposed to be this burgeoning heterosexual sitting here with people from my airline, where everyone knows I'm engaged to Amity because she announced it into a microphone. Yes, I was flattered that night of the award ceremony, and I liked being accepted by *the guys* for all of five minutes, but now I'm wondering if the flattery from Amity is bullshit—just like these homophobic faggot jokes. "Careful," I say, "you're sitting with a fudge packer."

The Eastern girls look at me with interest. They don't know whether to respect me or rip me a new faggot asshole.

"You're gay?" the captain says. "I thought you were engaged to Amity Stone?"

"Yes," I say confidently, "I am."

"Engaged or gay?" the precancerous gal asks, too interested for my comfort.

"Both," I answer matter-of-factly. "My fiancée and I love each other and understand each other. We have no secrets."

Julie looks at me, sips her mimosa, gives me the thumbs up.

"It's a modern fucking world," the melanoma model blurts.

The other Eastern gals decide to respect me. "I guess I won't tell my joke then," the original perpetrator says.

But the party soon breaks up. I've brought too much honesty to the table. The Eastern gals call it a day. They grab their stuff, give us their awkward, seldom used polite respects, and leave.

Why is my truth the one that breaks up the party? If I'm a liar and pretend I'm one of them and let them make fun of people like me, everything will be jolly. But I know I'll die a little inside if I do. I hate that other people, even my mother and father, would rather I live a straight life, so they can be more comfortable. It's asking too much. And now look where it's gotten me. There's a chance I'm engaged to someone I don't even know.

Back in Dallas, my phone is ringing as I walk through the door. I'm exhausted, my uniform stinks of cigarette smoke, it's late evening, and I still haven't eaten dinner. But I have a feeling it may be Nicolo, so I pick up the receiver and say hello. It's Amity. She's whispering and sounds desperate.

"Harry, it's your girl. Please pick up! Harry, your girl needs you!"

Amity tells me to get into my car and come get her at Kim's. She's frantic. I say I'll be right there. She can't remember the exact street or even the house number. "I don't know! I don't know! It's something circle or court! Just come get me!" She's almost crying now. Is this part of some scheme? Is she polishing my ego by making me feel like the white knight who rescues his damsel in distress? Whatever the case, I'd never forgive myself if she was truly in trouble and I wasn't there to help her. I tell her I'll come right away.

In my dented BMW, I jettison onto the Tollway and try to flash back to when I went to the condo with Kim and Amity. Intuition tells me when to exit. Then a right. And another right. Somehow I *do* find it, and as I pull up, Amity comes running out, her purse falling off her shoulder. Before I can even get out, she rushes around and jumps into the passenger seat.

"Go! Just go!"

I take off. "Amity, what the hell is going on?"

She's not crying, and she doesn't look as if she's been hit or anything, but her blouse is torn and she's shaking like an epileptic. "He's lost it, Harry. He's been on a cocaine binge for *days*." *Dies*. "I don't think he's had anything to eat. It was becoming a bad situation, Harry. He's threatening to kill his wife's lawyer. He keeps waving that gun around."

"Jesus Christ, Amity," I gasp. "Is it loaded?"

"Hell, yes. He shot out part of the chandelier. That's why we've got to get out of here before the police come."

"How long has this been going on?"

"Just a couple days, babe." She's grinding her teeth. She pulls the sun visor down and inspects herself in the vanity mirror, but it's dark in the car, and even in the lighted mirror she obviously doesn't see the coke on the side of her nose and upper lip.

I reach over and wipe it off. "A couple days? Shit, you should have gotten the hell out of there before now, Amity."

"I'm just so sorry, babe. Kim was going to be our opportunity to so many things."

I can't believe what I'm hearing. She's apologizing for losing our meal ticket—the one with the coke problem and the gun. The one who ought to be locked in a cage at the animal shelter with a sign that says, KOREAN PUSS HOUND. And she's insinuating that my inheritance wouldn't be enough. She'll have access to millions and it still won't be enough? Is everything Julie said true? Now isn't the time to get into it. She's too strung out. And I'm not sure how I want to approach it—I have no intention of playing my cards until I'm completely aware of the hand I'm holding. "Don't worry about it, Amity," I say. "We have jobs. We can pay the rent. Let's just go home."

On the way I stop for moo goo gai pan, hoping some food might straighten her up. Amity waits in the car while I run into the restaurant and get the food. When I return to the car, she's acting as if it's a different day. She's totally calm. The dome light is on, and she's repairing a chipped nail with her little bottle of nail glue. "Ready, babe?" she asks in an almost breezy tone.

I look at her sideways. She's acting as if we're out for a pleasure drive. I don't say anything. Now I'm freaked a little. Her mood swing is so faultless. We get home, and she puts on a Sade album and fires up a joint. After taking a toke, she offers it to me. I pass. She sings along with the ever mellow Sade.

"Amity, we've got to make some changes," I tell her, standing in the kitchen.

She stops singing, looks attentive. "Yes, babe?"

As I empty the Chinese food on plates, I look at the picture of the two of us having dinner at the country club in Kansas. It's stuck to the refrigerator by a magnet. Amity put it there after my mom sent it in the mail with a letter to us both. My mother no longer writes just to me, but to Amity and me. It's something she's never done with any of my boyfriends. "There's too much going on. We've got to simplify things here," I tell her. I'm rational, collected. "There're the waiters, and you've got some new mystery guy calling. I've been hearing him on the machine. And there's me. And there's Kim. I think we need to figure some of this out."

She tilts her head and softens, relaxes. "Harry, you just tell me what you want me to do, and I'll do it."

Too easy, much too easy. Why haven't I noticed this before? How fucking stupid can I be? It's all I can do to keep my mouth shut about what Julie said. Still, something tells me to play it cool until I get some backup on the whole thing, truly understand where she's coming from. "You know, Amity, you say it's just you and me. Well, it seems like there's an awful lot of other people involved."

"Babe, if you just want it to be you and me, then it's you and me."

I need to buy myself some time, steer Amity away from the cocaine and get her into a mental state that's workable. What I need is to get the gun-toting Korean out of the picture. ''Why don't you stick to me and Thomas for the moment, huh? Do you really need this Kim guy?''

''Of course not, Harry. Anything you say.''

Still too easy. It gives me a terrible feeling. ''Hand me that fortune cookie,'' I prod.

She picks it up, breaks it open herself, and reads, '' 'You will be happily married and wealthy beyond your wildest dreams!' ''

She hands me the crumbs.

That night, I tell her I have a bad headache and I think I'll sleep alone in my own room. When I'm sure she's asleep, I slowly leave my bed and go into my closet, where my little portable file box is. I open it and sift through until I find the will—the will that is washed in the slight scent of Amity's perfume. A dead giveaway. She's been here, all right. And Julie's dictation of the financial figures are almost dead on.

I'm a fool. A total idiot. I'm so stupid I can't even look at the current condition of my BMW and see that the ride I'm being taken for is radically off road. And Amity has been in the driver's seat from the beginning. I'm enraged that she's been playing me for a fool. My ego is bruised and I'm angry she thinks I'm stupid enough to stay in the car while she heads at 120 mph for a sharp curve on which my door will open and she'll push me out. I should go into her room right now and confront her about everything. But I'm not. It's a game, now, and I'm a player.

Is it the money? Is the money worth it? Is giving Winston the big *fuck you* worth the price of the ticket? Or is it my mother I'm trying to appease? Maybe, on some subterranean gut level, I want her acceptance. No matter how much sense of self my grandmother tried to instill in me as a kid, maybe I've never cut the cord with Mom. Even though I think it's a load of bullshit, maybe those pop psychologists are right about gay men and their too close connections with their mothers. Maybe I'm actually ruining my life for her.

One thing's for sure—the person I'm most angry with is my father. And I know why: For the first time in my life I'm acting *exactly* like him. I'm doing precisely what he would do in my shoes: retreat to a corner, keep recent enlightenment confidential, assess every angle of every player on the game board. Just as my father did (even at the end, in the garage with the motor running), I'll make a studied move to manipulate the desired outcome.

Great. I'm becoming my father's own son. What's next? Will I vote for Ronald Reagan and get Amity pregnant so that we can spawn a whole new generation of well-bred scammers dressed in khakis and Bass Weejuns? Christ, how am I going to get out of this?

CHAPTER EIGHTEEN

Nicolo and I are sitting under the shade of a tree, across from the library on campus. I brewed fresh coffee at home and poured it into a Thermos with ice, bought apple turnovers at the bakery, and met him at school on a break. It's a little ritual we started a couple of weeks ago: iced coffee and turnovers while sharing bits of our histories. Never in my life have I gone so slowly with a guy, but Nicolo is different from anyone. He's solid and honest. Kind and funny. Muscular and gentle. It's almost as if we're brothers, which sometimes worries me that we won't progress to lovers. I guess we're both too modest or inhibited by the world to kiss each other on campus. But last week he showed up at the house as I was leaving to go to work and before I drove away he leaned into my car and kissed me in a way brothers don't. It was the best damn kiss I've ever had from a man.

"Thomas says Amity is coked up all the time," Nicolo tells me.

"She's a party girl," I answer nebulously, as if her actions don't affect me.

He shakes his head. "I can tell you've been bothered by something lately, and I know it's her. She's out of control, Harry."

"How do you know?" I ask. I'm open to other interpretations.

"She is. You better watch out, amigo. Roommates like that always end up causing you difficulty."

I slug a shot of iced coffee, look him in the eye. "Why don't you like her? You're not very nice to her. To be honest, Nicolo, it's the one thing about you that has bothered me."

"Because she's not for real," he tells me evenly. The Latin macho stuff rises to the surface. "If you are going to become my boyfriend, I don't want you hanging around with people who are trouble."

I still can't accept that this whole thing with Amity has been a game. I *know* that somewhere inside her, regardless of her manipulating and scheming, she does love me. She can't help herself. Just like my father. Just like me. "If I become your boyfriend, you still won't *own* me. I'll hang around with whomever I want, and I'll always love Amity, whether you like it or not," I spout off, mostly in response to his macho posturing. At the same time, the scale has tipped so far that everything's falling away, and quite frankly I'm quite ready to plot my escape from Amity.

He laughs and slugs me on the shoulder. "That's what I like about you, Harry. That's the fire I saw in you the night we met when you came to my rescue at the restaurant. But have you ever thought that I may want to protect you like you protected me?"

Do I need protection from Amity? I could use someone else's opinion. Is this the time? Should I tell him about the engagement? Her scent on the will? Can Nicolo help me get out of this intact, emotionally and financially? I'd like to share my doubts, but if I do, then I'll have to confess that Amity and I are engaged, and there's a voice inside me warning against it. God, I'm a real shit. Where's my integrity? Here I am, ready to pass judgment on Amity, and I'm deceiving just about everyone I know. The truth is, I'm falling in love with Nicolo and I'm not able to tell her about it. Nor am I being truthful with Nicolo—that I'm engaged to be married to someone else while dreaming up a whole life spent with him.

"I appreciate your chivalry," I tell Nicolo, "but I don't need protection from Amity."

He raises his arms in surrender. "You are free to love Amity or anyone else." Then he lies back on his elbows, stretches his legs out, and crosses them. "Including me."

For someone who is moving so slowly with me, I'm shocked that he says it—and profoundly exhilarated. "Your permission is noted," I tell him, softening. "So when does summer school end?" I ask. It's now late July.

"Middle of August," he answers. "Then one more semester, and I'm a journalist," he states proudly, biting into his turnover.

"Just like your father," I say.

"That's right." His head rises more proudly still while he chews.

"Where do you want to go to work?" I ask.

"Argentina," he answers before swallowing. No hesitation.

If he goes to Argentina, I'll lose him. I instantly have a new motivation to get my share of the Ford windfall: to hold on to Nicolo. I know from family friends that American dollars can buy a person (or a couple) residency of any country. I could go with him. "Why go back?"

"The political climate is changing. I think I can return to make a difference."

"What if they disappeared you? You're Gianni Feragamo's son. Surely they'll have it out for you."

"My friends say it is different. The disappearances are ending. The country is opening up again. Raul Alfonsin, a lawyer who believes in democracy, is our new president. Argentina will be a democratic country. Of course, I can hear my father's voice. 'For how long?' he would say. 'Democracy does not last in Argentina,' he would say."

"So why go?"

"I do not want my father's and sister's deaths to be for nothing. If Argentina is to change, it must be documented and written about.

My English is good now. I can reach more people through both languages. But," he laughs sadly, "I may never make it back. I don't even know how I'm going to pay off all these loans I owe to the university."

"You're schooling yourself on loans?" I ask, sipping the iced coffee, letting it take a dent out of the humid Texas day.

"It took all of our money to come to America. I'll owe close to fifty thousand dollars for school. That's a lot of tips for an awkward waiter," he laughs, seemingly unworried.

Shit. Now I'm really determined to get the money. It's a drop in the bucket for me if my ship comes in. I'll finish paying off my student loans *and* his. Help his mother financially if she needs it. Live six months out of the year in Argentina with him, as long as he'll live six months of the year with me (and Amity?) in some place like California. I'm falling in love with this beautiful man, fully clothed. As I plot our future, a student in Wrangler jeans and a cowboy hat walks by, his boots clomping on the sidewalk. Nicolo follows him with his eyes. "Aha," I say. "You're into cowboys."

"Sí, senor. I used to fantasize about the gauchos," he growls sexily. "They are such an image. What is the word?"

"Icon?"

"Yes. Icon. I loved them as a boy. Only my aunt, Angelica, understood the depth of my attraction. When I was thirteen she sent me a poster of three gauchos mounted on their horses on the pampas. I still have that poster today."

"Well," I announce, "we have something in common again. When I was a boy, I loved horses. My parents bought me a pony when I was nine years old. He was large for a pony, about fourteen-and-a-half hands, more like a small horse. I boarded him at a stable a few miles outside the city. I loved him more than anything or anyone. I'd saddle him up and ride the dirt roads of the countryside. I'd race the wheat, and sometimes I'd win."

"What was his name?"

"Cinnamon."

"So you are a gaucho, and Cinnamon is your range horse?"

"Not anymore," I answer wistfully.

"Your horse is retired?" he asks.

"Yes," I answer simply, not wanting to dive into details.

"But you can still sit a horse, my friend, no? It's like riding a bicycle. Once you know how, you can always ride."

"True. How do you know?"

"I ride too. Aunt Angelica gave to me a horse of my own. He waits in Argentina."

"Maybe someday we'll ride together," I offer, aching for the opportunity.

Nicolo answers, "Perhaps in Argentina."

"Perhaps."

"Harry! Where have you been?" Amity shouts.

After my afternoon ritual with Nicolo, I've decided to confront her about the money involved in her last failed relationships. And with the fact that I've heard she's been bragging about my inheritance, in numerical detail. I won't tell her I smelled her perfume on the will—I'll wait to see if she confesses. "I was with Nicolo," I answer.

"Oh," she says, forcibly enthusiastic. "Great!" *Grite!* She adopts a strained expression whenever I mention Nicolo, and I realize she finds him a threat. I've got to be careful how I approach this. "Amity, I want to talk to you about something . . . ."

"Not now, babe," she says excitedly. "We've got to get Jackie to the airport. They're trying to fire her!"

"What are you talking about?"

"We'll explain on the way!" she says, jumping up and down. "Fire up the Beamer!"

She rushes me out the door, I start the car, and we drive three houses down to pick up Jacqueline, who comes flying out the door wearing a ridiculously large hat and carrying a cigarette in hand.

"I hope it's OK to smoke in your car, Amity," she pleads, trying to get her hat inside the car, "because I'm just really freaked out. I'm just freaked out because they're trying to fire me, and I really need to smoke when I'm freaked out."

"OK, girl!" Amity yells. "We get it. You're freaked out. Put the damn cigarette in your mouth!"

Amity explains that, while she and Jacqueline were flying together a couple of weeks ago, a muscular guy from Austin with gorgeous long hair came on strong to Amity, but she convinced him that her friend, Jacqueline, was the girl he wanted—because, Amity explains, I had asked her to keep her dalliances to a minimum, and she'd decided that any guy who comes on to her, she'd pass on to Jackie, and haven't I noticed what an effort she's making? Amity explains that after speaking on the phone, Jacqueline and the guy arrange a date, which happens to be on a day when Jacqueline's scheduled to work. Since lunch with a muscular guy with gorgeous long hair is preferable to passing out bags of dry-roasted peanuts to the irritable traveling public, Jackie decides to call in sick and go to Austin. And given that she's flying for free on a "pass," she feels the need to disguise herself since she's officially supposed to be sick. She goes to the airport in her "date clothes," but upon her head she wears a humongous, wide-brimmed black hat—the hat she's wearing now. It's similar to the style of hats Joan Collins wears on *Dynasty*, though it's even more outlandish than anything Alexis Carrington Colby would wear. While she walks through the terminal, I picture the hat knocking people over, downing pay phones, clearing shelves in gift shops.

Jacqueline jumps into the conversation to add that, in tandem with the hat, she wore a huge pair of dark glasses that were so dark she accidentally walked into the TV monitor near the gate podium, as well as the podium itself. At check-in, when the agent asked her to say her name, she whispered it. And when the agent asked her to repeat it, she merely whispered it again, she said, so that if any

other airline personnel were boarding the flight they couldn't iden-
tify her.

Apparently, after Jacqueline secured her boarding pass, the ticket
agent called down to the main offices and told them an off-duty
flight attendant, with an awning on her head and goggles on her
face, was acting awfully peculiar while about to board a flight.
Jacqueline was allowed to fly to Austin, but when her supervisor
checked it out, her illegal travel was exposed, and subsequently
she's been summoned to the airport to be fired.

So now she's in Amity's car, smoking like a wet log in a campfire,
knocking her hat against the roof, waving her cigarette like a baton.
"What am I going to do? Gila is going to fire me!"

Gila is the meanest of all the supervisors. When a flight attendant
class graduates, they assign the marginals and potential troublemak-
ers to Gila. She's known as the Gila Monster. Her fingernails are
sharp as knives and always painted bloodred. Her makeup is so
perfect her face looks like a mask—as if she's a player in the
Stewardess Kabuki Theater. Likewise, her hair is so immaculate
and oversprayed, it's a crash helmet. She used to work for another
airline, and she was actually a stewardess on a flight that crashed
into a residential area in Florida during thunderstorms. She was the
only flight attendant who survived, and the rumor is she got up and
walked away because of that helmet of hair.

"She's going to fire me, man!" Jackie whines.

Like the time the cop stopped Amity and me in the brand-new
Beamer, Amity slams into save-your-ass mode. "Girl, listen to me
good."

Jacqueline sucks the life out of the cigarette and thrashes in the
backseat.

"Jackie! I mean it," Amity says. "Pour some water on the fire
and listen!"

Jacqueline snubs out her cigarette. I watch the master go to
work.

Amity swivels in her seat, looks Jackie square in the eye. "This is what you do. First of all, take that damn hat off!"

Jacqueline hoists the hat off her head and wrestles it into the seat beside her.

"You walk into that office, no hat, no glasses, just *tears*," Amity coaches. "You sit down with that old Gila Monster, and you tell her you had to fly to Austin to get an *abortion!* You turn on those water works, girl. Get those tears going real good, and tell her your boyfriend got you pregnant, and left you high and dry!" *Haw and draw!* "You tell her you had *no one* to turn to and that you couldn't possibly have the abortion here in Dallas because you had to protect your anon—aninom—shit. Harry, say it."

"Anonymity."

"Right!" *Rot!* She turns to me. "I hate that word. I shouldn't use it." Back to Jacqueline. "You got it, girl?"

Jacqueline thinks about it for a second, then heartily agrees. "Yeah, that's it. That's what I'll say. I had an abortion. An abortion. Yeah, I had an abortion, man. I just had to take care of it, you know. Get an abortion."

We pull into the employee lot at the airport and wait while she goes in for her meeting with the Gila Monster. Amity puts Culture Club's cassette into the player, and I roll down the windows. "OK, Harry. What is it that you wanted to talk about?"

It's all adding up. Her out-of-control behavior, the coke, the professor, the marriage, Julie's claims, Nicolo's suspicions, and now this: this bogus story she's woven with master skill for Jacqueline from thin air. "Work up tears," she told her. "You had to have an abortion!" she told her. She's too quick. The duplicity comes too naturally for her.

"Well?" Amity asks. "Do you need to talk, Harry?"

My dad channels into me again. "Not now." Why tip my hand? Information is power. *Never exit the building until your car is waiting out front*, my father would say. I have to come up with a plan before I exit this charade. I turn on the radio, and the announcer's voice says, "Today, Soviet cosmonaut Svetlana Savitskaya became the first woman to walk in space."

"Jacqueline's been doing that for years," Amity says, reclining her seat for a power nap.

"Gila bought it, man!" Jacqueline says, returning to the car. "The whole thing. I took your advice, Amity, and I really cried a lot. At first, I didn't say anything at all, I just cried. Then I told her that I needed to tell the truth, that I had an abortion. She was *really* concerned. I can tell she's had an abortion herself, 'cuz she kept telling me I could have come to her, 'cuz, you know, she would have helped me, and that an abortion is something no woman should have to go through alone."

"Amen, girl," Amity says, as if it really happened. "It's just too scary for you to be alone."

Jacqueline agrees. "Right. You've got to have support."

"Is that all?"

"She offered to help me pay for it," Jacqueline said, taking out a cigarette. "She said she'd write me a check."

"Girl! Did you take it?"

I notice the flash of excitement in Amity's eyes. She *wants* Jacqueline to have taken the money.

"No," Jackie says, lighting her cigarette, " 'cuz I just would have had to pay her back, and I didn't want to have to do that."

"You wouldn't have had to pay her back, Jackie," Amity says slyly. "What's she going to do? Bug you for the money? 'Hey, Jacqueline. Where's my abortion loan?' No way. She'd have let it slide."

"I don't want her money," Jackie answers.

Amity finishes with conviction. "Well that Gila Monster has been mean enough to a lot of people, and it's time she helped somebody, Jackie. You deserve her concern *and* her money after all you've been through."

This is getting freaky. Like, where does the truth lie? So to speak. If I had any prior doubts about Julie's stories of the real Amity, I don't now. I can see the thrill Amity's getting from playing this game. It's Jacqueline's life that is affected, but Amity loves moving her and Gila into position, like pawns on a chessboard, until she can manufacture the best outcome.

"I'm just so glad it's all over," Amity finishes.

I can't tell if she means the conflict or the mythical abortion.

"You still have your job, and this calls for a celebration," I tell Jackie. "Let's go to Sfuzis and drink bellinis."

"Great idea, Harry!" Amity cheers. And before we're out of the airport drive, she pulls a little vial of cocaine from her purse and starts scooping tiny spoonfuls for everyone. I decline.

I'm declining, *big Tom*.

That evening, Amity has a date with Thomas, who has the night off from the restaurant. When he comes over, he mentions that, from the sound of it, Nicolo finds me to be serious boyfriend material. I'm so ecstatic to hear this news from someone he calls a friend that I want to dance on the ceiling. But I have to reel it in, stay cautious, as I don't want Amity to think I'm too far in until I figure out the best direction for her and me. I smile. Tell Thomas, "We'll see." But I can't quash the smile on my face, the smile that says it all.

"I'm so happy for the two of them," Amity chimes in as sweet as icing on the wedding cake. I'm paranoid around her these days. I know her happiness about Nicolo and me is an act. "Aren't you?" she asks Thomas, grinding her teeth from the coke she stuck up her nose when he rang the bell. "Aren't you happy for Harry and Nicolo?"

"Yes," Thomas answers. "Nicolo is my friend. I'm glad he has found someone."

"I'm glad you've found someone too," Amity purrs, locking

her arm in Thomas's. "How do you like my dress, Thomas? As Karl Lagerfeld said himself, 'Shaped to be Raped.' "

Thomas laughs, grabs her by the waist, and pulls her to him.

"We better go, darlin'," she cautions. "Our reservation is for eight o'clock. You know what happens when you're late for dinner in Texas—some hungry cowboy rides in and eats your meat!"

If only Nicolo would. Shit, I'm getting so pent up from no sex, I'm about to pop. I call him at work.

"I can't go out, Harry. I'm working late," he tells me. "But I have a surprise for us tomorrow. No coffee and turnover. No class. We're skipping out for the day, OK?"

Yes, yes, yes. Finally. "OK."

"Wear boots. *Mañana?*" he asks, his accent giving me a woody.

"Mañana," I answer.

A few minutes later, a guy comes to the door. Early thirties. Dressed in high-water slacks, a polo shirt, penny loafers, no socks, a belt that doesn't match, and his sparse hair in one of those comb overs on his mostly bald scalp. Gotta be a pilot.

"Is Amity Stone here?" he asks.

"No. She's out," I answer.

"Out? We're supposed to be having a date tonight."

Yep, a pilot. Must be a new one. First officer. Doesn't know about me. Definitely doesn't know about Amity. "Sorry, pal. You missed her. What's your name?"

"Chip."

"I'll tell her you were here, Chippy."

I close the door, go into the hall on my way to my room when I notice the light on her phone machine blink on and hear the cassette tape engage. I can't resist. I turn up the volume just in time to hear Kim demanding to know where she is and why she broke their lunch date this afternoon.

Thomas. Chip. Kim. Boy, is she fucking up. Her cocaine habit is starting to wreak havoc with her scheduling abilities. This is crazy. I'm being a fickle bastard. A couple of months ago I thought I was in love with her. I've got to talk to her, confront her. Surely we can work this out. I care for her and I don't want to see her self-destruct. Maybe I can help her change. Get off drugs. Stop lying. But do I have to marry her in order to help her? Do I have to marry her in order to help *myself*?

Maybe it's just not worth it. Maybe I need to cut my losses, move on, live a life of poverty and freedom with Nicolo. I know I'd be happy. Hell, I've been living like a poor kid ever since I was seventeen. Gay too. I've been mostly content. I never cared about money or what people thought of me before. Why care now?

Or is there an outside solution? The clock is ticking—I only have a month and a half until the big birthday deadline. Is there some girl out there who would help me out without cleaning me out?

CHAPTER NINETEEN

Nicolo is driving me into the country in his old Ford pickup truck. Instead of driving east from the city, we're driving west, to where there is nothing but the legend of "West Texas." It's an August morning, hot as Texas can be, and since the truck has no air-conditioning, we have the windows rolled down all the way to let the wind fly in as we soar past parched mesquite trees, rusty fences, huge wheels of hay, and an occasional naked mobile home. Our hair is whipping around, our eyes are dry, and we're having to yell to understand each other, but it's plain we're both as happy as two guys can be. Nicolo has brought a *bota* filled with sangria wine, and when he opens his mouth wide, like a baby bird, I shoot the citrus wine into his throat until he laughs and closes his mouth and the wine dribbles down his chin. I lick the remains from his chin, his short whiskers puncturing my tongue, and take a drink of my own from the bag.

"General Videla was indicted last week. They're detaining him for his part in all the disappearances," Nicolo tells me.

"Who's that?" I ask as we pass a dead armadillo on the road.

"Our former president in Argentina. Evil man. He's going to be on trial. Things are getting better in my homeland."

"I'm glad," I tell him. I'm also worried that he's going to leave the U.S. and return to his native country.

We drive for over an hour, passing a new corrugated barn standing next to an old splintered dead one, a satellite dish larger than the moon, a dry creek yearning for rain, and he still hasn't told me where we're going. Finally, following directions on a piece of paper he's taped to the dash, he pulls the truck off the highway and heads down a two-lane road that runs through a little town, then out into the countryside. He turns through a gate, where a Texas flag is flying, the entrance to a ranch. We drive down a dirt road for half a mile until we see the ranch house. He slows down, swings around the house, and stops the truck at an old green barn behind it. *"Estamos aqui, hombre,"* he says, turning off the ignition.

An old man comes out of the barn wearing dirty overalls and a dirtier T-shirt. There's shit on his work boots. As he approaches the pickup, he drawls, "One of you guys Nick?"

"That's me," Nicolo answers, reaching back behind the seat. He exits the cab with two cowboy hats in his hand, the *bota* around his neck.

"They're all saddled up, ready to go," the man says, itching an eyebrow. "Remember, I wanna see your ability 'fore you take 'em out on the land."

"No problem," Nicolo says. We follow the guy into the barn and Nicolo whispers, "Now do you understand why I say to wear your cowboy boots?"

There's a palomino and a bay waiting, bridled and saddled, both good-looking horses with fine conformation. Nicolo lets me choose, and naturally I pick the bay because he reminds me of Cinnamon. We walk them out into the sun, put on our hats, and let the old man hold them while we mount up. He directs us into the small arena next to the barn and puts us through a few paces. Walk, trot, canter. Turn them around. Do it all the other direction. As the man watches me ride, I feel as if I'm in a horse show, like when I was a little kid, and I remember my father as a good guy who stood on the side of the arena and gave me an approving nod of his head when I sat up correctly in my saddle and cantered on the correct lead. I look over at Nicolo, who has spaced himself across the ring, and I'm more in love than I ever could be watching my own handsome gaucho sit the palomino with ease and confidence.

"OK," the man yells. "Guess you were tellin' the truth. You both sat a horse 'fore. Take 'em on out. Just don't cross any boundary lines. Marked by fences all around, 'cept the west boundary—that's marked by the creek." He pronounces it *crick*, like a Kansan. "Don't taunt the cattle, and be back 'fore noon or thereabouts, 'cuz we got work to do with 'em later."

Nicolo tips his hat, I do the same, and off we ride, through the gate, into the pasture land. *Los gauchos son libres.*

We're dressed alike. Jeans, white T-shirts, and boots. Hats on our heads. Nicolo's muscles are bigger than mine, but I've been working on my body, and the results are coming in. I'm not at all the guy I was when the year started. I'm feeling, dare I say it, confident. Happy. Not without edges, but smoother than before.

We walk our horses steadily, through the prairie grass, toward what will be the sunset ten hours from now. The hot wind blows like a furnace, and a gust causes us to quickly reach for our hats and hold them on. "Are these your sombreros?" I ask.

"My brother's. I told him what I was doing and he dug them out of his trunk. We wore them as teenagers when we visited *Tia* Angelica and rode her horses."

"You don't speak much of your brother," I point out.

"I don't have to. He is my kindred spirit. We seldom need words between us, so I think that is why I don't speak of him so much. He's very special to me. What about you? You also never talk of your brother."

"My brother and I don't talk much either," I say, stroking my horse's mane. "But not because we're kindred spirits. We're more like Elizabeth and Mary."

"Who?"

"A couple of bitchy English queens. Liz was vicious and ugly— that's Winston."

He wrinkles his brow. "That's disturbing."

"Sorry. I wish I could tell you we're great pals, but we're not. If I could get the American government to *disappear* Winston, I would."

Nicolo stops his horse. His face tightens. "Don't ever joke about that," he dictates. His words are controlled, but discharged with force. Even his horse stomps his foot, as if to punctuate the point.

How fucking flip can I be? How *inappropriate*, as Matthew would accuse. "I'm sorry," I say, halting the bay horse. "I'm so sorry. I won't do it again."

"I believe you," he answers generously. "But why do you say these things, Harry?"

"I don't know," I sigh. "It's like I can't turn my brain off sometimes. It gets me into trouble, I know. Please know that I don't mean to be disrespectful. I really like you, Nicolo. A lot. I don't ever want to hurt you—if I can help it."

Nicolo says seriously, "Then I hope you will think before you speak."

We spur our horses into a trot and let the breeze wash our confrontation away as we ride. In minutes we're cantering, our horses enjoying the gait as much as we. In the distance we see a clump of cottonwoods, which tells us there must be a creek. We slow our steeds and approach the small creek at a walk, stopping to let them drink. After they're full, we cross the water, dismount, and lead them the hundred feet to the cottonwood trees, where we tie them to a tree with the rope from my saddle and let them graze.

We take off our hats, lean against the trunk of a tree. "This is incredible, Nick. Thank you, hombre. I haven't ridden a horse in years.''

He takes my hand in his and slips his fingers gently through mine. We hold hands and stare ahead, the way Amity and I did at the movie—only we're looking not at some manufactured world on a screen, but at the wide-open Texas sky that supports a cluster of thunderheads in the far distance. Below the clouds and sky is the infinite horizon of prairie and cattle land. In front of us, the creek moves slowly, like syrup. No sound. I realize now that my hand-holding with Amity while at the movie may not have been a political statement, but it *was* a statement as much as my hand-holding with Matthew during college. They both took on sociological meaning, and whether with Matthew or Amity, I looked to the outside world for some kind of reaction or nonreaction. But at the moment, I'm holding Nicolo's hand because he's reached for mine, and we simply like the intimate feel of our fingers being interlocked while the clouds grow taller and the creek slides by.

''How long did you have your pony Cinnamon?'' he wants to know.

''Eight years. Until I was seventeen.''

''And you say he's retired?''

''Not exactly.''

''Did you sell him?'' he asks, using his free hand to take the *bota* from his neck.

''No.''

''Did he die?''

''No. I didn't sell him and he didn't die. When I was seventeen I told my family that I was gay. They didn't take it so well. My mother wanted me to get therapy, to turn myself straight. My father just wanted to punish me. So he did the worst thing he could think of: He took Cinnamon away. He didn't even tell me. I went out to the barn, and he was just gone. I swear to God, Nick, I never cried harder over anything in my life. I wanted to kill my father. I drove straight to the hospital and found him. He was so humiliated that I was crying in front of his peers that he threw me into an empty room and backed me against the wall and told me that, as soon as I was ready to be a *normal man*, I could have my horse back. He made me choose.''

"You never saw your horse again, did you?''

"Why do you say that?''

"Because you have integrity. That is why I like you.''

For a moment I'm silent. I think about Amity and how much my lack of integrity has cost me. And I wonder how I'm going to tell him I'm engaged to her. "I never saw my horse again," I continue. "I knew I was gay, and there was nothing I could do about it. Nothing I *wanted* to do about it—other than just be it. I never found out where my father took him. Whom he sold him to. Or whether he gave him away. Or even if he just turned him loose. And I never forgave my brother for not telling me—because I know he knew. I wanted to run away. I used to dream about the year before, when I was sixteen—that I would be riding on him and he would fall while jumping a creek and we'd die together and spend eternity in heaven, like those brothers in Greek mythology, Castor and Pollux.'' I recite, by memory, the last seven stanzas of my poem I attempted to read to Amity.

Till the day arrived when off the trail
A shoe came loose, a broken nail.
It happened as they jumped the creek,
So quick that neither one could speak,

And down he went, onto the rocks.
The last he saw, his pony's hocks
And when he woke, the steed was gone
And light had washed from dusk to dawn.

Then lightning flashed, a cloud bore down
And took him high above the town.
And with the view of soaring birds
He searched the land for errant herds.

But nowhere did his pony run
Not on the earth, nor moon, nor sun
And when the boy did cry a tear
He heard a whisper, "I am here."

Upon the cloud, his horse stood by.
The two embraced, within the sky.
The boy climbed on and said, "Let's go!"
The pony's words: "One thing to show."

And back they rode, to the fateful creek
And hovered o'er to steal a peek.
And there they lie, in blood and stone,
Their bodies cold, no cry no moan.

And when he understood the sight
He grabbed the reins, and held on tight.
O'er wheat fields, and farms, and creek beds stony
He flew to heaven on his cinnamon pony.

Nicolo pats my leg. "Very nice, hombre." He lifts the bag of wine, and he fills my mouth with sangria. And this time, when the dribble falls down the side of my cheek, he gently laps at it with his tongue. I close my eyes and let him move his mouth to mine. He closes his lips over my tongue and softly pulls back, scraping the leftover wine into his own mouth. Then he gives it back to me, and we intertwine our lips and tongues and breathe. It's minutes before we separate and lie back against the tree again.

"Jesus," he says, pronouncing it the Spanish way.

"Sí," I whisper, exhaling every ounce of my breath. "You've been driving me crazy."

"I know," he laughs softly. "I'm going crazy too. But this is how I am when I truly like someone. If I don't care, I'll sleep with you right away."

"Don't care," I order.

His eyes grow wide.

"I'm only kidding," I tell him. "I'm glad that you care. But at this point you're never going to live up to the fantasies I've created of you."

He laughs again. "Do I have a ten-inch dick and an ass like Pele?"

"Yep. And beautiful brown *huevos,*" I claim, taking my own sip of wine. "So when am I going to see them?"

"I know. I'm dragging this out. I'm sorry, Harry. Sometimes Latin men are old-fashioned—even the queer ones. I've always dreamed that I would get married one day—when I found the right guy. And . . . well . . ." He turns shy, even red in the face. "It's weird, but that night in the restaurant, when you defended me, I *knew* we would be together. Forever."

The victory I feel when he says this to me is so complete that I'm speechless. Me. Harry Ford. It isn't like when Amity announced our engagement and I knew everyone was watching and that I was validated in their eyes and now free to be comfortable in their presence. No, this victory is personal, whole, undiminished by anyone's thoughts but my own. The roar of approval this time is silent and in my heart.

"You have not said anything," Nicolo says.

"I'm happy," I assure him. "More than you know. It's just that my brain is taking a ninety-degree turn again—at a moment when it shouldn't."

"What is it, Harry?"

"Well, *can* two guys get married?" I ask, ever the cynic even in my brightest hour.

"I first realized I was gay right before we left Argentina. The only person I told at that time was my sister, Graciela. I was so sad because I told her that I have always known that I wanted to be married one day, and now I couldn't be because of my homosexuality. She told me that was nonsense. That if I want to be married, then I must marry another man. She was sure of my rights. That was the last conversation we had before she was disappeared. I have never forgotten. And I know she is right."

"Well then," I say, laying my cheek next to his, "maybe someday, after we have sex, we'll get married."

A flock of enormous crows flies in, not intimidated at all by our presence. Some land in the cottonwoods, some next to the creek.

"After we have sex, huh?" he asks. "You are too modern."

"Hey, man, what if we suck in bed?"

"I hope we do," he laughs, hitting me on the thigh.

As I jerk, a couple of the crows look over, but none fly away. "You know what I mean. What if none of the parts fit? What if the smells are all wrong? What if we don't like the taste of each other?"

"We already know our mouths fit perfect," he says, running his thumb over my bottom lip. "I guarantee that every part of my body tastes like *dulce de leche*."

"Sweet milk?" I ask, translating.

"It is the thick, sweet caramel that Argentinos pour on everything for dessert," he whispers suggestively. Then he looks at his watch. "Uh-oh. We have to have the horses back," he says, sobering up. "The rancher said by noon."

"Or thereabouts," I stress, ready to strip off my clothes.

"Whatever that means. Anyway, it will be past noon when we get back, even if we run. And I planned this ride for the morning because I have to return for my afternoon classes."

"I thought you took the day off from school?" I ask, disappointed.

He shakes his head. "Not the whole day."

Foiled again. "Mount up, eunuchs, mount up," I moan, dragging myself up, untying the horses.

He grabs our hats. "What are eunuchs?" he asks, recoiling the rope.

"Dudes who don't have the problems we have," I say, positioning the bay gelding. He sticks the hat onto my head, and I climb onto my horse and take off like a rocket, spurring the cinnamon-colored bay over the creek. We jump it together and land on the other side. Alive.

At home, we climb out of the truck and head for the house. Because we smell like a couple of sweaty gay caballeros, Nicolo has agreed to take a shower with me, and I figure if I can't get him to sleep with me I'll at least soap his back. We're pure dust, grime, and sweat as we walk into the house and smell food. Cooking. Food cooking. I know if you combine Diet Dr Pepper, champagne, and nail polish on the stove, they don't smell like chicken, so I'm completely stumped. I'm additionally confused because I thought Amity was supposed to be out on a trip. I yell, "Hello," and as Nicolo and I round the corner into the kitchen, there stands Amity, wearing a gingham apron. She's stirring something in a pot on the stove.

And beside her is my mother.

"Harry!" Amity shouts nervously. "Look who's here: Susan!"

"Mother, what are you doing here?" I ask, friendly yet cautious.

"Well, I was supposed to fly down tomorrow on the airline as you know . . ."

No, I didn't know. And Amity told me she was working today and tomorrow.

My mother continues. "But Alexandra called to say she had to go down to Dallas to market to find fabric for some drapes, and she offered me a seat in her King Air, so here I am, a day early!''

Before I can say anything, Amity butts in. ''P'yew-eee, Aunt Bea! I can smell that horse fertilizer! Thank you so much for your work today, Raul.'' *Raw-ool.* She's talking to Nicolo, calling him Raul, motioning for him to take off. ''Fertilizing the rosebushes is all we need for now. You can go ahead. We'll call you if we have anything else.''

My mother smiles at me, nods to *Raul.* ''I'd hug you, dear, but it looks like you've been giving the gardener a hand. Why don't you have shower? Amity has made chicken and dumplings.''

Only Nicolo's eyes move. He looks at me with anger and warning.

I can't let this happen. He's too Latin, too proud. The insult could be a thorn forever embedded. ''Mother . . .''

''And after that, we're going shopping for Amity's wedding gown. You don't want to miss that, do you?''

''*Really*, Raul. You can go now,'' Amity states, not unkindly but with great urgency.

''Oh, for heaven's sake, what am I saying!'' my mother says, aghast. ''We can't let you see your bride in her dress before the wedding day—that's bad luck.''

Nicolo looks at me, then at Amity. She awkwardly washes her hands at the kitchen sink and avoids both our gazes.

My mother presses on. ''Sometimes I think I'm getting daffy. Since the day you were born I had hoped you'd find a nice girl like Amity and settle down, and now I'm about to jinx the whole marriage by inviting you to go gown shopping with us!''

Nicolo turns on his heel. ''Adios, amigo,'' he says over his shoulder.

''Nicolo, wait,'' I say, following him out of the kitchen and through the living room. ''Nicolo!''

He nearly shatters the front door on his way out. ''Did you plan to invite the gardener to your wedding?'' he spits, stomping over the lawn in his boots as I run along beside him.

''I'm sorry,'' I plead. ''Of course I was going to tell you.''

''When?'' he asks, opening his truck door, sliding himself into the cab. He slams the door hard enough to break it. ''Were you going to call me from your honeymoon?''

''There's a *reason* I was going to marry Amity,'' I tell him through the open window. ''Look, it's for you. You and me. And your mom.''

He starts the engine. ''You are marrying Amity for me?'' He laughs. ''Perhaps I have mistaken who you are.''

''No,'' I say. I don't want to break anyone's heart. How the hell am I going to explain this? That he and I can live happily ever after. That I can pay off his student loans. We can move to Argentina. Buy our own ranch with horses. Start our own newspaper. We can do anything—except get married because I have to marry Amity in order to make us *all* comfortable. I look into his black coffee eyes, see my own reflection in their light. I'm teeny tiny. Nothing really. Like a cartoon on a filmstrip.

He turns off the engine. It's eerily quiet. We're suspended in time for a moment while he wrinkles his brow. ''Do you love me, Harry?''

I take a breath. Exhale. ''Sí.''

''And do you love Amity?''

I take a moment and realize that I do. I love Amity, even with all her faults. ''Sí.''

''You love us both, but you're going to marry Amity.'' He squints at me, then closes his eyes altogether, then starts the car.

''Wait!'' I plead, pulling on his shirt. ''I can explain.''

But he grabs my hand and throws it off his shirt as if it were a deadly spider crawling toward his throat. Then he slams the truck into gear and takes off.

I race for the house to grab my keys and head after him. As

soon as I'm through the door I'm accosted by my mother. "That was no gardener! I heard you call him Nicolo. I know all about this Nicolo person!" she huffs. I look at Amity, and I'm ready to kill her. My mother follows my eyes, my thoughts. "It wasn't Amity's fault," she says, forcefully. "She never told me directly. I figured it out myself."

"I just said he was your friend," Amity clarifies in a neutral voice.

"So what?" I say, stomping into my room. "He is." I push everything around on my drafting table, lift up magazines and dirty T-shirts, throw junk mail on the floor. "Where are my fucking car keys?"

My mother follows me into my room, her hands on her hips. "Watch your language, Harry. Now you listen to me good and I'll tell you what I told Amity: This thing with this Nicolo better stop!" Amity comes into my room, and stands behind my mother, and gives me a shrug as if to say sorry. My mother continues. "I've told Amity there is no reason for her to try to cover for you and your foreign friend, and I've given her the same warning I'll give to you: I've never been more excited about a wedding in my entire life, even my own. But this wedding better be real or else! I don't like being made a fool of. And I won't allow either of you two to make a mockery of the Ford family name just so you can have enough money to pop bonbons on the back patio of your house in Highland Park—understand?"

Amity's eyes flash at the thought of having a house in Highland Park.

"Bonbons?" I ask incredulously. Then I push past them both and sail out of the house.

Nicolo's mother comes to the door, stands behind the screen, doesn't ask me in. *"Qué quiere usted, señor?"* she asks formally.

"Nicolo," I say. "I want Nicolo."

"No desea hablar con usted," she tells me.

"I have to explain," I tell her. "Please."

"Está muy enojado," she warns.

"I know he's angry. And I know he doesn't want to talk to me. But I can explain. *Please* tell him I need to talk to him."

"Wait on the porch," she says, converting to English. "He is showering himself. I'll tell him."

She closes the door and I sit down on the concrete steps, shaded by the large oak tree that rises from the lawn. The afternoon heat is just hitting its stride, and locusts are buzzing in drones. What am I going to say? I'd need a whole afternoon and a bottle of tequila to explain it all. I doubt he'll give me but a couple of minutes to lay it out. I try to collect my thoughts, but it's like trying to round up a swarm of flies.

Fifteen minutes pass, maybe twenty. I scour the trees, search for signs of the locusts in concert. And pan the sky, decide which clouds are friendly, which I would avoid. And watch the heat waves rise from the paved street until they dissipate into the atmosphere or scatter by the force of a passing car. And study the gait of the occasional pedestrian, determine his life circumstances by the way he walks. Guess the contents of his shopping bags or why he chose that particular breed of dog on the leash. I watch well-fed robins land on the shaded areas of the neighboring lawn and turn their heads sideways until they see movement in the earth and dive into the soil with their beaks and miraculously pull out a worm. And I watch the sun move in the sky, slowly, rearranging the lawn's shadows ever so slightly, but enough that I notice. An hour has passed, maybe more. He's not coming out. I knock again. No one answers. I leave.

When I return home, Amity and my mother are gone. I take the longest shower of my life because I don't know what I'm going to do when the shower ends. I hate washing the smell of horse off my body. It is so connected with my happiness—in the past and in the present. It's depressing to watch the suds slide the memory off my body and whisk it down the drain. I wash my hair several times, until my fingers eventually look like shriveled potato skins. I turn the shower off and reach for the towel.

After shaving and dressing, I pick up the phone, call Nicolo. There's no answer. No person, no machine. Nothing but endless unanswered ringing. I'm starving, so I drag myself to the kitchen and lift the lid on the chicken and noodles that are simmering on the stove. They smell heavenly. As I take down a bowl from the cupboard, I see a peach pie cooling on the windowsill, and the leftover flour remnants on the counter make me almost forfeit the noodles and go straight for the homemade pie. God, she's thought of it all, hasn't she? Dressed in that gingham apron, her hair pulled demurely back from her face with a yellow ribbon, she looked like some housewife from the 1950's. As if she was born to cook and clean and give friendly advice to her family. I'll bet my mother ate it up, just as she will the pie.

I scarf down the chicken and noodles, which are wonderful, and wash them down with the sun tea Amity brewed on the back porch. Then I take the pie down from the sill and cut a piece. I eat it. Then another. And when I'm through, I wash my plate and stick it in the dish rack, open the cupboard under the sink to access the trash, and reach in to throw my paper napkin away. Newspaper is sitting in the wastebasket almost to the top, which is strange because I emptied the trash this morning before heading out with Nicolo. I push down on it to make room, and something below it collapses with a crunch. I'm curious, so I lift up the papers to find the box the pie came in. Ha! She went to a bakery and bought a pie, then heated it until it was warm before my mother arrived. She even sprinkled the counter with a slight amount of flour and strategically placed the rolling pin to the side.

I dig farther, under the bakery box and find the container from Goldman's Deli—the container that held the chicken and noodles before she dumped them into the pot on the stove.

In other words, I've been eating a crock of shit. I can't help but laugh, though it's a bitter laugh at best. No one can serve it up like Amity, with such panache, style, and sincerity. The apron, the hair ribbon, the little bit of flour on the tip of her nose—which was probably cocaine. Amity is the most gracious manipulator. She slings as much shit as Winston, but she does it in a way that makes the recipient enjoy it. My contemptible lying brother should take lessons from my congenial lying girlfriend—he'd make swifter progress and ruin everyone's lives more pleasantly.

How smart of Amity to innocently thwart the possible consequences of my *corazón* being offered to Nicolo—a man who would desire my heart in full, not some package plan with triple occupancy and meal ticket included.

Now Nicolo has no interest in my heart, and why should he? I deceived him, let him think he was the only one for me, while all along I was engaged to be married to someone else. And why wouldn't Amity protect herself from me? I deceived her as well, telling her I love her and offering her a future, while freely leaving my heart open to attach itself to Nicolo. I'm a failure as a gay man and as a straight one.

I've got to get out of here. I grab my gym gear and head out to work off the decoy food.

At the gym, I hoist the weights as if they are Styrofoam, my anger providing me with greater strength than I've ever known. I heave them up and down, blowing out all my rage, then slam them down on the floor. And it doesn't go unnoticed by me that the weights on the bar can take all the slamming and dropping I can offer, but remain solid and unchanged. And I realize I'm going to have to get nimble if I'm going to outsmart Amity, Winston, Nicolo, and myself.

By the end of my workout, I'm completely drained. I shower, once again lingering under the hot stream of water, unable to formulate a plan, but aware that I need one. The guy next to me in the shower lets his eyes rest on my body longer than any straight guy would. When I look at him he remains absolutely still, his eyes not flinching, challenging me to make the next move. I do. I turn the water off and leave. I'm determined to get Nicolo back.

At home, I fall on my bed. A heavy sleep. Dead sleep with no dreams. The kind that feels as if it was induced by drugs. And when I wake, I hear the voices of Amity and my mother, and I know the nightmare has begun again. I drag myself to the edge of the bed and try to summon the energy to stand. "Yoo-hoo!" Amity calls. How the hell could I be attracted to someone who actually yells yoo-hoo? I'm angry that she's hoodwinked me and my family, so angry I want to shoot her, but the headlines would be too humiliating: GAY FLIGHT ATTENDANT SHOOTS GOLD-DIGGING FIANCÉE — ALSO FLIGHT ATTENDANT. I push off the bed, walk to the mirror on the back of my closed door, and peer into it. There are pillowcase marks on my face that look like scars—how perfect. Winston slices me up, Amity covers the gashes with powder, and my mother waits in the background with my account at Merrill-Lynch. And Nicolo is nowhere to be found.

I open the door, walk into the living room, and find Amity and my mother in matching outfits. Black stirrup pants, black little flat shoes, short-sleeved white cotton blouses with red polka dots, and matching small black leather purses on long shoulder straps. My mother is even wearing her hair down, which I've never seen her do in her life.

When she sees me, Amity commands, "Come on, Susan. Hit it!"

They put their arms over each other's shoulders to form a little kick line and sing while doing kicks:

> *We walk alike,*
> *we talk alike,*

we even shop for clothes alike.
What a wild duet!
We are Petries.
Laura Petries in our pants!

Mary Tyler Moore would sue. So would Patty Duke. Amity and my mother break from each other and laugh. They're both acting as if the whole scene with Nicolo didn't happen. No wonder my mother finds Amity to be such a great chum: They're two positive peas in a pod of denial.

The ladies who lunch are surrounded by shopping bags and boxes. On the fireplace mantel are two glasses of wine. Amity keeps sniffling, and I suspect she's been excusing herself to the ladies' room throughout the day and snorting little spoonfuls of coke, unbeknown to my mother. I don't know how she's obtained it. I haven't been giving her cash, and she blows her paycheck long before she sees any cash out of it. "The valet thought we were sisters," my mother giggles. "He must have been drinking," she adds, her hand to her throat.

You must have been drinking, I want to tell her. Instead, I say, "I don't blame him—you two *do* look like sisters. What did you buy?" I'm friendly, interested, eager to see the spoils. I can tell Amity doesn't trust it, but my mother is thrilled to model the spoils.

Amity joins with my mother to show off the skirts, blouses, cocktail dresses, and two Bob Mackie beaded gowns off the rack. "I know it's over-the-top," my mother says, "but hell, why should those gals in Hollywood get all the good stuff? And guess what? We have something to wear them to: your engagement party in Wichita, which is next month at the Oilmen's Club downtown! We've booked a Saturday evening—the first time they've allowed a private party to reserve the entire place on a weekend in the entire history of the club!"

Amity winks at me, like *isn't she adorable?* She takes her wine off the mantel and starts to take a sip. I walk over and take the glass from her hand. She smiles, but looks uncertain, wondering what comes next. I smile a huge mouthful of teeth, take a lusty swallow of her wine, and say, "Bravo, Mother! Amity and I are so lucky to have you!" I put my arm around Amity and kiss her on the cheek. And I look her in the eyes and wink back—let her know we're in this game together. She searches my gaze to see if the wedding is on and everything is going forward. I nod, and she nods in return. I realize how comfortable she is when playing a role. I decide the timing is good to continue. "I know you don't want to dwell on this, so I'll make it brief." I hand Amity her wine and walk steadily to the middle of the room, where I formally address the two women. "It's over between Nicolo and me. He wanted nothing to do with me—never to see me again. And though I admit I was wounded, I realized that he was actually saving my life. Saving it for Amity and the future for which we're intended. This is the only time I'll bring it up. I just want you to know I'm headed on the right course now, and none of us has to worry that I'll *deviate* again." I have to choke the word out for my mother's benefit, but I do it.

My mother, tears in her drunken eyes, raises her wineglass. I approach Amity, hold my hand upon hers, and raise our glass together. "Salud!"

CHAPTER TWENTY

O ver the next few weeks, Amity goes back and forth to her wedding gown fittings on her Vespa scooter—the one my mother had imported for her. Every time Amity steps into her stirrup pants, ties a scarf on her head, slips on her Ray Bans, and whirrs off on that scooter, I want to get into my car and run her down. She sabotaged my relationship with Nicolo, and now she's playing me perfectly by encouraging me to patch it up with him and offering her complicity—if I want to secretly see him, she won't tell my mother. She assures me she never told my mother anything other than that I have a friend named Nicolo. She reminds me that *Susan* had been calling us repeatedly and that I had been avoiding her calls—true. And when she resorted to calling Amity's number in order to find me, Amity told her I was out with my friend Nicolo. That's all.

I can just imagine how she'd put it. "He probably hasn't had time to call you, Susan, because *he spends all his time with Nicolo.*" Followed by a heavy sigh. And that's all it would take to start an investigation by my mother.

The night after I waited for him on his porch, I went to see him at the restaurant and followed him from table to table. "Nicolo, listen to me please!'' I begged on his heels, publicly humiliating myself.

"Congratulations,'' he told me, serving a man his steak.

"Thanks,'' the gentleman said, not knowing what he was being congratulated for. "But you forgot my baked potato.''

"He's talking to me,'' I explained to the steak eater, "but he doesn't really mean it.''

"How is everything here?'' Nicolo asked, rushing over to another table.

Before anyone could comment on their food I answered, "Everything is terrible! I need to explain myself.''

"More ice water?'' Nicolo inquired.

"In your veins,'' I told him.

"But not in my cup!'' the woman patron gasped as he poured water into her wine.

He went to the kitchen and picked up an order for two that was waiting: salmon in some kind of caper sauce and a huge piece of prime rib. I grabbed a baked potato and threw it on a small plate. "I *have* to get married,'' I told him as we exited the kitchen for the dining room, "or I'll lose everything.'' I dropped the potato off for the guy with the steak, then followed Nicolo out to a table for two, where a yuppieish couple was trying to enjoy a romantic evening.

Nicolo served the salmon to the man, the prime rib to the woman. I reached down and switched the plates.

"How did you know?'' the woman asked, looking sideways at me.

The cut of prime rib was a Texas-sized portion. "How can you eat that much meat?'' I asked the guy, ignoring his wife's comment.

Nicolo finally looked at me and imparted with great passion, "You are out of line, coming to my place of work! This gentleman can eat as much meat as he wants!''

The restaurant manager agreed and forcibly led me to the door and told me that if I returned he would call the cops—and Nicolo, who he said should have been fired long ago, finally *would* be.

For days I called, but either there was no answer or his mother picked up to say Nicolo didn't wish to speak to me and requested that I not come to the house. Against his wishes, I did—twice. Each time his mother appeared before I could even ring the bell and quickly ushered me away, telling me Nicolo wasn't home, even though his truck was there and I knew he was. I wrote to him, explaining it all, and the letter was returned to sender, unopened. His pride is making it impossible for us to reconcile, but I'm not giving up. I *must* explain to him why I'm getting married; it doesn't guarantee he'll come back to me, but it's my only chance.

In the meantime, my mother insists that Amity and I set a date since my birthday is approaching. "It's best you're married by your birthday, dear," she tells me. She and Amity decide the ceremony should be October 18, the same day as my birthday, because they believe it would be so wonderful for me to link the two events forever. I agree. My birth and my death, so to speak. Playing this game, acting as if everything is progressing right on schedule with the wedding, is making me crazy.

Jacqueline is hanging out with us a lot since the mythical abortion. She and Amity are in this stirrup pants phase together now, Jacqueline taking the place of my mother and looking more like Laura Petrie than my mother ever could anyway.

In between flight assignments, since I've lost Nicolo, I sulk around the house. The girls try to include me in their shopping and eating ventures, but now I find it all insufferable. I'm not the same weak little wimp I was when I arrived nine months ago, and frankly, I'm getting bored with everything I found interesting before. It's odd. I realize now that when I was in college my academics and friends were real, but I turned it all into a game. And now that I'm in the real world, everything is a game, and I have to find a way to make it real, which requires another game in itself.

Amity and Jackie insist on dragging me to the mall to see
Gremlins, and I realize the escape of a film would be good medicine.
We're driving in Jackie's Volvo to the mall, some innocuous song
by some innocuous British techno band is playing on the radio, and
I'm flipping through the *Penthouse* magazine that has now exposed
Miss America's clitoris to the American public.

"G'yaw," Jacqueline says as she looks into her rearview mirror
while I hold the magazine up in the backseat.

Amity turns around. "Can you believe Miss America's snatch?
It's not very pageantlike."

"What does Emily Post say a pageantlike snatch is supposed to
look like?" I ask sarcastically.

Amity checks the shape of one of her eyebrows in the vanity
mirror. "You know—fluffy, ladylike, pink. With a little crown on
it."

"Do black women have pink snatches?" Jacqueline asks, looking at me in the rearview mirror.

"I don't know. I've never seen one," I say, defending my
ignorance.

"You've never seen a black woman?" Jacqueline asks.

"Never," I say, defending Jacqueline's ignorance. I flip to
another picture and hold it up.

"Look!" Amity screams, turning around. "She's with another
girl. Miss America's eating her *beave!*"

Jacqueline's confused. "Her *beave?*"

"Beave, beaver, beavaronie. She's putting her tongue on that
girl's Libby!"

"Big deal," I remark. "Maybe she's hungry."

"Or thirsty," Jacqueline adds.

I can't believe I've been one upped by Jackie.

Suddenly Amity turns glum. "I can't believe she was ousted.
There's nothing sadder than a beauty queen taking a fall."

Just you wait, Amity. Just you wait.

* * *

Amity is back on the fast track, smoking more pot than ever and increasingly flying around on coke. As pissed off as I am, I don't want to see her disintegrate on drugs, so I try to caution her to cool it, but because I'm angry at her, it comes off sounding preachy, and she dismisses me and assures me that she's totally in control. Though she's seeing Kim again, she's pledged he's given up his gun and, better yet, is considering going back to his wife now that he has Amity on the side. She tells me she's encouraging him to reconcile since it would be much better for everyone involved. And somehow, she manages to continue seeing Thomas as well, because, "I just love his testicles—they feel so European!"

One Friday night, when Amity is going out the door with Thomas, I ask what Nicolo is doing, and Thomas kind of mutters, "Not a whole lot."

But Amity gets this concerned look on her face, the kind of face that Matthew used in the end and tells me compassionately, "Babe, Nicolo is dating someone."

She's so cruel. How can she tell me this? I want to die. There's no way I'll ever find anyone as good as Nicolo—I know it. And now, I've lost my chance at a future with him, because I can't help but assume that whoever he's seeing is funnier and smarter and has a better body—and isn't engaged to a psychopath. "Good for him," I say, nonchalantly. "I'm dating someone too."

Amity's eyes grow wide. "Who?"

"You," I answer.

There's a moment of silence before we laugh, Thomas included. Of course he's learned that Amity and I are engaged, and his European manner isn't fazed by her taking him as a lover. And even though I've repeatedly encouraged her to share the whole story of our *arrangement* with Thomas, assuming he'll pass it on to Nicolo, I'm sure Amity hasn't—just as I'm sure she doesn't want Nicolo and me to be together.

"So what's this guy like?" I ask, referring to Nicolo's new companion.

"Just an average guy, no doubt," Amity says nonchalantly.

"They've only been out a couple of times," Thomas assures me.

I'm not reassured. "So what does he look like?"

"No one's really seen him yet, because—Well, never mind," Amity says. "Ready to go, Thomas?"

"Because why?" I ask. Come on, Amity. You've set me up— now finish.

"Well," she says slowly, with a soft and compassionate look on her face, "from what we hear, the two of them never left the guy's apartment, if you know what I mean."

Ha! I sure do. If Nicolo's already hopped into the sack with this guy it means he doesn't feel about him the way he feels about me. I still have a chance. "I'm glad you told me," I tell her solemnly. "It's good for me to know."

After they leave, I can't stand it. I have to see Nicolo. I jump in my car and head over to the duplex he shares with his mother. Nicolo's truck is gone, but I approach the door and ring the bell. It's twilight, and the porch light wrestles control from the purple Texas evenfall as I wait for an answer.

"Buenas noches, señor Harry," his mother says, opening the door. She's stiff, formal.

"Buenas noches, señora," I answer. *"Nicolo está aquí?"*

"No, Harry."

"Is he on a date?" I ask, unable to contain myself.

"Yes. They go to a movie. *Amadeus.*"

It's a new film Nicolo and I planned to see together. "Can I come in?" I ask. She doesn't answer. "He can't force you not to talk to me," I claim. "It's time he understood my story. The only way is to tell you, because he won't hear it from me. Please."

She unlocks the screen door, allows me inside. "I am making

the dinner. You will have to talk to me in the kitchen.'' I follow her into the kitchen, where an array of vegetables are cut and sitting next to the stove. She opens the refrigerator and unwraps a piece of meat—veal, I think. ''What is your story?''

I sit at the kitchen table. ''It's nothing compared to yours,'' I admit, not wanting to offend her. ''My family is very different from your own.''

''Tell me,'' she commands, cutting the meat into squares. She's browning onion and garlic in oil, and the kitchen is coming to life.

''My father died.''

''I am sorry,'' she says coolly, placing the meat into the pan to sizzle with the garlic and onion. A minute passes while she turns the meat as it browns in the oil.

I exhale and take a long pause before filling my lungs again. ''He was hard on me. Hard on my mother, my brother. I don't think he was ever happy, at least not with us.''

She grabs the dish of chopped tomatoes and incorporates them into the pan, adds carrot slices, salt and pepper, and pours a broth over everything. Then she lifts the lid on a pot of thick white rice. Steam escapes, and she gives it a quick stir before covering it again, closing off the escape route. ''Himself? Was he happy?''

''When he was younger, maybe. But as he grew older, I always got the feeling he wanted out of his skin. That he wanted to shed his body and fly toward the horizon and disappear inside of it. He was the strangest guy. So controlled, so tight, yet totally exhilarated whenever he got lost—he loved being lost. And I couldn't figure it out, because he planned *everything*—down to the minute, every detail taken care of, leaving nothing to chance—every day of his life. But every once in a while chance won out, and those were the times he was happy. When my mother, brother, and I were upset that the road on the screwy map didn't exist and the car was out of gas in the middle of nowhere and there was no food and no way to get help because we were in the French countryside and we couldn't speak French—*that's* when my father would relax in his skin, light up a cigarette, and sit quietly on the side of the road with a smile he never wore otherwise.''

Nicolo's mother fills two small juice glasses with red wine, offers one to me, and sits at the table. I wait for her to say something, but she doesn't, so I continue. ''I always knew this about my father—that he respected, was even amused by, anything powerful enough to derail his force. That's why I thought it would be OK to tell the truth about who I was. I thought he'd respect that I was changing his blueprints for me. Oh, boy, was I wrong.''

''Nicolo's father never knew that his son is a man who likes men. He was disappeared before Nicolo spoke of it. I wonder how Gianni would react to this. He loved his manly sister, but perhaps it is different when it is your son, no?''

I refuse to cut slack. ''It shouldn't be. He should love Nicolo no matter what.''

Nicolo's mother takes a drink of wine and slowly lowers her glass to the table. She sets it down without a sound, as if she's well practiced at hiding her presence. ''It is one of the worst things about losing him. I don't know how Gianni would change. What he would think today. How he would look. My last memories of him are so sad. It was an awful time. The government was taking everyone. Teachers, students, priests, union leaders, journalists. Everyone knew what was happening, but no one would talk about it. People went on with their business as if all is well.'' She takes another quiet sip of wine and lowers her glass. ''When Gianni was taken, I went to our friend, who is a lawyer. But he would not help me. No one would. The lawyers are afraid they would be disappeared if they help. Gianni's friend at the newspaper helped me with the habeas corpus document. I took it to the judge myself. He read it. He stared at me and said nothing.''

''This sounds like the McCarthy stuff that happened in America,'' I tell her.

"Joseph McCarthy," she says with contempt. "Yes. And Hitler. But we had lots of McCarthys and Hitlers." She rises from the table and goes to the counter, where she takes two ripe peaches and cuts them into chunks. She transfers them into a bowl and pushes the bowl toward the back of the counter. She then slices the kernels off two ears of corn and cuts some potatoes, including a sweet potato, and adds them all to the pan. "They don't know what they do to the family," she says, slicing a piece of squash into chunks. "My dear Graciela was an artist," she says through slightest tears while putting the squash in with the rest of the ingredients. "What do they want with an artist? A sweet girl who sells her little paintings down on the *Caminito*? What possible threat is she? After her father disappeared, she paints what she feels in her heart. She paints these people, *los desaparecidos*, as angels that sacrifice their lives for the rest of us. She paints them leaving their homes, their cars, their jobs, their families, to fly to heaven. For this they kill her." She stands in the kitchen, shaking her head.

"If they killed these people," I ask, "why are they called the disappeareds?"

She sits at the table with me. "I have no answer. I only know that Gianni and Graciela were killed because my brother told me so." She takes the bottle of wine and refills our little glasses. "My brother was an officer in the navy. He had enough connection to know. He would not tell me how it was done. Only that it was. Nicolo will not forgive his uncle. He believes his uncle is guilty of their murders, even though it was not at his hands and he learned of it after. Guilty, because he does not speak. Does not speak to tell the truth and make a stop to what was happening to so many people."

The garlic, onion, meat, and vegetables are creating a delicious scent of steam that mixes well with the taste of the wine. I want to take off my shoes, stay, and eat. "And you, Mrs. Feragamo? What do you think?"

"I think that my family has seen enough pain," she says, stalwart. "I cannot allow you to hurt my son. I will continue to protect him."

"How? He's a grown man, señora."

She stiffens, changes expression. "I do what I must. I think that you should leave," she says, rising from the table.

Her word choice hits me. "How will you *continue to protect him*?" I ask, staying put.

"I will make sure he does not receive your calls—or your letters."

I spring from my chair. "Is that what you've been doing?" I ask incredulously.

"Yes, it is," she answers, her head held high in a righteous pose.

"Those times I came to the house—you didn't tell him?"

"No."

"And when I called?"

"No," she answers, still in her pose.

"The letter—did you send it back unopened?"

"Yes."

"Nicolo never saw it?"

"No."

"God, I can't believe this!" I shout. "You sabotaged me. You haven't even heard my story, and you sabotaged me!"

"I did what is right for my son," she answers, resolute. "Now leave this house."

I'm enraged. "What the hell are you trying to do? *Disappear* me?"

She looks horrified. "Leave now!"

"How dare you. What makes you any different than the Argentinean government?" She gasps, but I furiously charge on. "You think you know what's best for Nicolo, for me? You think you can control information? Judge who's right and who's wrong? Mold your own clandestine outcome?''

"Largo de aquí!" she hisses, running to the door. *"Largo!"*

"No!" I yell, my legs shaking with anger. My face is white-hot, and my brow is twitching in spasms, but I refuse her order to leave. "I've heard your story. Now you'll hear mine!"

"One minute—then I will call the police!"

I spew it out fast and furious. "I'm from a very wealthy family. And when my father died, he put a provision in the will that I had to be married by my next birthday if I wanted to collect. It's a lot of money. *A lot.* And I've decided I want it. Is there anything wrong with that?"

"Honest money or dirty money?"

"My family is honest. And the girl I'm marrying knows about Nicolo. And she's willing to marry me in order to help me get the money. Is that bad?"

"You are marrying for love or money?" she demands.

"Both. I'll use the money to pay off Nicolo's school loans. Help him—perhaps even you—get back to Argentina. Give him whatever he desires in life."

She brushes back her hair with her hand and answers indignantly, "You hardly know my son. He needs love, not money."

"I'm offering him both."

"By marrying someone else? You are playing Nicolo and this girl for being fools! I do not believe that you truly love either of them as much as you love your money, or you would have been honest with my son from the beginning. You are selfish. Your thinking is twisted."

"And what about yours? Have you learned nothing from your government, Mrs. Feragamo? How awful has it been—to be denied access to someone you love? To know you'll never see your husband again or your daughter because the government thinks it knows what's best? That's what you're doing to me and to Nicolo. You're playing God. You're guilty like your brother because you don't speak to Nicolo of what you know."

She cries, her head in her hands. Perhaps I've cut too deep. I walk to the door, stand beside her, put my hand on her shoulder, and quietly tell her, "I'm sorry. I didn't mean to hurt you. But that's how I see it." I am right about her and what she's done.

And she is right about me.

CHAPTER TWENTY-ONE

The wedding date is approaching. Amity's gown is chosen. My tuxedo, as well. The big engagement party is next week in Wichita, and I still haven't formulated a plan to escape this insanity with my pride and my inheritance. Why did my father do this to me? Hell, I never cared about money when it wasn't a possibility. But by dangling it in front of me with all these strings attached, he's trapped me. I'm caught up in the strings and can't free myself. I suckered into it all.

I've been off the hook with Amity lately because she claims to be flying a lot. The truth is, for just fifty dollars here, a hundred there, she gives her work trips away to other flight attendants in need of extra cash on their days off. And since Kim gives her the money, she can afford to bag the flying. She packs her luggage, puts on her uniform, pulls out of the driveway, and heads for Kim's condo, where she does lines of coke for days, before returning home with perfectly manufactured stories about her trip and how great the weather was in Florida or Maine or wherever she pretends to be.

It's September and school is back in session. Nicolo is somewhere on the DCU campus, but I can't seem to find him. I hang out on campus, constantly looking for him. It's not a large school, and it shouldn't be hard to locate him, but he seems to be hiding, since I can't hook up with him anywhere.

The day before leaving for the party in Wichita, I decide to devote the entire afternoon to scouting the campus. I look everywhere. The journalism school, the library, the classrooms, the lawns, the student union. Fruitlessly I comb the campus, mixing in with the squeaky young students in their shorts and polo shirts. They seem so happy and innocent, so without worry, as I was only a year ago. I'm charmed by their simplicity, their gullibility, but no longer do I wish it for myself. Nor do I yearn to return to academe. Even amid all this muck, I now take a small amount of pleasure in knowing that I've graduated, commenced my life. Even if it *is* fucked.

So far, September is just as hot as August, and the sun beats down with brutal strength. I go from hot to cold to hot, from the sun to the inside of a building to the sun again, searching for my Argentinean. No luck. I swear he's gone underground. And I'm sick of the smell of books and air-conditioning, polished linoleum and window cleaner, cafeterias and science labs. I kick the pavement in anger. It bruises my foot in retaliation, and I limp over to the football stadium and climb a few rows and sit in the bleachers.

The football team is in their practice gear on the field. The coaches are screaming at them, putting them through drills, and the big hulks are doing their best to be agile and run the drills. A trio of sorority girls in running shorts and bows in their hair, their tank tops adorned with Greek letters, are jogging the steps in the stadium. I can hear them gossiping about a sorority sister's weight problem as they pass. "If she eats dessert, she's not really *trying*." Far in the distance, I see a lone student sitting on the steps. A guy. Dark hair. Muscles. Reading a book. It's Nicolo. I step on a bleacher and start running on my sore foot like an injured gymnast limping across an endless balance beam. The closer I get, the more nervous I become. My heartbeat quickens from the run and my apprehension, and as I approach him from behind, I slow down, trying to gather my calm and good wits. I know I can make him understand. I'll devote myself to him, to us, as soon as this whole fucking scenario with Amity is over. Surely he'll believe that.

I'm almost even with him, and I walk down the four bleachers to where he sits, to face him, when I realize that it isn't Nicolo at all. It's someone else.

CHAPTER
TWENTY-TWO

The Oilmen's Club of Wichita, Kansas, has been spit-polished and shined into brilliance. An eight-piece band plays in the heart of the huge, multilevel dining room, and ice sculptures of swans, dolphins, and seashells are glistening next to spreads of raw vegetables, crab meat, Gruyère on toast points, and fruit. Flower arrangements of white roses, Peruvian lilies, and Birds of Paradise pour themselves over tables, descend the edges of stair steps, and fill all corners of the room. The tables are set with sea foam green spreads and white place settings, the silver cutlery shines so brightly it makes little stars on the ceiling.

The guest list is a who's who of Kansas society, and even some who aren't. The relatives on my mother's side are thrilled to see Amity again, and those on my father's side are making great efforts to speak with her and assess her character. A photographer from the local paper is making the rounds, exploding flashbulbs in everyone's faces as they freeze their good taste for the frame. When the photographer thanks them and moves on, they maintain their expressions for Barbie Botter, as she jots down their sentiments.

My grandmother, Queen Mother of the Plains, holds court at her table, and everyone drops by to pay their respects and compliment her in some way or another. Children, in particular, are fond of her. Since I was a child, my grandmother has kept nothing but candy and credit cards in her purse, and tonight there are several children gathered at her feet, waiting for a bounty of sugar.

It was the same for me at that age. There was always a magical Pied Piper quality about her, something that made me want to follow her and listen to whatever she had to say and imitate whatever she did. Every summer my grandfather would force me and Winston to go hunting with him and my father. And though Winston would gamely take a shot at a quail or even a deer, I refused to pull the trigger on my own gun. My father would remain silent while my grandfather berated me and called me a sissy. But I didn't care. I made it quite clear that I much preferred a day on the porch with my grandmother, learning Portuguese fishing songs, squeezing homemade lemonade, and making finger paintings with her from colors that matched the Indian Paintbrush and Lupine that grew on the ranch land of the Colorado house. If songs and cooking and art were the interests of a sissy, then I was happy to be one, though I certainly refrained from full-on disclosure as a boy. And Grammie would always defend me to her husband. She'd tell him there were enough hunters in the world, and that "gatherers of knowledge are esteemed over hunters of game."

Flitting about the party, Amity passes every charm test with flying colors. She is the belle of the ball, in her black strapless cocktail dress that contrasts with her blond hair and shows off her slender tan shoulders. It's the perfect amount of formality and sexiness for the occasion, and she's stacked herself into a black velvet pair of heels, pushing her slightly above the other women in the room. I'm wearing a dark suit and an emerald-colored tie. My shiny, flat dress shoes keep me just below Amity's height. Donald is overdressed in a tux, and my mother is in a black dress with a scooped neckline that shows off her new Sally Field breasts. Amity's parents were *unable to attend*.

When she nervously told me, two days ago, that her grandmother had suffered a stroke and that her parents wouldn't be able to make the party, I asked her if we should call it off. "Oh, no," she said, "it would make her feel worse—maybe even kill her!" When I suggested that we go visit her in the hospital, Amity claimed, "I just got back, babe. She's really weak. We need to let her rest." I sensed it was a scam, so yesterday I called every hospital in Fort Worth in search of Hazel Stone. No one by that name in any hospital. Then I called information for the James Raymond Stones, but there was no listing. If my father were alive, he'd have had them investigated by now. My mother has no intentions of rocking the boat and willingly accepts all information put forth by Amity.

My mother is taking us by the hand, leading us from couple to couple. "Harry, you know the Harmans . . ." and "Harry, you remember the McGriffs . . ." and "Harry, you've spent time with the Bennett-Strongs." I hardly remember any of these plastic people or their manufacturers. Some of these people should be melted down and turned into milk cartons. It's our maid's family I was really close to when I was growing up, and they weren't invited. Likewise, the Tuckers, the favorite family of my childhood, who lived down the street aren't present. While I struggle, Amity is working the room like a fund-raiser, shaking hands, making small talk, laughing on cue at stupid golf jokes. I want to stab her with a salad fork and see if she shorts out, like that gal in the *Stepford Wives,* but it's impossible to keep up with her, because she's far more energetic than I, and every free moment she slips away to the ladies' room to *powder* her nose.

Winston moves counter to us with balletlike skill, no matter what our position, making sure he steers clear of the feted couple. He has a woman with him—Patty, I presume. It's surprising that he hasn't made any major efforts yet to derail the evening with any of his Winstonisms.

"Amity dear, I want you to come meet my daughter Andrea.

She was married only months ago, and she's full of sensible advice!'' Mrs. Mahaffy says, spilling a little of her cocktail.

"Like how to fry an egg or cheat at bridge?" my mother asks gamely.

"I know how to do those things," Amity claims, sipping champagne. Her accent is so ramped up that she almost sounds British. "I want to cheat at frying an egg!"

"Nonsense," my mother tells Mrs. Mahaffy. "She's a wonderful cook. You should try her chicken and dumplings. And her peach pie!"

It's the best money can buy, I think.

"I insist you meet Andrea," Mrs. Mahaffy finishes, dragging Amity away while pouring more of her drink on the floor.

I escape to the television room, where Winston and I would sit with the other children when we were youngsters, drinking Shirley Temples and eating cheese popcorn while watching scary reruns of *The Outer Limits* or new episodes of *The Big Valley*. It's a grand old study with endless shelves of books, all the classics, and huge soft chairs made of buttery leather that would swallow us up. The children of other families would sit two to a chair, but I only tried it with Winston once. As I crawled into his chair, he pushed me out with his feet, and I hit the floor with a thump, spilling my Shirley Temple and landing in it. Everyone laughed and made fun of me, no one more demonstrably than Winston. From then on, we'd separate, staying on opposite sides of the room, sniveling at each other while digging the cherries out of our drinks.

I walk over to the immense glass windows and look to the street nine stories below. It's nothing now. Barely a view. Concrete and parked cars. An ugly brick office building across the street. But when I was a child, it was like being on top of the Empire State Building.

"Harry Ford," a voice says.

I look up, see a guy roughly my age. He's handsome, good bones, slightly thinning hair. His suit almost matches mine. "Hello," I say.

"You don't remember me, do you?" he asks, a grin on his face.

"Not really."

He puts out his hand. "Bob Valentine. We played together here as kids."

I shake his hand. Bob Valentine. I vaguely remember his childhood face. "Thanks for coming."

"Wouldn't miss it. I wanted a chance to see you," he tells me warmly. "I was really surprised to hear that you were getting married. I . . . had heard from friends that you weren't the marrying type."

Rich white people's code for *homosexual*. "I'm *not* the marrying type," I tell him, chuckling, "and Amity knows it."

"Interesting," he says, picking up the toothpick from his martini and using the olive to stir. He looks me straight in the eye. "My wife has no idea."

"Are you telling me you're gay?"

He smiles awkwardly and shrugs.

"But you married a woman anyway? Why?"

He takes a sip of his drink, gives a wry smile. "Isn't that what we're *supposed* to do? I mean, *you're* doing it."

"Not really," I tell him, plopping down in one of the leather chairs. "Not like you. It's not like I'm really getting married."

"Oh, you wait," he laughs, sitting down beside me. "It will be very real. Once you start down that aisle, you'll know what I mean."

"You're making me nervous."

He comes closer, speaks lower. "You were a cute kid, Harry. You still are." I have to admit, he's sexy in that well-bred, rakish way. "I liked you when we were boys."

It's an erotic statement, and it has its effect. I've had no sex with Nicolo and none with Amity in a good while. I'm tempted.

"I don't really remember you. If you liked me, why didn't you tell me?"

He raises his eyebrow the way Amity does. "Is that something a boy tells another boy?"

Physically, I'd have no problem sleeping with this guy. Mentally, that last statement tells me he's all wrong. "Yes," I answer emphatically, "it *is* something a boy tells another boy. There's nothing wrong with it."

He looks at his shoes, chuckles uncomfortably. "I wasn't *that* kind of a boy."

My voice is honest, not harsh. "No offense, Bob, but you aren't that kind of a man either. I am. I don't want to sneak around with you or anybody. I have no secrets about my love. His name is Nicolo."

He turns slightly colder. "Funny. *Nicolo* looks an awful lot like a girl tonight in that black dress and pearls."

"I told you, Amity knows all about him. My family too."

"So why the party?" he asks, biting the olive off the toothpick. "And why the girl?"

I sigh. "For my mother, the family name and all. And . . . personal reasons."

"*Financial* personal reasons?"

I nod affirmatively.

He chews the olive, swallows. "Then I guess you're not that different from me," he says bitingly. He sets his glass down and walks to the door. As he leaves, Winston appears, and the two of them bristle with recognition. "Hello, Winnie," Bob spits. "Honoring your brother with a visit from his big sister?"

Winston shows his fangs, mutters, "Nice to see you too, Valentino."

I have no doubt they've slept together—it's written all over their faces. I'm so glad I didn't jump into the broom closet with Bob, because I would be grossed out to think I could mess around with anyone who'd slept with my brother: male, female, or inflatable doll. And I realize now that it was probably Winston who told Bob about me. "When did the children's room become the snake pit?" I ask Winston as he plunks down into a chair.

"What's the matter, Happy. Aren't you having a good time?"

"Who wouldn't be? All these waxy people walking around. Music from someone else's generation. Food that gives you the shits. What more could a guy want?"

He raises his feet to the ottoman in front of him. "Nicolo perhaps?"

I want to punch him in his pretty face. "How do you know about Nicolo?"

"Mother and I are closer than you think. And of course Acidity and I have our little chats."

Oh, God, I can hardly handle the two of them separately. What are they *chatting* about?

"I'm sure Nicolo is *wonderful*, Happy. Far better than this silly girl running around shaking everyone's hand like she's running for governor. I really can't believe you're going through with this." He crosses his legs.

I stand over him. "Gee, it's so hard to figure out. If I do it, I'm fifty million richer. If I don't, *you're* fifty million richer."

"So shallow. Since when did you start caring about money? What is money?" he asks, picking up a paperweight from the end table beside him. It's glass with an Indian penny inside. He holds it to the light. "I hear things aren't going so well with your Romeo from South America. Why don't you drop this charade and reunite with your true love? I'd be willing to help you out, you know. Buy the two of you a house, another car, throw in some junk bonds, maybe even a *horse*."

He still knows where Cinnamon is. Somehow he knows. Cinnamon would be sixteen years old now. With good care, he still has half a life ahead of him. I can't believe Winston would do this to me. "What happened to make you so fucking mean?"

He stands, speaks very soberly. "Do you understand what I'm offering you? Nicolo. And the horse. And enough money to be comfortable." He squints. "Love *and* money. Are you refusing me?"

"Are you insinuating I don't love Amity?"

"Not the way you love Nicolo. It's not possible."

"Why do you say that?"

"When you're gay, you're gay. You can't love a woman fully."

I look him dead in the eye. "And you're the expert, aren't you?"

He blasts me with contempt. "Harry. Harry Ford. The perfect little man—so true to himself, true to the world." He walks over to the bookshelf and plucks out a book, which he holds in front of himself like a sword. "Wielding the saber of honesty since the age of seventeen. Forsaking all financial provisions in order to live peacefully. How peaceful was it, Harry? Driving around in that junk heap, in debt up to your ears just to attend a public university. Eating franks and beans with your middle-class chums. Working in a theater box office in order to pay for your books. And now you're tossing bags of peanuts to those animals in coach." He tosses the book onto a chair. "Was it worth it?"

I look at him and wonder how he can be so handsome and so ugly at the same time. "It was great," I tell him with pleasure. "I was poor, but I was happy. I loved my VW—it was the best car I've ever had."

"There's no accounting for taste," he sniffs.

"And franks and beans are just fine—better after you're stoned, but just fine. I loved working in the box office because I got to attend all performances for free, and it's how I met my college boyfriend. And the flight attendant job—well, it's kind of a drag, I admit. But I won't be doing it for much longer because now I'll be happy and rich."

"*Wealthy* is how we say it."

"I'll be more than wealthy," I assure him. "I'll be spending my life with someone who loves me." Nicolo, I hope.

"And you'll give up Nicolo and your horse for money?"

"I'm giving up Nicolo and my horse for *Amity*."

"She'll burn you, little brother. Mark my words."

I get up, leave. "I know what I'm doing," I spit over my shoulder. I wouldn't risk saying it if I weren't sure I could get Nicolo back. Never mind that I can't find him—I *know* I'll get him back, because if I have to, I'll call off the wedding.

"I ask for your attention please," Donald says into the microphone. "Your attention." He's a confident speaker—I guess because he's a general, and generals know how to give orders like, "Go out there and get killed!" So asking for attention is nothing to him. My mother stands beside him, wiggling and glowing like a firefly without an off mechanism. Amity holds on to me with one hand, her champagne glass with the other. "We'd like to make a presentation. As you know, we're here tonight to celebrate Harry and Amity's impending doom—I mean, wedding." Ha ha ha. The crowd chuckles on cue as if LAUGH signs are flashing in the corners of the room. "His mother and I . . ."

Who are you? I wonder, looking at Donald.

"His mother and I," he continues, "are very proud parents this evening. Needless to say, Amity has made quite an impression on our hearts."

"And our checkbooks!" Winston yells.

The crowd laughs, mistakenly thinking the imaginary LAUGH signs are flashing again. Donald nods, as if the remark was planned, and continues. "We also want to extend the regrets of the Stones of Fort Worth, Texas, Amity's parents, who had to cancel their plans to be here this evening when Amity's grandmother suffered a mild stroke."

The crowd gives one of those pathetically sad, "Oh" mixed

with "Ah" sounds, as if the flashing signs now say, SYMPATHY NOISE.

Donald continues. "But from what we understand, the damage was mild, and Grandmother Stone will be back to the horse races and her book club in no time. We must tell you, the Stones, with their kindest regards, have had their accountant send a blank check to cover the cost of this entire event."

The crowd is silent, but awash with impressed and approving looks.

I look over at Amity, and she looks back with slight nervousness and shrugs.

"Which we cannot accept," Donald adds.

Amity's shoulders fall as she exhales, relieved.

The room is peppered with several agreements of, "Of course not."

Donald takes a check from his pocket and tears it in half, then drops it to the floor. "Now, we want to do something special for these fine young people. Harry, Amity, will you please come up here?"

Amity sets her champagne glass down and dons that same look she wore when collecting her award at the airline ceremony. Pulling me up as she rises, she lets me take over, play the big man leading his fiancée to the forefront of people's affections. As we make our way, the band plays a few bars of Chopin's funeral march. The crowd laughs. My mother good-naturedly shakes her fist at the band, and they stop the music, then launch into "We've Only Just Begun." More rehearsed laughs. It's getting so trite that Rogers and Hammerstein are going to have to change the line to "I'm as corny as Kansas in September."

"Harry and Amity," my mother says, nervous to be speaking into a microphone, "I would like to present you with something that has been in our family for three generations." She opens a small velvet box, revealing a diamond-and-emerald ring of exquisite beauty. "Amity, this was my mother's engagement ring, and her mother's before that."

I look to the side of the room, where Winston and his date sit far apart. When Winston sees me he scoots closer to her and takes her hand, almost frightening her. He looks at me, at the ring, then at Amity. If he had a gun, he'd shoot the diamonds out of my mother's hands.

My mother continues. "Since I have no daughters . . ." I expect Winston to crack a joke, and obviously she does too because she barrels on. "I want you to have this ring and to become the fourth generation owner and, may I say, the most beautiful girl to wear it yet." She hands me the ring while Amity mouths a tearful *thank you* to my mother the way a pageant winner does as she first walks the runway with her new crown. "Harry," my mother finishes, "you may present the ring."

When I was in college, I did a scene from *King Lear* in which I played the king himself. I assure you, I look nothing like anyone who's ever played the character, nor do I have an accomplished voice or venerable manner. But I pulled it off, out of true commitment to the character. And that's what I do now. Commit. I take the ring, while smiling at Amity, and hold the diamonds into the light, letting them sparkle across her face. My mother places the microphone in my free hand, and I begin. "Amity, I feel so honored to have met you. I don't know what my life would be like today if we hadn't been brought together on this earth." By that other gold digger, Matthew, on the day he dumped me. Stop it, I tell myself. Concentrate. Look deep into her eyes. "I was lost, and you know it, until I met you. I didn't know what direction to take in life. But when I was down, you were there." Concentrate, Harry. "And now we're here tonight, less than one month away from sealing our fates together." Squeeze her hand. Kiss her on the cheek. Her eyes are misting up—is it the cocaine? Is she going to sneeze? Never mind. Get on your knees like those idiots in the movies.

"Amity," I say on bended knee, "I present to you, my future bride, this ring. From my family. From my heart."

She smiles and cries like Miss America, and as I rise to place it on her finger, the crowd contributes its tasteful applause while the band plays a jazz version of "Heart and Soul." She nearly has to push her eyes back into their sockets when she flashes those diamonds and emeralds for the crowd. I remember how she told me that, if we ever got married, all she wanted was a *thin gold band*. My ass. I'd have to saw her finger off to take back this ring.

After dinner, the lights go off and the band strikes up the "William Tell Overture" and the waiters come out in a line, carrying silver trays of flaming baked Alaska over their heads. They turn and snake through the entire dining room to great applause. I look across the table to my grandmother. Her eyes are sparkling in awe as she claps like a happy little child while the flaming desserts streak by in the dark, and for the first time tonight, I'm content. It heals my confused heart to see her smiling and clapping, oblivious to the subterfuge that brought this night to fruition. When she looks across the table at me, she stops clapping and nudges my uncle and whispers to him. He reaches into his breast pocket and produces a pen, and she takes it from him and writes something on the linen napkin she's pulled from her lap. Folding the pen into the napkin, she hands the napkin to my uncle and motions for him to discreetly pass it on in my direction.

It arrives from under the table on my right while Amity, to my left, applauds with the rest of the guests. I slowly unfold the napkin and look into my lap to read: "Are you happy?" I use the pen to scribble my response, given without hesitation. "No." And then I pass it back as discreetly as it came to me.

When the lights come back up, Amity is gone. Probably to the ladies' room to shove some more coca leaf powder up her nose.

But when I look over to Uncle Jack and Aunt Shirley's table, where Winston and his date are sitting, I see that Winston is also missing. A doubtful coincidence. I stand to excuse myself, and before I leave the table I see that my grandmother is holding up another napkin, her message written in plain block letters: "TO THINE OWN SELF BE TRUE."

I look at her and shrug, as if it's too late, then step away from the table. Before I leave the dining room, I walk toward the center of the room, letting people congratulate me as I pass by, and when I reach the speaking area where earlier I proposed on bended knee, I reach down and grab the torn check. When a few people notice, I make a joke. "She'll want to tape it back together and head to Maxwell-Grey!" Ha ha ha.

Barbie Botter calls out to me. "Is is true you'll be honeymooning in the Seychelles?"

"Of course!" I call over my shoulder. Where in the hell did she come up with that? I ascend the two steps to the top level of the dining room and wind my way out, piecing the check together. Kim Park is the account holder, and it's definitely made out in Amity's "Princess Modern" handwriting. She stole a check from Kim and forged it—banking on the fact that my mother would never cash it. I stuff the pieces of the check into my pocket.

If Amity and Winston are together, I'm sure they're in the TV room. I quietly approach the door and put my ear to it. Muted voices. A man and a woman. I slowly pull it open and peek inside. Children are frozen, two to a big cushy chair, staring at the flickering light of the TV screen while *The A-Team* thwarts a sabotage plot. The children, set free after dinner, are transfixed by the excitement of the small screen. They slurp their Shirley Temples with a frenetic pace that parallels the plot and root for Mr. T. If I weren't on a mission, I'd be happy to stay here with the innocents, but I've got a sabotage plot of my own to thwart.

I leave the TV room and head back across the edge of the dining room, through a hallway, and approach the men's card room. Again I hear voices. But no woman's voice. I stop at the doorway and steal a look inside. Fat cats my father's age are murmuring to each other, shaking hands, making an illegal business deal, no doubt. One takes two cigars from his breast pocket, and they start to light up. I hate the smell of cigars. I leave.

Maybe Winston and Amity actually went to the bathroom at the same time. I enter the men's and Bob Valentine is at the urinal. "Have you seen my brother?" I ask.

He laughs with contempt, shakes his dick clean, and goes to the mirror.

"How about my *big sister?*" I ask.

He fusses with his thinning hair. "Your sister's in the coat room with her future brother-in-law, Nicolo."

God, this is all getting confusing. "Thanks," I tell him. "It's too bad we both turned out to be jerks."

I walk down the hall again, toward the coat-check room, where I notice the coat-check girl standing nervously in the hallway outside of her station. She starts to speak, but I put my finger to my lips, telling her to shush. I open her little Dutch door, still conducting her to silence with my finger, and hear the two voices.

"Are you crazy?" I hear Winston ask. "I'm offering you your freedom and two million dollars. What more do you want?"

"Harry," Amity says. Is she talking to me? I freeze. How am I going to confront them both at once? I'm not ready. "I want Harry," she tells him. "We're in love." My heart is in my throat, but I realize she hasn't seen me. I duck behind a fur coat, grabbing its hanger to mute any noise. The fur is soft on my face, but it smells like mothballs. I'd prefer the smell of the cigars. Slowly, one-sixteenth of an inch at a time, I slide the coat over the rod, until I have a tiny frame of the two of them.

"You're more full of shit than that stupid horse of his. I know what you think you're doing, having this little agreement with my brother. But I'm telling you, it'll never happen. I know Harry. He won't go through with it. He's in love with Nicolo. You said so yourself to my mother, no doubt because you were worried he'd leave you. You *should* worry. We're Fords. We know how to take care of ourselves. This little quest for money isn't his style. If he thinks he'll lose Nicolo, he'll call off the wedding—I'm sure of it. And you'll be left with nothing." He holds out a business card.

"And you'll be left with *everything*. And there would be no problems for you," Amity points out, refusing the card. "So I don't think you're sure of it at all," she claims, giving him her best John Belushi eyebrow. "Or you wouldn't be offering me this *little* bribe."

"Let's just call it an insurance marker. Don't be foolish. Take it. Even if you win the gamble and he marries you, by the time you divorce him—two months later, I presume—our lawyers will be ready to destroy you, and you'll walk away with far less than I'm offering you now. Why put yourself through it? Besides, shouldn't he ride off into the sunset with his *true* love? If you love him, like I do, you should want to see him happy. Or are you more interested in your own happiness?"

"Scoundrels like you are horsewhipped in Texas," she says, throwing her shoulders back.

"Cut the Southern crap, *Amy*." Amity steps back, and she looks as if she's been slapped on the face. Winston continues. "Amy Stubbs. Surely you didn't think I wouldn't investigate your cave clan, *Amy*. Your grandmother's had a stroke, my ass. She's a pig farmer from Waco. The Stubbses didn't even know they were invited tonight. And even if they had, they probably wouldn't have arrived in time, considering they probably travel by pack mule."

"My name is Amity Stone," Amity says, her voice shaking. "Legally."

"You can change your name," Winston snarls, "but you'll always be Amy Stubbs, trailer trash from Waco. Shoplifting misdemeanors, hot checks, and booked on possession. My mother will never find you suitable.''

Amity's eyes are blurred with tears. "I'm in love with your brother and we're going to have a wedding,'' she states. But then she cautiously takes the card from my brother's hand and tucks it into her cleavage.

"Good girl. Now go home and change the lines in your little script and call me when you're ready to make a deal.''

I suck my stomach in and smash myself against the cloak room wall. Winston leaves first, and in a few seconds, after she composes herself, Amity glides out. I wait another minute before I exit myself, mothballs burning my nasal linings. I slip the coat room girl a twenty dollar bill—probably her third bill in two minutes.

"What a grand evening!'' my mother trumpets, walking through the front door of the house.

"What a grand evening,'' Amity echoes. "Thank you, Susan and Donald. This evening was a fairy tale. I only wish you'd have let my parents pay for this.''

"You never told me about their offer,'' I interrupt.

"I know you wouldn't have allowed it, Harry,'' she says.

"No, he wouldn't,'' my mother says. "None of us would.''

"If only Winston and Patty were staying here with us,'' Amity glows, "we'd all be together.''

"Yes. They were more comfortable in a hotel this time,'' Donald says, greatly relieved.

Amity and I head out to our room and peel ourselves out of our smoke-infested party clothes. I keep my underwear on, but Amity is naked. I kiss her poison cheek and head into the bathroom to brush my teeth. She follows me, puts the lid down on the toilet, and pees. "Harry, I have to tell you something.''

"Yes?'' I garble, my mouth full of spearmint toothpaste.

"Winston came to me tonight.''

Did she see me hiding in the coat room? Is that why she's

spilling the beans? No, it's just like her to tell me about it. That's how she duped me to begin with—and probably all the other guys too—by always being so painfully *honest*. I look angered, stop brushing my teeth, and slam my toothbrush down. "What happened?" I ask, spitting the paste out of my mouth.

"He's concerned that you still might be in love with Nicolo. Don't ask me how he knows," she says, winding the toilet paper around her hand about ten times rather than pulling off a few squares the way she usually does. "Your mother must have told him about Nicolo, and now he's afraid you might call off the wedding."

"Why would he care? He has everything to gain."

She wipes herself and flushes the toilet. "But he does care, Bubba. Oh, he acts mean and nasty around you, but he tells me he loves you, and since he knows you want to receive your inheritance, he's worried that you might forfeit the whole thing just for Nicolo."

I can't believe she's saying this shit, twisting the conversation, substituting the wrong pronouns again, misrepresenting my brother's misrepresentations. *She's* worried that I might forfeit the whole thing for Nicolo. "I assure you, he *hopes* I give it all up for Nicolo," I tell her, bringing the first amount of truth to this barren table. "He's even tried to bribe me."

She pulls her toothbrush from her toiletry kit. "Bribe you?" she asks calmly. "How?" She slowly puts some paste on her brush, but her hands are shaking.

I can see she's blown out of the water. "Yes, he offered to buy Nicolo and me a house, a second car, even give me back my horse. And throw in some junk bonds on top of that. *If* I call off the wedding with you and flee with Nicolo."

"G'yaw, Harry. What—" She stops.

"What am I going to do?" I wash my hands.

She shrugs and starts brushing her teeth.

"Of course I told him to fuck off. He thinks he can throw me a few crumbs while he walks away with the cake. Forget it. We said we would be honest with each other, me and you, and play this thing out, and that's what I intend to do. Besides, Nicolo doesn't love me—and you do.''

She brushes her teeth delicately, as if she's in pain—which I know is impossible since the cocaine has probably numbed her entire mouth. Meaning, I've gotten through to her. She spits, rinses. I wait to see if she comes clean, admits that Winston is playing us both against each other. ''Do you love Nicolo?'' she asks.

I'm stunned. I didn't think my feelings for Nicolo entered into her equation. ''What does it matter?'' I tell her, drying my hands. ''We're getting married—you and I.''

''It matters,'' she says.

''Yes,'' I tell her, unable to lie about it. ''I do. I love him. But the guy hates me. He doesn't want to see me. So I'm not going to chase him around like some pathetic puppy dog. I've got bigger fish to fry.'' That's one of her lines—I'm sure she'll appreciate it. ''We'll be married and have lots of money so we can see whomever we want. What's the problem?''

I watch the tension evaporate from her face as she relaxes, stands, and takes my hand. Then she squints, as if looking far off into the distance at something very beautiful. ''He shouldn't worry. None of us should. This is all going to turn out great.'' *Grite.* Her hair is naturally as blond as the ripest wheat. Her breasts are perfect little margarine cups. Her stomach is as flat as a kitchen counter. Her waist is so narrow you can practically put your hands around it and have your fingertips touch. And it's apparent that she has no intention of telling me about Winston's two-million-dollar offer, which means her little bush of light brown pubic hair is waxed into a perfect little V for victory. Victory over Winston, and victory over me.

CHAPTER
TWENTY-THREE

Jacqueline and I are driving in my car to the Highland Park Cafeteria. I check the rearview mirror often because my driver's side mirror was torn off when Amity borrowed the car two days ago to pick up her cleaning at the drive-through cleaners. Culture Club's "Church of the Poison Mind" is playing on the radio, and I talk over Boy George as I drive, explaining the whole story to Jacqueline. My family, the will, my brother, Amity, Nicolo, all of it. I spare nothing—because it's only two weeks until the wedding and Nicolo still won't see me, so I've come up with a plan. Actually, my friend Randy came up with it. Over a long phone conversation, as I described the cast of characters, he recommended I enlist Jacqueline to bail me out. "She's clay, Harry. Just mold her into what you need." It's weak and not really a great plan, and it's insulting to Jackie I'm sure, but it's the best I can do.

"So you see," I tell her as we snake down the line, past the wall of presidential photographs in the cafeteria, "I need you to marry me. Just for a month or something."

"Roast beef, uh-huh, roast beef," she requests from the server. She speaks to me without looking at me. "I thought you said you had to be married ten years."

"It's credited at ten percent a year. So we'll wait a month, get a divorce—that I'll pay for—and at least get a few hundred thousand dollars for our one-twelfth of a year marriage. Then we'll get on with our lives."

"Broccoli. Steamed broccoli," she tells the vegetable gal.

"See, the rest of my inheritance is forfeited to the estate in the event of a divorce, and my mother controls the estate, so at least Winston and Amity won't get anything."

"Zucchini bread, please. Zucchini bread."

"So what do you say?"

"Lemon." She picks up a glass of iced tea from the tray of hundreds of iced teas. "Lemon," she says.

We sit across from each other and I take her hand. "Jackie, please. I need your help. This is my life here. I've got to get Nicolo back. And I've got to out maneuver Winston and Amity. You're my only hope. Please."

"I don't know," she says, drawing her hand back. "I mean, I don't want to marry a guy unless he wants to have a baby with me. I want a guy who wants to have a baby with me, because I want a baby."

"Fine. We'll buy a baby. A doll. We'll get out of bed every two hours at night and pretend it's crying. Then after we get divorced, we'll throw it in the trash and you can have a real one with the guy you *really* marry."

She pulls off a piece of zucchini bread and puts it into her mouth. "I don't know, Harry. People are supposed to marry for love."

God, I hate it when uncomplicated people are earnest. And right. But I can't let Winston steal my inheritance. Or Amity. "I *will* marry for love. I'm going to marry Nicolo. And you're going to marry for love too. Just not this time."

"Well, what about a license and everything," she asks.

I fork one of my beef tips. "We'll get a license. Today."

She cuts herself a piece of roast beef. Then cuts that piece again. Then again. "I don't know if I can do this to Amity. She saved my ass, man. If it weren't for her, I'd have lost my job. She was a friend to me."

"And you'll still be a friend to her. If we tell her now, there's plenty of time for her to save face and bow out gracefully. It'll be fine. And after I get my money, I'll pay for Amity to go to the rehab center. We won't just abandon her."

"It's still mean," she laments, putting the roast beef in her mouth.

I squeeze my corn muffin as if it's her head. "Jesus, Jacqueline. I've told you what she's doing to me. She's a fucking crook. Worse, if she takes the two million my brother offered her, she'll spin totally out of control."

"She'll buy a lot of clothes," Jackie says, spearing a piece of broccoli.

"What she'll buy is coke, weed, and champagne," I warn. "She'll ruin her own life besides ruining mine."

Jacqueline sighs, sticking a broccoli floret into her mouth halfway and leaving it to look like a bonsai tree hanging from her lips. Finally, she sucks up the tree and answers, "I know. She ruined my life too."

"What do you mean?"

"She was fooling around with my boyfriend Arthur. Behind my back. It was her and Arthur together that wrecked my Jaguar. They wrecked it." She sips her tea, looks away, ashamed. "Together."

I remember Amity saying that Arthur has *no conscience.* "Jackie! Why haven't you ever told me this?"

"Friends shouldn't talk about friends," she says simply. "Friends are friends."

"Even if they fuck you over completely? Jackie, her name isn't even Amity Stone. It's Amy Stubbs. She's Amy Stubbs from Waco. Has she ever told you that?"

"Well, I don't know about the name thing, but I know she's from Waco."

"So she's still lying to you. And me."

"What does it matter what her name is? She is who she is, no matter what. Look, we all make mistakes," she says, taking a sip of tea. "You don't just dump someone out of your life when they make a mistake."

She's right. It's what Nicolo's mother is doing to me, and it's devastating. How could I do this to Amity? "You're incredible, Jackie," I tell her sincerely. "You *are* her friend, aren't you?"

"She doesn't have anybody really. Just you and me." She punctures the meringue of her coconut cream pie with her finger, then sticks her finger in her mouth and tastes the meringue. Turning her attention back to her broccoli, she thinks quietly to herself while munching like a turtle. I don't press her, but wait for her to finish and take a sip of tea. "Yes, Harry. You're a nice guy. And I think you're right. I think she'll probably fuck you over. She's had her sights on you since that day we all met. When the hospital called me, after they found my phone number in your pocket, Amity called about two minutes later and insisted I didn't need to go to the hospital. I could tell she wanted to get her hooks into you."

"She told me you weren't home when the hospital called," I say, shaking my head.

"Look, she can't help herself. I mean, she just can't help herself. But I can. I can control myself, and I'm not going to fuck her over just because she's fucking you over. There's too much fucking over going on. And it's against my principles to marry someone I don't love. See, that's what Amity needs. She needs your love. Then maybe she would get better. She'd probably get better."

I'm now feeling guilty for trying to get the upper hand. Maybe I should think about loving Amity, rather than trying to outsmart her. And who says Nicolo would accept my bogus marriage to Jackie any more than he'd accept my bogus marriage to Amity anyway?

Randy's plan is no plan at all.

* * *

After dropping Jackie off at the drugstore at the end of our block, I swing by the ATM machine, then head for home, feeling confused, angry, and hopeless. As I pull into the driveway, I see people at the back door sitting on the step. A middle-aged man and woman. They're dressed in church clothes, and the woman is holding something in her lap.

As I pull in and turn the car off, the man stands and puts his hand out to help the woman rise from the steps. They look at me and smile. I step out of my increasingly ragged new car; they walk toward me. "Hi," I say as they approach, the woman carrying a pie. "Amity's out of town. You're her parents, aren't you?"

"How did you know?" the woman asks, smiling. Her twang is softer than Amity's, and she's plain and sweet. Auburn hair pulled back into a bun. Forest green dress, brown flat shoes. She looks nothing like Amity.

"I knew she couldn't hide you forever," I answer honestly.

"She'd try," the man says candidly, just the slightest amount of hurt on his face. He's a large man in a big brown suit. His wingtip shoes are polished into a gleaming shine. "Jim Stubbs," the man announces, reaching out to shake my hand. "And this here's my wife, Erline." His Texas accent is thicker than his wife's.

I like them immediately. "Harry Ford," I say, shaking their hands.

"She's told us all about you," Mr. Stubbs smiles.

"We were so relieved to finally get a letter," his wife adds.

"Come on in the house."

"OK, but don't tell Amity," Mrs. Stubbs answers, giving me an impish wink.

I take them into the sitting room and seat them on the couch. After taking a folding chair from the hall closet, I sit next to them. Mrs. Stubbs puts the pie on the coffee table. "It's homemade peach, Amy's—I mean Amity's—favorite."

I smile. "I know. So did you drive over from Waco?"

"Yes," Mrs. Stubbs answers, "but we're supposed to be from Fort Worth," she chuckles nervously.

"I guess you're wonderin' why we're here," Mr. Stubbs says. Before I answer, he continues. "We'd been worried because she hadn't been returnin' our calls or letters, and in the past, that's meant she's fallen off the wagon."

"She has a history of substance-abuse problems," her mother says knowingly, as if she's spent time with a family counselor. "But that's all behind her now."

I smile and withhold. What good will it do to tell them she's gone wild with the cocaine again?

Her mother continues. "I know she'll want to kill us for coming unannounced, but we were so thrilled to learn all about you, and when she told us she would be getting married again, well, we wanted to do *something*, so we baked her a pie."

"That's very sweet. She'll be glad, I'm sure."

"You must be somethin' special, young man," her father tells me, "because she's never invited us to the other weddin's."

Weddings. Plural. How many? I wonder.

"We were so impressed with what she wrote about you," her mother says, in awe. "How your family background has made you the right man for her."

Oh, I'm sure. She probably couldn't wait to tell them that I was a *Ford* and how much my inheritance would be.

Her father looks at me with regard. "She says you're different from any man she's ever met."

What? Gay? Dumber than the others?

"Kind and sweet," her mother says softly. Then she grins, "But watch out for his sense of humor, she told us. 'He makes me laugh till I'm standing in a pee puddle,' she wrote!"

"We were surprised," her dad says honestly. "We never learn

anything until after she's married, and by then she's usually divorced.''

''We suspect you must have money,'' her mom laughs, ''but we don't give a hoot. Because this time we know it's right. She says you've overcome your family to be the man you are, and that's why she feels she knows you, because she's done the same thing.''

''What do you mean?''

''Oh, we don't take it personal no more,'' her father says.

''Nope,'' her mother decrees. She wears no makeup but has a few freckles on her nose, and they give her face a youthful quality for her age. ''It was like she was born to the wrong family from day one. She used to look up from my breast and just *squint*, like 'Who the hell are you? My *real* mother's a queen.' And I'd look down and think, 'Oh, Lord, this one's going to be trouble.' ''

''She was wearing makeup by the age of three,'' her father laughs. ''But Erline here don't wear any, so she had to steal it from her little playmate's mother next door. Can you imagine? Three years old and stealing makeup?''

''Don't misunderstand,'' Mrs. Stubbs says politely. ''We always loved her. She just wasn't like other kids. I mean, how many six year olds play the character of Blanche Dubois in a scene from *A Streetcar Named Desire* at their first grade talent night, *with feeling*?'' I can tell by Mrs. Stubbs's smile that she's reliving the scene in her head.

''She read *Gone With the Wind* from cover to cover at the age of seven,'' Mr. Stubbs gloats. Then he chuckles. ''She's always had a flair for the dramatic.''

''We're not stupid, Mr. Ford,'' Mrs. Stubbs says quietly, smoothing her skirt. ''We know there's an ache in her heart. We just don't know what it is. It's like she always feels she's missing something.''

Her father shakes his head. ''When we'd have tornadoes, I'd have to drag her to the cellar kickin' and screamin', because she always wanted to stay in the house and fly over the rainbow to Oz.''

"Yep," Mrs. Stubbs adds. "She's always thought there's something better than what she has, and if she moves fast enough, she'll catch up with it."

"We're thinkin' maybe she's finally caught up with it," Mr. Stubbs tells me sincerely. "Because she sure ain't never wrote a letter about anyone like she did the one about you. She makes it sound like you hung the moon, and she put no dollar figure on it. That's a good sign."

Her mother looks at me with soulful eyes. "We just wish she felt she had a family. Of course we *are* her family, but if we're not good enough, just 'cuz we buy our underwear at Wards and prefer beer over that imported champagne she drinks—well, then OK, we can accept that. We just want her to make a family of her own," her mother says tenderly. "And not just in her imagination. So when we got her letter, we realized it's finally going to happen. Thank you, Mr. Ford. Thanks for taming the beast in our little girl." Mrs. Stubbs leans over and hugs me. Mr. Stubbs pats me on the leg.

"Will you stay for pie?" I ask, my emotions more confused than ever.

"That would be mighty nice," Mr. Stubbs answers.

CHAPTER
TWENTY-FOUR

Amity has managed to avoid me during the past week. She's flying to and fro, crowing about the bridesmaids' dresses, the corsages, and all the preparations. She's on the phone with my mother constantly, screaming and laughing with joy. I haven't told her that her parents came to visit, because they made me promise not to. They told me she'll punish them for "ruining whatever tall tales she's spun on their behalf." And that she won't speak to them for an even longer period of time if I tell her what I know. I honor their request, but know that I have to speak to Amity somehow.

I've lost almost all hope of Nicolo. Though I'll be forever in love with him, and I have no doubt that he is my true soul mate, I'm afraid that his mother has won her own little dirty war, and that my fate is now with Amity, who I'm beginning to believe loves me in her own way—I'm just not sure it's the way I want to be loved.

I'm flying my last trip before Amity and I leave for the wedding in Kansas. My first flight of the morning is from Dallas to Shreveport, where we get delayed on the ground for three hours due to thunderstorms. Even on the ground, the aisle floor is moving beneath my feet, a lingering phenomenon caused by the turbulence of the previous flight from Dallas. And the aircraft cabin is a sweltering, humid prison because they won't let any of the passengers off the plane, in case we get clearance to leave on the spur of the moment. I have one guy tell me he is going to get the captain fired if he doesn't take off for Dallas right now. We're sitting at the gate, the sky is thundering and lightning as if it's Judgment Day and we've all been *very* bad, hail is smashing against the plane, and this guy wants to take off. And I know it's because he's bald, because those type-A bald guys have too much testosterone. They have to shave three times a day and get fucked three times a day, or they start yelling at flight attendants, insisting we take off in hurricanes.

Finally, after sitting for hours, we depart and some portly gal from Louisiana comes out of the rear lavatory, holding the in-flight magazine against her ass. "Mr. Steward," she says to me, "are you aware that you're out of sanitary napkins in there?" What the hell am I supposed to do? Ask the captain to land at a 7-11? I want to hand her a cocktail napkin and a Band-Aid and tell her to make herself a little minipad—with wings—but I bite my tongue and follow her up to the front lav to show her the compartment that holds those airline-issued rat mattresses we call sanitary napkins. When she tells me she'd prefer a tampon, I stop biting my tongue and tell her, "People in hell want ice water," before storming back down the aisle.

And then, as we smash around the clouds on our way back to Dallas, a seven-year-old child who's seated in the first row of coach, flying alone, throws up his airport hot dog. And when I go to help him clean himself up, he throws up again, on me. And the smell, and the feel, and the texture of regurgitated hot dog dripping off my face makes *me* throw up. And that makes the man in the row behind us moan, "Oh, God, I'm fixin' to puke." And the woman across from him says, "Myself!" and lets loose with chunks of creamed corn, causing the two children traveling with her to throw up. And I want to get on the P.A. system and announce, "Will everyone please throw up!" But instead I hold my head out in front of my torso and scurry to the bathroom—which is occupied. I bang on the door, but give up and turn to the galley, where I pull out the trash can and wipe my face off with a wet paper towel, while the stressed-out stewardesses who are still devoid of vomit frantically try to help all the heaving fools in their seats. When the ancient geezer finally exits the lav, I enter—and step directly into the puddle of whiz he's left on the floor. I try to unwrap the little soap, but it's glued so tightly shut that I consider going into the cockpit and grabbing the crash ax to hack it open. Finally, I smash it against the counter, rip it open, and use the little soap chips to wash my face.

When the plane lands in Dallas, I call the scheduling department from the loading bridge and tell them to send a replacement because I'm going home to run a screwdriver through my skull. But I don't go home. I drive Amity's car (she'd asked me to drive her car to the airport, so that she can "run wedding errands in the Beamer" while I was out of town) straight to Nicolo's house and park on the street. His truck is missing, but I don't care, I sit outside and wait. I won't try to win him back. I just want one, final, last, ultimate chance to set the record straight. And I wait for over two hours, nervously thrashing in the seat of Amity's car like a cricket caught in a jar, so that by the time Nicolo and his mother drive into their driveway, I'm drenched with sweat, my face still smells hot doggish, I have no idea what I'm going to say, and I'm so utterly exhausted, mentally and physically, I simply give up. I don't even get out of the car. I just sit there, my hand on the ignition key, ready to leave. Nicolo, after lifting out two bags of groceries from the back of the pickup truck, walks out to the street, and asks me, "What are you doing, Harry?"

"I'm going home, Nicolo," I tell him. "I've been chasing you forever, and I can't chase you anymore. I'm losing respect for

myself. All I've wanted to do is explain, but now I'm going home."
I turn the key, put the car in gear, and roll away. Believe me, my
love for him still endures, and I'll always wish that we could have
a life together, but the heat of the day seems to have melted my
ardor, and I can't get past his mother, nor force Nicolo's face into
a mold if it doesn't fit, so I'm just going to go home and wash my
own face for the eighth time today.

Minutes later I'm in the shower at my house when I hear a
tapping on the window. "Harry," a voice calls, "are you in there?"
It's Nicolo's voice. He's standing outside the slightly open bathroom
window.

"Yes," I yell, washing my face for the ninth time.

"My mother just told me! Your calls. A letter. How you never
gave up. Will you *please* talk to me?"

"That's my line," I tell him, rinsing the soap off.

"Please, Harry. I do want to talk," he tells me.

"The back door is open," I answer.

Not thirty seconds later, he pulls back the curtain to the shower
and stands naked in front of me. I look into his eyes and take a
quick glance at his body. He's gorgeous. "May I come in?" he
asks.

I smile and do an anemic, abbreviated version of one of Amity's
sweeping arm gestures, inviting him in.

He steps in, takes the soap from my hands, turns me, and soaps
my back. "I'm sorry. I'm an Italian at heart, my friend. I let my
anger and emotions keep me from you at first, but by the time I
realized I was wrong, you stopped calling or coming over. And I
thought you had left me. I didn't know that my mother was keeping
us apart. She feels guilty—she wants to tell you herself. I am
guilty too. I haven't been fair. I should have listened to you in the
beginning, and now my mother says time is running out."

His strong hands are moving the soap in circles around my back while the stream of hot water hits my chest. "All I want to do is explain," I tell him, leaning into his hands.

"I'm ready," he whispers in my ear.

"My father wasn't like yours. His principles were strong, but not in the way your father's probably were. He was short-sighted, only aware of his own little society. I guess what I'm trying to say is that he wasn't so concerned with people *living*, as your father was, but with people living *right*." I reach for the soap in his hands, and turn him around. His shoulders are big, like a swimmer's, and his dark skin is made shiny by the sheet of water passing over. I soap his back and massage him. "That meant the right school, the right car, the right house, the right neighborhood. And gay people just didn't live in that neighborhood—know what I mean?"

He nods. "Yes."

I move my hands down to his waist and over his ass, not in a sexual way, but with the strength of therapeutic massage. "You know about my horse, so you know what he's capable of. Anyway, he put it in the will that, if I'm not married by this week, my birthday, I lose my inheritance. And it's millions and millions, Nicolo." I knead his beefy ass, pressing my thumbs into it, and he braces himself against the tile.

"Where did you learn this?" he asks.

"From my father's attorney."

"No. Where did you learn the *massage?*"

"From my ex-boyfriend," I tell him. "He was a swimmer, and he used to have to get massages to work out his cramps." I look past his buttocks to the back of his powerful thighs and down to his calves. Man, even his heels are beautiful. "So at some point after meeting Amity, I realized I could still have my rightful claim, because she understood. Everything. And she was willing to help me, and I was willing to help her, and we could get married, but still have our relationships on the side. How was I supposed to know that I'd meet you and the whole thing would be tested?"

"Do you think she feels about Thomas the way you feel about me?" He turns around, faces me for the answer.

"Not at all," I tell him. I drop the soap and it hits the tub with a clunk. There's a moment of silence; then we both laugh.

"Pick it up," he orders, still laughing.

"No way. You pick it up," I tell him.

"Leave it for now," he suggests. "We'll decide who picks it up later."

"Good idea." I put my hands on his biceps, look him dead in the eye. "She doesn't love Thomas. But I love you. And I want to live with you and be your mate."

"I love you too," he says, pulling my hands off his arms and holding them. "So shouldn't the wedding be between you and me?"

I want it to be, but I don't know if it can. I'm suffocating in the steam, and I have no answer to his question. "Are we done in here?" I ask him. He nods, and I turn off the shower, realizing this is the stupidest move of my life. I could have soaped the front of him. What a fool I am. I step out, dripping, and reach for an extra towel. Hand it to him. And watch as he towels himself dry.

He's more than I imagined. The veins in his forearms run up through his biceps and continue into his chest until they disappear underneath the dark smattering of hair on his upper breast bone. His stomach has a line of hair that swirls around his belly button and runs down into his crotch. The v-shape of his abdomen above his genitals echoes the v-shape of his back and shoulders. His thighs are strong, and the hair underneath his knees, on his shins, is black and straight and luxuriant. I finally take a good look at his penis, and I'm completely magnetized by its beautiful, uncircumcised dark skin. It hangs heavily down, and his balls are darker still and full and loose.

"Can't I have this other wedding first?" I ask, toweling myself off as well. I'm thankful for the results from the gym, because I'm no longer unconfident with my body, but proud of its definition. My dick is slack, but extended in its relaxed state. "We can have anything we want. I'll pay off our school loans. We can go to Argentina, both of us. We'll take your mother and your brother with us. We can all have houses anywhere we choose. We can do volunteer work. You can write for anything you deem worthy. We can ride horses. It will be a life we could only imagine. Don't you want that?"

"Yes," he says honestly, "I do."

"Then come to my wedding. In fact, be my best man! You can stand beside me."

He slings his towel around his neck. "I want to be your best man—in life. Not at your wedding. If I go to your wedding, it is as your groom. Nothing else. What about Amity? You can't just marry her, take your money, and leave. It's not right. I would never respect you. And your mother would not allow it—I know this from meeting her. And my mother would not allow it."

"Gay men and their mothers," I sigh, shaking my head. "Why don't you let me worry about all that?"

He takes the towel from his neck and wraps it around mine, pulling me close. "Because you can't succeed at this. Even if we run away together, you will still be married to Amity."

"On paper," I tell him.

"In front of God," he counters.

"God will see we have our fingers crossed."

He closes his eyes, shakes his head no.

I realize he's right. I have to call it off. Follow my heart. The only reason to marry is for love. Only love. Just as I start to speak, we hear the sound of screeching tires and a loud smash and then a thump and then heels clicking against the sidewalk. "Help! Harry! Help me!"

Nicolo and I run naked into the living room and through the sun porch to the front door just in time for Amity to come crashing through. "Kim's going to kill us! He found out we're getting married!" she screams, slamming the door behind her and locking it. She turns around and sees Nicolo's dick. "G'yaw!"

Out the front windows we see Kim's Jaguar come skidding around the corner, hit the curb, jump into the yard, and smash into the BMW. "Fuck!" I yell, grabbing Amity and Nicolo and running back to my bedroom with them. "Shit!" I scream, realizing I've just run us all into a dead end. I turn them around, push them out. "Come on!"

We shoot through the hall, and out into the living room again. I look out and see him running toward the house with a gun. I push Amity and Nicolo onward, toward the back of the house so we can escape through the kitchen and out the back door. We make it to the sitting room, and all of us smash into the coffee table, but instantly pick ourselves up and dart through the kitchen, then charge through the little laundry room and throw open the back door, Amity in front, Nicolo behind her, and me in the rear.

Kim, cutting us off at the pass, stands there, pointing the gun at us. "Back in house!" he barks, like a strung-out pit bull.

We slowly retreat, facing him, and Amity starts desperately negotiating. "Now, babe. I told you, Harry is *gay*. I just give him a place to hang his hat."

"He hangs hat on your tits!" Kim spits.

"Don't be crazy," Amity says as we back through the kitchen. "These little titties couldn't hold a book of matches! Now I mean it, Kim. It's not what you think!"

"She's telling the truth," I say as we back into the sitting room. Nicolo and I are still without clothing, and my heart is pounding so hard I'm sure Nicolo feels it on his back. I'm scared because I can see the craziness in Kim's eyes. He's obviously on another cocaine binge. He's grinding his teeth, running his free hand through his greasy hair, and waving the gun as if it's a sword. "This is my boyfriend,'' I tell him, before I realize he may shoot me either way—for being Amity's boyfriend or for being gay.

Kim motions with the gun for us to get on the sofa. ''Why do I believe?'' he yells.

We reach back, grab for the sofa, and ease ourselves down. ''Look at them!'' Amity implores. ''They're nudie naked! What the hell are two guys doing nudie naked together in the middle of the day!'' *Middle of the die!*

''Waiting for you!'' Kim says, cocking the trigger of the gun.

''Jesus!'' Nicolo cries.

''Bullshit!'' I yell. ''This is the man I love.''

''Prove to me or you die!'' Kim decrees.

I look at Kim and read his sinister grin. I understand. Turning to Nicolo, I look into his eyes and press my lips into his, as I've been yearning to do since the day we rode horses. Nicolo kisses me back, and within a moment it's as if we're back in west Texas under the cottonwood trees, just the two of us—and at this moment I know we'll always be connected to each other, even if Kim blows us away.

''No good! Just a kiss!''

''What the hell do you want out?'' Amity begs.

''More!'' Kim says, his sinister grin now full on evil.

It's a matter of life or death. Without a word, I slide down off the sofa onto my knees in front of Nicolo and put his dick in my mouth. He doesn't move, nor does Amity, but I hear Kim's footsteps come closer and realize he's standing next to me. As I start to move up and down on Nicolo's trembling dick, I sense the cold, shiny, metal next to my temple. Waiting. Waiting to blow a hole in my head. From the corner of my eye, I see the gun. Nicolo, I'm sure, is too afraid to respond. He sits, motionless, and his penis is motionless as well, remaining soft and unresponsive in my mouth. *Please*, Nicolo. Work with me here, buddy. I pull back on his foreskin, close my eyes, and concentrate, knowing that I have to give the most intense oral sex of my life or I'm going to die. And so I do—I just do. I relax into the rhythm, open my throat, and swallow it the way I swallowed that hot dog at the baseball park when I was twelve. No inhibitions. I take it all. Praying that it's not my last supper.

And he responds. In kind. Unbelievably, for a guy who has a loaded gun pointed at his *head*. And I just keep going, fervently, madly, totally committed to saving all our lives.

"Stop!" Kim yells. I stop. Slowly raise my head. Nicolo's dick is standing straight up.

"G'yaw!" Amity says with wide-eyed approval of Nicolo's dick.

Kim points his gun at Amity. "He learned from you!"

"What?" she asks incredulously.

"He does just like you. You have been with him. You taught him!"

"Christ on a crutch, Kim! How the hell do you teach a heterosexual guy to give a blow job like that? That's like forcing an infant to eat a pork rib!" Amity is shaking with fear, and I don't think she or Kim hears the car door slam outside. "If I offered to teach you how to give a killer blow job, would you get down on your knees and stick this guy's dick in your mouth?"

Kim skews his face and spits on the hardwood floor. "No! Disgusting!"

"Well, OK then," Amity tells him, stomping her foot. "You can't teach a straight guy to blow like that!"

The front door smashes open, its lock broken by force. Kim wheels around and points the gun at Thomas. "Shit!" Amity shrieks. "What are *you* doing here?"

Thomas stands there, dumbfounded by his heroic entrance, realizing it's a stupid move since he's empty-handed and Kim holds the gun on him. "We're supposed to go to the movies! Why didn't you tell me to bring my gun?"

I look at Amity, see the scheduling screwup register in her head. "Damn."

"Who fuck are you?" Kim spews at Thomas.

"Who the fuck are you?" Nicolo butts in. Until now, fear and surprise have kept his Latin temper in check, but now it comes roiling to the surface. Or maybe he's just pissed that the blow job is over.

"Careful," I tell him. "He's not a member of PFLAG."

"What's PFLAG?" Thomas asks.

"Parents and Friends of Lesbians and Gays," Amity answers.

"That's right," Kim barks. "I'm not no member!"

All I can think is that he's used a double negative, which means he *is* a member of PFLAG. I'll never be able to explain it to him.

"G'yaw!" Jacqueline yells from the lawn. "Your new car looks like shit, Harry! It looks like shit. Your new car. What in the—" She enters through the broken door. "G'yaw! He's got a gun. A gun!"

"People shut up!" Kim yells, taking control of the room again. "Get in," he orders Jackie.

"For Christ's sake, Kim," Amity wails. "You can't shoot us all!"

I count. "Yes, he can. That thing's a revolver. Five bullets, five people."

Amity counts. "No, you gotta include Kim. People who shoot roomfuls of people always turn the gun on themselves. He wouldn't have a bullet for himself, which means he'd have to go to prison"— she turns to Kim—"*and get fucked up the ass for the rest of your life by big black men.*"

Kim winces.

The phone rings. No one moves. On the third ring, Amity walks to the phone, picks it up. "Hello? Susan! How are you?" she asks as if she's lounging on a chaise by the pool. "Of course, he's right here. Harry," she says, her hand over the receiver, "it's your mother."

I don't move. Amity extends the phone my way and looks at me like *take it*. I slowly move to her, grasp the phone. "Yes, Mother?"

"Hi, dear. I'm calling to say never mind your airline tickets tomorrow. I was able to call in a favor with the Goldmans and they're sending down the Lear jet for you. Isn't that marvelous?"

"Marvelous."

"So I want you two to be at Love Field tomorrow at exactly 10:00 A.M., the executive terminal, because they don't want to have to shut the engines down. They're just going to keep the Lear idling, and you two can hop on board, and they'll whisk you to Wichita!"

"Great."

"What time did I say?" she asks like a schoolteacher.

"Ten o'clock," I tell her.

"Wonderful! Donald and I will meet you at the airport when you land. Gotta run. I'm having some color done on my hair for the wedding, and Donald and I are making a surprise purchase today! Love your guts!"

She hangs up the phone. And I wait a few seconds, holding the receiver to my ear while the dial tone threads through my brain.

The police sirens are sounding now. Coming closer. Someone must have reported the two smashed cars on the lawn. Kim panics, runs past everyone, and flies out the door. He fires up his Jaguar, unhooking it from the smashed BMW as he backs out over the lawn, and floors it. We run to the window and watch as he drops over the curb onto the street and screeches away, heading north, away from the university.

Amity slams into save-your-ass mode. "Jackie, Thomas, you just got here. You didn't see *anything*. Harry, Nicolo, put some clothes on!" She brushes her hands over her face, sweeping off her nose. "Any powder?"

I check her face for cocaine. "No!" Then I grab Nicolo, drag him into the bathroom, scoop up his clothes, and pull him into my bedroom, grabbing the bong out of the hallway as I go. We hear the squad cars come screeching around the corner and shut down. Doors slam. Voices yell.

"Freeze!" we hear the cops scream into the living room as they come through the front door. I hear Jackie scream, "G'yaw!" in response. Then we hear the back door fly open. We're surrounded. "I'm sorry," I tell Nicolo. "I never meant to put you in danger."

"Officer," Amity cries, so loud we can hear her from the bedroom, "it was horrible! Did you see my car? Some strange man followed me home and tried to kill me."

"Is he gone?" the cop asks.

"Yes, he drove away," we hear Amity tell him.

The door to my bedroom flies open, a policeman points a gun at Nicolo and me. "Freeze!"

We stand there, both of us still naked, Nicolo holding his clothes.

"Harry!" I hear Amity scream. She comes running, pushing past the cop with the drawn gun. "This is my roommate and his friend!" she explains. The cop lowers his gun, looks at Amity. "What's the matter? Haven't you ever seen a couple of naked queers before?" she asks as if the cop lives in a vacuum.

"Quick!" the other cop says, barging in. "We need a description of the perpetrator and his car." He repeats Amity's descriptions into his radio as she talks.

"About six feet tall," Amity says, "with short red hair. Freckles. Irish looking. He wore wire-framed glasses. And drove a black car—you can see the paint his car left on the BMW. It was a black station wagon, American made. He went south through the university!"

The cops are gone. Jacqueline and Thomas have left—together. The trashed BMW has been towed. The front door has been nailed shut. And Nicolo and I are standing in the street, next to his truck.

He's laughing and rubbing his eyes. *"Dios mio,* hombre, that was one hot time on the couch."

"Yeah, well I was sort of under the gun, you know?" I answer, laughing myself. I blush.

"Nothing to be embarrassed about," he assures me. "I'll never forget it. Or the kiss," he adds softly.

"Me either. Look, I'm really sorry about everything that has happened. Honestly, I'd die if you ever got hurt. When that fool was waving that gun, I just kept thinking about your mother and how she couldn't bear to lose one more child."

"Don't worry. I've been through much more difficult times. Crazy, gun-carrying Americans don't scare me—not after what I've been through in Argentina."

"I guess that's right," I tell him.

He takes my hand, looks soulfully into my eyes. "Harry, you're *loco.* And I love you for it. You're my funny hero and a poet, and you ride a horse with skill, like the gauchos. These are the reasons I love you, and many more. But I can't live with you if you are married to someone else. I'll tell you one more time: If you marry her, you can not marry me."

Tears fill my eyes. I nod. Kiss his cheek. I have no way of responding other than gently patting his shoulder. Why the hell don't I get into the truck with him and ride away? What is it that makes me continue this alliance with Amity? Is it pity? Hardly a basis for a marriage. Is it the inheritance? If it is, then I've become as soulless and manipulative as I accuse my brother of being. Is it love? Is that why I'm with her? Do I love her enough to create the family we both desire?

Nicolo opens the door, steps up into his truck, fires it up, and slowly drives away, looking back at me from his open window.

I walk into the house and sit down beside Amity. "Harry," she says quietly, "where's the bong?"

I walk into my bedroom, retrieve it from the closet, and return.

She grabs the baggie of pot from under the sofa cushion and fills the bowl. I light the bowl for her, and she inhales hard, taking in a tremendous amount of smoke before handing me the bong. As I suck in, she exhales, and with her exhalation she breaks down into sobs. "I'm sorry, Bubba. I'm truly sorry. I've made a terrible mess of things."

I hold the smoke in my lungs, look at her, then exhale. I realize I've been awfully hard on somebody who probably has a good heart buried inside. I slide my arm around her shoulders and hug her to me. "It's OK, honey. You didn't mean for things to turn out this way, I'm sure." And I am. Even with all the subterfuge, lies, and manipulation, I doubt she planned on a shoot-out at the BJ Corral.

"Where's Nicolo?" she chokes, still sobbing.

"He went home."

She looks at me, her cheeks drowning in saltwater, mascara racooning her baby blues. "Is he coming back?" She sounds scared, almost childlike.

I answer with a sigh, "I'm not sure."

She sobs with shame and lights up the bong again.

Seeing her like this, so weak, so fragile underneath the bravado of her surface, I realize something I've probably known for a while now: Nicolo is strong. He'll survive without me. It may be painful and difficult at first, but he *will* survive. And Amity? Not a chance. She'll self-destruct. Even if she does make it out of the treatment center again, she'll snap right back to this place, this hallway, with her nasal linings throbbing, and her head in a marijuana cloud— even if her sense of humor prevails. She'll remain out of control, pushing her family away, while hunting out her next five-minute man to jump in and rescue her.

"What'll we do?" she sobs.

I look at her and smile. "We'll get married—that's what we'll do."

"Harry, you belong with Nicolo," she tells me, wiping the tears from her eyes. "You don't care about money like other people do. Fuck the inheritance."

I can't believe she says it. "It's not just the money," I say wistfully. "If I give up the wedding, I'll be giving up my family too. They'll abandon me. My whole identity, fucked as it is, like it or not, is still wrapped up in my family. How can I just let them go?"

"I can't answer that. I just don't know how that feels," she answers in a dazed whisper, "being a part of a family like that."

"Amity, I'm not supposed to tell you, but I met your parents. They're nice people. They love you. They told me great stories. Playing Blanche Dubois, reading *Gone With the Wind*. How you stole makeup from the neighbors when you were three," I tease, nudging her on the leg.

"I didn't steal that makeup," she says in a trance. "I earned it. From my friend's father." Tears stream down her face.

I get a sick feeling. "Oh, God," I whisper, after her statement hits me. "Is that why you're never having kids?"

She nods. "They might turn out like me."

I take her hand and hold it in mine. "I'm sorry." I let her cry for a minute, then explain, "I'm not trying to hurt you, Amity, but my guess is you've been running your whole life toward some kind of home you feel is good enough for you. Or maybe you're just running away from the neighbors' home because it was so bad for you. But the faster and farther you run, the more unhappy you become, and the larger your ghosts loom over your bed at night. If I leave my family, don't you think it's going to be the same for me?"

"But you've overcome all that. That's what's so great about you."

I shake my head no. "You're wrong. I haven't overcome them at all. You can't escape your family because your family is what makes you who you are. This whole year has showed me that."

She shrugs, the tears drip down her face.

I take her hand and push my fingers against hers. "I want to say I'm sorry. I've been thinking some pretty awful things about you lately. I sold you short. You've been a wonderful friend to me, Amity. Nobody else came to that hospital room when I was sick. And you pulled me off that couch at the airport and were willing to let me live here for free. You shared the spoils with me as they came your way and covered me in Padre Island when my credit cards were bum. You've become friends with my mother and made her feel younger than any face-lift ever could. You've confirmed what I've always known about my brother. And most important of all, you've taught me I can never escape my past—never outrun the Fords of Kansas. So how can you tell me to choose Nicolo over you?"

"Because you're gay. And you love him. Right?"

The tide turns. The tears recede into her eyes and flow from mine. "Yes, I love him. But he also has a family that loves him— just as he is," I say, wiping the tears away with my forearm. "Unlike me. And maybe through this whole sicko bullshit game, you and I can create some kind of new family we can live with. So I want you to marry me, Amity. But I have to tell you right now: If we do this, we do it for love. No money. Winston can have it. Or my mother or whoever. But no inheritance. It's the only way."

She looks uncomfortable. "Not a dime?"

"Not a dime."

"But you love me?" she asks, her brow wrinkled. "You truly love me?"

"Yes, Amity. I love you."

"Enough to give up Nicolo?"

"Yes," I tell her, wiping away more tears. "Enough to give up Nicolo." I wrap my arms around her and pull her close to me and hope that I'm doing the right thing.

CHAPTER
TWENTY-FIVE

When we arrive at Love Field, the Lear is idling. Amity, in her black stirrup pants and lemon-colored sweater, is radiant, carrying her wedding gown in one hand, a container of biscuits and gravy in the other. She's gone light on the makeup and left her blond hair straight and pulled back into a pony tail. I don't know how, but she looks ten years younger than I've ever seen her. Her eyes are clear, focused, even after the four bong hits she swallowed into her lungs before we left the house. Her complexion is luminous. There's a softness to her sense of purpose that I don't recognize.

I'm so nervous I feel as if I'm going to throw up, but she's as relaxed as the day we met. And just as ebullient. She'd insisted we stop at Butch's for biscuits and gravy, so the pilots of the Lear have a chance to eat a real Texas breakfast. The smell of the food while driving made me nauseated. As I lowered the windows to take in fresh air so I wouldn't vomit, she laughingly told me, "You're probably pregnant, darlin'!"

As we climb the little steps to the jet, Amity calls, "Hi, boys! Harry and I brought you some grub. Get it while it's hot!" The pilots are instantly in love with her and thank her kindly for the food.

She lays her dress in the seats across from us, and we buckle ourselves in. The jet takes off like a rocket, leaving Dallas in the dust. We streak past the skyscrapers of downtown, swing into an easterly turn that continues until we're heading north for Kansas. I look out the little window as we pass our neighborhood. The DCU campus is below, and I search the tiny sidewalks for Nicolo, knowing it may be the last time I see him. I choose one of the little antlike students below and imagine he's Nicolo and stay glued to him until he's slipped out of my windowframe.

We hurdle the sky at five hundred mph, passing over Oklahoma, moving toward our future at hyperspeed. Amity sits across from me and smiles, periodically holding my hand because she senses I need it. When the copilot comes out of the cockpit to offer us champagne, compliments of the Goldman family, Amity holds up two empty glasses for him and crows, "God bless the Goldmans and all their wonderful coolers." He accidentally spills a drop on her pants while pouring and quickly showers her with apologies. "For heaven's sake, darlin'," Amity tells him, "I'm a flight attendant. Considering all the drinks I've spilled on people, that's just a drop of my karma coming back to me." *Karma comin' back to May.*

"Thanks for being so nice about it," the copilot tells her, "and thanks again for the biscuits and gravy. Some of the best I've had," he says, blushing.

"I made them fresh this morning," she answers, winking at me.

As the copilot returns to the cockpit, I realize that the magic she offers doesn't come from her hands, but her soul. It doesn't matter that she didn't make those biscuits and gravy or the chicken and dumplings or the peach pie. What matters is that she offers them with so much love they *taste* as if they're from her heart. She hands me one of the glasses of champagne, but I decline, so she clinks them together herself and says, "Cheers!" Then she gulps the champagne from one glass, sets it down, and retains the other.

"Harry, would you like a scone?" she asks, taking one from the tray of catered breads left by the copilot.

"No, I'm afraid I'd just throw it up," I tell her honestly.

"Darlin', there's nothing to worry about," she assures me, confidently. "We're going to get through this together. You should eat."

She hands me the scone, and I pull a piece off and stick it into my salty mouth. At least I negotiated with my mother the forfeiture of the requisite rehearsal dinner. I knew I couldn't take another backslapping ceremony after the engagement party, and for once my wishes prevailed. No, today's the day. It's *straight* to the altar. *Straight* up the aisle. Straight straight straight.

Before we land, Amity announces, "Power nap!" and falls into a coma. She's eaten two scones and drunk half a bottle of champagne, and now she's out. How does she do it? Especially today. It's as if she's embracing our future with no trepidation, no caution, as if she's certain of its sanguine outcome. I look down to the squares of farmland below and realize that the summer harvest is gone and most of the land is relaxing into the coming days of autumn. Amity sleeps through the steep descent and touchdown, and as we're taxiing toward the private terminal, I wait, clutching my seat, preparing myself for her frightening rise from the dead. But instead, she slowly opens her eyes, like a baby bird in its nest, and blinks sweetly until she's awake. I relax, let go of my armrests, and smile at her.

"Let's go, Bubba!" she shouts, springing out of her seat.

"Shit, Amity!" I say, slamming against the back of my seat and grabbing my heart. Fooled again.

She takes a little carton of juice from the bread tray. "Drink some orange juice, Bubba. You're going to need your energy today!" she chirps, reaching across and grabbing her wedding dress.

She's right. I pat her hand. Sip the juice. Wait for my heart to descend into my chest again.

As we pull up to the terminal, we can both see my mother and Donald waiting by a shiny gold Mercedes sedan. The car is sitting right on the tarmac, next to several business jets. The pilots shut the engines down and enter the cabin to release the stairs. "After you," I tell her, and Amity steps out, the glamorous movie star making her return. My mother and Donald wave enthusiastically, and she waves back.

Now that it's autumn, the sun generously shares the sky with the cool dry air washing down from the Rockies that moves east to mix with the northern winds coming down from Nebraska. Autumn is my favorite time of year in Kansas. I usually welcome its arrival. Today I'm reticent, but Amity continues to hold my hand and lead me on toward the next season.

"There they are!" my mother cries, taking off her sunglasses and throwing open her arms.

"Hey!" Donald yells.

"Susan!" Amity answers, wrapping her arms around my mother. I shake Donald's hand and wait for him to slap a lung into my throat. He doesn't disappoint, and when we're done, I see that Amity and my mother are still embracing. Amity seems to be holding my mother with predilection, and when she finally lets go, she backs up to take a look at her. "You look great, Susan. Really great."

My mother's hair is down again, but pulled back in gold clips. And like Amity, she looks younger, more relaxed than in the past. The crisp breeze ruffles her ecru linen pantsuit as she reaches out to me. "How could anyone not love this girl?" she asks, referring to Amity.

I hug my mother, feeling her new breasts press against my own new built-up pecs, and answer, "I don't know, Mom. But we sure do, don't we?"

"Yes, we do," she answers as we watch Amity wrap Donald

in a hug. "Your parents are here already," my mother gushes to Amity. "We got a call from them. They sound very nice."

I look at Amity with surprise. She followed through and invited them. She turns to my mom. "They'll be very pleased to meet you."

The pilots deliver our luggage to us. Then Donald clears his throat in a nervous gesture, as if he's about to send us over enemy lines.

"Right," my mother responds, beaming. "Have you noticed anything?"

"The car?" I ask, pointing to the gold Mercedes. Mom and Donald nod affirmatively. "It's not yours, is it?" I ask.

"No, it is not," Donald answers. "It's yours."

Donald smiles, and my mother looks like the cat who swallowed the stomach-bursting macaw. "Well?" she gushes.

I look at Amity and wait for her eyes to spring out of her head and hit the windshield. But instead they mist over, and she most genuinely says, "Susan and Donald, you shouldn't have. Really. You've gone too far."

"What do you think, Harry?" my mother asks enthusiastically. "Have we gone too far?"

Well, it's not exactly like receiving money. And compared to the trashed, totaled-out BMW, it's certainly functional. "Not at all," I answer. "We were actually hoping for a little jet like the one we arrived in."

"Well, then you have something to work toward," Donald answers, not sure if I was joking.

"Come on," my mother says, handing me the keys. "Let's go home."

I hand them to Amity. "A man can live in a ditch, as long as he's driving a Mercedes," I tell her, smiling. "Let's go home."

"Home," she says, making magic of the word.

*   *   *

For the remainder of the day, Amity and my mother are occupied with last-minute arrangements. They leave to check the flower arrangements, sample the reception hors d'oeuvres, make sure the church is prepared, meet with the soloist.

I lie on my bed most of the day, thinking about Nicolo and what life with him would have been like. I imagine us in every possible situation. Riding horses on our land in Argentina. Feeding our dogs—two Labrador retrievers and a beagle. Nicolo, like his father, writing for a noble cause. Me studying Spanish and enrolled in law school, realizing my father's dream for me to become an attorney. My strictly pro bono practice would be for those who could not afford representation otherwise. Nicolo's mother and I would patch things up, and she would live in the guest house on our property. We'd equip her with a beautiful kitchen where she could create every piquant native dish of her desire. And Nicolo's brother, his kindred spirit I've yet to meet, could live in the house with us.

As the day passes, and I can't stand to lie in bed any longer, I stop by the kitchen to pour myself a beer, then move to a reclining chair by the pool. Donald approaches, pulls up a chair, and gets a look on his face that tells me I'm supposed to listen up. "Now, Harry," he tells me, as if I'm a soldier under his command. "I have some things I want to say to you." He sits sturdily in his chair, as if he's daring me to knock him out of it.

I want to run—through the yard, onto the golf course, and down the fairway. But he's caught me in a sand trap. "Yes, Donald?"

"Harry, I assume you've never *been* with a woman before."

This ought to be good.

"There are some things you should know about women." He stands and starts to pace back and forth along the edge of the pool. "Women have a different chemistry than you and I. You see, men think with their brains. Oh, sure, women like to tell us we think with our dicks, but we don't. No, our brains, and the chemicals inside our brains, are what motivate us, guide us, make us who we are. Right?''

"More or less," I say agreeably.

He stops. Points a finger at me. "But women are controlled by their vaginas."

What?

He starts to pace again. "Their vaginas make them laugh, and their vaginas make them cry. Their vaginas make them sad, and their vaginas make them happy. But only because their vaginas make them *think* first." He speaks with great commitment, the way he might when giving a speech at the officers' club. "You see, all the chemicals that control a woman's reasoning are right . . . down . . . there." He points at his privates.

I slowly ask, "Why are you pointing at your crotch?"

"Because this is where my vagina, *or my brain*, would be if I were a woman."

"I see," I tell him, with a wrinkled brow. "How high is your IQ?"

I hope he'll laugh. He doesn't. "That depends on how much stimulation *my brain* gets. Do you understand me, son?"

I'll *never* understand you, Donald. "Go on."

"If you want Amity to continue to be smart, outgoing, agreeable—then you need to stimulate her brain. And I mean stimulate it good. Because if you don't, it'll go dry on ya. Like the desert floor of Death Valley. And then you've got trouble on your hands, son. Because once a woman stops using her *brain*, it dries up, and she stops thinking clearly, and becomes nothing but emotion. And you'll lose control over her. I guaran-fuckin'-tee ya."

"So you think I should keep control over Amity?"

"Absa-fuckin'-lutely," Donald says, his eyes in a squint. "I don't give a shit what generation you're from. Women are women, and men are men. Now," he states, clearing his throat, opening his eyes, "I understand that your *soldier* is used to standing at attention for a different commander. But listen to me. I have no doubt your soldier is ready to fall in line and penetrate the foreign border with the rest of them. Don't be afraid, son—you can do it. And if you have any questions, don't be afraid to report back to me. You got that?''

I nod. Stand. ''Donald?''

''Yes, son?''

''Does my mother have a . . . high IQ?''

''She's a fuckin' genius, buddy.''

No wonder she married him in six weeks. I reach out my hand. ''Thank you.''

He shakes my hand while breaking nearly every one of my fingers. ''Don't mention it.''

Amity and I are in the large bathroom off our bedroom in my mother's house. I'm sitting on the edge of the tub, watching her poo up for the last time as a single girl. My mother has had a bottle of champagne sent out to us, delivered by Marzetta, who politely but sadly hands it over, and Amity forgoes the glass provided to swill out of the bottle. She's skipping a lot of the poo up steps. ''How come you're not curling your hair?'' I ask.

Her hair is still pulled back in a ponytail; she's lightly brushing mascara on her eyelashes. ''I'm feeling kind of natural today, Bubba.''

''Should I take you to see a doctor?''

''Stop!'' she scolds, picking up the bar of soap by the sink and throwing it at me.

I duck as the bullet flies past. ''This is going to be really weird,'' I tell her, picking the soap up from the floor. I don't say it negatively, just honestly. ''Whoever thought we'd *really* get married? God, I wonder what we'll be doing five years from now?''

She looks into the mirror, and instead of looking at herself, she looks at me—as she did on the first day she brought me home.

"Don't worry about it, darlin'. Life never plays out the way you think it will, I guarantee you."

"No shit. Whoever thought Jacqueline would turn out to be a shaman?"

"What's that?"

"In this case, it's a tall priestess who repeats herself while wisely sorting through all the muck."

"Besides you, Harry, she's my best friend."

"You're right." If I weren't afraid of hurting Amity's feelings, I'd tell her how I proposed to Jackie that she take Amity's place at the altar and how Jacqueline refused me on Amity's behalf. "She'd never do anything to hurt you," I tell Amity.

"I'd never do anything to hurt her either," Amity responds.

I want to tell her, "But you did!" She doesn't know I've been made aware of her tryst with Jackie's former boyfriend Arthur. And this is the thing that bothers me most about marrying her—her ability to revise her history at will. At the same time, I realize I'm the yin to her yang, since I'm revising my future at will. I wonder if we'll ever stop altering the past and the future and just let things be as they are.

"Do you think we'll be happy?" I ask.

Now she looks at herself in the mirror and smiles. "We'll be happy, Bubba," she tells me with surety. "We're going to cut the shit and get on with it."

Amity and I are driving to the church in our new Mercedes. My mother had ordered a limousine for us, but Amity convinced her to cancel it. She's insisted on traveling in full regalia in her new car. My mother and I practically had to sit on her huge dress to get the whole thing stuffed behind the steering wheel.

"You sure you don't want me to drive?" I had asked.

"No way, Bubba!" she'd told me.

We have the windows rolled down, and the fall wind rushes through the car, blowing the lace ribbons in her hair. "Look at us,'' Amity squeals. ''We're straight out of *Town and Country!* This would be the most killer ad for Mercedes!'' She's right. A brand-new gold sedan, the bride behind the wheel, the groom along for the ride. My mother and Donald are in front of us in their Cadillac, leading the way, and Jacqueline, after arriving at the house just an hour ago, is behind us in her rental car—a train of madness, with Jackie serving as the caboose. Tina Turner is singing on the radio, asking us ''What's Love Got to Do With It?'' It's a valid question. In the beginning, the answer would have been nothing. But now, love has *everything* to do with it, I can tell by Amity's repose. She's happy and at peace, rock-solid peace. But even in the cool breeze, I'm sweating. Amity looks over. ''Harry, for heaven's sake. Stop your worrying. It's not like you're going to the executioner. It's just a bunch of fancy-ass people in expensive clothes, and some nice old guy, who probably hits the sauce a little too much and fondles the altar boys, standing there in a big ole white robe, and you and me. Believe me, darlin', this whole thing will be over sooner than you think.''

''Good,'' I tell her, wiping my clammy palms on my tuxedo pants. ''How are you staying so calm?''

She glances over at me, takes my hand, and gives me a heartfelt smile. ''Because this is the most wonderful day of my life. You're doing something for me that no one else has ever done, Bubba. Ever. You're loving me for who I am. No conditions. No rules. You're putting my happiness before your own. And that's the meaning of true love, Harry. I want you to know how much you've inspired me.''

''But, Amity,'' I say, ''that's how your parents love you.''

She glances at me briefly, then concentrates on the road. ''I suppose,'' she sighs. ''And I love them too, but they just don't get me. It was the wrong family, the wrong house for me. I couldn't stand pork and milk. I hated riding that stinky old school bus for miles on dirt roads, just to get to *Waco* to go to school. My brother and sister thrived in FFA, while I thrived on THC. It was the only way I could accept my boring life. But I always knew it wasn't permanent. My cousin came to visit me when I was six, and she loved our farm, but I told her, 'This dump is just a place to hang my hat until I can strike out on my own!' "

"Jesus, Amity, you said that when you were six?"

"I was an honest six. And I wanted more than a farm family in Waco could offer. I wanted a family with a good name. A family who drank martinis instead of cow's milk. I wanted the clothes and the house and the style. I wanted to be famous. Oh, I know it's shallow and disgusting, but why not? It's not like I'm some horrible bitch."

"But, Amity," I say, impassioned, "you're not getting any of that with me! No house, no clothes, no style. There's only a small amount of name recognition. I'm not taking the money. I'll be poor."

She looks confidently ahead. "You're a fine man, Harry Ford. You won't be poor. I'm sure of it."

I'm in a side room, off the back of the main cathedral of St. Thomas Episcopal Church. I can hear all the guests in the pews, some murmuring, some speaking outright, some laughing. We have ten minutes to go before six o'clock—the wedding hour. My cousins, Ellie and Mary, look beautiful in their butter-colored, full-length bridesmaids' dresses. Jacqueline too. Brad and two other cousins, dressed in their long-tailed black tuxes, are nearly finished with their duties seating the guests. Most of the entourage are now standing in the back of the church, shifting in their stiff shoes, waiting for the minutes to pass until the music segues and they hear the bridal march that accompanies all of us down the aisle. I peer out into the church and see my mother and Donald sitting on the aisle in the front row. Next to them is my beloved Grammie, and next to her is Winston. Across the aisle from them sit Amity's mother and her brother and sister. I'm so happy she's invited them all, and Mr. Stubbs assured me again as they entered the church that this must be the "real deal" since they've never been invited to "any of her other weddings," and that this would be the first time he would actually give his daughter away. I still haven't found out how many other weddings there were. I guess I'll never know all there is to know about Amity Stone.

But all I need to find out about her at the moment is her location. I don't see her anywhere, and when I query Jackie as to her where-abouts, she shrugs, telling me, "I don't know. I'm not sure, because I don't know."

I walk back into the holding room, wipe my palms for the fortieth time, try to catch my breath, slow my heart down. None of it works. Fuck, if only I could breathe.

"You OK there, buddy?" my cousin Brad asks, poking his head into the room.

"Fine!" I answer, gulping more air.

"Five minutes," he says, counting it down.

Fuck. Where is she? I go back out and take another look at the crowd. It's too many people. Mother and Amity promised to keep it small, intimate. But there must be three hundred people here— which doesn't seem intimate in the least. I glance up at the family pew again. No Winston. He's gone.

No Winston. No Amity. Oh, fuck, I can't even think it. I turn back to the wedding party, ask my relatives and Jackie, "Has anyone seen Amity or Winston?"

"Winston just walked by. He went down the hall, that way," Brad answers.

"Your brother is handsome," Jackie tells me, smoking a ciga-rette in her bridesmaid's dress. "He's handsome when he walks. Really handsome."

"I'll be right back," I tell them all. "Don't start without me."

They all laugh nervously, and I start heading down the hall.

When I was a child, the limestone hallways of this church were sacred, holy, hallowed. They were so much larger than I was, and I always felt I was being led by them, that there was some mysterious force that determined my direction independent of my desire for control. And it still feels that way now—that as I aged and grew larger, so did these stone halls. And I'm still captive to their power. As when I was a child, I walk softly, with great care not to let my heels make any sound, lest I disturb God. And as I approach the voices of familiarity, they don't hear me any more than God does.

"Two million dollars. Made out to Amity Stone," Winston says.

"How thoughtful of you to pronounce my name correctly," Amity tells him coolly. "Is it *spelled* correctly?"

"The T's are crossed, and the I is dotted," he assures her.

I clutch my heart. I'm afraid it will disintegrate. My face flashes hot, and my ears ring. The one thing that made me believe in her was that she hadn't taken Winston's offer. I can hardly hear them as they continue.

"It better be a cash-equivalent check, darlin', or I'm fixin' to be Mrs. Harry Ford in about two minutes."

"Same as cash," Winston vows. "I couldn't put a stop payment on it if I wanted to."

"Hand me your pen, darlin'. I'm going to endorse this bad boy right now."

The muted sound of the wedding march, floating down the limestone hallway, begins.

"They're starting the music. How are you going to do it?" Winston asks her excitedly.

I hear her scribbling with his pen. "You leave that to me," she answers confidently.

God, what do I do? God, can you hear me? What the hell do I do now? You're telling me I made the wrong choice. Nicolo. It should have been Nicolo. Never do anything for money. But that's not what I did! I did this for love. For Amity. So that she could have a family and a life in which she'd be valued and loved. How could everything turn out like this? I start walking back down the hall toward the chapel, letting my heels smash against the floor so that God hears me—as well as that Texan Eve and my brother, the serpent she's cut a deal with.

"Harry!" Amity yells behind me. "Harry, come back!"

"Let him go," Winston calls after her. "It's easier this way. It's done!"

I hear her own heels clicking against the floor as she approaches. "Harry! Come on," she says, looping her arm into mine.

I throw her arm off. "How could you do this?" I hiss, keeping my voice low. I'm fighting to keep the tears in my eyes.

"Harry, you don't understand," she pleads. "This was the only way for all of us to be happy."

"I'm *not* happy anymore," I tell her, one tear falling.

"You will be," she swears as we round the corner to the chapel. Mr. Stubbs is waiting with an exasperated look on his face, and I turn to the left, to exit the church, but Amity shoves me with the strength of a defensive lineman and I fall splat on my face, Amity on top of me. The whole church turns and gasps to see us on the floor.

Amity stands, shrugs at the crowd, and nervously laughs. "I didn't have a shotgun." A few nervous chuckles arise.

As Mr. Stubbs comes walking toward us, I see my mother's horrified expression. Donald is holding her up. Mr. Stubbs pulls me up and sets me in the aisle. Amity takes my arm and pulls me in, then grabs her father's arm, and suddenly all three of us are linked to walk up the aisle together, Amity with a long-strapped white purse over her shoulder. I'm supposed to be waiting at the altar as he brings her to me, and he's thrown by the unorthodox style of this improvised trio. I dig my heels into the carpet. "Come on!" *Come own!* Amity implores, coaxing me forward.

I flash back to the first time we entered Suicide Express together. She spurred me on, swearing it wouldn't kill us although I was not so sure. The narrow road ahead dared us to enter its clutches, challenged us to hang on as we hurled forward into the world together. She pushes me again, and I step on the carpet, entering on the treacherous road with my heart in pieces. "What are you doing?" I whisper to her desperately.

We walk slowly, but it feels as if I'm moving seventy miles an hour, like on the expressway. People turn, smile at us, nod in recognition, whisper to each other, and I have to concentrate not to hit the side walls of the pews as I lurch recklessly forward. She's between her father and me, pulling us on, smiling like an angel who's earned her wings. The ringing in my ears is deafening now, and my legs are barely holding me up. I look for an off ramp, a chance to dash down a row and slide away. "Keep walking, Harry," she whispers.

As we reach the front of the church, I look to see my mother, finally relaxing and radiating with happiness and light, giving shine to all the beautiful hues of stained glass within the windows of the chapel. My grammie stands beside her, braced on a cane. Unlike my mother, she sees the panic and discomfort in my face, and she raises her eyebrows, then squints her eyes to ask me what is the matter. I can't answer. Winston has not returned to my grandmother's side, and I look behind us and see him standing at the back of the church in the shadows, like a vampire waiting to swoop down on his victim. Amity tugs on me, forcing me to look ahead and make the final steps to the priest, Father Warner.

"Dearly beloved, we are gathered here today to unite this man, Harry Ford, and this woman, Amity Stone, in holy matrimony. The union of a man and woman is a sacred covenant and shall not be taken lightly. If there is anyone present who has knowledge of any reason that Harry and Amity may not be joined in holy matrimony, let him speak now or forever hold his peace."

Amity inhales a huge breath, as do I. What is happening? Is she taking his money *and* mine? She's got the check. It's as good as cash. Is she outfoxing Winston and simply marrying me anyway?

No one speaks, not even Winston. I start to open my mouth . . . .

"Who gives this woman to this man?" Father Warner asks.

Amity and I release the air from our lungs.

"I do," her father answers proudly. He separates from Amity and steps directly into the pew with Mrs. Stubbs. Amity and I are left alone in front of God and everyone. My ears are ringing so hard and blood is flushing through my head so fast that I can't hear anything Father Warner is saying. I think he's educating us about the sanctity of marriage and telling us to be good to each other, or at least not to kill each other, but he's woefully late. It's all too late.

"Do you, Harry Ford, take this woman, to have and to hold, for better or worse, for richer or poorer, in sickness and in health, so long as you both shall live?"

I stare ahead, my vision tunneling, my face on fire. Amity pulls me to her and whispers, "Say *yes*, Harry." I turn, look at her. Search her eyes for any meaning. "Trust me," she whispers, her clear eyes promising me faith. I hesitate. She squeezes my hand, and at that moment, it's as if God squeezed it and the halls of the church open in my mind and God speaks to me loud and clear.

"I do."

As if held under water, then finally allowed to rise to the surface, my mother exhales with great force. Several of my relatives giggle at her relief.

"Good boy, Bubba," Amity whispers, her eyes filling with tears.

The priest starts again with Amity, requesting her pledge, her faith, her promise. "For richer or poorer, in sickness and in health, so long as you both shall live?"

I glance at my mother, who's now crying. She's trembling with an upside-down smile and wiping the tears from her cheek. Donald holds her free hand, and with his other gives me the thumbs-up.

My grammie, her head cocked, her wise eyes waiting, is now the one who holds her breath. I look into Amity's eyes. And she is crying as well. Such forceful tears, flowing without sound, streaming down her beautiful Grace Kelly face in sweet little streams. She squeezes my hand again and speaks. "No, Father, I'm afraid I do not."

CHAPTER
TWENTY-SIX

How can I possibly describe the look on my mother's face? She's waited rapturously for this moment, the moment that neither she nor I ever thought would happen, the moment when she sends her child into matrimony for the remainder of his life. And now, it's not coming to fruition as she had dreamed. The guests of the church are watching her almost as closely as the two of us standing before the priest, and as I look into her eyes, I actually detect quiet resignation that this is the natural outcome to everything that has brought us to this juncture. She doesn't even look as if she wants to flee the church and go running down a golf course fairway, as I had wanted when Donald had given me the man-to-man communique on vaginas and soldiers that day, which now seems a lifetime ago.

If she does want to flee, she doesn't show it. She stays planted. Her kind yet befogged gaze fixed on me and Nicolo, as the Argentinean breeze blows through the windows of the little open-air church.

"I do," Nicolo answers.

In the reflection of his almost black eyes, I flash back to the last time I stood before a priest in a church, in Kansas, with Amity by my side. Her wedding gown was a long, satin, off-the-shoulder dress that flowed over her body like water. She used white lace to pull her hair back into a pony tail and had forsaken her usual perfume to bathe herself in the scent of the fresh lavender necklace Jackie had made for her. And in this beautiful form she returned to me the unconditional selfless love I was offering. I should have known by her tranquillity, her repeated assurances that everything was going to work out for the best, that it would. But it wasn't until she told Father Warner that she did *not* agree to marry me and pulled that check from her cleavage and dropped it into my hands that I knew what she'd done. And as if that weren't enough, she turned and spoke to the congregation in my defense. "Y'all" she told everyone, through her tears of painful happiness, "I can't marry Harry because it wouldn't be right. Don't misunderstand me. Harry is a wonderful man. He's smart and sweet and good, and he makes me laugh all the time." *All the Tom.* "And I have no doubt that he loves me. As much as my parents have ever loved me."

Mr. and Mrs. Stubbs were grateful for the acknowledgment, but as confused as the rest of us.

"And I want everybody here to know that I love Harry too— just as much. I think he knows that now," she said. "But he's not *in love* with me, and that's because Harry is gay, and y'all know that. And if you don't know, it's probably because you live life with your head in the sandbox—which is a good way to get your head pooped on by a stray cat, so maybe you ought to pull it out. Because Harry deserves more than that from you. And he deserves more than even I can give him. And y'all, he's found it. And that's who should be standing here in my shoes today. Truth, his boyfriend is kind of a butch guy, and I don't think he'd be comfortable wearing my shoes, but you know what I mean. The problem is, most likely none of you would show up if Harry's true love were to join him here at the altar. And that's not right. We've got a phrase in Texas: 'Love me, love my dog.' And y'all need to learn how to love

Harry's dog." She turned to me. "Harry, I want you to know, if
you ever come back here with Nicolo, I'd like to be your best man.
Just don't ever ask your best man to wear an ugly taffeta dress."
She started to choke up about now, as she opened her purse and
walked over to my mother. "And, Susan, something tells me that
you and Donald will find it in your hearts to be here too," she said,
lifting a cold, watery, plastic storage bag out of her purse. She
handed the plastic bag, containing thawed ice and the engagement
ring, to my mother, and turned back to me with a stage whisper,
"Had to freeze the ring, Harry. Didn't want to be tempted to pawn
the family jewels." I laughed to keep from crying. "Listen," she
said to my parents. "I've come to know y'all over the past few
months, and I'm sure that you love Harry and ultimately want him
to be happy. If I'm wrong, forgive me. I hope I haven't hurt your
feelings. And Grammie Ford, I hope I haven't shocked you or upset
you, ma'am. I'm just doing what has to be done."

"Not at all, dear," my grandmother said, breaking the silence
of the frozen crowd. She then opened her purse while saying to
Amity, "Here, I want you to have a piece of candy and one of my
credit cards."

Amity refused the credit card, but gladly took the piece of taffy,
which she unwrapped while returning to the aisle to tell the entire
congregation, "I still think there should be a reception, because
we're all here, and the money's been spent, and my folks are all
the way up from Fort Worth. And I guess that's all I have to say.
So I'm going to walk out of here now." She walked over to me
and sweetly whispered into my ear, "I did it 'cuz I love you." She
started to walk away, but pulled back and added, "And I'd be
bullshitting you if I didn't tell you I can't stomach the thought of
giving up all that money and being poor." She then yelled up to
the soloist, "Darlin'! This is going to be the longest walk of my

life. I know we planned the song for last, but I need you to go ahead and sing it now—to kind of fill in until I make it out of here."

The accompanist started the up-tempo introduction on the piano. Amity looked me square in the eye, kissed me on the lips, and said, " 'Bye, Harry. Love your guts!" She then tossed the taffy into her mouth and walked down the aisle while the soloist sang Cole Porter's "Who Wants to be a Millionaire?" And as I looked at the check in my hands, I saw that she had endorsed it payable to me. She'd signed over the whole two million as soon as she'd gotten it from Winston.

I realized right then I'd underestimated her from beginning to end. And more than a few years passed before I realized why: I'd been so intent on holding my cards close, working every angle, manufacturing myself a preferred outcome—all the things I'd accused her of—that I'd lost my own heart along the way, as well as the hearts of everyone around me. We really were a lot alike, Amity and I. It wasn't until we gave it all up—the wedding charade, the money, the resentment of being born into our families—and just offered to love each other honestly that we started down the paths that would take each of us home.

To be sure, there were some bumps along those paths. Of course, after I signed the wedding check back over to Amity, she went on a clothes shopping and cocaine spree that nearly killed her. But I, Jackie, and Nicolo (who abruptly changed his opinion of her) stood by her as she went through her fourth rehabilitation program. This time, it was the Betty Ford Center, which I think motivated her by the very fact that she admired Mrs. Ford and her fairy tale life as First Lady—which Amity learned wasn't a fairy tale at all or the Betty Ford Center wouldn't exist. But it was definitely worth it for her to complete the program because it helped her to understand herself and be done with the drugs, and she got a chance to see

Liza Minelli without any makeup on. "She's kind of horsy," Amity wrote to me in a letter, "but she's real sweet."

For the next several years, Nicolo and I continued to live in Dallas, where he worked as a political reporter for the *Dallas Morning News*. I didn't go to law school, but opted to attend veterinary school after returning to undergraduate school to pick up my needed prerequisites. It was many years before Winston divulged the owner of Cinnamon, and even inheriting all my money didn't assuage his anger at Amity for duping him. So working with animals was my way of sublimating my yearnings for contact with my horse.

As the decade moved on, we all became increasingly aware of how powerful the HIV virus was and how AIDS would alter our lives forever. I was so casual, so careless, so cavalier that year I spent with Amity. And lucky. I didn't have safe sex with anyone— and I'm sure Amity didn't either—yet we both came out of it unscathed. Winston, sadly enough, contracted HIV in 1989. I was shocked, because by 1989 we all knew how to protect ourselves. But sex is a powerful thing—even more powerful than my omnipotent brother. His own cavalier approach to life was quickly commuted when faced with mortality. At first, he rebuffed my overtures. But as his term unrolled with prickly caution, each day becoming a lifetime, he let his edges soften enough to be approached. We formed ourselves a workable brotherhood, and though our interests were unlike, we made the effort to connect ourselves as best we knew how.

He's here today, with his partner, Chuck. Yes, two gay sons is a bit much for my mother. Not so much for Donald, surprisingly. He's been more adept at change than she. Winston, Chuck, Nicolo, and I have been grateful for Donald's support over time.

I haven't mentioned how I actually paid for my veterinary school. Given that I forfeited my inheritance to Winston and returned the full two million to Amity, I was penniless, right? Well, my dear grammie died the year after my aborted wedding, and after bestowing an even one million dollars on Marzetta, I was named the sole heir to the rest of her considerable fortune, a windfall that actually exceeded what I would have received from my father. She left me everything except a single item, which she bestowed upon Amity: her silk kimono from Japan.

Grammie explained to me, in a sealed private letter delivered by the attorney, that my grandfather had caught my father at the age of twelve in the barn of their country house *fooling around* with one of the ranch hands a few years older than he. She said my grandfather whipped them both so hard they had to see a doctor. The ranch hand was fired, naturally, and my father's relationship with his own father was never the same. She told me she tried to convince her husband that their son was doing what all boys his age do—just experimenting a little. She was sure my dad was straight as a Kiowa Indian's arrow. But my grandfather was so afraid that his son's behavior could be permanent he ruled him with icy formality and an iron fist for all of his days.

She said she hoped her words would help me understand my father in regard to my own situation, and they do. She concluded by saying that my grandfather was a cold and autocratic man who was difficult to live with or understand and that if it weren't for her friend Louise she may have never known love!

Nicolo's mother, who had long been yearning for her native land, ultimately decided not to return to Argentina, but to stay in Dallas, and in due time allowed me to buy her a small house. She and I mended our torn fences long ago, and she often comes to visit her homeland, but the ghosts of her past eventually overtake her, and she flies from their grip by returning to Dallas. On the ranch, Nicolo's aunt Angelica and her mate Aurora are our spiritual and land advisors since we've taken over the farming business, since they have many years of connection with the earth in a way we are only beginning to learn ourselves.

The truth is, Nicolo's aunt Angelica married us almost thirteen years ago in a grove of olive trees on the farm during our first visit to Argentina. But after all these years, my mother has decided, with Donald's encouragement, it's time she sees one of her children make a completed trip down the aisle. She readily agreed to come here, to Argentina, to have the wedding—probably because she's unfamiliar with the small gathering of locals in the church, save for Nicolo and his mother, and I assume she's imminently more comfortable having everyone speak Spanish so that she simply doesn't have to know what they're saying. To her happiness and mine, Amity and her latest boyfriend, a French-Canadian banking executive she met while working the first-class section of a flight to Montreal ("He's all natural and big big big!"), are attending the wedding, with Amity serving as my best man, of course. And they're staying with us at the ranch. Jacqueline and Thomas couldn't make it, because it would be a difficult distance to travel with two young boys, and Jackie is seven months pregnant with her third child. "I hope it's a girl. I really hope it's a girl, 'cuz I really want a girl," she told me last night on the phone, after wishing Nicolo and me *suerte*.

Amity is happy. Since her last dry out, she's managed to keep herself in control all these years, never spending money on a sub-stance more potent than champagne. She does go a little overboard on clothing, but that's OK considering she doesn't spend money on automobiles—she still drives the Mercedes presented to us on our wedding day, restoring it to mint condition after some bumps and scrapes acquired during her first wild months as a millionaire. She's never married, because, as she told me, "I'll never find a man as wonderful as you, Harry Ford." It made me feel guilty for her to say so, but then she added, "And besides, I'd get bored just sucking one dick for the rest of my life." Atta girl.

The priest concludes, "Then with the power of our creator, who we recognize to be all loving and all encompassing, I now pronounce you husband and wife—neither one nor the other—but both. You may kiss."

And so we do. And though our lips have had years to grow accustomed to each other's, it's a sweet kiss I take from Nicolo's lips, the sweetness of *dulce de leche*. And when our friends and family applaud, we break from each other and turn to them with smiles. *Tia* Angelica opens the doors to the small chapel, and waiting outside are our two horses.

Cinnamon is twenty-eight years old now, and he endured many miles on the freighter that brought him here, so I don't much ride him anymore. He's certainly earned the right to mingle in the field with the cattle in blissful retirement. But today is a special occasion, and *tia* Angelica has adorned him with a fine show saddle and buck-stitch bridle. Nicolo mounts up on his dappled Arabian, and I slowly swing onto my venerable old steed, and Nicolo and I ride slowly down the lane, side by side, hand in hand, as the golden wheat of the Santa Fe province rolls like waves beside us. As we look back, the congregation seems to be floating, drifting away, waving to us, singing a wedding song. Nicolo has promised he will play his guitar and sing the song for me tonight in our tent in the countryside.

I look back in my mind as well and see my buoyant Amity sitting on my hospital bed, visiting hours over, filling two glasses with the champagne she'd brought me, toasting to the "Us!" we had not yet become, and I realize our brief and shared paths ultimately provided the salvation that helped to shape our characters into something indelible and good.

Before I turn ahead, to the road in front of us, I take one last look at her and see that my manic ex-fiancée is the only person not waving, not singing. Her hands are in her pockets, and her hair is blowing in the breeze, and she's just watching us ride together on our horses. And I realize that 1984 was more than my year of heterosexuality—it was the year that I became a man. And if it's true that you get what you give in this world, then Amity is destined for more happiness than she could ever think possible, because that's what she's given to me.